COUNTRY OF UNDER

— A NOVEL —

BROOKE SHAFFNER

Mason Jar Press | Baltimore, MD

Cover design and layout by Ian Anderson. Cover concept by Niteesh Elias.

This book is set in Meta Serif Pro and Template Gothic OT.

Published by
Mason Jar Press
Baltimore, MD

Learn more about Mason Jar Press at masonjarpress.com.

We're not trying to become something, we're trying to un-become. We're trying to undo ourselves.

—Reverend angel Kyodo williams

We believe each other into being.

—Jennifer Michael Hecht

COUNTRY OF UNDER

CHAPTER 1

Marin taught Pilar to swim in the resaca. *Resaca* was the name Rio Grande Valley people gave the old riverbeds of the Rio Grande that were no longer part of the main channel. Rivers cut from their mother. Pilar had never known her mother. What she knew was the resaca buoying her, her father cradling her so that she stared up at the bowl of the sky, no clouds or houses to break its blue. All of it a womb in its still, enveloping edges. A world birthed by her father, its borders the ends of his arms.

La Llanura, Marin called it. The Flatlands. He'd bought a crumbling house on an acre of property outside of San Jacinto's city limits, the nearest gas station a mile away. Their neighbors were citrus groves and sugarcane fields, their visitors migrating birds. This was how Marin wanted to raise Pilar, how he wanted to live. The land's vast silence and ravaged beauty made sense to him—sun-dulled, windswept fields, patches of dirt overtaking the grass. Only the resaca—rippled by white birds lifting, blood-streaked by the setting sun—promised more. At night, it lapped the dock like a watery heart; the mournful wails of trains carried across its surface.

Marin had intended to take the swimming lesson slowly, to float Pilar on her back before turning her over and gliding her around on her belly, but with a sharp kick to his ribs, she wriggled free. Her head slipped under water for an instant and fear shot through him. But she popped up

like a cork, shook the water from her hair, smiled. He swam toward her
and she paddled backwards. Again her head slipped under; again she
popped up smiling.

Marin began to lose Pilar then, in the resaca. He had not been prepared
for the sharpness of her kick. He opened his arms and waited for her to return. He lifted her onto the dock and they sat at its end, Pilar in his lap. He
breathed heavily, as he did when he was anxious. He held Pilar too tightly.

What Pilar didn't learn from their rabbit-eared TV, she learned quickly in
school. She came to understand that her father spoke Spanish, a language
the tough kids reserved for swears. By first grade, she understood almost
everything in English. By second grade, she understood too much. Her
teacher talked about conjunctions, but those words didn't join anything—
the children unlearning their parents' language as fast as they could.
They moved her into the gifted class.

She understood that two worlds existed, La Llanura and the world
outside. Once a week, she and her father drove a half-hour to the supermarket. A cool blast of air hit them as the doors slid open and they
entered a fluorescent-lit labyrinth of colored boxes and cans. People were
dark-skinned and dark-haired. Their round bellies and breasts pressed
against their T-shirts. How easy they were with their bodies. They bumped
elbows and carts, chatting with people they knew. Even when they passed
strangers, there was some sign of community.

Marin and Pilar were a world unto themselves—silent, stark, pale. They
glided through the air-conditioned aisles like ghosts. Adults didn't seem
to see them; children stared at the strangeness of their pale skin and hair.
Pilar's hair would darken to her father's muddy wheat color when she
got older, but as a child, it was white-blonde. Her face, like Marin's, was
all Germanic angles—high cheekbones, strong jawline, straight nose. She
was the tallest in her class. When she'd asked her father why they looked
different, he'd said his father had come from Menonos. Mennonites. When

kids at school asked her what she was, she told them, without knowing what it meant, that she was a Menono. The word made them laugh.

Children in the grocery store stared at Pilar, and Pilar stared at their mothers. She loitered, watching them wheel their carts slowly through the aisles—hips swinging, singing to the Muzak, their voices floating out on clouds of vapor when they ducked their heads into the freezer. Their babies chatted happily to themselves in the cart seat, dimpled rolls of fat on their swinging legs. Pilar eavesdropped on the women's strangely accented Spanish: Mixed with English, it skipped like rocks. They were full of talk and laughter. Marin and Pilar laughed at home, like it wasn't something to do in public.

Marin had to circle back to retrieve Pilar. "Come on, mija," he whispered. His voice was so soft that Pilar, entranced with a louder world, didn't hear him. When he put his rough hand on the back of her neck, his palm was damp with worry.

The cashier spoke Spanish but couldn't understand Marin's Bolivian accent. Marin turned to Pilar. She began to translate but was distracted by the escalating tantrum of the boy behind them. The boy wriggled free of his mother and was soon writhing, red-faced, on the floor. "*I want it!*" he screamed. Pilar stared, open mouthed.

Still, Marin wouldn't use the English he knew. He pulled Pilar to him, kissed the top of her head, and whispered into her hair. His words were lost, but Pilar understood that he was saying, *You'll never scream like that. That language is not for us.*

Pilar knew that saying things aloud made them so. Two worlds existed, La Llanura and the world outside. The girls of Freddy Gonzales Elementary played house and the house had a mother, father, brothers and sisters. In the world of La Llanura, there was only a father. To ask about her mother would be to say aloud that something was missing, and then it would be.

La Llanura with its holes was home. Pilar tiptoed around the holes. She never brought anyone home. She kept the worlds separate.

That was the childhood Marin had known in Potosi, Bolivia. His father had left the Mennonite colony he was raised in for Marin's Bolivian mother and was dead to his Menono family. He'd learned Spanish and traded farming for mining. He'd reinvented himself for love. Marin's mother told him that his father had known only a few words in Spanish when they'd met. She said they hadn't needed words. To his sons, he was a mystery. He spent his days in a dark underworld that they did not speak about when he emerged. Marin and his brother Roberto would never have asked about their father's past. It was enough to survive the present. The mine's dust hung in his lungs until it killed him at 34.

A graveyard sprawled through the valley beneath Potosi's Cerro Rico Mountain. A sign over the graves read, *Silence for the men who lost their lungs.* Men died by 40 of the dust or the cave-ins or the backbreaking labor. They left a ghost town of wives and children who were then sent into the mines that killed their fathers.

Marin was 13, Roberto 11, when their father died and they took his place in the mines. They mourned underground, sadness a tunnel they felt their way through. There was catharsis in the work, an understanding. Marin led Roberto through the narrow passages; they threaded their way through death.

The light hurt their eyes when they left the mines. It pulled that shared dream—Marin and Roberto—apart. Their edges sharpened. Their mother did not ask about the mine, and they never spoke about it. She had dinner waiting for them. They prayed and ate and the ways of the world—the lightness of its touch—returned.

———————

Marin worked the graveyard shift in a graveyard. When Pilar was still a baby, he had driven past the sprawling San Jose Cemetery and seen a sign on the gate: *Wanted: Night Watchman.* The road was lined with knotted oaks in a climate only spindly palms and squat mesquite trees survived. Their boughs moved like the hands of God. Marin had wandered into the church at the edge of the cemetery with Pilar on his hip, shook his head when the priest asked if he had experience. The priest had looked at Pilar, who'd given him a toothless grin, and asked, "When can you start?"

Marin had worked the night shift his last three years in the mines. He was comfortable being at odds with the world's clock and more comfortable among the dead than the living. Though Holy Rosary Church paid him a pittance to guard the cemetery's 1,500 tombstones from vandals, thieves, and brujerias, the job allowed him to raise Pilar. When she was a baby, he strapped her to his chest in a sling and walked her to sleep among the dead, singing softly. She was a good sleeper and usually slept through his shift. When she got older, he would leave her and return before she woke. He gave up sleep until she started school, catching a few hours when she napped.

Marin was paid to guard the elaborate tombs of ex-mayors, doctors, and ranchers, but it was the unmarked graves he kneeled beside to mark with sugarcane. He returned to Potosi's graveyard, guarded the graves he'd left behind. The church didn't want visitors to see graves being dug, so they had Marin dig them at night. On hot summer nights, he took off his shirt and worked until sweat ran over his ribs. Because of his lungs, he stopped to catch his breath, but he was still strong, the muscles of his back and legs working in tandem, the arc of the shovel through the dark a dance that obliterated all other thoughts, even the thought of the motion's end—of the hole he was making and what it was for.

―――――――――――――

After those afternoons of trailing mothers through the supermarket, Pilar's father would cook a big meal of beans, rice, tortillas, and—one Sunday a month, when they splurged on meat—carne asada. Pilar couldn't eat fast enough. "Slow down!" Her father would laugh as she reached for another helping. How much pleasure he took in watching her eat.

When dinner was done, they would sit together in the old rocking chair on the porch, watching the sun go down.

"Háblame de los túneles." Tell me about the tunnels, she would say as the sky darkened.

"Buscamos la vena," her father would say.

"Vena?" Pilar had asked the first time he told her about the mines.

"We sought the vein," her father had translated. He'd run her fingers over the veins in his wrist.

Pilar understood now that he meant the vein of silver threaded through the mine's rock. Still, they always began this way. Still, she pictured the tunnels as pale blue.

Two brothers—Marin, 13, and Roberto, 11—enter a small, over-stripped mine, the kind left to child miners. They pass under a rickety wooden doorframe buttressing a stone arch. Inside, their carbon flame headlamps do little to cut the darkness. The arch gives way to jagged rock tunnels.

They feel their way through the shadows to the shrine to El Tio. He sits on a rock throne in a hollowed-out alcove, a clay devil with a mountain goat's horns and ears, eyes made of metal ore, teeth made of broken glass, and a man's body draped in pastel streamers. There are lit candles on his upturned palms and at his feet and offerings of coca leaves, cigarettes, and grain alcohol. In church, the brothers pray to Jesus and the Virgin, but El Tio is god of the mines. Marin and Roberto always kneel before him, light candles and lay candy at his feet. They ask him to pull silver from the vein, to protect them from cave-ins.

Marin remembered but omitted the blood of llamas sacrificed to feed El Tio. Every June, there was a fiesta at which the miners cut llamas' throats and smeared the blood over the mouth of the mine, where it dried to rust. He did not tell Pilar that the silver ore veins were depleted, that they were lucky to find tin. He told her the silver was there.

"Roberto never wants to stop at El Tio. Not because he's afraid, no. He hates El Tio. I make him kneel, leave candy. *Feed the Tio, or the Tio will feed on you*, I tell him." Marin remembered but omitted their first day in the mine when he'd opened his eyes mid-prayer to catch Roberto staring at El Tio's erect penis, his fist clenched around the candy. He'd passed his hand over his brother's eyelids like their mother had done when their father died. Roberto had knocked away his hand, kicked the candles down, marched up to El Tio and kicked him, cracking his clay balls. "Why'd you kill Papá?" he'd screamed and kicked El Tio again and again, tears trailing down his dusty cheeks. Marin had stamped out the fire spreading through the coca leaves and struggled to hold Roberto back. Their first day in the mine, when he kicked El Tio, was the only time Roberto cried for their father.

"The first time we went in the mines, Roberto marched up to El Tio and kicked him in the ribs—like you kicked me in the resaca. Locos—both of you!" Marin laughed, though it wasn't a joke: The Tio did not forget. In the telling of this story, he transmuted fear into wonder. He saw only the beauty of Pilar's head breaking the surface of the resaca like a seal's, of Roberto descending a three-story vertical shaft—a rock climber without a belay. In this story, he could save them both.

Pilar has Roberto's gray-blue, old soul eyes, the same intensity in her gaze and tight set of the jaw. She does not ask how he died. She has always known that Roberto died in the mines, that her father failed to save him, that his stories are pulled from that wound.

The story isn't about death, but about all the ways we can know and love someone, which are larger than death. Pilar closed her eyes and took the story into her veins. Like Roberto, she believed the silver was there. They move slowly through tunnels that snake and narrow, rise and dip, running their palms along the jagged walls, ducking under rotting wooden supports. They climb rickety ladders connecting the different levels. The passages tighten as they go deeper; the air thins with heat, dust, dynamite fumes, and toxic gas. Their eyes sting. They strip off their sweat-soaked shirts, hunch their shoulders then bow their heads then crawl on their hands and knees—a diagram of evolution in reverse.

They work as the Quecha Indians did, with picks, hammers, shovels, and brute strength. They chisel holes in the rock by hand, Roberto gripping the stake while Marin hammers. Their boss has taught them to listen for the silver in the stake's ring, for explosions in the distance. He's shown them how to roll green dynamite sticks in paper, insert the sticks into the holes, light the fuse and run. Hit the detonator too hard and the walls explode. They have only minutes to evacuate after lighting the fuse.

"Carefully," their boss says. "Con cuidado, nunca a la fuerza." As if he can protect them. He lowers Marin and Roberto by rope down narrow, 12-foot shafts. He watches them fumble for finger and footholds, rocks sliding from under their feet. Marin remembered but omitted the boss's cough. He had five years at best. He peers down the hole with dusty eyes, eyes like their mother's, like every adult Marin knew—sad and passing sadness. Marin knew it was in his eyes when he made Roberto kneel before El Tio. He hoped Pilar could not see it.

Marin wanted to pass a different story to Pilar, a story like La Llanura—flat and treeless, the past burned clean, a plane on which to make themselves. The making is in the doing, the cyclic motions of the present—cooking, swimming, rocking—stretching into the horizon.

The story was not in the plot twists, but in the twists, the tightening, of the tunnels; the ritual of lighting candles before El Tio, making their way through shadowy passageways, listening for silver inside the stake's ring. They do everything carefully—*con cuidado, nunca a la fuerza*. There is only the danger of intimacy, of working 16 hours in darkness beside his brother, days of threading their way along an empty vein. Sometimes Roberto's headlamp goes out and Marin leads him by the hand; they move as one over the uneven path. Even in darkness, Marin knows the crook of Roberto's grimace, the chip in his left front tooth, his awkward grip on the stake. He could single out the meld of his sweat with the dust from a mass of 100 miners. There is no question of what to search for: They seek the vein.

Because she was a good girl, because her dresses were clean, the girls of Freddy Gonzales Elementary let Pilar sit in their circle. But she remained on the periphery. When they played Duck, Duck, Goose, she was never picked to be Goose because she *was*—a gawky thing among so many sleek mallards. She did not want to be chosen. On the circle's border, she made sense. She listened to the girls talk of dance classes and roller-skating parties and stopped listening when they talked about their mothers. She unraveled cigarette filters believing they were woven by insects, pulled the fibers into wings.

One day as the girls compared the lunches their mothers had packed and rolled their eyes at their dichos, Vanessa Garcia, the most popular girl in the third grade, noticed how Pilar hugged her scraped knees to her chest and stared at the ground.

"What about your mother?" Vanessa asked.

Suddenly the circle's eyes were on Pilar, her face hot. "No tengo... I don't have a mother." Hearing the rawness of her own voice, she woke to loneliness.

"What happened to her?" Vanessa asked.

Pilar's pile of wings looked wrong. She buried them. The girls of Freddy Gonzales Elementary waited for her to say something, but she'd brought that wrongness into being with words and would not say anything else.

She left the circle.

Vanessa Garcia and her circle of ducks whispered when Pilar got on the school bus home. Pilar walked to the back and sat by Melinda, who played with the boys at recess. Melinda of the gnarled hair, oversized Selena T-shirt with ketchup stains, snot on her sleeve. Melinda did not turn from the window when Pilar sat next to her.

Fifteen minutes into the bus route, Pilar said, "I like your earrings." Her heart pounded. Melinda wore thin gold hoop earrings too big for her, the gold flaking off. Pilar was the only girl in her class whose ears weren't pierced. Marin had said no when she asked.

Melinda turned from the window and narrowed her eyes, like she thought Pilar was making fun of her. Pilar held her gaze, and there was a momentary softening in Melinda's face, an almost-smile. And then she shrugged, wiped snot on her sleeve, and stared down at the dirty rubber floor. Her hair parted to reveal a purplish lump at the base of her head. Melinda touched it, gently, as if to see if it was still there.

Dust rose as the school bus pulled onto La Llanura's long gravel drive. A rock flew up from the wheels and cracked their window. Through that cracked window, home looked wrong.

Pilar wanted to swim alone—to wash off that wrongness—but Marin insisted on watching from the dock. Pilar remembered the writhing child in the supermarket. She wanted to scream, *You never let me do anything on my own!*, but she never yelled. That red scream throbbed in her chest as she dove off the dock. She swam underwater for as long as she could, far from her father. She swam until the world was muffled and dim.

But when she climbed out of the water, her father was waiting. He handed Pilar a towel, but she did not take it. She stood, dripping, arms folded across her chest, her heart racing.

"What happened to my mother?" She stared at Marin in that unbudging way she had.

Marin wondered how long she'd wanted to ask, this child who asked for so little. "Sit down, mija," he said, wrapping the towel around her shoulders.

They sat together at the edge of the dock. Marin stared at the horizon, remembered riding, huddled with strangers, on top of trains and crammed between orange crates in truck beds. Walking through desert and brush. He kept to himself, migrated as a ghost does. His heart stirred absently at a sunset or a mother rocking her child, lifting like desert sand then settling back into oblivion, days dirt rocks trees sky running together, one country becoming another, dead so it didn't matter that the dust blew into his teeth, tongue, eyes. He hardly ate. Hunger had left him, he thought, for good.

Until he saw Luz.

He'd hitched a ride with a truck driver in Mexico City who'd agreed to drop him at the edge of the Rio Grande, where the river was shallow enough to walk across. Anticipation had kept Marin awake for the first half of the 11-hour drive, but sleep overtook him when night fell.

When the driver shook him awake, they were parked at the edge of a sugarcane field, the darkness thick as tar. The driver flipped on his lights and Marin saw Luz standing with five women. The women were afraid, but Luz shielded her eyes and stared at Marin—a halo of curly black hair, the curves of her silhouette engraved in his mind in that second before she grabbed the hands of the other women and slipped into the sugarcane. The stalks absorbed their bodies, sprang back as if they'd never been.

Even at first glimpse, Luz's pull was as magnetic as the moon's. Marin thanked the driver, hurriedly gathered his bag, climbed out of the truck. He could hear the women praying as they moved through the cane. *El Señor es mi pastor; nada me faltará. The Lord is my Shepherd; I shall not want.* Not wanting to frighten them, he waited until their voices were a distant hum before he stepped into the field behind them. He made his way slowly through the darkness, over the soft, uneven soil, the rough stalks cutting his face. He hadn't walked far before he lost all sense of direction. He listened for the women's voices, followed their prayers—*Sí, aunque ande en valle de sombra de muerte, no temeré mal alguno. Yea, though I walk through the valley of the shadow of death, I will fear no evil.*

It was like the mines, the men moving as one body through the tunnels. He'd come to know the other miners beneath words, sight. When his headlamp went out, he could trace the dimensions of their bodies, the parabolas of their pickaxes. Luz knew her way through the cane like that. Marin knew he was meant to follow her.

When he emerged from the cane, she stood with the women huddled behind her. She'd heard him. By the light of the full moon, he saw the switchblade she held against her thigh. She locked eyes with him, let him know she would use it. He loved her more. From the beginning, his love was sharpened by the knowledge that she would leave him.

"I won't hurt you," he said. She held his gaze a moment longer, then turned toward the river. It was spring, when the Retamal Dam raised the water from waist to shoulder high to irrigate crops on either side. Spring in that place marked by the bloom of white crosses along the riverbank, the corpses the Los Ebanos ferrymen hauled from the river, worms bursting from their guts.

The women waded into the river holding hands—a line of crosses—Luz at their center. It was 1984; Luz had been leading refugees of the Central American crisis across the river at night for months. She knew how to navigate the current and avoid the remolinos—whirlpools that toppled whole cows. The women's prayers carried across the water. They said the rosary, squeezed hands instead of beads. It was well past midnight, black sky bleeding into river, creating some confusion over which mysteries to reflect on. Thursday's rosary reflected on the Luminous Mysteries, Friday's on the Sorrowful. The pockmarked promise of the sorrowful, luminous moon called them across that dirty river.

Marin's mother used to pray the rosary when his father worked a double shift in the mines. He knew the prayers by heart but had not believed for years. Belief had dried up like the silver ore veins of Cerro Rico Mountain. *The mountain that eats men*, they called it. Marin left not because he believed in a better life, but because his old life caved in.

Something like belief welled up in him as he waded into the river behind the women. A baptism—their prayers merging with the current, ringing through the darkness, *As it was in the beginning, is now, and ever shall be, world without end*—their linked arms a line of crosses moving toward shore. They took the river into their veins, swallowed mouthfuls of raw sewage and maquiladora runoff as they prayed. Luz did not pray; she pushed against the current. She held fast to the women, dark rush of the river at her chin. When she rose out of the water, wet clothes clinging to her body, halo of curls still dry, Marin was filled with faith.

"Papá...?" Pilar searched his face with those deep-set, gray-blue eyes that would have made more sense in a grandmother's face.

Marin told the lie in English, which he understood but rarely spoke. "Your mother died giving birth to you." In that tongue not his own, it seemed true. He saw Luz wade into the resaca until the water closed over her. In English, the words had edges. They left his lips and hung separate from him, from the night he first saw Luz. In that darkness, there were no edges—one skin, river became another. It seemed that both worlds could exist, that world of shadows and this sun-raked afterlife in which everything was exposed to the light—his daughter's shoulder blades like broken things. Both worlds could exist: One made of language, that lie, and the other of feeling. The sharpness of sugarcane against skin might rise like a full moon in this desert. Two truths, like praying to the Virgin in church and El Tio in the mines. True that Luz brought him back to life; true that she left him for dead. She'd dropped them in these flatlands and returned to the river's dark current.

"Why did she die?" Pilar asked.

"She couldn't afford a doctor." That part was true enough. To deter undocumented patients, the hospital had bought green uniforms for their security guards like the Border Patrol's. Luz had seen a partera—a midwife.

The rest Marin told Pilar in Spanish: "Su nombre era Luz. She swam across the Rio Grande at night to give birth to you here."

"What was she like?" Pilar asked.

"She was beautiful." Marin's eyes went glassy. "And smart."

"Do I look like her?" Pilar asked to be seen.

Marin glanced at her—tall for her age, blonde, skinny, blue-gray eyes. "You look like me." He waved his hand as if that wasn't much to speak of, turned back to the resaca. He watched the patterns the wind made on the surface. "You're smart like her."

Pilar waited for more, but her father lay back on the dock and stared up at the blue bowl of sky until the edges of La Llanura folded around them. His breathing calmed, but the air in Pilar's lungs, the air of La Llanura, felt thin and not enough.

The girls of Freddy Gonzales Elementary did cartwheels on freshly cut grass while Pilar wandered through the sugarcane field that bordered La Llanura, listening for Luz. Luz spoke loudest there, the stalks over Pilar's head, a shelter that threatened to swallow her. If she walked too far in, she forgot where she'd come from, couldn't tell one way from another.

Do you see me? Pilar would whisper and wait—the stalks scraping her cheeks, arms, and legs—until a hot, dry wind hit her body, blew a hole in the distant cane, a hole in the shape of a woman, twisting. Pilar moved toward it and the hole closed over. She thought if she got close, she would see her mother. If she got close, she would be lost.

Do you love me? Pilar dared to ask, and some days there were answers in an upwhirl of glittering dust, the rustle of mesquite tree pods, the ripples on the surface of the resaca. Some days no matter, or perhaps because of, how much Pilar wanted her mother, she wouldn't come. Or she left suddenly, the way the light leaves when a cloud passes over the sun—warm on your shoulders, then gone.

On those days, Pilar tried to outrun the emptiness. She ran up and down the guttered rows of the nearby citrus grove—the trees strong and squat, their ragged limbs heavy with fruit—her heels digging into the soft soil until her calves ached. She reached her hand through halos of gnats to gather the fallen fruit, stretching her T-shirt into a cradle for a half-dozen bruised oranges. The citrus grove ran to the edge of the highway, the sharp clean smell mingling with the exhaust of old trucks. Pilar crouched between the last of the trees and waited for the trucks, the sound of loud boys laughing inside, hands dangled out open windows. She hurled the rotten oranges as hard as she could. The thud they made on a door, splat on a windshield, was satisfying. But when all the oranges were gone, the emptiness returned. It gnawed at her stomach, the taste of diesel and overripe fruit on her tongue.

————————————

That winter was a long, gray rain that kept Pilar from wandering through the sugarcane. On a day in late February, it beat against the school bus windows so that her father, waving, blurred as the bus pulled away. Pilar sat at the back of the bus with Melinda, who made room for her but stared out the window until they got to school.

Pilar's teacher, Mrs. Guerra, always read the class a story after recess. While everyone was grabbing a carpet square, Pilar saw Mrs. Guerra forcing Melinda to stand with her nose in the corner. When Melinda peered over her shoulder, Mrs. Guerra pressed her nose back into the corner and held her there until she stopped wriggling. Mrs. Guerra's cross swung on its chain. She was a small woman, but her hand seemed massive on Melinda's bird-boned back.

Mrs. Guerra sat in her rocking chair and began to read. Five minutes in, Melinda began to cry silently, her shoulders shaking. Pilar narrowed her eyes at Mrs. Guerra, who kept reading. The feeling of being pinned built inside her until it produced an equal and opposite reaction.

It thrust itself out of Pilar's mouth as if it had a life of its own: wet, insolent muscle.

At precisely that moment, Mrs. Guerra looked up. "Pilar!" Her brow furrowed. "I'm surprised at you."

Pilar stared back wide-eyed. She'd loved Mrs. Guerra, loved school until that afternoon. She bit her tongue and picked at her bug-bitten legs through the rest of story time. When it was over, she had no idea what the story was.

Mrs. Guerra made Pilar stay after school and write, *I will not stick out my tongue* a hundred times on the chalkboard. The words hunched their shoulders then bowed their heads then crawled on their hands and knees. When she'd gotten to 50, Mrs. Guerra put her hand on Pilar's back, gently, though Pilar thought of her hand on Melinda's back, and said, "That's enough." She let Pilar read while they waited for her father.

He looked tired when he arrived. His body was too big for the child's chair he sat in. Mrs. Guerra told him in broken Spanish what had happened. Her father leaned forward, struggling to understand. Pilar stared at the floor.

"You know you're one of my favorites," Mrs. Guerra said to her. "That's why your behavior this afternoon surprised me. Is Melinda your friend?"

Pilar shrugged.

"Pilar es una buena chica," Marin insisted.

Pilar was a good girl. She stayed in at recess to do homework. She stood aside as the other kids fought to be first in line.

She was supposed to translate for her father, but that wild child with her tongue thrust out had no language. Pilar held Mrs. Guerra's gaze—the bones in her face sharp as knives. Marin saw Pilar's refusal to look away and was afraid for her.

Marin and Pilar were silent as they left the school. Already the hallways were empty and dim. When they stepped outside, the rain had stopped and the sun had emerged from the clouds. The light was so bright that Pilar's vision went black. It seemed she was inside a dark bubble when her father said, "Mija, you can't do that." He scanned the parking lot, lowered his voice: "I am *illegal*." She had to be good or he would be sent back to Bolivia.

Pilar didn't really know what *illegal* meant, but she knew it had to do with the fear and the hiding. She knew not to ask questions. Her eyes adjusted. The rows of silent cars boxed into white lines, glinting tar, and fields of dirt beyond came into focus, and the red prickle of rage was pulled into dust.

Her father put his arm around her. "The Bible tells us not to take on others' battles," he said softly, but felt the hard prayer boards of his childhood. It was something his mother had said. To thank the priest who'd given him his job, Marin took Pilar to Mass once a month.

Her father's words dissolved like the story Mrs. Guerra had read. It seemed to Pilar that she'd been dropped from the sky into that glinting black lot and was seeing everything for the first time. She read her father's face—sad and passing sadness. She saw how the light shattered, dancing off the cracked mirrors and rusted chrome, how it broke before it was held.

They drove home in silence. The long gravel drive that ran to the house was riddled with puddles of rain.

A black car was parked beside the house. When they got closer, they saw a man in a dark suit at the door. Her father's knuckles were white on the wheel.

"Stay here," he said when he got out of the car.

Pilar sat motionless in the truck, promising so hard in her head that her lips moved that she would be a *good girl, good girl, good girl* if they didn't take her father away.

When Marin got to the porch, the man held up a badge. Pilar watched them talk; her father kept shaking his head, *No*. The windows were up, but by the way he shook his head, the slow movement of his lips, Pilar could hear him saying, "No, sir," the words misshapen in that language not his own.

He was breathing hard when he returned to the car. He told Pilar that he needed to talk to the man, to go play outside. "Yes, sir," she said.

Pilar walked slowly through the citrus grove, her tennis shoes sticking in the mud. She gathered all of the fallen oranges she could in her T-shirt, whispering, *Good girl, good girl, good girl*. The black car was still in the driveway when she returned. She rolled up her jeans and waded into the resaca to rinse the mud off the oranges. The water was cold and by the time she finished, her feet were blue.

When she walked into the house, her father and the man were sitting across from each other at the kitchen table.

"That was the last time I saw Luz," her father said, and the man wrote on his notepad.

Seeing her father's hand tremble on the table, Pilar again felt the red prickle of rage beneath her skin. "My mother is *dead*," she said to the man in the suit, her heart racing. The hardness of her voice echoed in her head.

The man stopped writing, raised his eyebrows at her father.

Pilar laid the oranges so gently on the table that her father kissed the top of her head and whispered, "Gracias, mija," before shooing her back outside.

Pilar wanted to press her ear to the door and listen but made herself walk down the long gravel drive, side-stepping puddles: *Good girl, good girl, good girl*. She lay in the grass staring up at the sky, her red windbreaker tied tight around her face. Thick gray clouds gathered, but the sky held its breath until finally the black car with its tinted windows drifted past like another cloud and drops began to fall.

When she walked into the house, her father was still sitting at the table, watching the rain beat against the windows.

One of the oranges had rolled onto the floor. Pilar picked it up and sat beside him. She peeled the orange and handed him slices, the sharp sweet smell overtaking the smell of rain.

After dinner, Pilar washed the dishes and got ready for bed while her father rocked on the porch and watched the rain. He did not come to tell her a story. Pilar tried to sleep but every time she closed her eyes, she saw dark puddles in the road, low-slung clouds, the black car.

She found her father on the porch. "Háblame de los túneles," she said and led her father by the hand into the house, into the story.

Her father tucked her in and they began as they always did: "Buscamos la vena," he said. Pilar held two fingers over his pulse as if she knew the story would keep him alive.

Her father led her by the hand through the mine. They did everything carefully—*con cuidado, nunca a la fuerza*—but he couldn't finish the story. He could not save Roberto. He stared at the dark windows.

The low, mournful keen of a night train stirred up questions. Would the man in the black car take her father away? Why had they been talking about her mother? The unspoken hung like clouds in her chest. She opened the window, breathed in the rain.

"How did he die, Papá?" The blood beat so loudly in her ears that she hardly heard her words.

When she turned from the window, her father looked at her like she'd killed Roberto.

The train was gone but the wind howled, forced its way into Marin's dead lungs. Dust caught in his throat. He coughed and couldn't stop. The cough tore through his chest, wrapped its fist around his breath. Still coughing, he slammed the window shut. "You're too old for stories."

He went back out to the porch, his cough trailing through the house. The porch boards were weathered and sagging. Pilar lay in bed listening to the creak of him rocking, the rasp of his cough. When he left for his night shift, silence filled the house. The weight of it sat on Pilar's chest. She cried without sound, careful not to break it.

CHAPTER 2

Who was Pilar Reinfeld? Where did that name come from? *Reinfeld*. No one could pronounce it. And why *Pilar* when she was white? The handful of South Junior High students who'd been in kindergarten with her remembered her approaching the teacher with her construction paper and scissors, asking her to repeat the instructions in Spanish, staying in at recess to finish. But Pilar didn't speak the Spanglish they spoke and her accent was weird. By junior high, she was still an enigma—slipping into first period late, always late, her long blonde hair wet—who knew white girls' hair changed colors when it was wet?—pulled into a tight ponytail, pale and gangly and dressed like a Catholic school girl, spit-shined penny loafers with spit-shined pennies in them, wandering the dusty lunch yard like a ghost, a taco in one hand and a book in the other. Why didn't she sit down? Why didn't she talk to anyone? Who were her people?

In the final days of seventh grade, in eighth period Texas History, Pilar tried to tell them. There had been the usual circus before the bell rang, everyone talking over each other, Smiley (Ismael) Palacios, the class clown, chasing Pilar around the classroom, pulling her ponytail. Pilar was a head taller than him, beauty blooming beneath the stark bones of her face and in the motion of her long, sinewy limbs. As Smiley leaned in close enough for her to smell his Cheetos-breath and taunted, "How come you're wearing a uniform?", she looked through him. She thought about how he'd never have caught her if not for the obstructions of desks and students. She thought about running through the citrus grove, the thud of oranges hitting trucks.

Now standing before the class in her black pleated pinafore and starched white shirt, she stared at some vague point above her classmates' heads and struggled to explain her origins. This habit of seeing her thoughts rather than the people in front of her made her seem distant. She found the visual distracting, was more likely to know a thing from its sound, feel, taste, smell. As her classmates waited for her to find words, she heard them breathe.

The Texas school system believed their state's history unique enough to merit an entire year of study. When Mr. De La Garza's students had copied all of his timelines from the overhead projector; color-coded all of his state maps according to climate, agriculture, and industry; and viewed every last slide of his family trips to the Alamo and Big Bend, he had fumbled for a project to fill the last two weeks of the year and settled on his students presenting their family trees. Pilar had nervously approached him after class. "I don't know anything about my mother's family," she'd said. "Just do your best," Mr. D had said. The students who presented before Pilar had traced their lineages back to great-grandparents, grandparents, or parents who'd come from Mexico. And then there was Pilar, whose family history wound back and forth across North and South America like a cat's cradle.

At ten, Pilar learned the name for her father's cough. She read about its bleakest prognosis, but never said it aloud: *Silicosis*. When his hands were calloused from digging a grave, Pilar used to peel the dead skin from his palms and hold it up to the light like a holy parchment. But now cyanosis had turned his fingers blue, and she was afraid to touch them. She grew too big to sit on his lap in the rocking chair. She woke to him coughing as he cooked breakfast. They tiptoed around its sound, apologizing when they bumped into each other.

At twelve, her first period arrived in the night. She awoke to blood, her own and her father's. Blood flowered in crumpled tissues Marin no longer tried to hide. He left piles of tissues to rust beside his rocking chair, the stove, his plate.

Pilar had hoped the family lineage assignment would open up new stories. Her father had seemed to want that. He'd made cocoa and pulled his chair close to hers. They'd worked late into the night, the smell of chocolate and cinnamon tangling with stale grease.

When Marin had explained to her as a child that they looked like his Mennonite father, Pilar had asked him if her grandparents were alive. He'd told her that his father had died when he was 13, which was when he began mining; and that his mother had died when he was 16. The fact that everyone her father had loved was dead, that she was his only family, became clear and sad and close as they worked on her family tree.

Pilar's assignment was just that for Marin; he wanted her to do well. He worked out the math of their relatives' births and deaths and wrote the dates on the branches Pilar had drawn. "Papá died when I was 13. He was 34. He was born in Manitoba, Canada and died in Potosi, Bolivia. Mamá died when I was 16. She lived in Potosi her whole life. Your mother died when you were born, in 1985. She lived in Matamoros." They walked through the graveyard of everyone her father had loved, and he read the tombstones as if they belonged to strangers. He protected the dead from the living and the living from the dead, making sure no vandals defaced the epitaphs he engraved. He sang Pilar a lullaby of birth and death and death and death.

Pilar didn't want to sleep. "How'd your mother and father die?" she asked.

"It was a hard life in Potosi." Her father sighed. "They call Cerro Rico the Mountain that Eats Men."

Pilar waited for more.

Her father shook his head. "It was a hard life."

Pilar watched him closely as he wrote *Luz Moreno, b. 1960, d. 1985*, his blueish hand like those of the dead. She'd thought again and again about the man in the black car, her father's hand trembling on the table when he spoke about the last time he'd seen Luz.

"Tell me about her." Pilar held his gaze.

Marin traced the bare branches of Luz's side of the tree. "Your mother didn't know who her father was. She lived in Matamoros and spent her days caring for her mother. At night she led women—refugees from Guatemala and El Salvador—across the river into the US. She led them through the sugarcane, so la migra wouldn't see. Luz's mother didn't know about that, or about us. She had many secrets."

Pilar remembered speaking to her mother in the sugarcane as a child. She felt that old tingle. She opened her mouth to ask for more, but the words evaporated.

"When I lost your mother, I gained you." Her father's mouth smiled, but not his eyes.

And so Pilar's maternal half of the tree was sawed off.

Her father's hand trembled on the table. He added a branch to the family tree: *Roberto Reinfeld, b. 1964, d. 1977. Potosi, Bolivia.* "Thirteen." Marin stared at his math, his fist wrapped around his pencil.

"I'm thirteen," Pilar said.

Her father nodded.

"You're the only one alive," Pilar said.

A beat of silence passed in which her father looked at the dark windows and the house held its breath. "I survived because I left," he said.

"Why'd your father's family move to Bolivia?" Pilar asked.

"I told you he was a Menono, yes?"

"But I don't know what that means."

"Papá didn't talk much." Her father's eyes grew distant. "Mamá was Catholic. She kept statues of saints in every room. When Papá worked the mines, she said the rosary over and over. *As it was in the beginning, is now, and ever shall be, world without end.* I asked Mamá how come Papá didn't go to Mass, how come he spoke Spanish in a funny accent."

"Like you," Pilar said.

Her father looked surprised, then smiled. "Like me... and like you." He mussed Pilar's hair.

"Mamá told me Papá grew up a Mennonite, that they believed in the Bible and lived the old way, without electricity, cars, or telephones. They lived away from the world, in colonies. When Papá was 12, my grandparents left a colony in Canada and moved to Bolivia, where the government gave the Mennonites land and religious freedom. They traveled in horse-drawn buggies, used tractors with steel wheels, sewed their own clothes, and spoke German. Mamá said she and Papá didn't need words, that she loved him in his silly overalls and straw hat. He left the Mennonites for her. 'When you leave the Menono Colony, you leave forever,' she told me. 'You are dead to your family.' Some days Papá did seem dead."

Pilar thought of how often she'd felt the same about her father.

"How come you live here, Papá?"

"Your mother gave birth to you here. She wanted you to be an American."

Marin looked out the windows into the night and saw La Llanura in his mind, the resaca and the flat fields, the emptiness he'd chosen, as if he'd conjured it out of the darkness, as if it was the only world he could have created. Like the swarms of Monarch butterflies that migrated from Canada to Central America, generations of their descendants instinctively returning to the same tree in the jungle after their parents died mid-migration, Marin returned to the world of simplicity and seclusion that his father had run from.

"What's a Mennonite?" Smiley Palacios asked after Pilar presented her graveyard of a family tree. Mr. De La Garza looked at Pilar blankly, waiting for an explanation, himself.

"They believed in living like people did in the Bible... without cars or electricity or TV," Pilar fumbled, staring into space. "They grew their own food and sewed their own clothes."

"Like you." Smiley smiled his oily smile.

"That's enough, Smiley," Mr. De La Garza said.

Pilar felt the blood rush to her face. "Their kids went to school until they were 12 and mostly studied the Bible in German. Then they started farming. My great grandparents left Canada for Bolivia because the government passed a law that required them to learn English and send their kids to public school."

"If they wanted to speak German, why didn't they move to Germany?" Smiley asked.

Splotches bloomed on Pilar's face like red birds crashing into windows. Her panic elicited a barrage of questions: *How come you don't look half-Mexican? Did the Menopeople have telephones? How come your mom's half of the tree is blank?* Mr. De La Garza made futile attempts to shut down the feeding frenzy. He took his glasses off, closed his eyes, and pinched the bridge of his nose. Her classmates' faces blurred. The confusion of her family lineage was writ on her skin: the ghost-pale reserve of the Mennonites, and the wild dance of the Potosi miner festival with its buckets of llama blood thrown over the mouth of the mine. It was hard enough to contain that strange tangle of blood, never mind explain it.

How to explain that she was the product of La Llanura—an old-souled ghost girl born out of her mother's death, raised in a world of resacas, sugarcane, and songs that sang only in her head? She was a Menono without the comfort of religion—speaking her own language, at odds with society. She shuffled her feet as she walked the perimeter of the dirt lunch yard and dust rose behind her—the tail of the long migration that plunked her down in that South Texas school yard. She longed to belong to some flesh and blood circle of soulmates, but she descended from a long line of defectors and didn't believe one existed.

Pilar stood, paralyzed, in front of her Texas History class until their questions died down and they stared at her with faces blank as pancakes. Her panic quieted and she woke to loneliness.

"Asking why the Mennonites didn't move to Germany if they wanted to speak German is as stupid as the people who say, 'If you want to speak *Mexican*, why don't you live in Mexico?'." The boy who said this was short and chubby with dark, curly hair. Wire-rim glasses framed his cherubic face. Pilar had never noticed him.

"That's right..." Mr. De La Garza scanned his grade book for the boy's name. "Thank you, Carlos. It was an excellent presentation, Pilar." Mr. De La Garza smiled weakly. "You can take your seat."

Pilar wanted to turn to look at Carlos after class. Her heart pounded as she gathered her things. When she finally looked up, he was gone.

At lunch, she glanced up from her book to see him at an outdoor table of drama kids who laughed hysterically as he told them some story.

In high school, Pilar was still perpetually late. The school bus got her there early, but she would get lost in some book at the library, starting when the librarian tapped her shoulder. Emerging from the glassed-in quiet of the library into the chaos of the cafeteria was like her father emerging from the mines. The fluorescent light was too bright, the voices too loud. Pilar read until the halls emptied. She walked to class slowly, thinking, like Esperanza in *The House on Mango Street*, about how her name meant different things in English and in Spanish. Pilar: a sturdy column of stone, wood, or metal. But what was her strength for? Always she moved less through physical space and time than through a private interior landscape of memories and musings, a subterranean tunneling known only to her.

She'd slink into first period Geometry 15 minutes past the bell, her long blonde hair pulled into a tight ponytail at the base of her neck, her black dress buttoned to the collar like Emily Dickinson, the sharp cut of her cheekbones, jawline, widow's peak, everything about her so severe except for the wild red blotches painting her skin when the boys called her name. Smiley Palacios no longer chased her around the classroom; rumor had it that he was medicating his ADHD with cocaine he bought from one of the school security guards. The boys were more cunning. *Pilar, Pilar, Pilar* they whispered, coughed, peeped, and bellowed when she entered the classroom, one boy at a time in rapid succession, a censontli birdsong flitting around the room until Mr. Encinea, who would have rather been coaching golf, wearily directed their attention back to points, lines, and planes. Pilar refused to look at the boys. She slid into a desk and opened her textbook, but the boys had gotten what they wanted: red blotches flowered on her cheeks and forehead, deepening until her face was tomato red.

She never spoke a word in Geometry and sometimes slept face-down on her desk, while in English, she raised her hand when no one else would. She talked shyly about *The Scarlet Letter*, color rising and falling in her face—a scarlet alphabet of its own. She used words none of them understood, talked about Hester Prynne like that stock-entangled Puritan was her best friend. Mrs. Alvarez looked at her blankly when Pilar concluded her impassioned discourse on Hester's desire to determine her own identity. Her classmates loved that Mrs. Alvarez read aloud and let them sleep; they loved getting her talking about her dachshund, Mighty Max, for whole class periods, *begged* her to again tell the story of Mighty Max's Halloween costume: a giant hotdog bun with little holes for his legs.

Pilar smiled at this photo of Mighty Max the first time, but when Mrs. Alvarez had passed it around so many times that it was creased and covered in fingerprints, when she'd read aloud to her AP English class for the whole of a six-week grading period, Pilar left her class and went to the library. She read the end of *The Scarlet Letter* slowly, delaying the bereavement that descended upon her when she finished a book she loved. She mourned for Hester and Pearl and Dimmesdale, then wandered through the stacks in search of a new love, trailing her fingers along the books' spines.

Some days the security guards barred Pilar's entry to the library, demanding a pass from a teacher. "My teacher isn't teaching," she said. Her words echoed in her head as they did in the rare times she spoke her mind.

"Those are the rules," the security guard said, blocking the library doors.

Pilar gave the security guard the same unflinching stare she'd given Mrs. Guerra in third grade.

"Do you want to go to detention?" he asked.

"Can I read there?"

And soon she was in detention, writing an essay on the misuse of authority in response to the question, "Why are you in detention?" A security guard walked around making sure that everyone was silent and writing and collected their papers. Pilar knew no one would read them.

Carlos Gomez, the boy who'd come to Pilar's defense in Texas History, was in her junior year Spanish class. Pilar had kept an eye on him as he transitioned from glasses to contacts, from the Tommy Hilfiger polos and jeans that everyone else wore to a Mod look—skinny ties, vests, and blazers. The cherubic baby fat of his adolescence had fallen away to reveal a face that belonged in a Renaissance painting—olive skinned with dark, bottomless eyes and lips like a butterfly. On Football Fridays, when the other students wore red and blue to support the Bobcats, Carlos dressed like Ziggy Stardust in a red and blue striped jumpsuit and red pleather platform boots, a red and blue lightning bolt painted on his face. "I'm rooting for a different team," he said. It was 2001; San Jacinto High's senior song was Christina Aguilera's "I Turn to You". Since no one knew who Ziggy Stardust was, they assumed Carlos' striped jumpsuit and lightning face paint were of his own invention. In a way, they were. No one could have made more mad sense as the Cheshire Cat in San Jacinto High's staging of *Alice in Wonderland*, or been more heartbreakingly honest as Biff in *Death of a Salesman*. Word of Carlos' stardom spread until closing night was standing room only, football players who might otherwise have gone their entire lives without seeing a play, spilling into the aisles. Carlos' classmates and fellow thespians loved him for his wit, and his Math and Science teachers loved him for his brilliance. Mr. Cancino and Mrs. Bonura, his UIL Math and Science sponsors, were in a constant tug of war with his drama teacher over whose practices and competitions Carlos would attend. When security guards harassed him about the dress code, these teachers were quick to plead his defense.

As many people as there were who loved Carlos, there were plenty who hated him. "Hey, maricón!" they'd call as he walked down the hall. They'd spit in his face. Luckily, Carlos had undergone 12 years of intense surveillance training. His Mexican mother had crossed the border to leave him with his grandmother when he was five. No matter how many times his grandmother prayed to Saint Anthony or cast her curandera spells, his mother never returned. His mother had laughed and exclaimed, "¡Qué bonita!" when he came out of the bathroom wrapped in her silk robe and draped in her jewelry. It was her boyfriend who tried to beat that beauty out of Carlos. His mother thought he'd be safe with his grandmother.

Abuela tried to keep him safe, constantly warning him about drawing El Mal de Ojo—an admiring stare that led to bad luck, sickness, or death. Carlos' beauty was so feminine that the admiration was always mixed with confusion, which prolonged the stare and, in Abuela's diagnosis, deepened the evil. *Don't sit cross-legged; don't play house, especially not with Enrique; don't use glitter on that card; I'll rip up i's dotted with hearts; no, you can't have light-up tennis shoes, a hula hoop, an E-Z Bake Oven; how about this toy train, this water bazooka, this lizard cage?* Later it was, *Don't cross your legs, talk with your hands, read* Vogue, *watch musicals, wear cologne, style your hair, or file your nails!* When Carlos tried to sneak out of the house dressed as Ziggy Stardust, his grandmother stood on the doorstep shouting, *Tights are for ballerinas and Dios mío, the lighting struck your hair!* Abuela's surveillance produced the keen powers of observation and chameleon-like transformation essential to Carlos' survival at San Jacinto High. If some jock should harass him, Carlos could ape his bow-legged swagger and slow-rolling baritone within an inch of identity theft. He kept wit like a switchblade rolled in his sleeve; he kept a switch-blade for when wit didn't work.

Pilar and Carlos had a working relationship in Spanish class. They were the only students who could read and write in Spanish. Their classmates' Spanish had crumbled like the window-front shops of San Jacinto's Main Street—panaderías replaced by Starbucks, taquerias by Taco Bell, farmacias by Walgreens. Scolded for speaking Spanish in school as children, given the message that Spanish was for low-class cholos, they'd unlearned it. If their parents spoke Spanish, they sounded a lot like Char-lie Brown's parents by high school. "Slow down, Mamá!" they complained and answered her in English.

Carlos didn't want to forget. He remembered his mother in Spanish. Pilar didn't have the words to convey the nuances of her thoughts to her father. This was why they listened to Mrs. Sepulveda's 15-minute mono-tone lessons. She completed her assignments, then spent the rest of class transcribing her father's stories of the mines.

Mrs. Sepulveda, for her part, did require her students to turn in their assignments, though it didn't concern her that, with the exception of Pilar, they all copied from Carlos. She believed it was for the best that they forget Spanish. It would do nothing but drag them down.

Carlos facilitated a smooth assembly line of copiers. He supervised the pushing together of desks and moved the neatest writers to the head of the line. He flitted around the classroom, humming songs by The Smiths, offering assistance with a mix of sweetness and sass. "Accent over the e," he corrected Ruby Rojas, a mezcla mix of New Waver and nerd who wore tattered flood pants and edited the yearbook. "Love that amulet!" Carlos leaned in to look at the deep purple vial around her neck. When he reached the tail end of the copying line to find Hector Hinojosa, the Varsi-ty quarterback, lagging, he clucked his tongue and scolded, "Hector, mijo, you can do better!" Carlos fidgeted through Mrs. Sepulveda's 15-minute lessons so that it seemed he wasn't listening, but when she called on him, he'd offer up the answer with some twist of wit that momentarily dredged Mrs. Sepulveda out of her boredom and made her imagine, in a fit of laughter, a world where she loved teaching. Accent by tilde, Carlos won over the football players, cheerleaders, new wavers, preps, and kickers. When he didn't know the answer, he asked Pilar. She gave it to him, and he made sure that she was left in peace to fill the pages of her notebook.

At the end of each grading period, Mrs. Sepulveda called students up to her desk to ask them what grade they felt they deserved and how many absences they had. Every student claimed they deserved an "A," which they got.

"Pi-*la*-ar!" Mrs. Sepulveda sang. "How many absences?"

Pilar was writing about the time a pale-footed swallow flew into the mine and got trapped in a vertical shaft. Marin had made a net by tying Roberto's red bandanna to the end of a rope and scooped up the swallow. As soon as he'd lifted it out of the shaft, it broke free. Disoriented, it flew into the tunnel's walls until it collapsed in a bloody heap. Marin and Roberto had thought it was dead. Marin wrapped its humped body in the bandanna, and Roberto carried it toward the exit, crying. But as they approached the mouth of the mine, the swallow's beak poked through the bandanna. Roberto held out the swallow and it beat a smooth course out of the mine.

"Pilar, *yoo*-hoo!" Mrs. Sepulveda called as she did to football players in the hallways. "Pilar está en otro mundo." Mrs. Sepulveda shook her head. The class laughed. "I need to know how many times you've been absent, mija."

"How many times I've been absent?" Pilar asked foggily and stared at Mrs. Sepulveda in her unnerving way. Either she didn't look, or she looked too closely. Once, waiting for a bathroom stall, she'd watched a girl primping, mesmerized as the wet red heart of her lips emerged from a cloud of Aqua Net, until the girl caught her eye in the mirror, snapped, "What are you looking at? Pinche puta güera." Güera: white girl. One "r" short of war.

When Pilar went up to Mrs. Sepulveda's desk, Hector Hinajosa swiped her notebook. Pilar froze, turning, somehow, a whiter shade of pale. Hector opened it to find pages covered in Spanish and demanded that Carlos translate. Carlos handed it back to Pilar.

Wandering through the library stacks during lunch weeks later, Pilar stumbled upon Carlos. He was hiding from two football players who'd shoved him against a locker after everyone had gone to lunch. Carlos had realized, as a Master padlock lodged in his back, that he'd left his switchblade in yesterday's jeans. His tormenters had leaned in close enough to kiss him, their breath on his butterfly lips when they spat, "Pinche maricón." They would have done worse had they not been distracted by a fight between girls from rival gangs that broke out in the cafeteria. As a chant of *FIGHT! FIGHT! FIGHT!* spread through the lunch pit, Carlos' bullies had craned their necks to get a look, and Carlos had escaped to the library. Still out of breath, he'd collapsed against the stacks opposite Pilar.

Pilar thought, for a moment, that Carlos' breathing was seeping from the books. Then she rounded the stacks to find him sitting on the floor, hugging his knees, eyes closed. The anima drained from his body, he became a stranger. Pilar fought an instinct to turn away.

Carlos opened his eyes—dark and still like the resaca at night—and Pilar held this stranger's gaze. She extended a hand, and he took it.

Carlos dusted off his *Rebel Without a Cause* red windbreaker and walked dazedly over to the library's windows, which looked out on the cafeteria. Students circled around the fight or stood on the stools bolted to the cafeteria tables, pumping their fists in the air, chanting.

When Carlos turned to Pilar, the electric energy she thought of as him had returned. "If we slip out before the crowd breaks up, they'll never notice," he said.

"Where will we go?" Pilar asked.

"Trust me." Carlos pulled Pilar by the hand out of the library. *FIGHT!*
FIGHT! FIGHT! rose as they pushed through the glass doors. Through the
crowd, Carlos and Pilar caught glimpses of the security guards struggling
to pull the girls—thrashing on the ground, their faces scratched, scalps
torn bald in patches—apart.

They slipped outside unseen and made their way through the parking
lot until they came to a brown 1988 Chevette with a rusted fender and a
dent in the back door. It was freshly washed.

"Meet The Bitch," Carlos said with a flourish.

"She's nice," Pilar said.

"You're the first to call her nice." Carlos moved a pile of CDs off the passenger seat. The inside of the car was otherwise spotless. He popped a CD
into his stereo, and soon they were speeding past lopsided shacks, trucks
on blocks, and rows of shriveled tomatoes, Lou Reed crooning through
the scratchy speakers: *Hey babe, take a walk on the wild side.*

The Bitch had no air-conditioning, so they drove with the windows
down, dust rising. Carlos sang and Pilar inhaled the words. Until then,
she'd listened to her father's Bolivian *canciones*. She had no interest in
the sugary pop on the radio, but David Bowie, Patti Smith, and Lou Reed
breathing angst into burning worlds spoke to her like an oracle. After
listening to the choruses a couple of times, Pilar sang, too. Her vocal cords
vibrated, but Carlos had the volume turned up so loud that only the sound
of "Gloria" crackled from The Bitch's speakers, so that Patti Smith's voice
became her own, the bass line thumping in her chest like a truer heart.

Carlos drove through downtown San Jacinto, past the crumbling shops
of Main Street, *Farmacia* and *Costurera* chipping from their hand-sten-
ciled window-fronts, over the railroad tracks, and onto a nowhere road
lined by brush, road kill, and a string of concrete warehouses so nameless
that they called them what they held. They called them Ropa Usadas.
Used Clothes. He parked in front of the warehouses and turned to Pilar,
his face serious.

"I thought we could do something about this." He waved his hand over her pleated black pinafore.

Pilar looked at her dress as if seeing it for the first time. "My father buys my clothes..." She hated shopping.

"My treat," Carlos said. Pilar's chiseled face and willowy figure, more like the models in *Vogue* than the curvy cheerleaders crowned Homecoming Queen, had not escaped Carlos' eye. He couldn't resist a makeover.

Clothing hung on round metal racks, but Carlos led Pilar to the back of the warehouse, where there were massive mounds of clothing—men's and women's, fat and thin, summer and winter lumped together on the concrete floor. A forklift periodically rolled in and pitched more clothing onto the piles. Pilar pictured a long line of Ropa Usadas stretching from the no-where-lands of northern Alaska to the nowhere-lands of southern Texas, each succeeding warehouse filled with the picked-over remnants of the previous warehouse. She imagined the piles of clothing before her had been shuffled through a long purgatory of increasingly dingy secondhand stores until they were laid to rest at this last ditch stop before Mexico, this unloved crotch of America.

Carlos had picked his way through the piles and was now digging through the tallest mound of clothing on his hands and knees. "Come on in, the water's fine!" he called to Pilar. He flopped backwards and waved his arms and legs, making ropa usada angels.

Pilar hesitantly waded into the strange smells, stains, and souls of the ropa usada.

Carlos held up a maroon gas-station attendant shirt with *Walen* stitched over the pocket. He put his ear to the name and listened. "Walen saved his gas-station pennies for a Harley he rode all the way from Alabama to Panama. When this shirt blew off along the way, he knew he'd never again pump gas for anyone but himself. What d'ya say, a little walk on the wild side with Walen?" Carlos cocked an eyebrow and handed Pilar the shirt.

Pilar draped it over her arm and stared out across the foothills of clothing. The strangeness of never having chosen her clothes dawned on her.

Carlos swept his arm over the mounds of clothing. "Who do you want
to be, Pilar Reinfeld?" he called across the mounds as if she was out there
somewhere. "*Who? Who? Who?*" he hooted, cupping his hands around
his mouth.

Pilar fished a pair of green corduroy bellbottoms out of the pile. She
rubbed the corduroy between her fingers, inhaled the dusty, mothball
smell. The lump in her throat loosened. She unbuttoned her collar. She
reached for another pair of bellbottoms—jeans—and a white butterfly-col-
lared shirt, sunflowers embroidered around its buttons. She tried the
shirt on over her dress, her skin tingling at the synthetic slide of polyester.
"Where are the dressing rooms?" she asked Carlos.

"No dressing rooms. That corner does the trick." He pointed. "I'll
shield you."

They made their way through the mounds to the corner, picking up
clothes along the way. Pilar picked out several bold-printed 70s shirts and
a faux-leather bomber jacket. Carlos handed her a turquoise sequin mini-
skirt. "You should show off your legs," he said. Pilar raised her eyebrows,
but took the skirt.

When they got to the corner, Carlos turned his back to Pilar and extended his arms. Shielded, Pilar pulled on the bellbottom jeans and sunflow-
er-embroidered shirt. The jeans simultaneously held her body, as nothing
she'd ever worn had, *and* a stranger's body—a history curving around her
ass, creasing around her thighs.

Carlos was her mirror. He gave a deep nod of approval and Pilar took it
in. She became a woman who stared back without blushing. She worked
her way up to the turquoise sequin miniskirt, which was short, stretchy,
and tight. When she pulled it on, the surrounding world of the Ropa
Usada fell away. There was only the skirt and her. She admired her long,
sinewy legs like they belonged to someone else. A man's eyes trailed her

as she stepped through the piles of clothing. She saw him and knew those legs were hers.

Carlos let out a wolf whistle.

"What about you?" Pilar asked.

"Lil ol' fabulous me? At 60 cents per pound, I wouldn't turn down a treasure dive." Carlos squatted and arced his arms over his head like a diver. "Whatever I come up with, I wear." He dove into the mound and tunneled for several feet before his sleek head emerged like a seal's. He held up his haul: a spaghetti-strap champagne-silk floor-length dress with gray eagle's wings over the bodice. Pilar had never seen anything so beautiful. How that delicate dress could have survived beneath all those patched trousers, she couldn't fathom.

Carlos kneeled in the pile, bent over the dress like he was praying. He bit his bottom lip.

"Shield me," he said.

Pilar turned her back to him and extended her arms.

Carlos stripped off his heavy black work boots, snug-fit Lee Riders, red windbreaker, and white T-shirt. He shivered, though the air in the Ropa Usada was warm. The dress slipped over his head like a skin. Inside its silk, he felt newborn. Abuela's all-seeing Ojo fell away, and lightness descended upon him.

When he turned to show Pilar, she caught her breath. He seemed to swim toward her in slow motion, all that anxious, crackling energy fallen away to reveal grace.

"Carla." Carlos extended her hand, like he'd always held her. "Pleased to meet you."

Carla's dark eyes glittered. The dress lifted when she twirled, her long neck and freckled shoulders so delicate it hurt to look.

"It's you." Pilar held Carla's gaze.

Carla grinned. "Let's get out of here."

They hopped a ride on the back of the forklift. The forklift driver kicked them off, but not before they'd drawn everyone's attention. People stared at this boy in his eagle's wings dress and this girl in her turquoise sequin miniskirt, but their stares were a skin that Carla and Pilar had shed.

In The Bitch, Carla pulled a deep red lipstick out of her backpack and ordered Pilar to pucker. She painted Pilar's lips and her own, and they headed for the highway. As they ascended the overpass, rose from that cracked mouth of earth into the cloudless blue sky, they opened their blood red mouths and sang.

CHAPTER 3

Pilar floated on a tide of warm air and music until she saw signs for
Mexico. Beyond his fear of deportation, Marin had filled her head with
cautionary tales of American teenagers who'd crossed the border to be
tortured with electric cattle prods by prison guards.

Pilar looked worriedly at Carla.

"We're not going to cross." Carla exited the highway and turned down
a dirt road dotted with shacks and trailers—flashes of river between
them. Pilar didn't ask where they were going. She liked being driven into
a mystery. Carla pulled off the road, drove The Bitch through a dirt lot
of brush and rusted cars, and parked at the edge of the Rio Grande. She
spread a faded quilt over the hot hood of The Bitch. They sat and stared
at the river—that dirty vein for maquiladora chemicals, raw sewage, and
drug runners that was nonetheless beautiful in its determined course. A
sugarcane field lined the Mexican side.

"People cross here," Carla said. "At night, they come through the cane."

"My mother helped women cross through the cane," Pilar said.

"She died giving birth to you?"

Pilar looked questioningly at Carla.

"Texas History. I sat in the back. Small, chubby, glasses?"

The fact that Carla had remembered, that Pilar sat in a sequin mini-skirt beside a boy in a dress on the bank of this fluid border, let her say: "I sometimes think she's alive."

"What's worse—that she's out there somewhere and doesn't want to know you, or that she's dead?" Carla looked at her with a still gaze. "My mother dropped me off with Abuela when I was five and never came back. She's still in Mexico somewhere, I guess."

"I used to wander through the sugarcane field near our house talking to her," Pilar said.

"We used to play dress up," Carla said. "She'd put on her fanciest dress and I'd wear her silk robe and jewelry and we'd dance. She was... *We* were so beautiful. Then her boyfriend tried to beat the maricón out of me. When he knocked me unconscious, Mamá brought me to Abuela. 'You'll be safe here, mijo,' she said. I didn't know she meant forever."

Pilar almost said, *I'm sorry.* It was what teachers said when she told them she didn't have a mother. She hated the pity in their eyes.

"I was going to look for her after I got a car. I had this dream of seeing her on a street in Reynosa. She'd open her arms and I'd be that free again." Carla stared across the river, her lips turned up but her eyes vacant. "Then I go to get my license and the lady hands back my green card and whispers, 'This is fake—don't show it to anyone else.' I was like, 'What the hell, Abuela? When did you plan on telling me?' Of course all of this happens a year after fucking 9/11. I might make it to Reynosa, but I'd have to stay there."

"My father's undocumented," Pilar said without looking at Carla. "He drives without a license. He shakes when he sees a cop."

"Why doesn't he do what I did?" Carla explained how she'd used her fake green card to apply for a Social Security card. She'd covered the part that read, *Valid for work only with I.N.S. authorization*, made copies, and used the doctored Social Security card to get her license and job.

"I don't even know if Papá has a fake green card. He won't see a doctor because he's afraid to fill out the forms."

"Fake ID only gets you so far." Carla shrugged. "If I get pulled over, I could still be deported. I'm never going to be a prep, but I drive the speed limit and keep The Bitch clean. I'm supposed to be meeting with Mrs. Bonura and Mr. Cancino about colleges right now. We've been meeting all year. I don't know how to tell them that I'm probably ineligible for all the scholarships we've been working on. Definitely for financial aid. I tell them I have drama practice and come here. I wait until night and watch people thrash across. I hope they make it. I hope I make it."

"Me, too." Pilar squeezed Carla's hand. She wished hard for both of them.

"Something about this ugly river." Carla smiled.

Pilar felt it—a current under her skin.

The wind blew up Carla's dress. She mock-gasped, demurely tucked her knees beneath her.

Pilar laughed. Carla threw her head back and laughed with her. The sound carried across the water.

They watched the sun set, strata of deep pinks and oranges piling up from the horizon, reflected in the river. They sat until darkness dropped over everything. Carla's voice came to Pilar on the rush of the river: "I know a drag bar where we can show ourselves off."

"My father—" Pilar said. She heard his cough.

"Your father doesn't need to know," Carla said.

"I don't know."

"You're not listening to the skirt." Carla leaned toward Pilar's skirt, cupped her hand over her ear. "Can you hear it?"

Pilar heard the rustle of cane. She felt unattached to anything but the air when she said, "Yes."

As they drove back to the city, the red and yellow lights of cars streamed into the distance like their true lives radiating outward.

Carla took Pilar to a gay bar on 10th Street called 10th Avenue. Colored spotlights streamed through machine-generated fog. Disco balls with missing rows of mirrored tiles hung from the ceiling. A drag pageant was underway when they walked in.

An MC in a tux with a sequin cummerbund and tie that matched Pilar's skirt announced: "Next up we have the reigning Mz. 10th Avenue, Betty Crocker! As many of you know, no one can backflip like Betty, and she's ready to give you the full 360 degrees of her audacious, bodacious queenitude. Who's ready for a 'round the globe LOVE tour?" The audience cheered and whistled. There were skinny, voluminous, and all sizes in between queens. Most were hyper-feminine in snug formals with big hair, bird-winged brows, heavily made-up eyes, impossibly long lashes, and deep red mouths, but Pilar noticed a couple of outliers: a gothy queen in a witch's hat with a crystal bindi; a half-man, half-queen in a powder-blue 80s-style prom dress covered by half of a tuxedo shirt and bowtie, a black line dividing their face into half-masculine and half-bighaired queen. There were clean-cut and tattooed men, many in tank tops and tight jeans with sculpted arms and hair. There were boys indistinguishable from the boys at San Jacinto High, except that they looked past Pilar to eye each other.

Pilar and Carla squeezed through the tightly packed room to find a spot near the stage. At school, Pilar felt painfully self-conscious in a crowd, her tall, angular body heavy and separate until she left it for some daydream. Here she sank into the fog and music. "Great skirt!" someone called. She felt seen but not threatened.

"Watch out for those hips, bah-dum-bum!" the MC said as Betty Crocker, who looked to be six-foot-three and had squeezed her voluptuosity into a form-fitting plush leopard-skin jumpsuit that zipped from her crotch to her considerable breasts, sashayed to the stage.

Pilar and Carla watched Betty Crocker perform Missy Elliott's "Get Ur Freak On", which had climbed its freaky way up the Billboard chart and was a regular on B-104. "I love this video." Carla did its jab, slide, and hammer dance. Pilar smiled dazedly at her, having never seen Missy's or any other music video. Mesmerized by Betty's blend of breakdancing and voguing, she swayed with the audience, warm skin brushing hers. She felt at once intensely inside her body and free of it. She grinned at Carla in gratitude for this escape from the barbed wire monotony of La Llanura. Eyes on Betty, she raised her hands and swizzled her hips. Carla laughed and butt-bumped her.

When Betty Crocker ended her performance with a 360-degree backflip in which she somehow managed to land square on her platform shoes, her black beehive still intact, Pilar understood that you could do anything you dreamed. If you did it boldly enough, the world bent to your dimensions. She didn't know if she'd ever own that boldness, but she knew that she wanted to be close to it.

Carla shook her head in amazement. "I've seen her before, but she never gets old." Betty Crocker owned the stage, the audience, the sweat dripping down her face. She looked regally apart from the standing ovation she received. The applause and whistles went on for so long that the MC had to shush the audience to announce the next contestant.

A queen in a glossy black bob named Raspberry Beret performed to the Spanish version of "Hey Mickey". The queen after her sang Janet Jackson's "All for You". She was reedy in body and voice and cloying. She periodically stopped singing to mug, pulling her obscenely long purple nails through the air toward her face, until the audience clapped.

"I never liked that song," Carla said. "Come on, let's get a drink."

Their hands had been stamped UNDER AGE, but Carla knew the bartender. She winked at him and ordered Flaming Dr. Peppers. He dropped a shot of amaretto into a mug of beer and lit the shot on fire.

"Where's the Dr. Pepper?" Pilar asked.

Carla laughed. "There's no Dr. Pepper. Blow the shot out and slam it before the glass cracks," she instructed Pilar.

Pilar liked that none of the rules made sense in this through-the-looking-glass world. She slammed the shot, the heat of amaretto hovering in her throat.

"If you really want it / All for you / If you say you need it / All for you," Purple Nails crooned with excessive vibrato.

Carla gave her the side-eye. "I don't need it." She excused herself to go to the bathroom.

Pilar drank her beer, the golden edge of it descending, and surveyed the hazy fantasia of shiny wigs, silver lashes, and glittering costume jewelry drifting through machine-generated fog. She was no longer the tallest in the room. Next to her, a queen a full head taller than her in a beaded silver dress laughed and said to the olive-skinned, platinum bobbed queen next to her, "Honey, those are the *Perezes*, not the Parises!"

Carla emerged from the smoke. She'd parted her hair to the side, shadowed her resaca eyes, darkened her long lashes, dusted her cheekbones with bronzer, and glossed her butterfly lips. The champagne-silk dress hid her feet so that she glided toward Pilar. Pilar was dumbstruck.

"You look like you've seen a ghost," Carla said.

"You look beautiful," Pilar said.

"A queen named Bianca made me up. She even shaped my brows." Carla raised her eyebrows. "Abuela'll have a fit, but—"

"You're like... glowing."

"I'll have what she's having," Carla said to the bartender.

They watched as more drag performers took the stage, none of them as mesmerizing as Betty Crocker. Finally, the MC announced, "And that concludes the 2002 Mz. 10th Avenue Pageant, unless some brave soul from the audience wants to step up to the mic." Whisperings and beehive shakings rippled through the crowd. "Anyone? *Anyone?*"

"You should do it," Pilar whispered to Carla.

"That Flaming Dr. Pepper went straight to your head," Carla said.

"Who do you want to be?" Pilar whispered.

Carla stared at the stage. She squeezed her eyes shut as if she were making a wish, opened them, and downed her drink. She pulled a CD from her backpack and walked to the stage with majestic grace. The crowd parted, the patrons of 10th Avenue turning toward Carla like a field of sunflowers. Queens nodded in approval. Men called, "Hermosa!"

Pilar's heart raced as Carla handed the MC her CD and whispered in his ear. He announced her as El Ojo. The crowd buzzed. When Carlos left the house dressed like Ziggy Stardust, Abuela would scold, "You draw the stare de chicas y chicos, confuse the Ojo. Ojo that doesn't know what it wants is the worst kind." With Patti Smith's first words—*Jesus died for somebody's sins, but not mine*, somewhere between a snarl and seduction—El Ojo stared back. No one questioned her when she growled, *My sins my own.* She strode the stage with a bow-legged swagger, her knees pummeling that silk dress like fists as she sang, *People say "Beware!"/ But I don't care / The words are just / Rules and regulations to me.* Her swagger became a jagged shimmy as the song sped up. She rocked between "Come here" and "Beware," relishing the sin of being both.

El Ojo pushed the borders, choosing androgyny in a world of hyperbolic femininity. The room embraced her so fully that Carlos' anxious energy dispersed in its sea of body heat. *I walk in a room, you know I look so proud / I'm movin' in this here atmosphere, well, anything's allowed.* El Ojo grinned around the room. Hoots and whistles rose. *I go to this here party and I just get bored / Until I look out the window, see a sweet young thing...* El Ojo blew a kiss to Pilar. *Ooh I'll put my spell on her.*

The crowd fell away and Pilar believed that El Ojo sang to her. The song pulsed in her chest. *And I said darling, tell me your name.* Pilar moved her lips in sync with El Ojo's. El Ojo motioned for the audience to sing. The chorus rose from the audience: *G-l-o-r-i-a.* El Ojo bent the world around those letters. Like a woman possessed, she rolled her eyes up to the glittering disco ball with its missing teeth. Her body a vessel to hold whatever she wanted.

When the song ended, Pilar stood in the center of the howling audience, crying at El Ojo's fierce beauty. The three judges, former Mz. 10th Avenues, held up 10s. El Ojo leapt down from the stage, and the audience cleared a path for her, still clapping as she walked toward Pilar.

"It's a tie between El Ojo and Betty Crocker," the MC said, "so have a drink and a dance while the judges confer."

Carla took Pilar by the hand and pulled her over to the DJ, whom she handed the Squirrel Nut Zippers' *Bedlam Ballroom* album. She taught Pilar to swing dance. They practiced off to the side until Pilar got the hang of it. Mostly Pilar held on tight while Carla slung her around. They made their way into the center of the crowd, which circled around them and cheered when Pilar put her hands on Carla's shoulders and Carla swung her to one side of her waist and then the other. She looked around at the towering queens in sequined formals, stilettos, and pancake makeup, drunk with their shiny, spinning world. For the first time, Pilar liked being the center of attention.

The MC called Betty Crocker and El Ojo up to the stage. Pilar wondered how El Ojo would take it if she lost. The MC paused in suspense and Betty and El Ojo squeezed hands. Carla would later tell Pilar that Betty had been a figure at 10th Avenue for many years. Impressive as her backflip was, it was no match for the revolution El Ojo ushered in.

"It was a tough decision, but the judges have chosen a winner. Mz. 10th Avenue 2002 goes to... *EL OJO!*" Betty Crocker hugged El Ojo, accepted her runner-up sash, and sashayed into the audience with impervious elegance. El Ojo's smile wobbled as she stared out at the audience, but she did not cry. Mz. 10th Avenue 2000 placed a tiara on her head and handed her a trophy. El Ojo kissed the trophy, raised it high, and pointed at Pilar.

How to take off that tiara? To shake off that fantasia of sequins and freedom? Carla couldn't bear to change back into boy clothes there, and it wasn't safe to drive home in a dress. Betty had told her about assholes following her in their cars just to shout slurs. So she changed at the 76 Truck Stop across the street. The rapt attention of 10th Avenue's queens became the aggressive leer of truckers; its machine-generated fog became the stale haze of cigarettes. Carlos changed into his jeans and T-shirt and scrubbed his face with a wet paper towel. Pilar changed back into her black pinafore. Carlos drove Pilar home cautiously, the music off. He avoided an intersection where there'd been a roundup of undocumented immigrants two days earlier.

Her father left to work in the graveyard at 9, so Pilar hoped he'd be gone when she got home. But as they neared the end of the long gravel road that led to La Llanura, Pilar could make out the silhouette of him waiting on the porch. She kissed Carlos on the cheek, stepped out of The Bitch and walked toward her father—rocking, coughing, waiting. Moths circled the porch light, ringing a mouth, the old silence rushing in.

"Where've you been?" her father demanded. He stood to get a look at Carlos as he backed out of the driveway. "Who's that boy?"

"He's on the lit mag staff." Pilar lied in English, which they almost never spoke. "We've got an issue going out, so we had to work late. No one answered when I called."

Marin squinted at Pilar, like he was struggling to see her. "I didn't hear the phone." Even from the porch, he would've heard the phone. Who was this daughter looking him in the eye and lying, her breath smelling of beer? With a sharp pain in his rib, he realized she was the child he'd made with his own lies.

"Pilar, I am—You can't be out running around at night. You can't..."

What they did not speak about hung in the air. Pilar felt her father's fear, heard him saying, *Can't, can't, can't*. But the world she'd come from was louder and said otherwise.

"I understand, Papá," she said so softly that the words didn't seem to come from her, but from some pale ghost of a self she no longer believed in.

CHAPTER 4

Standing in the doorway, silently watching her father at his morning ritu-al—his eyes on the white birds on the resaca—Pilar used to feel a love that pained her. Now the resaca was a mouth, the white birds words waiting on its tongue.

Now she danced alone in her room to Patti Smith's "Birdland". Carlos had given her *Horses*. Each song was a strange, raw poem, but it was "Birdland" that she listened to again and again. She was mesmerized by its bedtime story of a New England farm boy losing his father, languid pi-ano exploding into a spaceship hallucination. The words spoken, crooned, warbled, howled—Patti's voice stretched to hold a vision.

No matter how many times Pilar listened, it remained otherworldly. In the end, it didn't matter what Smith was saying, the words a vessel for the force inside her. You were riding in that shining black ship, shooting through the atmosphere. She loved it without understanding—the truest kind of love.

Listening in her room, she strutted and tossed her hair. Catching a glimpse of herself in the mirror, she cringed. But then the music took over. The bravery, though you were not a singer, to sing your strangeness. She took on Patti's tough, sultry, take-no-prisoners look. Her gawky teenage body, built like Patti's, filled with her defiance. She thrashed herself invincible.

Headphones in her ears, she cried out, *"Take me up quick, take me up, up to the belly of a ship / And the ship slides open and I go inside of it, where I am not human."*

Her father cracked open her door, hesitantly peered in. "Everything okay, mija?"

She opened her eyes and tried to explain, but he looked like he'd seen an alien—strange squawking swirl of black feathers.

Her father rocked on the porch, watching snowy egrets glide over the resaca, and Pilar stood on the threshold, listening to "Birdland" as she waited for Carlos.

I see them coming in, Patti sang as The Bitch pulled onto the long, dirt drive that led to the house.

Her father turned to see her in green corduroy bellbottoms, a butter-fly-collared shirt, bomber jacket slung over her shoulder.

"Where'd you get those pants?" He squinted at her like he had the night she came home from 10th Avenue.

"Carlos bought them for me at a Ropa Usada."

"Why is my daughter wearing used pants when I bought her new?"

Pilar hated how he said *my* daughter. "Carlos is waiting, Papá." She grabbed her backpack.

"What time will you be home?"

"I don't know. I've got Yearbook."

"Call me after school. If I find out you're running around with that boy," he flipped his chin at The Bitch, "I'll be driving you from now on."

Pilar hiked up her green bellbottoms like it was an offensive gesture and strode toward Carlos' car.

They drove with "Birdland" blasting and the windows down and that prophetic vision rose from the dust. The dry, flat fields were aflame as far as the eye could see, but they were rising out of the land, out of their bodies, into that explosion of sound. The birds were migrating south—blackbirds bunched together along sloping telephone wires, swarming over fields, bursting from treetops. Pilar and Carlos sang their futures into being as dark birds rose around them.

That hallucination drained when they pulled into the San Jacinto High parking lot, that daily checkpoint. Carlos parked and glanced at himself in the visor mirror. He ran his hand through his hair, his curls sticking up at odd angles like antennae seeking messages. "I look like shit," he said.

"Impossible," Pilar said, though he'd worn the same slept-in jeans and T-shirt every day since winning Mz. 10th Avenue. If he couldn't be El Ojo, he didn't want to be anything. He showed enthusiasm only for Pilar.

"I'm a lost cause, but *you*—" Carlos pulled mascara and lip gloss from his backpack. He tilted Pilar's chin up, painted her lashes and lips and pulled her hair out of its ponytail, utterly absorbed in this makeover. But as they walked toward school, his arms hung like a rag doll's. "SJH just feels so," Carlos looked around, dull-eyed, at the rows of cars, "anticlimactic."

When they sat with the drama kids at lunch, he remained aloof from their frenzied banter, making no attempt to vie for the spotlight. Pilar absorbed every detail of their thespian antics. Then, in the last five minutes of the lunch hour, she'd say something that sent Coke spurting through their noses. Carlos would cock an eyebrow like, *Who* are *you?* Pilar would stare back innocently until the corners of his lips turned up. That glimpse of the old Carlos made her spend whole lunch hours wracking her brain for something funny to say.

Carlos pulled Pilar into his world while he backed toward its edge. He took her to garage band concerts, coffeehouse readings, and parties of rainbow-haired misfits siphoned from six high schools across three cities. The more Carlos withdrew, the more Pilar tried on his bravery, wit, spontaneity. While he sat on an ice chest, listening with a look of disdain (*I come to this here party and I just get bored*) to the redundant chords of a punk band playing in someone's backyard, Pilar talked to the cute bass player. Never mind that the boy's disaffection was far less interesting than the way he tucked his shoulder-length hair behind his ears. The point was in crossing the yard to talk to him. The point was in reporting to Carlos afterwards, who wanted every detail of the he said, she said, who rolled his eyes when Pilar imitated the boy telling her that they'd gotten their band name—Automatic Drip—off the coffee cans they used as ashtrays. The point was not the shoring, but the crossing.

Pilar was taking Driver's Ed, but her father was too afraid of being pulled over to let her practice and didn't want her driving anyway. She and Carlos skipped Spanish so that Pilar could practice driving The Bitch in empty parking lots and on quiet streets. Carlos feigned novela drama when she made a mistake. "¡Ay, cuidado! ¡No magulles a La Puta!" He took her to the DMV to get her license. "Watch out, San Jacinto!" he cried as they left. "She's a licensed woman!"

Pilar was the sole hippie at San Jacinto High, her bellbottoms and butterfly collar shirts an anomaly in those hallways of preps in their polos, kickers in their Wranglers and ropers, and New Wavers in their Cure T-shirts and flood pants. Before, her pale looks had been washed out by her father's pinafores. But when Carlos lined her eyes and painted her lips, her beauty was undeniable. Before, the boys had called her names to make her blush; now they wanted her to stare back. Pilar believed that they were making fun of her and mostly refused to make eye contact. But some days, when she wore the bellbottom jeans that hugged her hips, she stared back defiantly, until the blood drained from her face. In those moments, she became El Ojo. No one looked at—*through*—those boys like Pilar did. They sought out her searing stare the way they ran tackle drills until their knees buckled—to find out who they were on the other side of that pain.

Locking eyes with Pilar was a welcome clearing from the frenzy of prom that engulfed San Jacinto High that spring: the Darwinian scramble to pair off, the huddles of gossiping girls, new couples drifting aloofly through this frenzy, fingers interwoven to signal their withdrawal from the prom date pool. Though Pilar might find her way into boys' imaginations, asking her to prom never crossed their minds.

"They're like mosquitoes," Carlos griped as he and Pilar wove around the slow-moving couples on their way to class. "Come spring, they're everywhere." In years past, Carlos had been happy to take dateless female friends to prom, to borrow the drama department tux, pin corsages, and pose for parents' photographs. "Bettina asked me, but I just can't bear it another year," he confessed to Pilar. "I can't watch other people having this magical night without wanting my own."

Pilar raised her eyebrows, surprised at his sentimentality.

"I *know*," Carlos groaned. "Clearly I've been brainwashed. It's just that nothing ever changes in this town."

As if in protest, a five-foot teacher with springy black curls grabbed Carlos by the arm.

"Mrs. Bonura!" Carlos' eyebrows shot up. He grinned sheepishly.

The springy pyramid of ringlets framing Mrs. Bonura's youthful face did not detract from the ferocity in her eyes. "Where have you been? Mr. Mendez came by to ask *me* why you'd been missing drama rehearsals. I said you told us you were with him."

In spite of the fact that Pilar was not Mrs. Bonura's student—she was in Honors Chemistry I, while Carlos was in AP Chemistry II—Mrs. Bonura turned her coal-black eyes on Pilar, as if she might know something. Pilar stared at the ground, chewing her lip.

"I'm sorry, Mrs. B." Carlos wriggled free of her grip. "I just—"

"This is no time to slack off. This is your *future*. I want to see you after school today. Capiche?"

Carlos stared at his Converse but nodded.

"I've got to tell them," he said to Pilar as soon as they were out of earshot.

"Probably they can help," Pilar said.

"Doubtful. Mrs. B only thinks she's The Godfather." Carlos sighed as a tide of red and blue washed by him. It was Football Friday. Again.

The first sign of real enthusiasm Pilar saw from Carlos came when she spotted the canoe. As he was driving her home from school, they passed a ramshackle antique store they'd never thought twice about, the canoe moored amidst lawn statuary and weeds.

Carlos pulled into the dirt driveway. El Ojo's tiara had sat on the floor in front of the passenger seat since they'd gone to 10th Avenue. Pilar set it on Carlos' head before he climbed out of the car. Carlos held his tiara-clad head regally upright as they walked through the yard overgrown with weeds, weaving through Virgin Mary and gnome statues. Wind chimes sang, making their path toward the canoe feel fated. It was a green Old Town canoe, belly up, well-made if well-used. Carlos ran his hand over the wood. He and Pilar flipped it over to reveal bench seats at either end.

A woman with Coke bottle glasses and ratted bird's nest hair came out of the store. "Nice tiara." She stood on tiptoe to appraise the tiara, pushing her glasses up.

"Not for sale." Carlos protectively clasped his tiara. "We're here about the canoe."

"It's a very good canoe," the woman said.

"Not much use for a canoe in the Valley." Carlos straightened his tiara and narrowed his eyes. He bargained fiercely, until he'd talked her down from $250 to $50. Pilar grabbed Carlos' arm as he went to shake the woman's hand, mouthing, "It's too much." She knew the canoe would wipe out his savings from working at Sprouts, San Jacinto's struggling health food store.

"We *need* this," Carlos said with irrefutable seriousness.

All that remained was the matter of transporting the canoe to Pilar's house. The store owner brought out tie-downs. Carlos placed his tiara on the front seat and he, Pilar, and the woman struggled to lift the canoe onto the roof of The Bitch. Strapping it down was like bathing a greased heifer. Faces flushed and dripping, they secured it as well as they could. The canoe made The Bitch a good four feet longer and three feet taller. Broader, too, since the ends of the paddles stuck out the back windows.

Being that big made Carlos bold. He drove carefully, beneath the speed limit, letting Pilar guide him through his blind spots, but insisted on cruising San Jacinto's main drag. The canoe sailed past Wal-Mart, Dairy Queen, Sonic, Whataburger. Children pointed from backseats and their parents turned to look, dwindling at green lights.

"I'm hungry," Carlos said and pulled into a Burger King drive-through. He donned his tiara and ordered an extra-large fry in his best Queen Mum accent. He'd given up meat after reading Sprouts' nutrition books—another source of conflict with Abuela.

The cashier squinted up at the canoe when Carlos pulled up to the window. Such a big load for such a little car. "Will that be all?" she asked.

"My friend here needs a crown, too." Carlos patted his tiara.

Pilar put on her paper crown and they sat in the parking lot eating fries before resuming their cruise. After school hours were prime cruising time, and as they drove down 10th Street, they were flanked on either side by pickup trucks with five-star hubcaps and murals custom-painted on their back panels: *REYES* airbrushed amidst purple clouds of dust, howling wolves, and bouquets of AK-47s. These gussied-up trucks cruised down the main strip, their drivers catcalling at girls and revving their amped-up engines. The cruisers momentarily squinted at the canoe, before turning their attention back to the girls. A driver leaned out his window and called to a group of girls standing outside the Sonic, "Ay-Way, Hermosa! ¡Ven aca!" He motioned to the girls.

"Do they think the girls are just going to hop in a stranger's truck because they've got an extra-loud muffler?" Carlos asked. "Check out *our* sweet ride!" he called, pointing up at the canoe. "We can paddle all night, baby."

The girls cocked their heads at the canoe.

Pilar laughed so hard she nearly peed her pants. They were the only parade they'd want to join, the green canoe perched atop Carlos' battered brown Chevette their banner of anomaly, their procession of one stretching beyond that strip of fast-food joints and big box stores, deep into the country, until the canoe drifted through fields of burnt grass, brush, and barbed wire.

The canoe rumbled over the gravel road that led to La Llanura and tipped precariously forward when Carlos pulled to a stop.

Her father came out on the porch and frowned. "What's that?"

"We bought a canoe," Pilar said. "For the resaca."

"I got it for nothing," Carlos said.

Marin wouldn't look at Carlos—this boy who'd turned his daughter into someone he hardly knew. But at least they were here, where he could keep an eye on them. "You know how to use that thing?" he asked Pilar.

"I know how to swim." Pilar smiled the same wide-open smile she had when she'd kicked free of him in her first swim lesson. This boy—with his androgynous cologne creeping into Marin's nostrils—made her happy.

"Alright, be careful." Her father gave the canoe a skeptical look. "Come in for dinner before dark."

Wrestling the canoe off The Bitch was a bitch, but gliding through the resaca was magic. The water was smooth as glass. Egrets lifted as they paddled into the center. Quiet came over them, the dip of their oars and the shudder of wings the only sounds. They lay back in the belly of the canoe, their feet intertwined, and stared up at the sky, cirrus clouds drifting like breath through the blue. Buoyed by the resaca, drifting through its center while staring up at the sky felt like a kind of dreaming—*merrily, merrily, merrily, merrily.*

The air cooled as the sun sank, the palms rustling in the breeze. They lay for a long time in silence until the sun was gone. Until they'd swallowed that red belly and were left in a shadowland.

"I miss Carla," Carlos said.

"Me, too." Pilar said. "What if we took Carla to prom?"

Carlos sat up and stared out at the thin pink glow along the horizon—a thread to unravel the world. The air held its breath for whatever he wanted to birth. "I've been dying to wear that dress again," he said. "But I don't think San Jacinto High can handle it."

"You've already brought them Ziggy, Biff, and the Cheshire Cat," Pilar said. "Carla's your strongest role."

"She is," Carlos said. He opened his mouth to say something more, but Marin came out to the porch and called for Pilar.

They paddled back to the dock. Even after they'd tied the canoe to the dock and stepped ashore, even after Carlos had turned down the driveway to make his way home to Abuela and Pilar had stepped into her father's kitchen, they were still buoyed by their idea. Still gliding.

"I asked you to come in by dark," her father grumbled. "I made carne asada, but it's cold now."

"I told you I'm not eating meat." Carlos had converted Pilar to vegetarianism. She folded her arms over her chest. She blamed her father for the way the buoyed glide of the canoe fell away.

"Sit down." Her father roughly set heaping plates on the table. "You'll eat what I've cooked."

Pilar sat down and pushed her plate away. She tore off pieces of a tortilla, sullenly popping them into her mouth.

The silence was sharp as glass.

When her father finished eating, he started to clear the table but was seized by a coughing fit, his thin body wracked by it. He turned his head, held a napkin to his mouth, and wadded it up in his fist so Pilar wouldn't see the blood.

Pilar's anger crumpled into guilt. "I'll clear the table, Papá," she said.

She joined her father on the porch when she'd finished the dishes. Together they rocked, staring out at the resaca, the palms silhouetted against the pink sky. The fire swirled through the resaca grated against the creak of his rocking chair, saying, *This is all and this is all, forever and ever, Amen.* How maddeningly free of desire he seemed, resigned to move through his days as an olvidado. He loved as a ghost loves: Pilar was everything to him and not enough. She wanted him to love the bright fire in her blood.

"I'm going to prom with Carlos," she said.

Her father's expression was one of physical pain. "No, you're not."

"Why, Papá?"

"Did you hear me?" Her father cut her off. "I said *no*. And I'll drive you to school from now on."

Pilar looked defiantly at her father. The flat world of La Llanura was the only thing he could love, and that world was a lie—the line of the horizon a tripwire.

Pilar became the olvidada. She pushed her dinner around on her plate, said nothing, ate little. She offered monosyllabic replies to her father's questions—*Yes. No. Fine.*—glaciers shifting under the smallest words.

She returned to life only after her father left for the graveyard. He left at 9 each night and Carlos arrived soon afterwards. Pilar and Carlos rocked on the porch, planning what Pilar would wear to prom. Given Marin's lockdown, Carlos would have to find the dress without her. He'd already begun combing the Ropa Usadas.

"No ruffles." Pilar stared up at the sky as she rocked, conjuring the dress. "No lace. No bows... No sleeves."

Carlos cocked his head as if to picture the dress and nodded.

"No sequins."

"*None*?" Carlos' large, dark eyes pleaded with Pilar.

Pilar stopped rocking, planted her feet on the porch, and gave Carlos a stern look. "*None*."

Carlos sighed and threw up his hands. "We'll do what we can."

Pilar stared up at the moon—hung at the edge of the skyline like an egg that had hatched the half-light for them. "White," she said.

They swing-danced through the yard, then went for a night canoe, the water dark and still, stars swimming on the surface. In darkness, there were no edges: The resaca might have still been part of the Rio Grande. Pilar and Carlos might have been explorers discovering the New World—the shadows theirs to shape.

Thus began a double life, the two of them gliding through a dream that disintegrated when they moored. When Pilar returned to her father, Carlos to Abuela, they were not the same.

As Pilar became more distant, her father became more controlling. He picked her up in his truck as soon as school let out, refusing to let her stay after for lit mag meetings. He made her do her homework at the kitchen table, where he could keep an eye on her while he cooked. But even when he yelled and slammed his fist on the table, his eyes were sad. As if he knew he'd lost his daughter when she was becoming her most beautiful.

All those nights of canoeing bound Carlos and Pilar like Marin and Roberto. Carlos could trace Pilar's dimensions in the dark. He swam through the mounds of clothing at the Ropa Usadas as Pilar, knowing what she would love and hate, knowing the dress mattered enough to hold out. Knowing when he'd found it.

It was not just a dress, but a birth skin. A sleeveless white cotton tunic, embroidered along the neckline, it was nothing like a prom dress and everything like Pilar. She slipped it on and walked barefoot across the yard—a sliver of moonlight over the blue grass.

Carla picked Pilar up for prom after her father left for the graveyard Friday night. She knocked on the door and called, "Carla's here. Get your prom on!" She'd pinned a gardenia in her side-parted pixie cut, the whole of her in bloom in the champagne-silk dress—her long, sinewy arms tanned honey, her large eyes lined and shadowed, her eyebrows plucked into perfect arches, her glossed lips like petals. She lifted her dress to reveal gold-trimmed scalloped cream heels. "The one thing my mother left me. I used to walk around in them when I was little. Lucky for me her feet were unusually large, and mine are unusually small."

Carla had made Pilar a crown of white bougainvillea flowers. "Couldn't see you in a corsage," she said as she placed it on Pilar's head. She appraised Pilar, her tallness turned elegant by the flowing tunic. "The dress is perfect, but let's work on your face."

As Pilar led Carla into her bedroom, she realized that Carla was the only person who'd been in the house since the man in the black car. She saw it through Carla's eyes: clean, spare, unlived-in. Pilar sat on her bed and Carla tipped her chin up. Carla lined Pilar's eyes and painted her lashes and lips, then stood back and wolf whistled.

They drove to prom as they had to school every morning before her father put an end to their ritual, with the music blasting and the windows down. The immovable world a blur through the dark, it was possible to believe in the word of Billy Corgan: *Our lives are changed; we're not stuck in vain.*

Prom was at the Echo Hotel, a remnant of old San Jacinto with its 1950s marquee and mildewed conference rooms that had survived the influx of Marriotts and Holiday Inns by becoming the go-to locale for high school dances, graduation parties, and Elks Lodge meetings. Carla's transformation was so complete that she slipped by the security guards at the entrance without a second glance. She managed her heels with considerably more grace than the girls teetering past. Student Council had chosen an Under the Sea theme and blue streamers and colored fish dangled from the ceiling. Many of the girls looked like mermaids in snug sequin dresses with ruffles at their ankles. The DJ was playing Cumbia music, mermaid-girls swizzling their sequined hips with boys in ill-fit tuxes. Some accessorized with black cowboy hats and boots. The preps had no idea how to Cumbia and wouldn't admit it if they did. They sat at the tables, gossiping and sprinkling glitter in one another's hair, waiting for the DJ to play pop or country. The drama kids were all at some house party. They'd invited Carlos and Pilar, who'd said they might come. Without speaking about it, they'd agreed to keep their prom plans a secret.

Their friends would have thought going to prom was an ironic stunt, when it meant so much more.

Pilar and Carla stood in the back of the room observing the scene. Pilar noted particularly bad examples of the following: *Ruffles. Lace. Bows. Sleeves. Sequins.* She gave Carla an *I told you so* look.

Carla sucked in her cheeks to make a fish face and did the Cumbia with flapping fin-hands.

"You're good at that," Pilar said.

"My mother taught me," Carla said.

The DJ eventually played pop and country and the kids from their classes got up to dance.

When they'd heard all of the sugary pop they could stand, Carla pulled *Bedlam Ballroom* from her beaded silver purse and said, "It's time." Pilar took the CD and crossed the room to talk to the DJ. It wasn't like the other times, when she tried on Carlos' bravery for size. When the DJ squinted at the CD and shook his head no, she leaned in to whisper in his ear. Her words were inconsequential. The warmth of her breath lingered. She looked at him with those gray-blue eyes like the sea in a storm and waited for *yes* to float in on the tide.

When the Tim McGraw song ended, the big band drumbeat of "Just This Side of Blue" rose. Couples let go of each other in a disjointed daze, gooey-eyed smiles sliding from their faces.

They left the dance floor to Carla and Pilar. Carla curled Pilar to her and then flung her out. Carla then Cumbia-stepped with fish-lips and flopping fins across the floor toward Pilar. Carla pulled Pilar close, then dipped her; Pilar threw her head back and laughed. Carla swung Pilar around the dance floor, then flung her out again until they stood on opposite corners. Carla raised her perfectly arched eyebrows like, *Hey, good lookin'* and pantomimed reeling Pilar in with a fishing rod. Pilar fish-flopped toward Carla and Carla whirled her around. They were two undiscovered planets in their own wild orbit.

But soon the stares of the watchers circling the dance floor penetrated that world. Unlike the circle of love that held them at 10th Avenue, their prom spectators furrowed their brows and wrinkled their noses as if they smelled a bad smell, which might have been the profusion of Aqua Net and Axe Body Spray awaft in the air, but was more likely the tangle of two prom gowns.

"That's Carlos Gomez," some guy bellowed. A murmur traveled through the crowd. "In the pink dress."

"It's *champagne*, you plebian," Carla snapped. She Cumbia-stepped in place, staring at her mother's shoes, adjusting the gardenia in her hair. Pilar gripped both of Carla's hands, pulled her close, smiled encouragingly, and flung her out again. The thing was to keep dancing. They took their routine from the top—swinging through the stares and murmurs. They finished with their signature stunt, Carla wrapping her hands around Pilar's waist, lifting her into the air, and swinging her to her left side and then her right, even as the talk rose: *Who? Carlos Gomez, that pansy from Spanish. SHE'S a HE. So what's Pilar?* When they'd done this stunt at 10th Avenue, Pilar had felt like she was flying. Now her body felt like lead. Carla's fingers dug into her hips.

"Just This Side of Blue" screeched to a halt. Carla set Pilar down and they saw that two security guards were talking to the DJ. One of the guards crossed the dance floor to talk to Carla.

"Party's over, son," he said.

"Says who?" Carla pulled a tissue from her bra and patted her forehead.

"You've violated the dress code. Come on, let's go."

Carla adjusted her spaghetti straps, stood up straighter, and looked around. "This dress is the classiest act in this muck pond."

Students who'd laughed uproariously at Carlos' plays, leered. They were happy to let Carlos play the fool in his Ziggy Stardust jumpsuits, but Carla's beauty cut into them.

"Let's just go," Pilar pleaded.

Carla sighed and began to walk toward the door. Pilar noticed the fragile notches of her spine beneath her silk dress. Carla walked at a regal pace, her head held upright. The guard pushed her forward and she stumbled in her heels. She batted his hand from her back.

The onlookers trailed behind. One of them threw a plastic fish at Carla's back. Pilar put her arm around Carla, who lifted the hem of her dress and continued to walk at a measured pace. At the door, Carla turned to look her classmates in the face. Pilar would not look at them. She saw only what Carla's large, dark eyes swallowed. It made Pilar's eyes fill.

Once he'd ushered Carla and Pilar out the door, the security guard headed back inside. He let the onlookers usher Carla and Pilar into the parking lot. Groups of boys leaned against their cars, chugging spiked Coke. "Don't let the door hit you on your way out, you fuckin' faggot freak!" a boy in a cowboy hat and unraveled bowtie bellowed. His friends laughed. Pilar felt sick. She tried to hurry Carla toward The Bitch, but Carla walked slowly, leering at the boys.

"What the hell are you looking at?" the boy in the cowboy hat yelled. "Don't you have some pansy party to be at?"

Carla looked him up and down. "I guess you have to talk big, Alfonso. Your dick looks so much smaller when it's not crammed into skintight Wranglers."

"What did you say, you little faggot?" Alfonso lunged at Carla. His friends halfheartedly held him back. "I'm 'bout to smash your pansy face in."

Carla wagged her perfectly manicured pinky at Alfonso and slowly curled it toward her palm.

"Are you out of your mind?" Pilar hissed. She yanked Carla by the hand and they ran toward The Bitch, parked at the back of the lot. They were too slow in their heels and Alfonso and his friends barreled toward them like linebackers. As they closed in, Pilar could smell the sour alcohol sweating through their pores.

Alfonso shoved Carla to the ground and punched her. "You can't talk to me like that, you little faggot." Carla had forgotten to put her switchblade in her bra. Alfonso pummeled her, fists flying. Pilar threw her body over Carla. A boy pulled her off and held her back, his sweaty hand over her mouth. Pilar kicked at the boy who forced her to watch in silence as Alfonso kicked Carla.

Some of the boys' dates came to see what was happening—girls whom Carlos had tutored in math, who ran student council, fed the hungry. Alfonso's girlfriend, a girl named Melissa who'd been Carlos' co-star in the seventh-grade play, screamed at Alfonso to stop until her voice went hoarse. The girls begged their boyfriends to do something, pleaded with the part of them that kneeled at Sunday Mass and visited the Vannie Cook Children's Cancer Clinic with their football team—that vibrating cord between sweetness and violence its own border.

But it was already over. Carla curled up into a ball. Pilar bit the hand covering her mouth hard enough to break the skin and felt the warm gush of blood. The boy jerked his hand away.

Carla lay in the parking lot, curled on her side, her knees pulled to her chest. Pilar kneeled beside her, put her hand to Carla's swollen face. Her lip was split, blood trickled from her mouth, her right eye was swollen shut.

"Do you want me to get someone?" Melissa asked, tears in her eyes.

Pilar shook her head. She didn't want the security guards involved. "Please just—leave us."

Carla's left eye roved over Alfonso and the watchers heading back inside, then closed.

"Carla?" Pilar held two fingers over Carla's wrist.

Carla opened her good eye and pulled at her dress, bloody and pitted with gravel. "Look what they did to my dress."

Pilar was so relieved that Carla was coherent that she smiled. "Don't worry about the dress." She gently touched Carla's swollen eye. "Can you walk?" She scooped Carla up and helped her hobble into the back of The Bitch.

Carla curled sideways in the backseat, and Pilar drove slowly. She leaned forward, her knuckles white on the wheel. "I'm taking you to the emergency room."

"I'm illegal," Carla said as if Pilar had forgotten.

"It doesn't matter. I've taken my father."

A long silence passed and then Carla said, in a voice so plaintive that Pilar hardly recognized it, "I can't stand another stranger touching me."

Pilar took the road that led to Carla's house.

"Abuela can take care of me," Carla said. "She has before."

"This happened before? *Who?*" Pilar looked at Carla in the rearview mirror. She would find him.

Carla closed her good eye and pulled her knees to her chest.

"I tol' you, mijo. I tol' you," Abuela said as she swabbed Carlos' wounds with witch hazel. She'd made him change out of the dress. He lay on the couch in pinstriped boxers. "I tol' you not to mess with el mal de ojo. You make too pretty a girl. And God made you a boy." She looked up at the crucifix hung over the couch, crossed herself, then went to the kitchen. Pilar stabbed her turned back with the evil-ist eye she could muster.

Abuela returned with a raw egg in its shell and a tall glass of water.

"What's that for?" Pilar asked.

"The egg absorbs the bad energy of el ojo. It pulls the color from the bruises. Watch," she commanded and slowly swept the egg over Carlos' entire body, working her way down from his head to the soles of his feet. She repeated this process seven times, saying the Credo, Lord's Prayer, Hail Mary, and Glory Be. *Hail Mary, full of Grace, the Lord is with thee. Blessed are thou among women...* The long hairs sprouting from the mole on her chin trembled. Pilar wondered how Carlos' beauty could have come from such an ugly woman. "You draw the ojo de chicas y chicos. Ojo that doesn't know what it wants is the worst kind," Abuela said as she rolled the egg over Carlos' eyes, lips, chest, and legs. Carlos trembled, crying without a sound.

"That's enough." Pilar grabbed Abuela's wrist.

Abuela jerked her wrist away and gave her a stubborn look. "You'll see when I crack the egg." She waited a few minutes before cracking the egg into the glass of water. The yolk quickly settled to the bottom of the glass. A stream of egg white erupted out of its orb and spread towards the rim of the glass. "There!" She tapped the glass. "Abuela knows."

Pilar sat beside Carlos, swiped her thumb under his eyes. She helped him into bed. He turned on his side and Pilar kissed the bruises on his back.

"The other time, three of them cornered me backstage after school. I was practicing the monologue where Biff asks, 'Why am I trying to become what I don't want to be?'" Carlos' voice was soft, the edges dulled.

"Why won't you tell me who?" Pilar asked.

"There'll always be someone."

Pilar cried silently, so Carlos wouldn't hear.

"Will you put on Patti—low so Abuela won't hear?" Carlos asked.

Pilar put on "Because the Night."

Abuela drove Pilar home. She talked in rapid Spanglish: *El ojo* this and *if Carlos had a father...* Pilar stared out the window. The bright lit fast-food restaurants and revving mufflers of cruisers seemed jarringly ugly. Slowly the streets turned silent, dwindled into empty roads running past fields until they drove down the long gravel road that led to La Llanura.

Her father was waiting on the porch. He headed for Abuela's car in long, swift strides. "You went to prom with that boy," he said as soon as Pilar got out of the car.

"Yes," Pilar said stonily.

Abuela got out. "Ay, Dios mío, they were both dressed like girls!" She shook her hands at the sky, crossed herself. "My Carlos got beat up bad." She shook her head at Pilar, the hairs of her mole quivering in the car's headlights. "They get each other into trouble."

Marin nodded as if none of this surprised him. "I came home because I knew," he said to Pilar. "Wait for me on the porch."

Pilar sat in a rocking chair but did not rock. She watched her father and Abuela talk—a tall, still shadow and a squat, frenzied one. Abuela's hands waved in the air; her voice rose and fell, strains of it reaching the porch: *Dios* this; *Santo Cristo* that.

Pilar promised the cratered face of the moon that she would get Carlos out of this godforsaken place.

Finally Abuela left and her father strode toward Pilar. He stared down at her in the rocking chair and said, "You won't see that boy anymore." As he spoke, his voice hard and triumphant, Marin let himself believe that getting rid of Carlos would bring his daughter back.

The way the bones of Pilar's face closed over obliterated that belief.

Carlos wore his Ziggy Stardust jumpsuit to school Monday. He'd tried to cover up his black eye with a white lightning bolt, but everyone had heard about what happened. Some students turned away, but many of his GT classmates, whom he'd known since third grade, offered support. Girls asked how he was, told him that Melissa had broken up with Alfonso and called her parents to pick her up from prom. Boys slapped him on the back in solidarity before they took their seats. Guillermo, the marching band drum major, clasped Carlos' hand in a high five and said, "That guy's an *asshole*."

Gibby Valadez, Show Choir Captain and Carlos' rival for the lead in every one of SJH's musicals, winced at Carlos' black eye when he sat down at their cafeteria table. Everyone knew that Gibby was gay, no matter the Shakespearean intensity of his crushes on female co-stars. A beat of awkward silence passed before Gibby launched into the opening lines of "It's a Hard Knock Life". He looked around the table for accompaniment and Jose, Bettina, Dominic, and Steve sang, *For us!* Carlos joined in: *'Steada treated, we get tricked! 'Steada kisses, we get kicked!*

In the absence of sense, there was song. In the absence of safety, there was the ritual of canoeing through darkness. Carlos came over after her father left that night. He and Pilar paddled into the center of the resaca, lay back in the belly of the canoe, and let the low, sad keen of a night train speak for them.

Carlos hummed the opening of "Because the Night". He sang and Pilar joined in. They rose as the chorus built—sitting up, then standing, then climbing onto the canoe's bench seats. They spread their legs wide and shifted their weight from foot to foot, the canoe rocking as they belted.

They can't hurt you now-ow-ow, Carlos scream-sang until his voice was hoarse. He ripped off his T-shirt and raised it above his head like a mast, a flag for that inky country in which the bruises covering his back were invisible.

They canoed through the watery black eye of the resaca—let the blackness bleed into them—no longer a wound to tiptoe around, but a space of gestation.

"We're getting out of here," Pilar said. The words felt as if they'd materialized from the dark mouth of the resaca. "We're getting scholarships to colleges far, far away."

Carlos stared up at the vast city of stars and said, "New York City needs me."

"New York City will have you," Pilar said. For the first time since she was a child, saying things aloud made them so.

They heard the crunch of gravel under wheels.

"Uh-oh," Carlos said at the sight of Marin's pickup winding up the drive.

Pilar shrugged. "It doesn't matter anymore."

Her father stood at the dock, waiting for them with his arms folded over his chest, but they took their time paddling back. His tall silhouette against the sagging backdrop of the house seemed a thing that had little to do with them.

When they moored, they were not the same. The charred shore was an afterworld. They'd left their bruised bodies behind and slipped on the skin of night.

"You think you can lie to me," Marin said to Pilar.

"This life," she stared out at the dark, silent fields, "is a lie."

"Go," Marin said to Carlos with the fury he felt for Pilar. "I don't want to ever see you here again."

Pilar put her arm around Carlos and walked him to his car. Before he drove off, she leaned in through his window and said, "We're getting out of here."

"How dare you disobey me?" her father roared when Pilar returned.

Rage spread through her body and when she opened her mouth, black words flew out like stones. "My mother didn't die. She left you. You tried to control her. You drove her away." Her voice shook. Her words shocked her. "She left you and *you* died. You live like a dead man, apart from everyone."

"¡Cállate! ¡Cállate!" Marin's trembling hand flew against Pilar's mouth, hard enough that she stumbled backwards. His voice rose, amassed a force beyond the bounds of his broken body. "You live in *my* house! On *my* land!"

Pilar steadied herself and stepped toward her father, her heart pounding. "La Llanura is just another graveyard you guard, you'd be happier if I was a granite slab."

Marin remembered the cave-in, how he'd grabbed Roberto's hand and they'd run, stumbling through the darkness, for the exit as the tunnel walls crumbled around them. How Roberto's hand had slipped from his as the dynamite exploded and a rockslide began, how he'd dog-rolled out of the mine just before the entrance collapsed and unfolded himself to find Roberto gone. Fallen boulders sealed the entrance. His boss had held him—kicking and screaming his brother's name—to keep him from going back in.

He remembered reaching for the kicking, screaming, red-faced new life that was his daughter. The partera's dark, smoky house—everywhere candles, a shrine to the Virgin—had made him think of the mines. He'd picked up Pilar and she'd stopped crying. He'd wanted for her to know only light. He'd tried. All those graveyard nights of inventing stories. But she'd become a changeling. She'd stopped believing in his stories.

In Marin's silence, Pilar's words hung in the air.

Her father looked at her without love.

Pilar held her hand over her mouth and cried without sound.

"I've been wanting to talk to you, too," Mrs. Bonura said when Pilar approached her in the hall between classes. When the bell rang, she ducked into her classroom to give her students an assignment, then returned to Pilar. She put her hand on Pilar's back, scanned the empty hallway, and said in a low voice, "Let's have what the Mafioso call a walk-and-talk." Mrs. Bonura steered Pilar down the hall. "I need the details on what happened at prom," she said. "Mr. Cancino and I want those boys expelled."

"Mr. Cancino?" Pilar asked. Mr. Cancino, Carlos' and Pilar's soft-spoken Calculus teacher, seemed to cower behind his dark beard and smudged spectacles.

"I know." Mrs. Bonura raised her eyebrows. "I haven't seen him this riled since we lost the Mathlete district tournament."

Pilar told Mrs. Bonura about Alfonso kicking Carla until she curled into a ball, about the boy, whose name she'd learned was Rey Ramirez, who'd held her back and forced her to watch.

Mrs. Bonura's hands balled into fists. "I want them tried for assault."

"I don't know. Did Carlos tell you he's not—?"

Mrs. Bonura looked blankly at Pilar.

Pilar checked the hallway and whispered, "Carlos isn't a citizen."

Mrs. Bonura didn't bat an eye. "The police aren't allowed to ask for ID from people reporting crimes."

"Carlos wouldn't want to get dragged into some drawn-out trial. He'd be furious if he knew I talked to you about prom. What he wants is to go to college in New York. He needs a full scholarship since he can't get financial aid. I thought maybe you could help him get into Columbia." The fact that Mrs. Bonura had gone off to college at Columbia, then returned to teach at her high school alma mater was known by everyone and alternately praised as devotion to her community and pitied as a failure to live up to her potential.

"We'll talk more about going to the police. But I want Alfonso and Rey out of this school, so Carlos can focus on his grades. He's a strong enough student for Columbia, and they'll love that he's star of the drama team, but it wouldn't hurt for him to bring up his ranking. Getting full funding for Columbia without federal aid will be tough, but I'll look into private scholarships unconcerned with immigration status. I'll also call Columbia, Cooper Union, and some other New York schools to find out their policies on undocumented students."

"I need to get out of here, too," Pilar said.

Mrs. Bonura's eyes held Pilar's. She must have seen that Pilar's use of the word *need* was not an exaggeration. "I've got to get back to class, but I want to see you and Carlos in my room Friday after school. We need to get started right away. Capiche?" Mrs. Bonura's clasped fingers flowered.

Pilar again had a sense of her power. When she'd fought with her father, she'd been terrified by the world her new voice carved. Now the baby hairs trailing down the back of her neck sang electric. "Capiche," she repeated, though she had no idea what it meant.

That sinking feeling returned when her father picked her up after school. He stared straight ahead and waited for her to close her door. Its steel slam reverberated in their silence. Pilar didn't work up the courage to tell him she needed to stay after school Friday until they pulled up to the house. Her father gave her the slightest nod of acknowledgement. Dust enveloped the pickup when he pulled to a stop. Her father climbed out into it, coughing as he walked into the house.

There were no more dinners together. Her father prepared simple meals that he ate on the porch and left Pilar to eat what she wanted. Pilar carried her meals into her bedroom and ate absentmindedly while she pored over books. They pressed their ears to their doors and listened for one another to leave before coming out. It hurt to be in the same room.

Carlos and Pilar met with Mrs. Bonura, Mr. Cancino, and Mrs. Alamia, Pilar's AP US History teacher, after school every Friday to work on college and scholarship applications and tackle whatever difficulties they were having in their classes.

Principal Adame was noncommittal about taking disciplinary action toward Alfonso and Rey. "That old dinosaur was more concerned with *tradition*," Mrs. Bonura made angry quotation marks with her fingers, "than with the fact that we've got two psychopaths on the loose."

"The Administration is not on our side," Mr. Cancino said gravely. "That means you guys need to lay low. You can rebel all you want in college, but we've got to get you in."

Carlos and Pilar were always good students, but in the end of their junior year they became machines. They locked themselves in their rooms as soon as they got home and studied in silence for hours. They double-checked their homework, then took practice AP tests. They stayed up late into the night, writing and rewriting scholarship essays. Pilar called Carlos for Calculus help and edited Carlos' scholarship essays. They wore the polos and jeans worn by everyone, distinguished only by the wry twist to Carlos' mouth, the ferocity in the set of Pilar's jaw. Carlos got Pilar a job at Sprouts and they spent their summer racking up hours in the cool, fluorescent-lit aisles, working out SAT practice questions when they weren't helping elderly customers distinguish between mustard greens and kale.

By the time they sent in their applications senior year, they'd scored 5s on all of their AP exams, aced their SATs, and brought up their rankings. An extremely smart girl named Aracely, relentlessly driven by a mother who'd sacrificed her own ivy league scholarship to marry, was slated for valedictorian. Beyond Aracely, a handful of students, who'd end up at MIT, Stanford, Princeton, and UPenn, jostled for the top spots. In the end, Carlos and Aracely tied for valedictorian; salutatorian went to a quiet, wry-witted girl named Edna; and Pilar learned to schmooze her most lackadaisical teachers and moved her ranking up from fifth to third. Abuela expected that Carlos would go to the local college, The University of Texas-Pan American, that he would continue to work at Sprouts and help her with money. Carlos let her believe this—one of so many lies she'd made necessary.

Marin knew Pilar would go away to college. She was Luz's daughter. He steeled himself in silence. He sat on the porch in the mornings and watched flocks of blackbirds dense as locusts scatter and converge. He thought of leaving Bolivia, of Roberto leaving the world. He imagined his grandparents leaving Canada for the strangeness of Bolivia, his father leaving the Mennonite community for love. He thought about how birth— that first arrival—was also a departure. How he'd known the mines like a womb, running his palms along the damp rock walls; known Roberto beneath sight. How the late afternoon light pulled them separate when they left the mine. How the light hurt his eyes. *Luz*. How their silver-veined love emptied. Pilar's leaving looped backwards on all those other leavings like barbed wire. Cirrus clouds tore and drifted—in the sky and in his lungs. He coughed and the cough was connected to that first cough in the mines as he plugged a hole with dynamite, lit the stick and ran, though he could not run because every leaving looped backwards. The birds would circle from south to north and return in winter, the old replaced by the young.

Though his father never spoke of his Mennonite life, Marin knew the listening in rough-hewn pews, the waiting for light to seep—stained— through glass and skin. The blue light of what he must do: Let go of Roberto, Luz, Pilar.

Marin made Pilar vegetable tucumanas instead of meat. He let Carlos drive her to and from her summer job at Sprouts. He let her study at Carlos' house. They ate dinner together then rocked on the porch. The barbed wire uncoiled and the breath between them loosened.

Carlos and Pilar had used Mrs. Bonura's address on their applications. Spring of their senior year, Mrs. Bonura brought an armful of envelopes from their prospective colleges to school. Carlos and Pilar opened them in her classroom after school with their trio of college application coaches.

Pilar waited for Carlos to open his first. He opened the scholarship fund's—
it didn't matter which colleges accepted him if he didn't have financial
support. He'd been awarded funding for tuition, lodging, books, and
other expenses at whatever school he chose. He got into Cooper Union,
Fordham, NYU, The New School, and Vassar. He saved Columbia—his first
choice because of its strong engineering program and the cache that an
ivy league school held in the Valley—for last. He read the first sentence
and climbed on top of his chair. Grinning with his eyes closed, he swizzled his hips and raised his fists. Mrs. Bonura jumped up and down with
Pilar, her curls springing outward. Mr. Cancino hugged Mrs. Alamia, then
stepped back awkwardly and cleared his throat.

Pilar got into Barnard, Fordham, NYU, and The New School, but they'd
offered her only partial scholarships. She'd been awarded a full scholarship and stipend that included a work-study to Santa Agostina University,
a Catholic school in Los Angeles that she'd applied to at the last minute.
She was sad that she wouldn't be in New York with Carlos, but excited by
the idea of California. She had in her what was in Luz—that pull toward a
shore where she knew no one. She imagined herself walking alone on the
beach at night. She looked up to see Carlos mold his mouth into a smile,
like he was doing an impression. The bereft look in his eyes surprised Pilar. It would never not surprise her—the revelation of how much this bold,
beautiful boy needed her. She hugged him before he reached for her.

When Carlos told Abuela that he'd won a full scholarship to the college of
his choice and was going to Columbia, she narrowed her eyes and asked,
"It'll be enough to live in Nueva York?" Carlos steeled himself for a barrage
of questions, but when he assured Abuela that his scholarship would cover everything, her face crumpled. "It broke my heart when your mother left.
I was so scared about how I'd raise you. And now—my little nieto going off
to a fancy college in Nueva York!" She shook her head, wiped her eyes.

Carlos' body loosened. He exhaled, laughed, and his eyes filled.

"I was going to wait until your graduation, but... I have something for you, mijo." She went to her room and returned with a delicate necklace with a 50 pesos gold coin pendant. "Your mother left this for you." Carlos took the coin from Abuela's palm and turned it over to find, *por mi belleza, Carlos* engraved over the angel.

When Pilar told Marin about getting a full ride to SAU, his eyes grew shiny. "I'm so proud of you," he said and held her until his breath slowed.

New York City and Los Angeles existed solely in Pilar's and Carlos' imaginations, since they could not afford to visit. Carlos was additionally deterred by the story of the undocumented valedictorian who'd been stripped of his shoes and belt and hauled into an underground ICE compound when he returned to the Valley from visiting colleges. If the boy's teachers hadn't rallied in his defense, the judge would have deported him.

Carla came over the night before Pilar left for LA. They offered themselves one last time to the resaca. They dressed for her. Carla had managed to remove the blood stains from her eagle's wings dress through a laborious method she found online involving glycerine and dishwashing powder. "Driver's licenses, bloodstain removal—what *doesn't* the internet do?" she asked as she slipped the dress over her head in Pilar's room. Pilar put on the white tunic and Carla did her makeup. She tipped Pilar's chin up, lined and shadowed her eyes, coated and delineated every eyelash, and looked long and hard into those gray-blue grandmother eyes before painting her lips dark red.

Pilar painted Carla's full lips the same dark red. Red-mouthed, they fed themselves to the resaca's dark mouth. They pushed the canoe off the dock and glided into the oil-black water. They stared up at the sky and imagined New York and LA—as far off as that map of stars. They promised to call each other, to tell each other everything. In darkness, Carla's red mouth became Pilar's became the resaca's and it seemed they could put 3,000 miles between them and still hold onto their oneness. They lay back in the belly of the canoe, their legs intertwined as the palms swayed goodbye.

Pilar's scholarship paid for her plane ticket to LA. Even if they'd paid for her father to accompany her, he wouldn't have been able to fly without identification. Her scholarship advisor would pick her up at the airport. Marin insisted on going inside the airport with Pilar, though he nervously eyed the border patrolmen lined up in front of the airport security scanner. Before she left, he took her hand in his and traced two fingers along the vein in her wrist. "Busca la vena," he said. *Seek the vein.*

CHAPTER 5

The air in LA was dry and barely there—an insincere kiss. Pilar missed the warm swaddling of the Valley's wind. She unpacked what little she'd brought, while her roommate's parents, plump, cheerful Midwesterners, hauled trunks of things up from their minivan. When they left, taking with them their talk of weather and food, silence settled in between Pilar and her roommate. Kristie was a shy, pre-declared chemistry major who was asleep by the time Pilar returned from the library and up before she woke.

But the revelation that Pilar's brilliant, passionate professors ushered into the classroom was enough to make her cry. She pushed herself to speak in class, her voice quavering but ardent. Mostly she showed her gratitude for what her peers received as a matter of course in her papers. Between the 20 hours a week she spent at her library work-study and the study carrel she claimed on the basement quiet floor, she essentially lived in the library. She worked on papers past midnight, re-reading and underlining, peeling back layers of meaning until the essay glowed whole in her mind and she had only to bring it to life on paper. *Only.* She wrote and re-wrote sentences and paragraphs and pages. She wrote ten pages instead of five. When she surfaced, the world shone.

She took off her shoes and walked slowly through the cool grass of the darkened, empty campus. The founders of Santa Agostina University had planted a walkway of oaks which had grown tall against the proclivities of the LA climate, their branches tangled in an arch overhead. The line of a George Oppen poem she'd written about echoed in Pilar's head as she walked barefoot through this tunnel of trees: *help me I am of that people the grass blades touch.* The oak boughs moved against the sky in a kind of breathing, then released her, down the hill, around fraternity row, and up the stairs to her dorm hall, where the shine disintegrated in the fluorescent lights, gossip of huddled girls, smell of nail polish. They smiled as she passed and Pilar silently held up a hand, but couldn't find the words—about boys, parties, clothes—to make herself part of them.

Kristie snored softly. Pilar undressed in the dark, trying not to make too much noise. She'd had too much coffee and lay awake in bed. She thought of her father. From a distance, she understood the largeness of his love. How when they'd rocked on the porch without speaking, their worlds had pulled close—bubbles that touched but did not burst.

But when she called him the next day, they struggled to find words.

"Are you getting enough to eat, mija?" her father finally asked. "Do you need money? ¿Estás bien?" He asked like all those days he'd dressed her for school, braided her hair, packed her lunch, and sent her away.

Pilar was suddenly hungry for his stories of the mines, stories she hadn't heard since she was nine. She ached to trade the cool glass box of the SAU library for the dark, humid oblivion of the tunnels, to feel her way by hand along solid rock. She almost said, *Tell me about the tunnels, Papá.*

But her father started coughing, the sound like some machine breaking down.

"Papá? How long has it been since you went to the clinic?" Her father's only option was a clinic that served people who were undocumented, unhoused, or living with mental illness or addiction. He hated waiting for hours among so many sick, desperate people—rocking, crying, mumbling. Fearing deportation, he was distrustful of the forms he had to fill out.

"They can't do anything," her father said through the coughing. He couldn't stop. He could barely get out goodbye.

Pilar dreamed a dust storm swallowed him.

She called him when she woke and got a message. *No estoy en casa. Silence for the men who lost their lungs.*

But soon after, he sent her a postcard of a Ringed Kingfisher—the first of many postcards of birds of the Rio Grande Valley. *This guy was perched on your canoe the other day, already taking over. But I miss you, mija. Love, Papá*, he'd written. Her father had pointed out Kingfishers before— big-headed blue-gray birds with shaggy mohawks, reddish-orange bellies, and long, sharp beaks. The intensity of their stare reminded her of her father, looking out at La Llanura.

She missed him and she missed Carlos. She failed at the motions that bound SAU's student body, failed to mill around outside of the library complaining about the *insane workload*. She was feeling particularly raw in her loneliness one night as she made her way back to her dorm from the library when a boy leaned out of his third-floor window and called to her in a Southern twang. "Hey, beautiful! Party on 3rd Belk!" 50 Cent's "In Da Club" drifted out the window. The music sounded loud enough that Pilar would only need to dance, not talk. The boy dropped down his key card and Pilar climbed the stairs to the third floor. The lights were off and the narrow hall was packed with bodies swaying and sloshing Solo cups of beer. Pilar moved into their movement, closed her eyes. She absorbed the heat of all those bodies until her loneliness fell away.

At midnight, the RA turned off the music and flipped on the lights. People groaned but made their way toward the stairs. As the hallway emptied, Pilar was dropped into that well of loneliness again.

"Pilar!" someone whispered from the room at the end of the hall.

A tall, cherub-faced boy with curly brown hair stood in the doorway. He wore a bowler hat, a Hawaiian shirt, khakis, and two-tone Elvis Oxfords. "I've been looking for you," he said with a Southern twang.

Pilar recognized him as the boy who slept through her Literature 201 seminar. Pilar loved that class and hated him for sleeping through it. Still, she went to his room.

"Buster," the boy introduced himself. "And this is my roommate, Matt." Matt sat on the floor in front of a pile of cards. "Join us—BS is better with three."

"BS?" Pilar asked.

"Where are you from?" Buster's brow furrowed. "And are all the girls there as tall as you?" He grinned, a dimple blooming in his right cheek, his teeth large and pearly-white.

"Texas," Pilar said. "And no."

"Matt's from Dallas."

"Texas proud." Matt pointed to the Texas flag hung over his bed. "Where in Texas?"

"The Rio Grande Valley," Pilar said. "In the southern tip."

"I bet you've got more wetbacks down there than in LA!" Matt said.

Pilar imagined the dome of her mother's pregnant belly pushing against the Rio Grande's current. She was still standing and now she turned to leave, mumbling something about an 8 a.m. class.

"Did I say something?" Matt swigged from a Jack Daniel's bottle.

"Wait, don't go." Buster followed her down the stairs.

Pilar hurried down the stairs, the sour beer smell nauseating her. Outside, she stood for a second beneath the rustling trees, letting them breathe for her.

Buster waited for her to turn, to wonder why he was still there. "What you said about 'Sonny's Blues' blew my mind," he said.

"How would you know what I said?" Pilar asked. "You're always asleep."

"I'm just resting my eyes. I mean it. I loved that story so much. That's the problem, see. I love them so much that I read them and I just start writing... I stay up all night writing. I'd love your opinion on this one story, actually."

That anyone would want her opinion blew Pilar's mind. She gave Buster her email.

"Okay." He grinned. "Okay."

Pilar read Buster's story on the library's basement quiet floor. It was about a rodeo clown who ate frozen dinners in a rusted trailer and drank himself to sleep. But staring into the bull's watery eyes, the clown knew when it would charge by the ripple of its ribs, the rhythm of its breath—the aliveness between them a kind of love. The clown puts on his red overalls and walks white-faced through the night. He sees lopsided trailers, trucks on blocks, cats mating in the dumpster—their cries like babies'—as if for the first time. His neighbors' dreams tumble out of windows, spill over sod squares not yet grown together. Feathers from a chicken coop swirl around him. He slips into the bull's pen. Its eyes open; its nostrils flare. He lets it into the ring, heart full as he thrusts it toward the bull's horns.

Pilar re-read the story, underlining her favorite lines. She imagined reading those lines to Buster, finding words for what they made her feel—both the bright light of her life radiating outward when she drove with Carlos, and her father's dwindling figure, swallowed by dust. They made her feel she'd found someone who'd understand her.

Buster missed two classes and the next time he came, a dark-haired, birdlike girl dropped him off. She stood on tiptoe to kiss him. They kissed shamelessly, oblivious to Pilar and the other students entering the classroom.

Pilar had seen the birdlike girl before—transported like driftwood by a giggling, gossiping current of girls. Pilar wasn't that sort of girl. She thought Buster must want something more, that this was why he'd asked her to read his story. She stole glances at him—the three watches on his wrist, his eyelids drooping, chin bobbing beneath the bowler hat—looking away if he caught her. She would not want anyone who wanted anything but her particular strangeness.

Pilar and Carlos spoke every Sunday night. Columbia was challenging, but Carlos was doing well in his math and science courses and planning to major in engineering to please Abuela. Now that he was out of her grasp,

Abuela pleaded with him rather than ordering him to do things. She left voicemails about serial killers and rapists, begging him to be careful.

"It's all students and campus security guards in Columbiaville," Carlos assured her.

"Por favor promise me you won't go down to the Village, especially not on weekends," Abuela pleaded. "And don't be hanging out with any artistas. Go to church and make *nice* friends. Meet a nice girl you can marry and get your papers! I worry for you, mijo, but I am so proud. I tell all the women at the panadería about my grandson in college in Nueva York!"

"The least I can do is major in engineering," Carlos told Pilar. He'd cast off Carla as high school rebellion. "What else was there to do in San Jacinto? No one would so much as blink at Carla here. Yesterday, this hipster showed up to Logic and Rhetoric with raw fish safety-pinned to his clothes. Everyone just held their hands over their noses and changed seats." It was enough to be the scholarship kid from a Texican border town. Though there were other students from modest backgrounds, Columbia felt overwhelmingly white and monied compared to the Valley. Carlos' mind drifted in Art Humanities as students discussed trips to the Colosseum, the Louvre, and the Parthenon.

"I was in literature class and someone used the word *furtive*, which I'd never heard in my life," he told Pilar. "People were throwing it around like it had been a staple at their nightly Socratic family dinners. That was the third word in that class I'd never heard. Suddenly I was fighting to keep my head above water as the ocean dragged me out, all these meaningless voices talking on and on."

"You're smarter than all of them," Pilar said. "Half the time I've read the word; I've just never heard it. One time I was reading a quote and I pronounced 'unabashed' *un-a-ba-shed*. Two people jumped to correct me. I didn't speak in class for a month."

"Just say it like you know what you're talking about," Carlos said. "Say it like—"

"Them?"

"I know." Carlos laughed bitterly. "Easier said than done. Even the kids who dress like trash are walking ATMs. *Especially* the kids who dress like trash." He dressed preppy, tucking his mother's necklace inside his shirt. He touched the coin when he was anxious and remembered dancing with her.

Pilar and Carlos went home for Christmas break, exchanging gifts of books and music and details of their new cities. Carlos' scholarship didn't fully cover his living expenses and his undocumented status meant that he couldn't work on campus, so he tutored four students a week. He rode the M79 crosstown bus across Central Park to his students' Upper East Side apartments and was shown into their bedrooms by a housekeeper or personal assistant. There they waited at their desks like miniature hedge fund managers in their Trinity or Horace Mann uniforms. Carlos laughed to Pilar about studying *The Communist Manifesto*, which he'd only just read in his Contemporary Civilization course, with a surly but driven Horace Mann sixth grader while the family's housekeeper served them tea and cookies.

What Carlos talked about most was Mask and Wig, the all-male musical comedy troupe he'd joined—the only realm in which he crossdressed. He went on and on about brainstorming sessions with Abe, his hilarious co-writer.

Pilar told Carlos about Buster. "He's with one of those fragile, needy girls."

"Nothing like you."

"But his writing made me think he's more interesting."

"Maybe he's not. Maybe you read too much into things." Carlos thought Buster seemed a little too smooth.

Pilar learned to make small talk with the girls in her hall and joined enough of their late-night study sessions and ice cream runs that they now grabbed her when they headed down to the court. Even in the midst of dancing in an alcohol haze, flanked by squealing girls and bellowing guys, some part of Pilar held separate, observing. A tall stone column, true to her name.

She watched Buster gallop into the Kappa Sig house with the birdlike girl riding piggyback. She watched the aftermath of their fights—Buster running after her, calling, "Cass, wait!" as she hurried out of the house, her shoulders shaking.

She watched Buster when he swaggered, alone, through the dancing, wearing nothing but cowboy boots and a gunless holster. Her eyes moved over his chiseled chest and stomach, glanced down, winced away. She thought of Celie in *The Color Purple* saying men looked like frogs when they took off their pants. She watched Buster drink and play pool with his fraternity brothers, who laughed as if his nakedness were pure comedy. He wore a bemused half-smile, as if there was some secret to his performance that his brothers could not understand. Pilar tunneled under the skin, thought: *He's the rodeo clown.*

"That's some compelling literary analysis, Pilar, but he was walking around *naked*," Carlos pointed out. "Did you even look?"

"He's good looking. I told you that," she said, annoyed that Carlos had gotten snagged on the superficial. "What I'm saying is it's not enough for him—the whole fraternity facade. Walking around in nothing but boots and an empty gun holster... there's both a desire for raw connection and a parody of its impossibility."

"Oh, Pilar." Carlos laughed. "You're hopeless."

Pilar thought, *You're no better.* She knew not to press Carlos about his feelings for Abe, to let him stumble into himself at his own pace.

Pilar thought her observation went unnoticed until Buster walked toward her one night. He was so drunk that he stumbled in his cowboy boots, frog penis flopping. Pilar wanted to be seen, and his eyes were half-lidded. She wanted him to call her name from a third-floor window again. Or to call her by some name not her own—to be remade in a softer, more malleable form.

She straightened her shoulders and walked out of Kappa Sigma. She took off her shoes and walked barefoot across the lawn, sinking her toes—

body—into the cool grass. She removed herself from that middle ground of wanting. She didn't have any classes with Buster her spring semester. The base of her spine tingled when she passed him, usually interwoven with Cass, but she would not look.

She was her father's daughter—practiced in self-denial. Of course, alcohol loosened her resolve. Some boy always asked Pilar to the fraternity formals. Though she never went all the way, she endured as many fumbling hookups as the next SAU co-ed. Brain severed from body, thoughts dispersed in the eau de cologne of beer and sweat. Worse than the averted eye contact or awkward small talk when these boys checked out books from her in the library were the thoughts that returned as she struggled to study. She re-read the same page seven times, a nauseating guilt flooding her body as the night's drunk grab and tangle spiraled through her mind.

Pilar confessed to Carlos. "I don't know why I did it. This is a guy who has *nothing* interesting to say."

"It's *okay*, Pilar. That's what people do in college. You know, except me, wasting away my precious youth! As someone who's acing Chemistry, let me remind you that this is largely the effect of chemicals leaving your body. A mere case of the Sunday Night Blues—nothing to do but dance it off. Put on 'A Town Called Malice',"—Carlos had given her a mixed CD before they left for college—"put your phone on speaker, and dance with me." Pilar only had a CD Walkman, so she borrowed Kristie's untouched boombox. Kristie usually didn't get back from the chemistry lab until late. Pilar closed the door and cranked up the volume. As the song climaxed, Carlos screamed into the phone like a crazed Richard Simmons: *"FOOT-BALL RUN! ARMS TO THE SKY! JAZZ HANDS!"* Pilar was doing just as he commanded when Kristie walked in, her blue eyes wide. Pilar froze, her face hot. "Sorry!" she yelled over the music and hurried to turn it off. Carlos' tinny screams still came through her phone: *"RUN DOWN THOSE SUNDAY NIGHT BLUES!"*

"Call you back," Pilar said to Carlos. "I hope it's okay that I borrowed your boombox," she said to Kristie. Kristie dug her fingers into her jean pockets, her face waxy and red. "I'm just glad someone's using it." Red-faced, they stared at each other until Pilar took her phone into the hall.

That summer, Pilar and Carlos worked at Sprouts and watched the sun set from their old spot by the Rio Grande. Carlos would blast music from The Bitch's speakers and they'd swing dance through the dust as the sky darkened and the sweltering air cooled.

Their Sunday night talks continued through sophomore year. And then it was first snowfall in New York, Carlos' heart flopping like a dying fish when Abe brushed snow from his hair and admonished with his sweet smile, "You should wear a hat." Pilar hugged her knees around a beach bonfire with a bunch of other students when Buster came up behind her as if he'd walked out of the ocean, and said, "Hey, I have something for you." He handed her a worn copy of Raymond Carver's *What We Talk About When We Talk About Love*, said, "Let me know what you think," and then walked off alone down the shore.

Pilar finished *What We Talk About When We Talk About Love* and went on to read *Cathedral*. She preferred the more expansive stories in *Cathedral*. She imagined talking about this with Buster but talked to Carlos instead.

It was in the sunny 70s when they returned to San Jacinto that Christmas. Over gingerbread and pumpkin spice lattes at the recently opened Barnes and Noble, Pilar talked to Carlos about Carver and Carlos told Pilar funny stories about Abe. Pilar returned home that summer, but Carlos stayed at Columbia as a teaching assistant in a summer drama program for high school students. That solitary summer in the Valley, she started writing poems about her father and the mines, La Llanura and her mother, dust, sugarcane, and graves. She kept writing them when she returned to school, showing no one, not even Carlos. She wasn't sure he'd understand.

Christmas of their junior year, they drove to their spot by the river. Pilar had tucked a poem she'd written about the first time he took her there into her satchel. She'd meant to give it to Carlos. But her heart pounded and her palms sweated when she reached for it, and she didn't. It felt like the first secret between them.

She took her first writing workshop spring semester of her junior year. Buster was in it. They were vocal about their appreciation for one another's writing during workshop, but they didn't talk outside of class. It seemed that they never would, until one day toward the end of the semester, Buster ran after Pilar as she was leaving class. Pilar was a fast walker.

"Hey... Pilar," Buster called, a little out of breath or maybe nervous.

Pilar gave him a questioning look.

"Do you think we could maybe get lunch? I'd love to talk... about writing." He was nervous—Pilar hadn't imagined it.

"Me, too," Pilar said. "I still have your copy of *What We Talk About...*"

"*When We Talk About Love*?" He hadn't forgotten.

Buster would graduate in a month, while Cass was still a junior, and rumor had it that their on-again, off-again relationship was permanently off. Pilar tried to act casual, switching her overstuffed backpack from two shoulders to one, as they walked to Buster's vintage blue pickup. She was already imagining scenarios in which their lunch became more. "I have *Cathedral* with me," she said. "I'm reading it again."

"I love that one, too." Buster held her eyes a beat too long.

He drove Pilar to a mom-and-pop spaghetti house through congested streets striated by the tall shadows of palms. Not having a car, Pilar didn't leave campus much. She looked out her window at sunshine dripped over endless strip malls and traffic, then stole a glance at Buster. He turned to her and smiled. She looked back out the window, the light now beautiful, hedging the distant outline of mountains.

Buster joked with the waiter, who seated them next to the window overlooking the parking lot. It wasn't long before they were having the conversation Pilar had imagined. Two years' worth of unspoken spilled out: Her mouth moved seamlessly from one idea to the next. She had never talked so much or so easily. Buster sat on the edge of his seat, leaning toward her, laughing when his white Western shirt dipped into his spaghetti sauce.

They talked about the final jazz scene in "Sonny's Blues," Creole waiting for Sonny to strike out for deep water. "Lish cuts off Carver before he fills his lungs," Pilar said.

"I don't know," Buster said. "Stories where the big things live in the silences are true to the people Carver writes about." His drawl made unspoken things breathe between his words.

Pilar compared "The Bath" to "A Small, Good Thing". "It's the difference between metal and breath."

"You don't think the ending in 'A Small, Good Thing' is too soft?" Buster asked.

Pilar read the ending of "A Small, Good Thing". She'd hardly touched her spaghetti and now she pushed her plate away and held *Cathedral* like it would feed her. Her eyes filled.

Buster smiled crookedly at her, his right cheek dimpling, and shook his head.

Pilar looked away from Buster's smile. She held fast to her thoughts. She told Buster about her father's stories of the mines—how though death was a constant presence, their meaning was in the two brothers working together in darkness. "The stories were about everything their bond held—the sorrow and the light—like the old folks in 'Sonny's Blues' telling stories as the windows darken."

She looked at Buster, surer now. "The best stories hold what Baldwin talks about when he says that Sonny filled the air with his life, but that life held so many others. 'He had made it his: that long line, of which we knew only Mama and Daddy, and he was giving it back, as everything must be given back, so that, passing through death, it can live forever'."

Buster's eyes widened. "What d'you memorize these things?"

"I wrote my paper on that line," Pilar said. "What I'm saying is that there has to be room for the going back and that stretch into forever. You have to hold all those other lives and find your way inside. Sit with pain and then pass through it—into something larger."

"And if you can't find your way inside?" Buster searched Pilar's eyes.

Heat rose in her cheeks. She turned toward the window, not seeing the parking lot, but her father. "When I got older, my father's stories became something else. All action and heroism. It became unbearable to sit with each other's pain. To be that close. We knew the story was a lie, but we couldn't find our way back. So we stopped telling it."

She was still staring out the window, squinting at the rows of silent cars, when Buster tucked a strand of hair behind her ear, grazed her cheek with his thumb. She turned to find him looking at her with wonder. "Where did you come from?" His mouth spread into that wide, white smile.

The feeling of being seen was so raw that Pilar closed her eyes. That feeling—between drowning and stumbling into something larger—swelled. The image of her legs wrapped around Buster's back surfaced like the imagery that filled her mind when she read. When she opened her eyes, he was still looking at her.

After lunch, Buster drove Pilar to the library, Dylan crooning on his stereo. They'd talked themselves into a silence where everything held meaning. They drove with the windows down. "Tangled Up in Blue" seemed to waft in on the breeze.

He insisted on opening Pilar's door as he'd insisted on paying for lunch. He took her hand to help her down from his truck. He searched her eyes, took her face in his hands, and kissed her. Pilar pulled closer, wrapping her leg around him.

That same spring, Carlos and Abe were nominated to co-write and direct Mask and Wig's end of the year performance. Cue smoldering glances in the dressing room, electrified touches during rehearsals, all that pent-up desire fueling their writing sessions. They could hardly write their ideas down fast enough. Carlos would come up with an idea and when he'd pushed it to a dead end, Abe would twist it into hyperbolic absurdity that had Carlos rolling on the floor. They were like cocaine-fueled copywriters chasing down a million-dollar deadline. Never had they been more brilliant, hilarious, in sync.

The actors absorbed that magic and took the script in still more hysterical directions. The night of the performance, everything that had been amiss during rehearsals fell into place. The actors squeezed last minute punchlines and comic gestures into every last cranny until the audience held their aching sides, begging for mercy, wheezing, tears squeezing out of the corners of their eyes. The 2006 Mask and Wig end of the year performance was all anyone talked about for awhile. Lines from the performance became staples in the student body vernacular; the graduation commencement speaker, considered by many to be the most renowned postmodern author of his generation, opened with a quote from their performance. But all of that—and then some—was yet to come.

The actors bowed first and then ducked backstage. The stage manager came out, announced Carlos and Abe, and presented them with jesters' hats that read, *Writer/Director: Mask and Wig, Spring 2006.* Carlos and Abe donned their hats, after which the stage manager joined the cast backstage, leaving them for a solo bow. They clasped hands and bowed. The audience stood and the curtain closed on torrential applause.

Carlos and Abe hugged—applause thundering through the curtain— and then pulled each other tighter. It was impossible to tell who kissed who first, elation enveloping them in a utopia of entwinement. Carlos discovered that a kiss didn't just involve your mouth, but your whole body, electrified. Abe clasped the back of Carlos' neck and pulled him closer. Their bodies became tongues—seeking, touching, tangling.

The curtain opened. The cast returned for a second bow and Carlos and Abe froze in the midst of disentangling themselves. The cast froze in the midst of discovering them. For a split second, they were locked in this Coming Out Diorama. The audience, confused by the diorama, stopped clapping.

But then the applause rose. This was, after all, Columbia University in the City of New York. They whistled and hooted and clapped as if the survival of New York City's thriving Gay Pride tradition depended on their stinging palms. In this way, the audience entangled themselves in Carlos and Abe's kiss and in the creation of this historic Mask and Wig performance. It was a performance, after all, that satirized Columbia, which is to say that *they* were the raw material from which it was molded. And what was Columbia if not a community where they could relish this queer theatre kiss in a kind of voyeuristic orgy of good will and thereby insert themselves into Mask and Wig's moment of artistic triumph?

There was at least one person in the audience who did not cheer for this early offshoot of the Pride Parade. Abe saw his imperious mother, whom he'd lovingly caricatured in the original draft of the script and then thought better of it, wearing her Orthodox garb of wig, calf-length skirt, and stockings (Abe had stopped wearing his yarmulke and tzitzit the year before), clasp one hand over her ample bosom and the other over her mouth.

———————————

Pilar's lunch with Buster had been on a Tuesday. In Thursday's workshop, they sat at opposite ends of the long table, but stole glances at each other. They talked to other students on their way out of class, but Pilar felt Buster's closeness as a pressure. They kept walking, until the other students had dispersed, and Buster slipped his fingers through Pilar's. "I thought workshop would never end," he said.

He kept walking and Pilar walked with him, not caring where they were going. He pulled her into the tunnel of oak trees and kissed her. "I wanted to kiss you here," he said. Pilar slipped her hands under his shirt, ran her palms over the smooth muscles of his back. He had to go to work—he worked as a line cook at In-N-Out Burger—but asked if he'd see her at PiKA's Glam Rock party the next night. Pilar hadn't known about the party, but nodded. She would ask Carlos what to wear. She stood very still and watched Buster walk away, his figure dwindling beneath the arch of oaks.

He turned to look back at her before he emerged from their shade into the late afternoon light.

The next night, Pilar put on the turquoise sequin miniskirt, as Carlos had advised. She hadn't worn it since he won Mz. 10th Avenue. It still hugged her curves. "Careful with this Buster character," Carlos had said.

"Why do you say that?" Pilar had asked.

"I worry about you, Pilar. You don't know your own beauty. Trust me, Buster's interested in more than your writing."

"I'm not beautiful," Pilar said matter-of-factly. She was interesting looking at best—her face too pale and angular, body too lanky. Men didn't want women who towered over them.

"Yes you are, and men are pigs," Carlos said. "Plus it's hard to trust anyone named Buster."

"Oh my god, where did you get this?" Pilar's hallmates exclaimed over the miniskirt. They listened, rapt, as she told them about swimming through mounds of Ropa Usada clothes, paying 60 cents per pound. Pilar watched herself in the mirror as they teased her hair and lined her eyes, wondering if Buster would like her this way. She went down to the PiKA house with these squealing girls, danced in their cluster of soft arms, legs, and ratted hair, but kept looking for Buster. He never came.

She slipped out of the head-banging revelry at some point past midnight. She took off her heels and walked barefoot through campus until she'd gotten to the tunnel of oaks. The tangle of branches made her think of tangled limbs. She pretended that the stars peeking through the rustling boughs were enough.

She was headed back to her dorm when Buster leaned over the balcony of his third-floor senior apartment and called to her as he had her freshman year, "Hey, beautiful! Where're you going?"

Pilar stared up at him.

Buster leaned over his balcony and sang, "Tangled Up in Blue": *Every-one of them words rang true / And glowed like burnin' coal / Pourin' off of every page / Like it was written in my soul.*

"Shouldn't I be on the balcony?" Pilar asked.

"Yes. Come up to 3F."

Pilar didn't move. She'd settled into her disappointment and was think-ing of staying there.

Buster leaned over his balcony and drawled, *"Please,"* so that the word seemed to hold more. "I want to tell you something."

Pilar tugged down her miniskirt and climbed the stairs.

Buster wrapped her in a red kimono to ward off the wind on his balco-ny. He brought her a gin and tonic.

"Why weren't you at PiKA?" Pilar stood at the opposite end of the balco-ny. She leaned back against the railing and sipped her drink.

"I was writing. Ever since we talked, I've been writing. I want to show you when it's ready." Buster crossed the balcony and pulled her toward him. He kissed her neck and her body loosened. "Why so far away, Pilar? You're all I've thought about these last few days." He slipped his hand through hers and led her inside. He sank into a battered armchair and, though Pilar was nearly as tall as him, pulled her into his lap. His arms felt made to hold her.

The anthology they used in their writing workshop lay on his coffee table. They read passages they loved. Pilar wanted to go on sitting in Buster's lap, reading to each other, words sinking beneath the warm swell of gin, *forever and ever, Amen.*

"What'll you do when you graduate?" she asked.

Buster shrugged. "Maybe take a train across the country. Or live on a boat. Or work on a cattle farm. What do you want to do when you're out of here?"

Pilar wondered what it was like to feel such freedom. She didn't want to return to the Valley, but worried about her father. She couldn't see past being steeped in books in her basement library carrel. "Maybe I'll do this the rest of my life." Pilar smiled.

"I want to do more than this." Cradling her, Buster lifted her out of the chair and kissed her. "Let's drive somewhere," he whispered.

They walked down to the parking lot, Pilar still wrapped in his red kimono. Soon they were flying up the 405 in his pickup, his hand on the stick shift. Pilar remembered the euphoria of night drives with Carlos. Buster exited onto Mulholland Drive and careened along its winding cliffs. He pulled to a stop under a tree with a large, low-hanging canopy. They got out of his truck, stood at the edge of the cliffs, and looked down at the lights of the Valley below. "This is my favorite spot," Buster said, and it became Pilar's favorite spot—floating in this sea of lights with this boy she had longed for before she knew him, when she was still standing in the sugarcane, whispering, *Do you love me?,* that wanting suddenly so loud that she thought it would rupture her skull.

Buster answered as if he'd heard. "*I LOVE YOU, PILAR REINFELD!*" he yelled into the sea of lights. He cupped his hands around his mouth and yelled it into the tangle of tree limbs, which might have been the synaptic tangle in Pilar's brain. "*I LOVE YOUR MIND, YOUR WORDS, YOUR PAS- SION.*" Her father more often showed than said those words. Carlos had said them, but it was this boy's love that seemed to answer all those days of waiting in the cane. She felt—for the first time—known for the parts of herself she'd labored to make known. Staring out at the lights of that oth- er valley with Buster, she felt she'd found the place where these valleys converged. She felt his breath on her face when he pulled her to him and whispered, "I love you."

Buster picked her up and she wrapped her legs around him. They lay beneath the tree; its tangle of limbs became their tangle of limbs. The hardness, the reality, of him was wonderful until he unbuckled his belt. "Wait, I've never..." Pilar said. Buster kissed her protesting mouth. He leaned his whole weight against her while he wriggled out of his pants.

Pilar woke, goosepimples sprouting on her skin. "Don't," she said as Buster pulled down her underwear, her panic swelling like the moon. She tried to shove him off of her, but he pinned her shoulder to the ground. The moon pulled large and close as he thrust himself inside her and she knew—with cold, metal clarity—that Buster did not love her mind, words, passion. Her mind left. She was a bag of a body for him to shove himself inside. A body under water, holding its breath, kicking as hard as it could as Buster thrust, until a sharp pain shot through its pelvis and its mouth let out a small animal cry.

Though she'd been taught not to, she screamed until her throat was raw, the sound sucked into the black sky.

"Okay, okay." Buster held his hands up in the air. Pilar was still kicking after he rolled off of her, still fighting against air. She gasped for it and it caught in her throat. Buster stood, buckled his belt. He stared at Pilar lying on the ground as if she were a stranger. He backed away, a lumbering shadow against the dark sky. "I should go. I have a girlfriend." He waited for her to get up, to pull up her panties, pull down her skirt, brush herself off.

Pilar felt shaky and faraway as she got into his car. Buster drove her back to campus, fast through the winding hills, everything a blur through the windows. She stared out the window, the sky whitening, the moon emptying slowly. She didn't look at Buster as she climbed out of his car. She walked toward her dorm, an ache at the back of her throat and white noise ringing in her ears. Even when she got to her room, she did not cry. She lay in her bed with her clothes on and her eyes open, listening to her roommate's snores until morning.

CHAPTER 6

After that brief bliss when Carlos and Abe kissed, everything went to hell. Abe dropped out of Mask and Wig and wouldn't return Carlos' calls, emails, or texts. When Abe blocked his number, Carlos hoped without hope that Abe would contact him. He checked his phone and email to find nothing, then checked again. The withdrawal he felt was bodily. He'd invested so much energy, creativity, electricity in Abe and now that he was gone, he moved through a flat, gray world. His engineering classes were painfully dull. He'd find himself halfway down a page having no idea what he'd read. He'd come up with a hilarious idea for a Mask and Wig sketch, but upon realizing he couldn't tell Abe, it was no longer funny. The club wasn't surprised when Carlos dropped out, too. Without his collaborations with Abe, his comedy fell flat. What remained was a weird tension with the troupe. Carlos told them he'd picked up more tutoring because he needed the money, which was true. He bargained with Abuela's god: If he could just see Abe—his big brown eyes, full lips, curls—he'd go to church, become a successful engineer, buy Abuela a new house.

A few days after the performance, Carlos was crossing the quad, listening to Arthur Russell's "A Little Lost" on repeat, tears welling up as he sang, *"It's so unfinished / Our love affair... I hope your feeling isn't diminished / I hope you need someone in your life / Someone like me."* He blinked to clear his eyes and spied Abe in the distance, coming out of the library. He'd started wearing his yarmulke again. Carlos' heart pounded; his voice caught in his throat. Abe froze when he saw Carlos, then walked hurriedly toward the Broadway campus exit. Carlos ran after him. The red hand went up at the crosswalk just as Abe arrived. Carlos slowed to a lope, catching his breath, wracking his brain for what to say. I love you? What could this flood of feelings be but love? Abe looked wild-eyed over his shoulder at Carlos approaching, blotches blooming on his face until it was beet-red, then walked straight into traffic. "Abe!" Carlos screamed wildly, but Abe just kept walking across Broadway, drivers blaring their horns.

Pilar went to the campus doctor and peed in a plastic cup. She imagined having to tell her father that she was pregnant. She wondered if her nausea was morning sickness. The pregnancy test came back negative, but she tested positive for HPV. The doctor explained that nearly all sexually active women contracted HPV at some point in their lives, but she felt dirty. Marked.

Her creative writing workshop was divided into two critique sections, and Pilar asked Dr. Adams if she could switch out of Buster's section and into the other for the few remaining classes. "Of course," Dr. Adams said, seeing how upset she was. His eyes held hers; he put his hand on her face. He had a daughter her age. Pilar wondered whether she'd ever deserved his praise. Dr. Adams swept a tear from her cheek.

Buster sent Pilar an email saying he'd had too much to drink that night and hoped that they could still be friends. Pilar couldn't so much as picture him. He was a black hole against a backdrop of bruised sky. He told Cass that it was just a kiss, but she wept for anyone who would listen. There were stares and whispers when Pilar walked into the dining hall, so she ate frozen dinners alone in her room. Out of the corner of her eye, she caught the girls in her hall frowning at her, though they pasted on smiles when she greeted them. Even alone, she felt like she was being watched.

The solitude she'd always found comfort in felt perforated, sharp objects slicing through. She lost the ability to slip out of her skin, into her thoughts. The silver running through things dried up. She moved through a cold, metallic world. Girls cried into their flip phones as they walked across campus, carrying on disembodied half-conversations about their grades or boyfriends or eating disorders. They made Pilar sad. Then tired.

Her poems had been the place where she found language for things too raw to touch. Now Buster wound through the lines, hand on the stick shift and head out the window, looking for what he could take. Poetry was soldered to that night: screams swallowed by black sky. Pilar revised poems for her final portfolio but wrote nothing new. She focused on keeping her grades up so she wouldn't lose her scholarship.

Some days the repetition of checking out books for her work-study cleared out other thoughts. Sometimes she heard Buster's words—*I LOVE YOUR MIND, YOUR WORDS, YOUR PASSION*—felt him pinning her shoulder as he unbuckled his belt. One afternoon, her hands started shaking as she checked out a boy's books. "I'm sorry," she said, but finished somehow before telling her supervisor that she didn't feel well. She locked herself in a bathroom stall, hunched over and coughed, gasping for air. Then she walked hurriedly outside, as if someone was following her, toward shelter, any shelter. She ended up in the campus cathedral, gripping the wooden pew in front of her and waiting, with closed eyes, for light—stained—to seep through glass and skin.

Nights were worse. She'd look out the library windows and see the white moon swelling. Her vision would char at the edges, then the racing heart, the sweating palms, the sharp pain in her chest like she was drowning. Her body shook as she walked through the darkened campus. She thought of her father's hands shaking on the wheel when a cop passed. She felt his fear in the pit of her stomach, her bones, behind her eyes. The words came like something hard she could hold in the dark: *El señor es mi pastor; nada me faltará. Sí, aunque ande en valle de sombra de muerte, no temeré mal alguno.* She said the words over and over, moving her lips, though no sound came out. She polished them smooth like stones at the bottom of a river. She stepped from stone to stone.

She got herself home just like her father had, through the garbled voices of the girls in her dorm hall and into her room, where she shut the door, slid down it, and cried with her hand over her mouth.

After that, she never left the library after dark.

She understood her father as she never had. The vibration of his pain in their silences on the phone made her think of windows breaking.

Pilar stopped returning his calls. She used her father's story to lessen her own: No one had died, she told herself.

———————————

Carlos filled his flat, gray days with worries about Pilar. She didn't have a cell phone, so he left messages on her college voicemail—at first demanding the glamrock update; then, *Pilar, I'm worried,* talk *to me*; then, *This is about that asshole, Buster, isn't it? I swear I'll find a bull to gore him.* He called until her voice mailbox was full, then left messages with her roommate, then sent emails. Pilar didn't respond.

The only one who wanted to talk to Carlos was Abuela. She left a dozen messages, at first saying that she missed him and wanted to know if he was coming home for the summer. She could get him work at the bakery, or he could work his old job at Sprouts. He could take classes at UT-Pan Am. When he didn't call her back for two days, her panic escalated: "Mijo, call me! I'm afraid you've been kidnapped by some loco!"

Carlos couldn't bring himself to call her back, to hear again how all she wanted was for him to get a good job, marry a nice girl, and get his papers. How did he get trapped in this sad-ass Shakespearean triangle where everyone pursued someone who didn't return their love?

Abuela somehow got through to the Dean of Undergraduate Student Life. Carlos had had to jump through flaming bureaucratic hoops when he'd been given the wrong class. None of the administrative departments seemed to communicate with each other; no one seemed to care that he needed the class to fulfill his engineering requirements. And yet Abuela had not only spoken directly with Dean Schaefer; she had him calling her *Abuela*. Carlos skipped through her messages to listen to this voicemail: "This is Dean Schaefer calling for Carlos Gomez. Abuela's very concerned about you and has called our office multiple times. If you don't respond, we'll be forced to investigate..."

"I don't know yet whether I'm coming home," Carlos said exasperatedly when he finally called Abuela back. "But you can't go to the dean when I don't call for two days!"

"How should I know if you're okay?" Abuela demanded. "So much crime in that city—shootings, riots, locos everywhere. Mijo, I've been praying to Saint Antony. I was worried. I was ready to do la brujería."

Carlos sighed, then wondered if he should contact SAU's dean about Pilar or do la brujería on Abe. "I'm fine, Abuela. You have to stop worrying. I'll let you know about summer as soon as I know."

———

Pilar remembered running the rows of the citrus grove when she was upset as a child. She went for an early evening run through the neighborhood surrounding SAU. Even as her muscles and breath pushed forward, her body felt raw, exposed. She kept checking over her shoulder. On the way back to campus, an SUV ran a light and nearly slammed into her body. She never swore, but fear pushed a jumbled obscenity from her mouth—*MOTHER OF FUCK*—as she slammed her fist down on the hood. By the time she got back to her dorm, her hand was bruised. Anxiety's frayed wires had shorted out and she was exhausted.

Kristie had left her another message from Carlos: *Call me or I'll fly out there*. She wanted to crawl into bed without showering and sleep until morning, but she forced herself to call Carlos. She begged him not to fly out. Though he flew home for holidays, it was a risk.

"What happened, Pilar?"

Pilar was silent for a long time and then she was crying—loud, shuddering sobs that didn't sound like her. She couldn't stop.

Carlos knew without her saying. He felt the sharp kick in his ribs that came when Pilar's body was pulled from Carla's. He stopped himself from punching the wall. "Please tell me you reported that asshole. *Pilar...?* Have you talked to anyone? Let me fly out—I can be there tomorrow."

Pilar stopped crying. "No. It's too risky and expensive. I'm fine, Carlos. Don't worry, I'll be fine."

Carlos pushed some more, but Pilar was unbudging. "Okay, call me anytime. I'm here for you. I love you."

"I love you, too," Pilar said, though reclaiming those words made her eyes fill.

The sound of Pilar's sobs echoed in Carlos' head as he lay in bed, staring into the dark. In the middle of dinner in the cafeteria, he pushed his plate away and left to call her.

"Are you eating?" he asked. (Because he had no appetite.)

"I'm eating right now," Pilar said. She was eating a microwave dinner in her dorm room. She told Carlos she'd decided to stop drinking.

"Pilar, what happened is *not* your fault."

"I never really liked drinking anyway," she said.

Carlos did like drinking, but he sipped seltzer at parties in solidarity. Still the sound of Pilar's sobs echoed in his head at night. He took his phone into the hall so as not to wake his roommate and called her at 1 a.m., 2 a.m. It was three hours earlier in LA.

"Why are you up so late?" Pilar would ask.

"I—was thinking of you. I just called to say I'm here."

"I know. I promise I'm okay. Please don't worry, Carlos."

Pilar got a cell phone and a switchblade like the one Carlos had carried in high school. She ran with them in a waistpack. Conversations with Carlos took the place of conversations with her father. Carlos asked if she was eating enough, sleeping enough. Pilar answered when he called but didn't call Carlos first until a month after the night with Buster. She still wasn't writing poems, but she'd started running the cross-country trails until the borders of her body fell away, the particles of her dispersed into breath and light. After calling Carlos, she was able to call her father—the familiarity of their stilted conversation more comforting than painful. She told him that she'd started running and he sent her a postcard of a Greater Roadrunner in motion, both feet off the ground.

She was looking forward to going home for the summer.

"It'll be nice," she told Carlos. "Valley life is so simple."

Carlos was silent.

"Papá, is that you?" Pilar asked.

It was the first joke she'd made since that psychopath Buster. Relief flooded Carlos and he laughed.

"You're staying in New York," Pilar said.

"I can't go home to Abuela right now," Carlos said. Everything that had happened with Abe tumbled out.

"I'm glad you're staying in New York," Pilar said. "You should resurrect the eagle's wings dress."

"I was thinking it was time for Carla to come out of the closet," Carlos said. The old electricity crackled in his voice.

Carlos looked for a summer sublet in Brooklyn. A bunch of Mask and Wig guys had gone in together on an apartment in Harlem, but he needed to put 11 miles between himself and Abe. He found an apartment in Crown Heights, close to Prospect Park, the Brooklyn Museum, the Brooklyn Botanic Garden, and the Central Brooklyn Public Library. He liked his roommate, Timon, a softspoken Trinidadian DJ whom he recognized as a fellow dreamer. Timon spent most of his time at his girlfriend's apartment, which gave Carlos too much time to think.

Pilar encouraged him to write to Abe. "Even if he doesn't respond, it'll give you a sense of closure." Carlos wrote Abe about the memories he'd hold, saying he wished things between them had had a chance to grow. Abe didn't respond, but Carlos knew, somehow, that he'd read, and re-read, his letter.

The Eastern Parkway Mall—wide, bench-lined sidewalks shaded by an arch of old oaks that stretched for two miles along either side of the neighborhood's main boulevard—was a catwalk of convergences. On Sundays, Carlos liked to sit on a bench with pumpkin roti and coffee as El Ojo—a giant eye taking it all in. He watched Black families make their way to church in their Sunday finest; Hasidic mothers trailed by children in old-man suits and hand-sewn dresses; shirtless Rastafarian runners, dreadlocks swishing over their muscled backs; a bearded man harvesting bottles.

Rollicking bass-beat gospel songs spilled out of the tiny red stucco church next to Carlos' building. Some part of him wanted to sink into that joyful swaying and clapping, but he subscribed to the gospel of the Senegalese man who guarded the car lot across the street. "I talk to everybody who passes," the man proudly told him. "The street is my church."

In the evenings, old folks and young couples sat on the benches lining the Eastern Parkway Mall, talking until the sky turned pink and fireflies rose. Carlos watched the lights of cars stream by and remembered driving at night with Pilar. It made him sad that she was living their old life in the Valley, stocking vegetables at Sprouts. He pushed into the unknown for both of them, auditioning at Lucky Feng's drag cabaret, touted on its website not only as the first restaurant in the world to feature drag-queen servers and performers, but as the *Drag Queen Capital of the Universe!*

An excitement that he had not felt since kissing Abe tingled along his spine as he slipped the eagle's wings dress over his head. He hadn't worn it since prom. Riding the subway to the East Village, the people in his car did a double-take—first at that inimitable evening gown paraded out on a Wednesday afternoon and Carla's equally extraordinary beauty; then, more slyly, they gave her the side-eye over their newspapers, read her flat chest, absent hips, faint Adam's apple, their glances not so much disapproving as unsure. Carla leaned against a pole, adjusted her spaghetti straps, and folded her arms over her gray-winged chest. She hummed her audition song: "Because the Night".

Lucky Feng's was in a brick rowhouse painted bright red with gold dragons over its windows. A silver-haired, queeny man who introduced himself as Nathaniel let Carla in. Nathaniel led Carla up a stairway and through red velvet drapes into a performance space lit by Chinese lanterns. The bar was adorned with gold dragons. Rows of long tables led up to a small stage.

Carla sat center stage on a stool with a microphone. She had ten minutes to do a stand-up routine and a musical number. Her standup was rough, but passable. She impersonated Abuela befriending the dean, the dean insisting in his voicemail that he call Abuela and go to Mass, and *not* some sham of an Episcopal Mass! But her performance of "Because the Night" was achingly beautiful. She closed her eyes before she began and remembered singing it with Pilar in the canoe, Pilar saying, *We're getting out of here*. When she sang, *They can't hurt you now*, her voice was broken with the knowledge that neither the night nor their bodies belonged to them.

Nathaniel gave a few halfhearted claps. "You've got raw talent we can work with. We'll have to get you a new look, though." He looked the eagle's wings dress up and down.

Nathaniel's blasé pragmatism was exactly what Carla needed to move forward. "Does that mean I have the job?" she asked. She couldn't wait to tell Pilar.

"Sweetheart, if you want this job, it's yours. Of course, you'll start with waiting tables. It'll be a while before we can work you into the show."

Nathaniel ushered Carla into the back office. The only ID he asked for was a driver's license. Carla marked herself free for every shift over the summer and listed singing, dancing, comedy, and acting as skills. "It's not often we get a Columbia girl," he said. "A *Colombian* Columbia girl!"

"Texican," Carla corrected.

"I think I've got a look for you." Nathaniel squinted at Carla, nodding slowly. "A vision is coming to me…" He made a slow arc with his hands.

Soon after Carla's audition, Nathaniel combed through second-hand stores and costume shops with Carlos to pull together a Carmen Miranda look involving a fruit and feather turban; a gold sequined halter and gold lamé slit skirt; red, gold, and green bicep-tutus; bangle bracelets to his elbows; a necklace of red and gold beads the size of Christmas tree ornaments; dangling watermelon earrings; a gold globe of a pinky ring; and towering gold strappy platforms. This was topped off with red acrylic nails, false eyelashes, arched charcoal eyebrows, blue eyeshadow, heavy rouge, and glossy red lips.

Carlos sent a photo to Pilar captioned: "Carmen and Carla would never be friends."

It was the first time Pilar had seen Carlos in a dress since prom. She looked right through all of the gaudy accessories to the bravery beneath. "I'm so proud of you," she wrote. "And I think Carmen and Carla would be friends."

Carlos smiled at his phone. When Carmen looked again at herself in the full-length mirror of Lucky Feng's dressing room, she held her turbaned head a little higher.

On his first night of waiting tables as Carmen, Carlos twisted his ankle in her towering gold platforms. Limping around his new neighborhood the next day, an Antiguan woman with a beautiful, lined face suggested home remedies and helped him cross the street. When he got caught in a summer shower, the Indian man who ran the dollar store he frequented let him pay later for an umbrella. Another time, the man's wife had wrapped a Band-Aid around Carlos' papercut finger. Carlos knew that Crown Heights embraced him because he dressed the part of a preppy student. Extravagant costumes were for the Labor Day Carnival and Purim.

The Eastern Parkway Mall was a prime catcalling gallery. Carlos had seen men trail women for blocks as they speedwalked to the subway entrance with their arms folded over their chests and their heads down. There were Alfonsos in Brooklyn, too—no telling what they'd do if they found out the woman they'd trailed for blocks was a man.

It was safest to become Carmen in the Lucky Feng's dressing room. Plus, he needed help. The Sisters strutted their lithe, naked bodies around, waiting until they'd finished their makeup to dress in the cramped, over-heated space, the air thick with aerosol hairspray and aswirl with glitter. It was impossible not to get glitter on your limbs, cheeks, eyelashes, and lips; impossible not to swallow a little glitter. "Swallow a little glamour, you'll shit it out!" Bama Dee Light, their six-foot-three Black Drag Mother from Tuscaloosa, hooted. Bama, who'd been doing drag since the 80s, often arrived fully dressed, with a makeup kit for touchups, and helped the younger queens who hightailed it to Lucky Feng's from retail jobs, restaurant shifts, and night classes with roller suitcases in tow.

Carmen, especially, was a communal creation. When Carlos attempt-ed his own makeup based on a Sephora makeover, Bama, whose face looked like an impressionist painting, scolded, "Cute as you are, that baby face won't do." She wrapped her red-taloned hands around his hips, exclaimed, "What I wouldn't do for this waistline!" and spun him around. She opened a valise of lipsticks and brushes arranged like a tiny skyline and dove into the three-hour creation of Carmen's face. As she widened Carmen's eyes with white makeup in the corners, Carlos remembered the queen in the 10th Avenue bathroom who'd made up El Ojo. How that stranger became a caretaker as she cupped El Ojo's face in her hands, sealing it from Abuela's slap.

———————————

Pilar had never in her life been a morning person. She used to have nightmares about her father tumbling into the graves he dug. She'd sleep lightly until he came home and kissed her forehead at 5:30 a.m., then sink into a deep sleep in the last hour before her father woke her for school. He had to wake her two or three times, and then she was slothlike, non-verbal. Her softspoken, gentle father, patiently waiting for her on the porch, was everything she needed in the mornings.

That summer in San Jacinto, she dragged herself out of bed at 5 a.m. and had breakfast waiting for her father when he returned from the graveyard. They ate together on the porch, watching the sun rise before he went to bed. Pilar ate lightly, then ran up and down the rows of the neighboring orange grove. The humid air enveloped her, making her body feel heavy and present. She pushed through the heaviness. Or she swam long, underwater laps in the resaca—to be submerged, held.

She drove her father's pickup to Sprouts, her thighs sticking to the cracked vinyl seat, past burnt fields of brush. She felt laid out and dried like that. When the register was slow at Sprouts, she wound through the aisles checking prices and restocking shelves. The produce misters thundered before they watered the vegetables. Pilar found the tiny rainstorms comforting.

She helped her father make dinner. She was so hungry by the time they ate that she ate meat again, a metallic taste in her mouth. Afterwards, they watched the sun set from the porch. When the sun streaked the resaca with blood, her father rocked beside her, the rhythmic creak of the porch boards promising, *This is all and this is all, forever and ever, Amen.* While her father got ready for work, she'd go for a night canoe. She pushed off from shore, dipped the paddle into that dark wound, and pulled through it.

She asked her father if they could go to Holy Rosary's Sunday Mass. They walked through the graveyard together on their way there. He told her again how he'd strapped her to his chest as a baby and walked her to sleep among the dead. The pews were tightly packed, mostly with women and children. The women's plump arms brushed Pilar's as they turned the pages of their hymnals. The Mass was in Spanish, which she now spoke only with her father. The cathedral's vaulted arches echoed. The words washed over Pilar and she did not try to pick them apart. She became a child again. The barbed wire at the back of her throat loosened and a sleepy warmth overcame her. When Mass was over, she didn't want to leave. She went every Sunday for the rest of the summer. Most Sundays her father slept in and she went alone.

She started praying before she fell asleep, in that time when her father used to tell her stories. "Make me better," she prayed over and over, her lips moving in the dark. Three words to undo three words. *Make me better.* She meant: Make me stop hurting, hating, doubting. Make me the kind of person who transcends this—make beauty of this clawing in my gut. Don't make me say those three glass-sharp words, let these three—*Make me better*—resurrect them, remake them in a form that does not cut.

She meant: Let my fists unfurl, let me breathe easy, let me sleep. She didn't know who she was asking, or if anyone was listening, but she shaped and released those words over and over, until they left her body and dispersed in the surrounding dark.

CHAPTER 7

Pilar took a religion course called Introduction to Mysticism her senior year and language again became capable of conjuring up worlds. When Sister Mary Jo McQuarry, a nun from Mother of Sorrows, LA's oldest Carmelite monastery, spoke to their class, she felt called by some name not her own.

Dr. Weaver had invited Sister McQuarry to talk to Pilar's class about how the Sisters of Mother of Sorrows managed to be mystics in the modern world. She looked to be a youthful 60-something in a knee-length chocolate skirt, white pointy-collared shirt, and brown vest. Somehow, she made this adult Brownie uniform look comfortable. She had a tanned, apple-cheeked face and silver hair pulled back in a ponytail. She was small but made her way to the front of the classroom with an athlete's stride.

"Augustine said that 'No one should be so immersed in contemplation as to ignore the needs of his neighbor; no one should be so absorbed in action as to dispense with contemplation of God.' That's exactly Augustine, isn't it? Endlessly pragmatic, endlessly idealistic, endlessly fascinating. What a wonderful paradox to wrestle with! I mean you might as well take on the biggies, right?" She laughed a deep, throaty laugh, lines crinkling around her eyes.

Pilar loved that she began with a quote from Augustine, but mostly she wanted to crawl inside that laugh.

"I never thought I'd be a nun. The nun teachers I had in Catholic school were bitter women who'd joined the cloth because they were poor or past marrying age. They rapped our hands with rulers and had a dumb row for slow students. Even as a child, I knew they had nothing to do with God. In 1960, I joined my college's outdoor program and nature became my religion. I led Outward Bound trips for middle and high school students for five years after I graduated. I loved helping young people. I felt close to them—still unformed and searching, myself. I was pulled into their discoveries. But between trips, I was lost. I slept on the couches of friends whose lives were moving forward in ways that mine was not.

"I was sleeping on a friend's couch in LA and she invited me to a contemplative retreat with the Carmelite Sisters. For a week, we meditated, prayed, and kept a vow of silence for the first half of each day. That stillness was my greatest fear. But I sat through my fear and gradually the stillness moved inside. Sitting in silence with those women was the first real miracle of my life."

Sister McQuarry had this lively but matter of fact way of speaking that made miracles seem widely available.

"We didn't speak until the midday meal, and then there was so much to talk about. It was 1969. In the early 60s, Vatican II pushed the Church to make itself relevant to the modern world. The Sisters faced the challenge of reconciling their contemplative practice with social engagement. Part of the Carmelite pact is to pray ceaselessly. At the retreat, we talked about how we might move through the world in ceaseless prayer—mystics knee-deep in the world's sorrows."

Pilar had always moved knee-deep through the world's sorrows. But she wanted to know how Sister McQuarry did it laughing.

She called the Carmelite reformer Teresa of Avila *a total badass for her time*. "A community based on Teresa's experience had to be open to newness and fearless in the face of challenge. 'I hold that love, where present, cannot possibly be content with remaining always the same,' she wrote in *The Interior Castle*. I felt a call to join the Carmelite community like people fall in love. Every day since has been an adventure. Soon after I took my final vows, I began overseeing Mother of Sorrows' immigrant outreach program, Project Luz."

The hairs on the back of Pilar's neck prickled.

"We're in Angelino Heights, and Latino immigrants make up the majority of our congregation. We run a food pantry and teach English and job skills. We also connect immigrants to housing, healthcare, work, and legal resources. I've pushed for more political involvement, but there's been a fair amount of pushback from my superiors."

Something like love washed over Pilar. She rode the wave of it up to Sister McQuarry after class and said, "I want to volunteer at Project Luz."

"Wonderful!" Sister McQuarry smiled. "Come to Mass Sunday—we'll talk afterwards." She gave Pilar her card, which simply read *Sister MJ* and had Mother of Sorrows' address. "Everyone calls me MJ." She grinned again, gathered her things, and was gone. Pilar turned the card over to see: *It is impossible to love Christ without loving others, and it is impossible to love others without moving nearer to Christ. —Pierre Teilhard*

Sunday morning, Pilar took a bus to Mother of Sorrows. It took her an hour, the light changing as mansions and manicured lawns drifted into taquerias and bodegas. She got off too early, in Echo Park, a neighborhood of mission-style houses built into hills, panaderías next to markets with signs in Mandarin. From there, she walked up the hills into the Angelino Heights district, where the monastery was. She bought a papas con huevo taco from a taco truck and sat on a bench by the algae-slicked pond that made up most of Echo Park. Pilar ate the taco slowly—the tortilla warm and thick like her father's—and watched ducks paddle through trash-strangled lily pads. Then she began the steep climb to the monastery. Cracked stucco tenements and lopsided wood-frame houses bordered beautifully restored Victorians. She passed a Latino family dressed for church, an elderly Asian man hobbling on a cane, and a tattoo-sleeved hipster smoking and walking his pit bull. She passed a yard filled with polyvinyl Catholic statuary; a purple and green house with a mannequin wearing a shredded Pi Kappa Alpha T-shirt flailing over the porch railing; and a butter-yellow Victorian with white trim, sprinklers arcing over tulips, sunlight glinting off twin Beemers in the driveway. As she got higher, she could make out Mother of Sorrows' imposing walls.

When she reached the top of the hill, Pilar gaped at the monastery, which looked like a massive medieval castle with stone towers, turrets topped by crosses, and landscaped grounds full of oaks and willows, all enclosed behind tall stone walls. To ponder how Mother of Sorrows Monastery grew up beside Hollywood's cocaine-addled actors and tabloid photographers, Venice Beach's silicone-breasted rollerbladers and stoned surfers, was to meditate upon one of life's great mysteries. Pilar followed the line of cars pulling through a wrought-iron gate with a peacock design, taking leave of LA and entering a sepia-toned dream.

She trailed a dozen families as they made their way to the tall stone cathedral towering above the monastery. Church bells rang from its dome-capped steeple. Standing in the crowd outside the church, Pilar might have been in the Valley. There was the same Spanglish, laughter, warm bump of bodies.

The cathedral doors opened and the crowd filed in. The air darkened and cooled. The chatter echoed and dispersed—the vaulted ceiling breathing it in. The church warmed as it filled. Pilar wedged herself between two mothers in a packed pew. The skin, bone, and separateness of her dissolved.

There were English Masses at 8:30 and 10:30, but Pilar went to the 12:30 Spanish Mass. She stared out at the rows of bowed heads during the prayers. The words became theirs as they spoke them; they became something larger. Voices melded to lift history, then dimmed as they rose into the arches—a lesson in letting go.

When Mass was over, Pilar stared up at the choir and picked out MJ's apple-cheeked face from the wise, wrinkled moon faces of her Sisters. Pilar waited for her outside, watching blackbirds gather in the trees. She started when MJ put a hand on her shoulder.

"It's such a lovely day." MJ gave her that wide-open smile. "Let's talk in the courtyard."

MJ led Pilar down a gravel path to a courtyard surrounded by long, arched corridors. "When I first came to the monastery, I was afraid to walk down these corridors at night. We only had candles to light the way and our footsteps echoed." Pilar wanted nothing so much as to follow one of those corridors wherever it went.

They sat on a bench beneath an old oak and MJ told Pilar about Project Luz's programs. "We're still developing a youth program. Maybe you could help with that?"

"I could lead a writing workshop?" Pilar's heart pounded. It was a question not just to MJ, but herself. She still wasn't writing poetry.

"I like that idea!" MJ said.

They worked out that Pilar would start with a Saturday workshop from 12 to 5 with a meal provided. Students would do the bulk of their writing in class.

"I could stay later." Pilar dreaded the squealing, vomiting bass thump of Saturday nights at SAU.

"Let's see how you feel as the semester progresses. I don't want you taking the bus back in the dark. Come on, I'll show you where you'll be teaching."

MJ led Pilar down a corridor, their footsteps echoing. At the end of the courtyard was a heavy oak door and a rusted iron bell. "The older Sisters had to answer this bell with a veil draped over their heads. Up until the 70s, no one from the outside could see inside and vice versa. See all these windows?" She pointed up at the line of arched windows with their shutters open. "My first year here, they didn't open."

Inside they walked down a hallway past a library filled with magazines, newspapers, and books. "Can you imagine reading the news for the first time in the 60s? All that revolution and death—Vietnam; Civil Rights protests; Watergate; JFK's, Martin Luther King's, and Bobby Kennedy's assassinations; the Cuban Missile Crisis, the first man on the moon. Either we pushed our way into the world, or we'd be buried by it.

"So we tore down the walls between the sewing room, altar bread kitchen, and chapel to create Project Luz." MJ led Pilar into a cavernous space divided into classrooms, offices, a computer lab, and a nursery. Bright signs hung on the walls: *I can do all things through Christ who strengthens me.* They peered in a classroom where a petite woman with black hair to her waist was teaching English. "That's Sister Soledad," MJ said. "She taught in a bilingual school before coming to Mother of Sorrows." MJ showed Pilar the computer lab, where a dozen immigrants bent over desktop computers. A tall, reedy nun with short white hair looked up from helping a woman and smiled. "Sister Robin can tell you about going from answering the door in a grate veil to teaching computer classes," MJ said. "We dove into this work before we knew what we were doing. It was frustrating, endless, overwhelming... and transforming."

The rest of Pilar's senior year passed in buses to and from Mother of Sorrows. She'd chosen to live alone in a dorm room instead of a senior apartment with roommates, so as long as she showed up on time to her work-study, no one paid much attention to her comings and goings. She started out just going on Saturdays to teach the workshop, but then the Sisters would insist that she stay for dinner afterwards. They'd invite her to Sunday Mass the next day, then lunch. When she became a regular at Sunday Mass, MJ said she was welcome to spend the night Saturday, as long as she didn't mind sleeping on the Visiting Room couch. Soon Pilar was spending entire weekends at Mother of Sorrows, then calculating whether she could squeeze in a weekday meal between her classes and work-study. When she wasn't teaching, helping out at Project Luz, cooking, gardening, or cleaning, she studied in the convent library. Streamlined with purpose, cushioned by community, life felt lighter. She felt useful, needed, held.

On the hour-long ride to Mother of Sorrows, Pilar would see how long she could read her students' writing before she felt the edge of dizziness. Then she'd stare out the window, listening to the iPod that Carlos had pre-loaded with songs and sent her last summer. She loved this free time to daydream. Most Saturday mornings, there was a woman with a crinkled map of a face who got on about halfway through Pilar's ride, carrying cloth bags with vegetables peeking out. She must have been 70, but bounced on the balls of her feet like a dancer. She looked like the world amused her, one corner of her mouth quirked. She caught Pilar watching her one day and her near-smile spread into a grin. Pilar grinned back. After that, they always smiled at each other when the woman boarded. What kind of life might the woman imagine for her? That she was a college girl having an affair? She *was* having an affair—with nine nuns, she thought and laughed.

She had 20 students, ages 14 to 18, in her writing workshop. They were wonderfully earnest, but when she asked them to write about themselves, they stared at her, silent and wide-eyed. Pilar chose excerpts from Sandra Cisneros, James Baldwin, Jamaica Kincaid, Audre Lorde, and Mary Oliver for their honesty, beauty, and strength. She arranged the desks in a circle. She asked her students what the words made them feel. Not to spur discussion, but because she wanted to know.

Pilar was scared by how intently they listened. She asked them to write what they couldn't speak. She kneeled beside their desks and asked in Spanish, encouraged them to write in the language of home. The first one to respond to the readings was Ceci, a 14-year-old girl who wore her dark hair in a long braid. She was small for her age and spoke in a whisper, not looking up. When she fumbled, a boy picked up the thread; and when he hesitated, others jumped in. Most of them had known each other for years. They'd learned English together and now they were learning a new language—their words searching and fractured.

Dr. Weaver had assigned a research paper on a topic of choice as their final project. Pilar decided to write about Mother of Sorrows' movement into the world under Vatican II. When she wasn't teaching, she interviewed the Sisters.

She talked to Sister Robin, who was 73 and had entered Mother of Sorrows out of high school. Robin divided her time between Project Luz and answering a phone where people called in prayer requests. Pilar dragged a folding chair into the small, windowless phone room. Robin sat in a worn armchair, the room's only furniture besides an end table, on top of which sat the phone and a box of prayer request forms.

She was 29 when Vatican II began and she'd lived in cloister since she was eighteen. "On the good days, I surrendered myself to contemplative life, and the small joys were sweeter amidst all that deprivation."

"And on the bad days?" Pilar asked.

"I really struggled with the deadening of the mind. The way you got to holiness was blind obedience. I was praying, but I wasn't intellectually stirred. Back then the habit was three and a half yards of brown wool serge and our minds were bound up like our bodies. We had this hilarious Sister, Claris. We were walking out of Mass one hot July day and a lady said, 'Oh, look at those sisters. They always look as fresh as daisies.' 'What's that rolling down my leg?' Claris whispered. We were puddles of sweat!"

Pilar laughed.

"Claris was a Latina with bright red hair. I think she was from where you're from."

"Really?" Pilar hadn't met anyone from the RGV at SAU.

"She used to say, 'Where Texas ends and the fun begins!'"

"I'll have to steal that," Pilar said.

"She was a *talker*." Robin shook her head. "She barely survived our six-week vow of silence. Two weeks in, she snuck out to a payphone and called her sister. Thankfully only sweet old Father Joe found out. 'Your prayer is people,' he told her. A week later, she dragged me up to the roof to smoke in the middle of the night. Without speaking, she put two cigarettes in her mouth, lit them, and handed one to me. We smoked and stared out at the lights of the city. I can still see Claris blowing smoke rings—the last of our old lives hovering like open mouths."

Pilar told Robin about highway drives and night canoes (but not drag pageants) with Carlos. She imagined that MJ and the younger Sisters saw the Church's views on homosexuality and plenty of other things as outdated, but Robin had lived in cloister for so long that she might not have any frame of reference. She might just say, "It's not for me to say."

"So you understand." Robin smiled. "Don't tell Mother."

"Mother Connie hates me." Only the Mother Superior had refused Pilar's interview request. She looked like a white-haired Olive Oyl, was the only one of the Sisters who still wore a long, veiled brown habit, and spoke like an old screen star, overly articulating her words. "I've serious academic work to do," she'd warbled. "I'm one of the foremost scholars on Carmelite life."

"Don't mind her," Robin said. "She became a nun when friendships between the Sisters were frowned upon."

"Anyway," Robin continued, "Claris' father got sick when we were choosing whether to take our vows. 'I have to go home,' she told Mother. 'Family's everything to me.'"

Pilar shifted uncomfortably, thinking about her father.

"Father Joe understood, but Mother said, 'If you go, don't come back,' so Claris became a teacher. We fell out of touch after a couple of years, but I know her students must love her. MJ reminds me a lot of Claris—her energy, laugh, and love of people. She struggles with the separation, too. Of course back then, we talked to people through a double grille. They'd tell us these heartbreaking things and we couldn't touch.

"When we tore down the Visiting Room grille, it was like the fall of the Berlin Wall! I wept when I hugged my mother for the first time in ten years. That hug was *God*. During the days of blind obedience, we had to say a prayer and kiss the floor before we broke silence. We were assigned our ministry and Mother had to approve any book we read. But now we were

free to read and talk and choose our service. I took classes at SAU and
Mount Saint Mary's, not just on Christianity, but on Buddhism, Sufism,
social justice. We founded the Association of Contemplative Sisters and
women from contemplative communities all over the country came together to wrestle with what it means to be a feminist and a nun, to balance a
contemplative practice and outreach. We talked about women becoming
priests. It wasn't going to happen in our lifetime, but what could we do
to push that change from the inside? Those gatherings felt every bit as
revolutionary as what was going on outside of the church."

Pilar talked to Robin about how books had blown open the world of La
Llanura. "I know it's not the same—"

"No, it *is*," Robin insisted. "We were reading to figure out who we wanted
to be."

Pilar had that under-the-skin feeling of reading words that ventrilo-
quized her feelings. Only now did she understand the drama and tears
surrounding her freshman hall dormmates' pledge for sororities. This was
the Sisterhood she felt a part of—this fire sprung out of darkness. "Do you
feel like you've missed out on anything?"

"I was always so impetuous that I think the cocoon of cloistered life
was a good place to grow. In my 20s, I went away to a school of religious
education where I met a priest. He was handsome and had a fine mind
and we were drawn to each other. He wanted to marry, but I knew I was
not on a path where I was going to fall in love with somebody and marry
them. If you're in a sexual relationship, that becomes central. If you've
got a family, they come first. You can't be for everybody. I wanted a love
outside of myself."

Pilar remembered her obsession with Buster and her face grew hot. All
that pining and analyzing. What had she been so drawn to? His writing?
His freedom? Wasn't "freedom" just another way of saying irrresponsible?
She jumped when the phone rang.

Robin smiled apologetically as she answered. "This is Sister Robin. Tell
me how I can help."

"Thank you," Pilar whispered. She shut the door softly and stood outside, listening to the murmur of Robin's voice. Her favorite caller, she'd told Pilar, was a woman who said, "I'm out of hope. Can you hope for me?" Fifteen years later, they were close friends, though they'd never met.

She thought of two women's voices stretched over 15 years—that communion beyond the body's borders. Of Carlos listening to her cry, the sound traveling across cities, rivers, fields: a country. She thought about what it would feel like to be what people needed.

Her father sent her a Laughing Gull postcard. That summer, he'd caught teenagers playing a Ouija board in the graveyard. Seeing him, they'd screamed, tossed the board into the air, and run off. She'd laughed when he told her, but the image of teenagers running from him—like everything that summer—had made her sad.

Walking through Mother of Sorrows' shadowed corridors, Pilar passed rooms, once walled off, that were open now. She felt herself opening—to the fall of light through leaves, her students' pens moving across their notebooks like waves, the Sisters' laughter after morning silence. Again she was *of that people the grass blades touch*. And here was the help.

She was no longer afraid to cross campus alone at night. She passed like a ghost through SAU's streaking, drinking games, and theme parties—a dog-eared copy of *The Interior Castle* under her arm. She was thinking about Teresa as she walked past the freshmen dorms when a vending machine toppled out of a third-floor window and crashed at her feet. Pilar looked up to see a petrified group of boys standing at the window. "*Woah.* Sorry!" they called down. Pilar squinted up at them as if they were aliens emerging from a spaceship. When they saw that she was safe, they burst into laughter.

The following Sunday, over a post-Mass meal, Pilar reported to the Sisters on this strange lifeform. "Do you think it was a sign?" she asked jokingly.

"Free chocolate from God!" MJ said.

"Tell me you brought us some," Robin said.

"Sorry." Pilar shrugged.

"We have fresh kale from the garden!" Sister Letitia, who ran the community garden, said.

Robin sighed. "My favorite wartime food."

But Sister Margarita was an incredible cook, and everyone oohed and aahed as she set steaming dishes of enchiladas, bowls of guisada, sopas, salsas, guacamole, and salad on the long table.

They bowed their heads and blessed the food, thanking God for Margarita's cooking, a plentiful garden harvest, and the small wins in their days. "And thanks God for gettin' some young blood in here!" Robin added, winking at Pilar.

Looking around at the Sisters' white hair and creased faces, Pilar did feel young, for maybe the first time in her life. They were leading her out of that hungry, desperate, in the dark prayer into something lighter. She smiled over the fact that these celibate septuagenarians just might be her soul sisters.

MJ rummaged around in the refrigerator and returned with an ancient-looking bottle of salad dressing. She held the bottle up to the light, searching its eroded label for an expiration date. "Lord knows we need some young blood given this dressing has been around since Carter was President. Remember listening to his 'Crisis of Confidence' speech? God, I loved that speech." She stared up at the dressing. "You too, huh?"

This sent them all into fits of laughter, even Pilar, who'd never heard the speech but would watch it that night in her dorm room and be moved to tears.

The Sisters were giddy with these first words to each other. Soon the dining hall buzzed with conversation—about an asylum clinic at a partner church and the science behind meditation. Pilar looked forward to these conversations, which flowed between the silly and serious, personal and philosophical, temporal and spiritual. When something struck her in her classes, she saved it for the Sisters.

Mother Connie walked in and they fell silent for a moment before greeting her.

"Is there dressing?" she asked, piling salad onto her plate.

Pilar and the Sisters glanced conspiratorially at each other and burst into laughter.

Carlos had stopped cutting his hair when he started working at Lucky Feng's, and by the time his senior year started, it reached his chin. He kept his sublet in Crown Heights, which was more affordable than staying in the dorms. He decorated his room with posters of Patti Smith, Lou Reed, Laurie Anderson, and David Bowie. They reminded him to stoke the B-side dream life even as he was steeped in upper-level engineering courses.

He did take US Lesbian and Gay History as his elective, but the class dynamic was off from the get-go. Dr. Devlin looked to be fresh out of the PhD mill. She had short, bleached hair, buzzed on the bottom and long on top; wore black oxford glasses and dark red lipstick; and had a hint of a Southern accent. On the first day, she briefly explained gender-neutral pronouns and asked their pronouns when they introduced themselves. Stating pronouns seemed new to the majority of the class. "*She*... or *they,* I guess," Vic, not Victoria, a dimpled Black student from Hattiesburg, Mississippi said in a soft Southern twang. Samantha, a blonde trans student from Vermont used *she*. Several students forgot, absentmindedly adding, "Oh, *he*" or "Oh, *she*" when Dr. Devlin reminded them. "*He,*" Carlos said, but flashed back to the moment in the Ropa Usada when she'd introduced herself as Carla. Carlos was unfamiliar with *they* as an option. He wondered what the Queens of 10th Avenue would have thought if El Ojo had insisted upon *they*. He imagined trying to explain it to Abuela and almost laughed.

When he returned his attention to the discussion circle, Calliope Goodloe was introducing herself. She was a redhead with dreadlocks and a pointy face, blue veins showing through her translucent skin. She wore all black with black combat boots and was painfully thin.

In spite of claiming *she*, Calliope launched into a longwinded diatribe on people's unwillingness to truly disrupt the biases of the English language by using the gender-neutral pronouns *ze/zir*. She spoke with a self-assurance and fluidity that Carlos had come to associate with a prep school background. "Ze is a writer and wrote that book zirself. Those ideas are zirs. I like both zir and zir ideas," Calliope demonstrated.

Zzzz, Carlos thought, relieved to see faces furrowed with confusion as he looked around the circle.

"We're open to all pronouns," Dr. Devlin said, "but let's finish up introductions. Lots to cover today."

Calliope raised her voice over Dr. Devlin's and continued to expound, at length, upon the biases of the English language and linguistic theory in general.

Dr. Devlin cocked her head and squinted at Calliope as she spoke. Her expression of disbelief passed into listless absence. She chewed the cap of her pen, sighed resignedly, and looked through Calliope.

"Why isn't she shutting that stage whore down?" Carlos whispered to Jyoti, the purple-haired Indian girl next to him.

"Calliope's Dean Goodloe's daughter," Jyoti whispered back. "Devlin's brand new and afraid of losing her job."

As in James Goodloe: Dean of Columbia College. Carlos glanced back at Calliope, words streaming from her thin, determined lips as the rest of the class' eyes glazed over.

He raised his eyebrows at Jyoti, who nodded deeply, as if to say, *It's gonna be a* long *semester.*

It was, indeed, a long semester. Calliope took every opportunity to disagree, correct, contradict, and monopolize discussion. If she was allowed to do her thing, whether that be endlessly haranguing on some pet peeve only tangentially related to their reading, sermonizing on the semiotics of something or other, or annihilating any shred of hope with her relentless doomsday narratives, class might pass in a civil, if deadening, way.

But if anyone upstaged her, watch out. One day, as Calliope harped about Columbia's inequities—a valid critique, if one likely fueled by Dean Daddy issues—Áine, an environmental engineering major with whom Carlos had taken a couple of classes, said that she was starting a group for first-generation and low-income students, to talk to her after class if you were interested. Áine was the oldest of seven sisters and the first in her Irish Catholic family to attend college. While Calliope criticized Columbia's imbalances from her tuition exempt recliner, Áine was actually doing something.

Calliope did not forget. When Áine used the wrong pronoun a few classes later, Calliope cut her off as she scrambled to self-correct, barking, "When you do that, you *disappear* someone."

"We get better with practice," Dr. Devlin said. "That's what we're here for."

Carlos gave Áine a look of solidarity across the circle, but her gaze was held by Calliope, who stared her down like an ant sizzling beneath her magnifying glass.

Carlos would have liked to offer Áine more, but he, too, felt overwhelmed by the crash course in queerspeak. Dr. Devlin had given them a multi-page glossary of terms for the myriad ways in which one's gender might interact with one's sexuality, but it wasn't just a list of random vocabulary words he could memorize. The terms elicited emotions, memories, questions. Was he gay? Or CAMAB (Coercively Assigned Male at Birth)? If CAMAB, who'd done the coercing? Was he femme, androgynous, bigender, gender expansive, gender non-conforming, non-binary, gender fluid, or some complex Venn diagram of these? The only term that Carlos could claim with any certainty was "questioning." Only he couldn't hear his questions because he was drowning in an Ocean of Confusion while Calliope sped by in her 50-foot yacht, throwing those terms around with eloquent abandon.

A memory Carlos had tamped deep down surfaced:

He begged his first-grade teacher to go to the bathroom, but he didn't have the words. "Miss, tengo que ir al baño." He'd been holding it for so long it hurt.

"¡Cállate y siéntate!" Mrs. Salinas yelled.

Warm wetness ballooned over his pants.

"Eww!" Mrs. Salinas wrinkled her nose. She dragged him roughly by the hand to the bathroom. Her disgust made him cry. "Why did I have to get stuck with a class of retards?" she asked.

He'd looked up the Spanish translation of retard *when he got home.*

Just say it like you know what you're talking about, he'd told Pilar. *Say it like...*
  Them?

Instead of speaking up, Carlos resorted to sarcastic comments under his breath when Calliope launched into a tirade, like, "Oh, goody." He glanced repeatedly at his nonexistent wristwatch.

His stage kiss with Abe had disintegrated like a firework that briefly shimmered before it vanished. There'd been nothing more than unspoken crushes since his summer weekend with the Fengs in Fire Island, where he'd kissed a man on the dance floor. As far as he could tell, no one in US Lesbian and Gay History had seen him *unmask* and *unwig*. Given he'd made no formal declaration of his sexuality, Calliope, who began every other sentence with "As a Queer Radical Feminist..." would label him *closeted*. Wasn't one dramatically staged uncurtaining (plus one San Jacinto High beatdown) enough? How many times did he have to come out? Actually, Calliope would call him *doubly closeted* as he hadn't come out as undocumented to anyone besides Pilar, Mrs. Bonura, and Mr. Cancino. Secrecy felt safe. But he might have opened up if not for Calliope. He mourned for the space he'd thought the class would be—to stumble into questions, into himself... or herself... or themself... or zirself?

Carlos had come to this class in search of a tribe, and he knew he wasn't the only one. He felt that yearning when Jyoti double-underlined the same passage in Walt Whitman's "Song of Myself": "Every kind for itself and its own... for me mine male and female, / For me all that have been boys and that love women, / For me the man that is proud and feels how it stings to be slighted, / For me the sweetheart and the old maid... for me mothers and the mothers of mothers, / ... / Who need be afraid of the merge? / Undrape... you are not guilty to me, nor stale nor discarded, I see through the broadcloth and gingham whether or no, / And am around, tenacious, acquisitive, tireless... and can never be shaken away." Jyoti was a political science major, and it was her first time reading it, too.

She closed her book when she saw Carlos looking.

Then Carlos opened his book to the same passage and pointed to where he'd written *AMERICA IS QUEER!!!* in the margin.

"Always was and always will be," Jyoti whispered.

They grinned at each other.

Dr. Devlin, in the rare moments in which she charged ahead of Calliope, blew Carlos' mind with the connections she made across history—between the pain, defiance, rebellion, and discoveries of the past and that of their own lives and time. From Ma Rainey and Bessie Smith to Marsha P. Johnson and Sylvia Rivera to the young men of ACT UP protesting government inaction while dying of AIDS, she made Carlos feel like walking history. While Calliope leaned back in her chair with her arms crossed, calculating her next power move, the rest of the class leaned in, scribbling notes.

Dr. Devlin grew breathless as she sprinted ahead of Calliope, her Southern accent thickening as she shed her imposter syndrome, but she only ever got so far before Calliope caught the back of her blue blazer, tackled her to the ground, and stampeded over her in her combat boots. Carlos, like the rest of the class, stopped listening. Calliope was always saying the same thing: *I am very smart and very angry, and if you challenge me, I will mow you down.* Dr. Devlin tried to wrest discussion back from Calliope's denunciations to more nuanced inquiry. She called on students who tended to be thoughtful in their contributions, but they offered hesitant, minimal responses, then sank into a silence that Calliope was all too happy to fill.

As unnerving as Calliope's attacks were, their class's true captor was sadder than fear. You could smell it in the air—the malodor of steamrolled hope. They'd come to this class wanting not just history, but a sacred lineage illuminated. They'd wanted radiant beauty, community, celebration, exploration, and enlightenment and instead got stuck in a rut like a loveless old straight couple arguing over the dishes.

People started to skip class. Those who showed, including Dr. Devlin, were absent in all but body. Carlos looked around their gap-toothed circle to see classmates staring blankly into space, sleeping face down on their desks, or reading for other classes. Calliope didn't seem to notice; she didn't seem to need an audience. Not wanting to jeopardize his scholarship, Carlos came to class, but under the dark drone of Calliope's diatribes, his mind drifted far and wide.

Though he'd never been nostalgic, he found himself reminiscing about San Jacinto High. For all he'd felt SJH stifling, there'd been a sibling-like solidarity within the cadre of 50-odd students he'd shared classes with for 10 years. They'd vied, teased, and annoyed each other, but there'd been a gentleness to their competition. They'd been in it together, all of them branded *nerds*—far from a compliment at SJH. Pilar was of course very much in his life and he still exchanged messages with the drama kids, but he found himself thinking, with real affection, about students he hadn't even been close to. Like Edna, the wry-witted salutatorian. He imagined her deadpan face and droll internal monologue as she sat in a similarly besieged Stanford classroom. His eyes grew damp remembering how his classmates had leapt out of their seats to give him a standing ovation after his graduation speech. He pressed the heel of his hand to one eye and then the other. He looked up to see Dr. Devlin staring vacantly out the window, shoulders slumped.

Sometimes he went further back, slipped his mother's coin pendant between his lips and longed for the freedom he'd felt before he knew there was anything queer about slipping on her silk robe and jewelry—when there was only beauty.

Did he have to have all of the right words to exist? *Were* there right words when he was trying to discover, claim, create his life?

Dr. Devlin's eyes flitted around the "discussion" circle as Calliope rattled on, beaming this message: *I'm sorry. Everyone will pass.* Finally, she gave up and dismissed class early. Students fled the classroom like people evacuating a bomb site.

Outside, Carlos gulped in the Calliope-free air. He swung his arms and legs wide as he crossed campus, a liberation march of one. When he got back to Crown Heights, he got off at the Brooklyn Museum stop. The museum was open late on Thursday nights and mostly empty. Carlos walked through the cavernous lobby to the elevator. There was an exhibit of emerging Brooklyn artists' work on the fourth floor that he wanted to see. The museum's vast emptiness was the perfect stage set for his melancholy. He wandered through its deserted galleries, half-looking at the art.

He sat on a stool and watched a video with big, cushiony headphones. It began in the desolate dunes of Fire Island, panning to the gray roll of waves. Two doe stepped tentatively through the dunes. Slow, somber piano notes reverberated as the sun set. A plaintive voice, at some register between sorrow and resignation, sang, *We have always been on fire, we have always been let down, we have always been an island.* A man with tousled brown hair wearing sparkly silver eyeshadow, a black T-shirt, and rolled-up black pants stood barefoot, singing alone amidst the dunes. He gripped a microphone with both hands. He closed his eyes and sang his heart out to no one.

Current images of Fire Island were interspersed with footage from Nelson Sullivan's video from July 4, 1976, the halcyon days before the AIDS epidemic: solitary shots of the dunes, the sun sinking into the horizon, the dip and stretch of telephone wires, a tattered Puerto Rican flag waving from a pole, beach grass blowing, waves graying, shadows lengthening, a montage of darkened houses broken by lone lights. Then came the slow turn of a disco ball, the man in a sparkling shirt singing again and again, *Come get us.* 1976 footage of people dancing at the Ice Palace, disco lights, slow-motion fireworks. *Come get us*, the singer pleaded, his face shadowed amidst the slow-turning projections of the disco ball.

It had been such a magical feeling to take the Fire Island ferry, on which everyone was queer, to an island where everyone was queer. Carlos didn't know the name of the man who'd kissed him on the dance floor, but he'd been beautiful. The man had pulled him close, dug his fingers into Carlos' back, kissed him greedily while drag queens gyrated on elevated platforms. It had felt good to be gripped, pulled, wanted inside a mass of sweaty, dancing men.

Now he was this solitary man standing amidst the dunes, singing his heart out as dark fell. Carlos' face was wet; he realized he was crying, but he kept watching the video on loop, hunched and hugging himself, the cushiony headphones cocooning him in his lonely blue world. He remembered Abe fleeing into traffic, Abuela rolling an egg over his bruises, his mother's hair swishing against the seat of her Wranglers. All the things he'd believed were the answer, all the people he loved, all the places he was supposed to fit in felt prickly and wrong. He didn't understand anybody, least of all himself.

He watched the video on loop, cried, and unconsciously started to sing: *We have always been on fire, we have always been let down, we have always been an island.*

He didn't hear the guard announcing that the museum was closing until he tapped Carlos on the shoulder.

Tears streaming down his cheeks, he stumbled down the museum stairs and out into the gray November dusk. He walked through the darkening trees of Prospect Park, through whirling brown leaves and trash, his shadow stretching beneath the park lamps. He walked and walked through the disappointment of the city, all the dreams that had never materialized, all the ways he'd been let down, until he was shivering in his too-thin trench coat.

Timon was out and the apartment was unbearably quiet when he got home. Carlos turned on the small radio tuned to WNYC in the kitchen. "New Sounds" was on—its strange, sharp squawks more anxiety-inducing than comforting. He started to pour himself a glass of Fireball and then just carried the bottle over to the window. The whole world had gone dark and he was the only one left. He took another swig and called Pilar.

"Hi…" Pilar said a bit absently, probably working her way out of some book.

"I'm so glad you answered," Carlos said. "It's been a *day*." He updated Pilar on *The Calliope Goodloe Show*. "Like a third of the class even bothers to come and the second class ends, we bolt for the door."

Pilar couldn't understand why he was cowed by Calliope. This was not the Carlos she knew. "Why even care about her?" she asked. "Read Baldwin on your own. He didn't fit in anywhere either."

Rise above or withdraw: Pilar's solutions to everything. Easy to do when all you needed were books. But she used to need *him*. Carlos wanted suddenly, desperately, to make her laugh. "Because Calliope's my *NEMESIS!*" he roared.

Pilar let out a loud, full laugh and Carlos felt lighter. "Can you see me wringing my imaginary sweat towel?" he asked. It was a joke that went back to his SJH thespian days. He and Gibby, who were always rivals for the lead in school musicals, would say this to each other. When Carlos nailed an audition, Gibby would shake his fists at the sky and cry, "You're my *nemesis!*" Gibby always shook his fists at the sky, while Carlos always wrang an imaginary sweat towel.

"It's not Calliope," Carlos continued. "It's what she gets in the way of. These are supposed to be my people, Pilar. My tribe. We're supposed to be figuring out who we are together. Asking the big questions. But my *nemesis* keeps burning our village to the ground! I have you on speaker so I can wring my sweat towel, by the way."

Pilar didn't laugh, but asked in her exasperating NPR Lady voice, "Could you find some way to say that in class?"

"I don't know." Carlos wasn't even having the conversation he'd hoped to have with Pilar. He wanted words to lift the weight of what he still felt for Abe. He wanted someone to swim out into the in-between and rescue him, or at least sing with him: *We have always been on fire, we have always been let down, we have always been an island.* He didn't want to find himself in a queer lexicon, to be packaged and labeled—for whose safety? Labels were for gravestones. He wanted to figure it out as he went, to touch things and see how it felt. He wanted a tribe with whom he could talk about that.

Pilar waited for him to say more.

"Anyway, enough about me. You still chillin' 'n' illin' in the nunnery?"

Pilar laughed halfheartedly. "Yeah, I'm still leading the workshop and interviewing the Sisters. They're not what you think, Carlos. They were teachers, nurses, Outward Bound instructors before becoming nuns. They're *fun.* Sister Robin used to sneak up to the roof to smoke with this rebel Sister from the Valley. I told her about you." Pilar cracked herself up recounting some longwinded story about expired salad dressing and the head nun walking in.

Carlos raised his eyebrows. *This* is what made her laugh now? "I guess you had to be there," he said. "That head nun lady sounds like she's as much of a drag as Calliope. I guess you have a *nemesis,* too!"

"The Mother Superior? She's just really old school. She joined the Sisterhood in different times."

"She's called *Mother Superior*? So humble," Carlos said.

"Mother for short," Pilar said.

When was Pilar going to give up her mother obsession? Any armchair shrink could see she'd found nine mothers to replace the one she never had. "Doesn't it bother you that this Mother Superior bi-atch gets to call the shots?"

"She doesn't, really. The Sisters sort of work around her."

"Good strategy," Carlos said, sarcasm creeping into his voice, though he tried not to be sarcastic with Pilar.

"The Church isn't perfect," Pilar said. "The Church, as Vatican II said, is the people."

Not my *people*, Carlos thought. "I should go. I've got an early morning class."

"Get some sleep," Pilar said. "Don't worry about Calliope. Just figure out a way to get what you need from the class."

"Thanks for listening," Carlos said. "¡Besos!"

"On both cheeks," Pilar said.

Carlos stared at himself in the mirror as he pulled his hair into a ponytail and brushed his teeth. He raised one perfectly plucked eyebrow and remembered the gentleness with which the queen in the 10th Avenue bathroom had plucked his eyebrows for the first time. He thought of Bama cupping his face as she painted, of painting Pilar's lips red. The feeling of someone who cared enough to transform you.

"*Queer* is people," he said aloud.

CHAPTER 8

Carlos read *Borderlands/La Frontera* on his hour-and-15-minute subway ride to Columbia. As the train swerved, he looked up from his book to see all kinds of people, most of them listening to headphones, swaying and bobbling in a kind of conjoined dance. He wondered what a mash-up of their soundtracks would sound like. The train grew crowded as it moved into Manhattan, Anzaldua's sentences tangling with the blood and breath of packed bodies. On weekends, he'd read on a bench beneath a tree on the Eastern Parkway Mall, thinking about the borders and crossings in Crown Heights, the words weaving through the passing people. He thought about parking with Pilar at the edge of the Rio Grande in the eagle's wings dress.

He finally got how she felt about books. He'd been smart enough to get by on CliffsNotes at SJH and the books he'd read for his core courses had all seemed pretty distant. But when he read *The Fire Next Time*, he called Pilar just to read sentences aloud: "But renewal becomes impossible if one supposes things to be constant that are not—safety, for example, or money, or power. One clings then to chimeras, by which one can only be betrayed, and the entire hope—the entire possibility—of freedom disappears."

Pilar found her heavily annotated copy and answered with her own underlined sentences: "Love takes off the masks that we fear we cannot live without and know we cannot live within. I use the word 'love' here not merely in the personal sense but as a state of being, or a state of grace—not in the infantile American sense of being made happy but in the tough and universal sense of quest and daring and growth."

Hearing this, Carlos better understood Pilar's enthrallment with the Church—a quest of sorts, however misguided.

Still, books weren't enough. He kept hoping for exchanges in class that felt like these conversations with Pilar: They'd read quotes ecstatically to each other, then do the queer version of football players body-slamming after a victorious game (actually, that was already pretty queer).

But Calliope continued to hijack, harangue, and dominate until it was the second to last class, the handful of students still attending relieved that the semester was coming to an end. In Carlos' hurry to flee after class, he forgot his notebook. He was nearly to the subway when he realized and went back for it.

As he climbed the last flight of stairs leading to the classroom, he thought he heard Calliope's voice. He almost turned around, but the notes he needed for his Senior Design exam were in the notebook he'd left.

When he got close enough to make out her words, he wasn't sure it was Calliope. It was like her voice had been distorted; it broke and quavered and rose. "But *why*? Why can't you... Why can't I... Why can't we just... *try*?"

Calliope never asked questions, never questioned herself.

Carlos froze at the top of the stairs when he saw her talking on the phone outside of their classroom. It was as if the raw clay of her features had been molded into a different person, her fierce face scrunched up and red as a newborn's. "No..." She shook her head again and again, stopping only to drag the back of her hand across her dripping nose. "No, no, no." Her mouth trembled; her fingers flew to her lips. "*Please* don't leave me." She was oblivious to everything else—Carlos at the top of the stairs, students passing in the hall, staring. Nothing was real, nothing mattered but that voice, leaving her.

Carlos watched this total eclipse of Calliope—sobbing, begging, inarticulate—unable to look away.

She hunched over like someone had stabbed her, letting the phone fall from her ear, and released a heaving, guttural sob. Then she cradled the phone to her ear again. "*Please*," she cried. "Please don't—"

She was quiet, waiting, listening.

Then her knees buckled and she slid slowly down the wall, sobbing, "I LOVE YOU, I LOVE YOU, I LOVE YOU."

Her fingers fell open, her phone clattered to the floor. "I love you," she said softly, plaintively, to no one.

Carlos remembered running after Abe, breathlessly screaming his name.

Calliope sat slumped on the floor, her head in her hands, sobs choking out. When she looked up, her bloodshot eyes were swimming.

Carlos put his hand over his heart.

Calliope gave him the barest of nods before she struggled up from the floor.

Carlos extended his hand to help her.

Calliope shook her head, gathered her satchel, and walked shakily down the stairs.

Calliope's red, scrunched up face returned to Carlos as he tried to study. He couldn't unsee it—her aching ugly-cry heartbreak radiance. That last-gasp attempt to save things. *I LOVE YOU, I LOVE YOU, I LOVE YOU.* To no one, anyone.

At least Calliope had played it full out. Their class had never made it to first base, never even made it through a first date. If Calliope was this terribly vulnerable human under her tyrannical facade, how much was there to discover about the rest of his classmates? With just one class left, Carlos found himself desperate to know them. He wanted to know whether he and Jyoti continued to underline the same passages; what it was like for Vic to transfer from Ole Miss to Columbia and switch from pre-med to history; he wanted to learn about the polyamorous commune that Maddie lived in; to know more about Gio, a Puerto Rican activist and economics major who planned to enter politics; about Samantha, who'd exchanged dungarees for dresses in second grade and was a leader in Columbia's International Socialist Organization.

In her syllabus, Dr. Devlin had emphasized her commitment to inquiry-based discussion, with the overarching questions, *How can we understand the world? How should we live together?* Their class had long since given up on living together, but Calliope's last-gasp questions hung, unanswered, in Carlos' brain: *Why can't I... Why can't you... Why can't we just... try?*

He removed Dr. Devlin from the class email list and asked his class-mates for a first date on the last day:

> *I know we don't really know each other, but I want to. I'd love for us all to show up and speak in our final class. Who knows—it could be great. We could be great together. Or at least we could try?*
>
> *Yours 'til the end,*
> *Carlos*

Eighteen of 20 students came to the final class of US Lesbian and Gay History. Dr. Devlin had gotten a running start by the time Calliope arrived— her skeletal frame drowning in a baggy gray sweatshirt, eyes shadowed by dark circles, dreadlocks matted. Carlos smiled at her and moved his desk back from the circle to make space. Tala, the Filipino girl next to him, widened her eyes, but made room. Calliope gave them a dead-eyed stare as she moved her desk into the space between them.

Undeterred, Dr. Devlin walked around their discussion circle encourag-ing them to relate the class to their lives, and they did. They talked about chosen family, about activists from the ballroom scene creating Kiki Hous-es for queer youth facing houselessness, how the gay rights movement wasn't just about marching in the streets, but also mothering people dying of AIDS when care was an act of resistance. Students who hadn't spoken all semester spoke. Vic talked about what it felt like to chant with their Nichiren Buddhist community. A tall, broad-shouldered girl named Gabi talked about her volleyball team, Tala about her chamber pop band.

Only Calliope was very quiet.

Carlos looked at her, picking at pink patches of scalp between her dreadlocks. He chewed the corner of his lip, took a deep breath, and said, "I broke down at the Brooklyn Museum the other day." He talked about the video he'd seen. "But I think what Dr. D's been trying to teach us is, whatever we are, we are *not* an island. This fire was always burning; the world is queer."

"Always was and always will be," Jyoti blurted, reddening when the class looked at her.

Dr. Devlin nodded at Carlos, the corner of her mouth quirking up.

Carlos smiled tentatively at Dr. Devlin, grinned at Jyoti, then looked around the circle. "I grew up in a tiny Texican bordertown in the Rio Grande Valley," he continued. "As smalltown, Catholic, and machismo as the Valley was, the gay scene was liberating. We welcomed everybody because we *needed* each other. We didn't have all the labels. We were just making it up in the dark. My inspiration was a plus-sized queen named Betty Crocker who could backflip and land on her platforms. She was so beautiful.

"I was 17 the first time I did drag. I sang Patti Smith's "Gloria", which was a far cry from the songs the other queens performed. I danced different and chose a weird drag name. I'd dug up my dress from a pile of used clothes, and a queen I'd never met made me up in the bathroom. I'll never forget how she held my face as she painted—like we'd always known each other.

"My best friend Pilar pushed me onstage. I'd only sang "Gloria" in my bedroom with a hairbrush for a mic, but everyone sang with me. *Held* me. Sometimes I think that's what we need most—a space that holds you until you figure out what questions to ask."

Jyoti snapped and the other students echoed her.

"I mean, don't you have *questions*?" Carlos asked.

"A million!" Jyoti cried. "I'm *paralyzed* by questions."

Deep nods moved through the circle.

"This is great." Dr. Devlin resumed her professorial pace around the circle. "What are some questions you're wrestling with?"

"Can I be out as a politician?" Gio asked.

"Why is the International Socialist Organization dominated by straight cis men?" Samantha asked.

"Will I ever find love?" Maddie asked.

"Why don't men—*cis straight* men," Áine corrected, glancing at Calliope, who stared into space with her arms folded across her chest, "aspire to feminine norms like reflecting, listening, and apologizing when an apology is due?"

"What if it's not one gender I'm attracted to, but feminine qualities?" Jyoti asked.

"Will my mother ever accept me?" Vic asked softly, then pulled the brim of their cap down over their eyes.

Dr. Devlin looked at Vic, her eyes shiny. "Who am I to answer that when my mother hasn't spoken to me in five years?"

"What if bodies don't even matter?" Gabi asked. "The first girl I kissed was four-foot-eleven with these tiny hands, but the force with which she gripped my hips and pulled me toward her was so *sexy*."

A wiry girl with a skater haircut named Casey brushed her long brown bangs out of her eyes and asked, "Years from now, will straight people have to come out?"

Questions piled up unanswered until Carlos thrust his fist in the air and declared, "We've got to reclaim the *questioning* in queer!"

"¡Pa'lante!" Gio cried and the other students snapped.

"I love this idea of a holding place until you figure out what questions to ask," Dr. Devlin said. "Did y'all have a place like that growing up? Or maybe, hopefully, you've found one? In Mobile, we went to a bar called B-Bob's with mounted deer heads wearing dangly earrings."

The class laughed.

"The skate park," Casey said. "Guys talked shit until I nailed a rocket air. After that, they had my back."

"When I was five, my aunt Bess bought me the pink dress and white patent leather Mary Janes I begged for," Samantha said. "She kept them at her house and let me come out to my parents when I was ready."

"There was this big old oak in the empty lot down the street that I'd spend hours under when my mom and I fought," Vic said.

"I met my best friend Aaron at a teen support group at the White Plains LGBTQ center," Tala said. "We went to a gay bar in the village for the first time and all these possibilities for how I could live opened up. All night, I was on the edge of my seat. Aaron pulled me onto the dance floor. In the middle of all those strobe lights and glistening bodies, I became free."

Students cheered and snapped. Carlos felt that opening: joy. His eyes welled up as the class became what he'd hoped for on its last day.

Out of the corner of his teary vision, he noticed Calliope shaking. He wondered how long it had been since she'd eaten. He offered her half of a muffin from his satchel.

Calliope's eyes filled. She stared at the floor, her face reddening as tears spilled down her cheeks.

Carlos watched his classmates' faces slide from elation to perplexity, then crumple like Calliope's.

Calliope blew her nose and looked up at Carlos, the class. "It's just so hard for me to let anyone in. It's so hard for me to trust—"

Dr. Devlin nodded consolingly.

The class was quiet, waiting for Calliope to say more. Maddie cocked her head. Jyoti leaned toward her.

Carlos saw in their faces what had happened when he'd watched Calliope's breakup. That hardwiring for connection, against everything.

Calliope shook her head, puffed air through her lips.

"You won't even take my muffin." Carlos pretended to wipe a single tear and danced the muffin toward her.

Calliope sniffled and raised her eyebrows at the dancing muffin. "What kind is it?"

Not wanting to be late, Carlos had grabbed the last lonely muffin from the café downstairs and taken a few bites as he jogged up the stairs. It was some cross between bran and morning glory. "It's still figuring it out, but I think it's, um, gender expansive?"

"Well, in that case—" Calliope took the muffin, unwrapped it from its plastic, and took an enormous bite. "Thank you." She held her hand over her mouth as she chewed.

Carlos laughed and Calliope did, too.

The class tentatively echoed her laugh, looking to her for permission.

Calliope looked around at them and laughed louder, disbelievingly. She took another enormous bite and smiled sheepishly, her mouth full.

CHAPTER 9

Carlos called Pilar and recounted what he'd come to think of, just a wee bit melodramatically, as the Metamorphosis.

"I knew you could create the class you wanted to be in," Pilar said.

"It was a collaborative effort. Anyhoo, what's up with you besides balmy weather and better tacos?"

"I'm okay," Pilar said flatly. She didn't want to bring Carlos down.

"What's wrong?"

Carlos pressed, Pilar said she was fine. He pressed some more until she came out with it in a single breath: "Papá told me yesterday that he was hospitalized for a lung infection this fall, he's still paying off the bill, and I can't afford to fly home for Christmas."

"Oh Pilar, I'm so sorry. Is he okay now?"

"He says he is, but he didn't even tell me he was hospitalized. He wouldn't have gone to the hospital unless it was really bad. I feel terrible."

"How is this your fault? He didn't tell you."

"If I'd worked another job, maybe I could fly home. I wanted to take the bus, but it takes two days and Papá would worry himself to death."

"I worked two jobs and it wasn't enough," Carlos said. "Why are tickets so expensive? You can either fly to Paris or the Valley."

"I'm worried about him."

"How about I ask Abuela to invite him to her orphans' dinner?"

"I don't know if he'll go, but thanks." Pilar fell quiet.

"Guilt doesn't do him, or you, any good."

"I know... I've been researching whether I can petition for his green card," Pilar said hesitantly. "I should have done it when I turned 21, but I was struggling just to keep my scholarship. I couldn't have handled it if it wasn't possible. I'm ready now, but what if something's changed? What if I waited too long? I'm sorry, I know you hate talking about this, but you're the only person I've told. I stay up reading all this conflicting information online. I lay awake worrying, then wake up in the middle of the night and research."

"Oh Pilar, I *want* you to talk to me. I just hate talking about it because I can't do shit. I'm a model citizen with no path to citizenship. But maybe it's possible for your dad. Just prepare yourself for the fact that it might not be, okay?"

"I have to try," she said.

"Try, but it's not your fault if it doesn't happen."

Pilar went silent.

"Do you know anyone who's staying on campus over the holidays?" Carlos asked.

"I'm going to spend the month at Mother of Sorrows. The Sisters make all their Christmas gifts—I'm excited."

"Oh... good." Carlos worried that Pilar was going to spend Christmas steeped in Catholic guilt, obsessing over her father.

Pilar knew the Church was condemnation to Carlos. But like MJ said, that had nothing to do with God. "What about you?" she asked.

"I'm also doing Christmas with the Sisters. Or Chinese food anyway."

"That's great... Be careful if you're out late." She worried about Carlos walking the streets in drag. He was so slight.

"You sound like Abuela. You've got to stop worrying, Pilar. Let's plan on talking Christmas, but I want to hear from you before that, okay? And text me the address of your nunnery!"

"Will do. Same address for you?" The thing was, she had stopped worrying. She usually dreaded Christmas, felt guilty about her father struggling to fly her home. She futilely insisted every year that she be the one to give the gifts. But her only worries this winter had been about how she could spend more time at Mother of Sorrows, be of use. For once, she wasn't worrying about her father. And look what had happened.

"Yep. ¡Besos!"

"On both cheeks."

Before Buster, Pilar had loved the solitary immersion of the reading period during finals week—having this one road laid out before her to drive. After, she'd had panic attacks while studying. So she took MJ up on her offer to study at Mother of Sorrows. She spent the weekend there as was her ritual, but arrived Friday evening so that she could wake early and study before leading the Saturday workshop. MJ unlocked the Sunday school hall, where Pilar had her pick of bright, cheerful rooms with long tables, beanbags, hula-hoops, blocks, and colored chalk. "Nothing like a little hula-hooping to get the blood flowing to your brain!" MJ said and Pilar laughed.

She'd spent Saturday morning and evening studying for exams and left Sunday for her paper on Mother of Sorrows' movement into the world during Vatican II. The warmth and laughter of her post-Mass lunch with the Sisters had melted her anxiety, but as she made her way alone down the long, shadowy corridor that led to the Sunday school, she felt cut off and adrift. A buzzing filled her chest as she set out her books, notebooks, pens, highlighters, notecards, and laptop.

She re-read, then laid out her father's latest postcard, a Snowy Egret. *Good luck with finals, my love. I believe in you.* These were the white birds that her father watched in the mornings. She and Carlos would lay still in the canoe as the sun set and watch them roost in the palms circling the resaca. When they paddled back to shore, the birds lifted out of the trees all at once.

She opened her paper—still just a jotlist. Carlos hated that she'd stopped writing poetry, but there was the same uncertain space when she began a paper. She never knew whether she'd settle into a groove where her mind smoothly unfurled ideas or spend the day trudging through sludge.

Pilar stared at the blinking cursor, the words on the screen disconnected. She saw her father coughing up blood in the hospital, overwhelmed by doctors and nurses bustling around him. Their silent sign of love—two fingers over the wrist—seized by a stranger.

She stood up and shook the image out of her head, shook out her arms. She listened to "Some Kinda Love" on the iPod Carlos had given her. The song was spare and jangly, more spoken word than singing, Lou Reed's intonation largely monotone with slight shifts in emphasis and rhythm, but not volume. He didn't need to scream. Pilar loved that he couldn't really sing, but managed, by some trick of magnetism, to hold her. He sang like Carlos' bow-legged swagger across 10th Avenue's stage.

Pilar had sometimes listened to a song on repeat while drafting a poem. The song became familiar enough to move into the background, but its music kept her thoughts moving. She drew on the Sunday school chalkboard as she listened to "Some Kinda Love"—the resaca circled by palms, birds. The song moved steadily forward, steadily into. We're here to touch, taste, do, dance, it said. To bend and break and bend again. To miss any of it *would seem to be groundless*. Pilar hula-hooped and the music swirled loose through her hips. "Some Kinda Love" was how Carlos moved. Not her. Even before she called it prayer, she'd promised to be good if they didn't take her father.

But amidst the Sunday school room's sidewalk chalk, tiny chairs, and beanbags, she felt the safety of other children. She slipped on the lightness of Lou Reed's shoes and strode around the classroom with a cheeky heel-toe roll. The fact that Lou Reed couldn't really sing and didn't give a damn let her dance her gangly, awkward dance. She duck-walked and shoulder-shrugged to the bass drum beat. There's some shit and some beauty out there, "Some Kinda Love" said. Walk into it with curiosity;

walk through it with a smirk. That beat rolled right on through to the end of the song. "Some Kinda Love" was unsinkable.

Her body and mind loosened. Lou Reed's voice wove with the voices of the Sisters, her father, Carlos. She went inward and heard the lyrics in the imploring register of hymns, then outward to hear them in Lou Reed's mischievous dare. *Some kinds of love / The possibilities are endless.* Baldwin: Love *in the tough and universal sense of quest and daring and growth.* Teresa: *Love, where present, cannot possibly be content with remaining always the same.* MJ: *I felt a call to join the Carmelite community like people fall in love.* Robin: *I wanted a love outside of myself.* Carlos: *Who do you want to be, Pilar Reinfeld?* Her father: *Seek the vein.*

She sat down to write and the words rolled out steady and sure. She titled her paper "Between Thought and Expression" and wrote about how the Sisters moving into the world under Vatican II was the expression of years of contemplative thought. If that contemplation had never lived in the world, it would never have become whole. But the deep belief needed to move through the world in ceaseless prayer could only be conjured in solitude. The Sisters needed their contemplative practice to release the world's sorrows and restore their belief. It let them move lightly through heavy things. Pilar loved how often she heard laughter at Project Luz.

She imagined tearing down Mother of Sorrows' grilles and walls, throwing open its windows and doors. She dreamed herself into those first meetings of women from contemplative communities across the country: their furious reading, talking, searching. She thought about her own emergence from the blankness of La Llanura into Carlos' world of speed and sound. How the Ropa Usada, 10th Avenue, the river, The Bitch, the canoe, prom, "Birdland" birds *scattering like roses*, and the birds waiting on the resaca's tongue tumbled together just as the wonder and terror, freedom and disconnect of the 60s had for Sister Robin.

Climbing into the crackly blare of The Bitch, Pilar hadn't cared what kind of noise was playing. She'd been grateful to be swallowed by its whir and boom as they drove out of the dust. She didn't care where they were going. It was enough just to be in the car with Carlos. She wrote herself into gratitude for the isolation of her childhood, just as Sister Robin believed that the 11-year cocoon of cloistered life had been a good place to grow. Her long gestation in La Llanura let her walk into punk and grunge and drag with childlike wonder, more eager to understand and connect than to differentiate and judge. Carlos understood how one album, song, artist, genre bled into another, while Pilar listened with blind love to one song until she knew the lyrics like a prayer. Only then might she move on to another song, and it took her a long time to love it as much.

Carlos had a gift for classifying and cataloguing, Pilar for unexpected connections. She loved how two seemingly opposed things read, illuminated, *ignited* one another. That gift was boldest in her writing, her teachers' praise always some version of, *I never would have thought to make that connection.*

The Velvet Underground and Carmelite nuns! She thrilled at the echo of her strange life through the telephone wire between them. She wrote and danced—shimmying her shoulders, flapping her elbows, swinging her hips. She piled blocks into a tower and toppled it, flopped backwards onto a beanbag. Carlos studied efficiently so he could go out afterwards. But this was freedom to Pilar—this crescendoing chorus in which Lou Reed, the Sisters, Teresa, Carlos, her father, and her professors harmonized. A lightness in her body returned when she laughed with the Sisters, a warmth in her lungs when Ceci proudly read a poem. This was the power that Buster had stolen. Quiet as it was, this paper was Pilar's Metamorphosis.

She lost herself in the writing and then realized, with a jolt, that she needed to catch the next bus if she was going to make her work-study. She stuffed her things into her backpack and ran back down the long corridor, "Some Kinda Love" blasting on her headphones, tennis shoes slapping the stone tiles. "Late for my bus, see you tomorrow, thank you!" Pilar yelled breathlessly as she ran past Project Luz.

MJ popped her head out and called back, "See you tomorrow!", her laughter at the messy aliveness of this girl with her shoes untied and papers and socks spilling out of her backpack, echoing down the time-worn corridor.

Pilar ran after the bus as it pulled away, waving her arms until the driver stopped to let her on. She listened to "Some Kinda Love" while shelving books in the library. All through that song ran Carlos' question: *Who do you want to be, Pilar Reinfeld?* Her classmates were applying for jobs and graduate schools, but Pilar couldn't see past her next exam, paper, workshop. What was the expression of all her reading, searching, connecting?

Securing her father's status was the first thing that felt like a worthy use of her life. The vein between them—the reason she'd been born.

Her library shift ended at midnight and Lou Reed walked her back to her dorm. *Let us do what you fear most,* he crooned in her ears and she quietly sang it back. She'd wanted her father to feel safe for so long—the possibility of his citizenship a hope she held close when all else went dark. She imagined walking into something other than loss. She breathed in the cool night air, letting the space between thought and expression shrink with each exhale.

Bellows and whoops slashed through the song. She was on the sidewalk that ran past the court—a horde of pale bellies, patchy chest hair, flopping penises, and sloshing Solo cups barreling toward her. It was the night of the Naked Run, in which fraternity pledges ran naked through the sorority houses and the sisters received them in their underwear. Pilar froze, her heart pounding, as they stumbled around her in a tang of beer and sweat. They hooted in her face and raised their fists.

The night with Buster came back—moon swelling through a tangle of limbs. When the last of the pledges had passed, Pilar brushed herself off, her hands shaking. That black cavity opened in her chest. She sucked in air, but there wasn't enough. She hunched over, hands on her knees, and wheezed. She sank to the ground, hugged her legs to her chest, and rocked. Her phone fell out of her pocket. Her shaking fingers dialed Carlos.

Carlos texted back, *At a holiday drag ball! Call you later?* He sent a picture of the Lucky Feng's Sisters dressed in red and green kimonos and cheongsam and holding folding fans, massive synthetic buns piled on top of their heads. Pilar searched for Carlos among their garishly painted faces but couldn't find him. She closed her eyes to clear her head. *Sure,* she texted slowly. *Have fun.*

She shakily stood, zipped her iPod and headphones into her backpack. If there was another stampede, she wanted to hear it coming. Again the dark became a blade. She made herself walk into it. One step and: *What if she'd waited too long to petition and it was no longer possible?* Then another: *What if it was possible, but her father wouldn't let her?* One fear: *What if she mangled the paperwork and couldn't re-apply?* And then another: *What if she did everything right but was rejected anyway?*

The one that kept her awake was: *What if her father died while waiting?*

Pilar caught a few fitful hours of sleep, then dragged her heavy body out of bed to catch an 8 a.m. bus to Mother of Sorrows. She slept on the way, chin bobbing on her chest.

She got off outside of the monastery, rubbing the back of her neck. She walked through the open peacock gate, and along the gravel path through the still empty, sun dappled yard. She stared up at the row of open windows and tried to open herself, to slow, let go. She rang the rusted iron bell and MJ opened the heavy oak door, all bustle and warmth. She'd been up for hours.

"Hello, love!" She gave Pilar a snug hug. "There's coffee in the kitchen, and Margarita made the *best* morning glory muffins. Take a couple with you. The Sunday school's unlocked. You can join us for midday meal, or grab something quick if you don't want to break. Help yourself to whatever's in the fridge and stay as long as you like."

"Thank you." Pilar threw her arms around MJ again, squeezing back tears before she let go.

"Your students love you and you've been an enormous help. We don't want to lose you—at least not for another semester."

Pilar smiled a tightlipped smile. She couldn't see a life beyond the Sisters. If she opened her mouth, she'd cry.

MJ squeezed her arm. "You look tired, my dear. Feel free to nap in the Visiting Room."

"Thank you, I'm okay. I'll let you get back to work." Pilar adjusted the heavy straps of her backpack and headed to the kitchen. She spread butter on the still-warm muffins, wrapped them in a paper towel, and put her headphones on. Warm bread in her hands and "Some Kinda Love" in her ears, she made her way to the Sunday school.

The Sisters took their midday meal from 1 p.m. to 2 p.m. When one o' clock neared, Pilar had filled a half-dozen pages of her notebook with disjointed ideas. She stood on the shoreline and squinted into the distance—fragments converging to shape some hazy whole. She ached for the Sisters' warmth and laughter, but knew that if she joined that louder world, this quiet one would never become real.

She pushed for two more hours, until she was far from shore. It was like nights in the resaca, when she and Carlos stopped paddling and lay quiet, sealed inside the still, humid air. Their drift through the dark became all and enough. When her father came home, she was both too far and too close to worry. The body of him, the mouth yelling her name, just a shadow on the shore. His fear had fallen away, its call incomprehensible birdsquawk. She heard only the heart of him, the resaca lapping the dock.

She was paddling out into the oil-black eye of the resaca, where she didn't miss the Sisters or worry about her father because they were with her. The night that she and Carlos claimed as their own, she'd told her father that La Llanura was a lie. But what he'd wanted to give her—a flat plane on which to make herself—was not. The stories he'd told were true. He'd taught her how to light a tunnel out of sadness, plug the holes with dynamite and explode the walls.

She broke around three when hunger dulled her focus. She put on her headphones and listened to "Some Kinda Love" as she walked to the kitchen at the opposite end of the corridor. She spread chunky peanut butter on a cool, crisp red delicious apple and it tasted like heaven. She found egg salad in the refrigerator and made two sandwiches, with baby spinach from the garden and pickles. She ate one and saved the other, along with a muffin, for dinner. She quickly drank a cup of coffee and headed back to her Sunday school room, thoughts percolating.

She put away her headphones, but "Some Kinda Love" thrummed under her thoughts until the music dimmed and she moved into herself. As she worked, the Church's emergence became connected to her father's. Change happened over generations. For all his isolation, her father had walked out of the mines, left Bolivia for America, and raised a daughter who'd gone across the country to college. If she'd found her way into a larger life, hadn't her father? She was bone of his bones, flesh of his flesh. And if she could secure his status, she could lead him by the hand, finally, out of the darkness of the mines. Roberto's story was alive in her.

Her father had taught her to how to make a home with words, submerged beneath the skin. In the sanctuary of a Monday night in Sunday school, she wove herself into a story full of light. Carlos, her father, Roberto, the Sisters, and Lou Reed were in it; everyone and everything connected by a silver vein, so that no one ever died. She wrote herself into the courage she needed to wrestle with the world.

She tied everything into an ending that sang, proofread the paper, then thrashed around one last time to "Some Kinda Love". She leapt onto the table, raised her fist, and scream-sang, "*Some kinds of love / The possibilities are endless!*"

Mother Connie burst into the classroom. "What in the—?" She stared up at Pilar in angry consternation. "I heard a terrible racket."

Pilar yanked out her headphones, glanced up at the light fixture above her head, unclenched her fist and untwisted and twisted a decorative brass knob. "Just, uh, checking the light." She nodded assuredly at Mother Connie, brushed off her hands.

"It looks perfectly fine to me." Mother Connie stared up at the light with furrowed brow. "Well, get down, girl." She waited for Pilar to climb down, shook her head, and bustled off.

Pilar laughed after Mother Connie was out of earshot. She was usually terrible at lying, but she'd absorbed something of Lou Reed's mischief. Carlos would have been proud of her. She wouldn't feel guilty for rousing this ghost of the Church's past. You could ride the change, or be left behind.

It was nearly 9 when Pilar left Mother of Sorrows. The Sisters were in Private Contemplation. She stopped to read a flier, posted in English and Spanish, on Project Luz's door:

New Sanctuary Legal Clinic led by Padre Bob Fernandez, La Placita priest and immigration lawyer:

As immigrants, we all face deportation in some way. But we should not hide our faces in fear of an unjust system. Instead, we should lift our heads and rally our communities to fight for justice. Our goal is for individuals facing immigration proceedings to plan for and understand your own case.

Join us!
Thursday, January 4, 2007 from 7–9 p.m.
Project Luz: Classroom 2

The flier had been on the door all weekend, but somehow she hadn't read it until now. Pilar took one of the fliers from the shelf outside Project Luz. The clinic was right after her workshop. She tucked the flier inside her notebook and resolved to talk to Padre Bob about her father: the expression of all that thought.

She listened to "Some Kinda Love" as she made her way out. She felt in her bones that she was meant to walk down that shadowy corridor—a tunnel through time. Her father's salvation would come through Mother of Sorrows. All she had to do was believe.

She walked out into the courtyard. The trees moved in the night breeze, the sound like the movement of water. She stood on the shore and peered out at the twinkling downtown skyline in an inky cobalt sky. "*Let us do what you fear most,*" she sang breathlessly.

She jumped when her phone rang. It was Carlos calling her back. She didn't pick up. Her belief still felt fragile. She needed to hold it close, inside that story of light.

Pilar wasn't ready to talk to Carlos, but she took on extra work-study hours assisting professors with review sessions so she could buy him Laurie Anderson's *Night Life*. She'd taken a bus to Skylight Books over Thanksgiving break and seen it in the window. She didn't know much about Laurie Anderson, except that Carlos loved her. She'd flipped through the book, in which Anderson had drawn her dreams during a year of performing a solo show on the road. She'd woken in the middle of the night and attempted to capture the dreams—"heavily charged atmospheres, sensations, emotions; depictions of bewilderment, ecstasy, weightlessness, abandonment, freedom." The drawings and their captions were haunting, whimsical, luminous, strange. It was the perfect gift.

Carlos called her again while she was assisting with a review session. She meant to call him back, but ended up studying late. She'd call him once finals were over. Meanwhile, she liked to think of him flipping through Anderson's illustrations—which ones he'd lean in and study, which ones would make him laugh.

She bought her father a photography book on the birds of south Texas. His real gift, she hoped, would arrive in the new year.

CHAPTER 10

After a semester full of self-doubt and searching, Carlos took comfort in Lucky Feng's routine. It was a relief not to overthink everything. Admittedly, the bachelorettes from New Jersey and Long Island were highly inebriated and easily pleased. They never tired of attractive, attention-hungry Joey, who entertained the audience with erotic balloon sculptures while Carmen and the other drag queen servers took their orders. But Carmen teased and fawned over them, and they tipped her well. At Lucky Feng's, all was play: Wigs and eyelashes, faces and selves, opinions and boobs could all be put on and removed. Carlos leapt into that lightness as soon as winter break began. During the fall semester, he'd worked a couple of shows on the weekends, but he worked as many as five weekend shows and a few during the week over break.

Nathaniel promised that they'd incorporate a Carmen Miranda samba into the cabaret, but Carlos knew it would be a while. Nathaniel clung to some private notion of a narrative arc that no one cared about, especially not the drunk tourists, birthday girls, and bachelorettes that made up most of their audience. The Sisters had all put in a year or more as servers before they performed solo and advised Carmen to get *real* comfortable serving Cosmos in platforms.

They complained that Nathaniel's unbending ideas about performance order, lighting, and blocking cramped their stardom, but they threw themselves into their acts no matter how many times they'd performed them. The show began with a choral performance of Celine Dion's "My Heart Will Go On"; Lady Bangcock's falsies toppling out as Bama Dee Light held her up like Rose at the prow of The Titanic; Cher Noble lasciviously wagging her tongue as she lip-synced vibrato; Helluva Bottom Carter shaking her amply padded ass at the audience, faking flatulence as Celine sang, *Once more you open the door*; Juana Bang performing fellatio on a recorder during the instrumental interludes. Following several solo performances, the Sisters called drunken brides-to-be up to the stage to do lap dances for the hot gay bartenders. When the Sisters forced the brides' heads into their laps, the bartenders pretended to be turned on. Occasionally a birthday party of metrosexuals, the sort of straight men who'd been in Carlos' Mask and Wig cast, diversified the bachelorette audience. "I'll show you a lap dance!" the Sisters would call to the bachelorettes while straddling the metrosexuals and pinching their nipples. The metrosexuals would laugh good-naturedly and halfheartedly squirm to go along with the show. Next came a standup monologue, a couple more solo numbers, and finally, an audience-participatory sing-along of "We Are Family", which Carmen and all of the drag queen servers joined.

What made Carmen pause with a full tray of Cosmos and grin, starstruck, at her Sisters on stage was not the canned jokes, but their unmitigated, undeniable, contagious enjoyment of themselves and each other. It was big or bust in this world—big hair, eyes, mouth, heels, boobs, hips, ass, and sass.

Carlos learned about the layers that went into that largeness. Bama had taught Carlos to paint, but Cher Noble/Max taught Carlos about shaving, tucking, padding, corsets, tights, and wigline blending. Raised on the Upper West Side by an art history professor father and a Montessori teacher mother who'd met as socialist activists in the 70s, Max inhabited the middle ground between idealism and realism. "Until America supports its artists like Scandinavia, I'll take the rich daddies for all they're worth." He'd graduated from Tisch's musical theatre program two years earlier and had been working the drag circuit since his senior year. What he liked best was theatre drag—performing musical numbers from *A Chorus Line*, *Kinky Boots*, or *Songs for a New World*. When he wasn't building his drag career, he was auditioning for Broadway musicals. He performed a minimum of six drag or cabaret shows a week, nannied, and taught voice and dance. He hairdressed, sewed costumes, and painted shoes for other queens. He'd leave a drag gig at 3 a.m., crawl into bed around 5, then wake at 9 for his day job. His acting and drag careers demanded constant, confident networking. "There's a reason Ru sang, *You better werk!*," he told Carlos.

Max wasn't the most beautiful boy in the world, but he was a master of seduction, on stage and off. He'd pick up a hot actor at an audition, squeeze in a dressing room hookup with another queen before squeezing her into her corset. Carlos listened to his Lothario tales with the same rapt attention with which he absorbed his drag instruction. He had a lot to learn, and Max was a willing teacher.

Cher Noble gave Carmen her first corset, a garment she affectionately called The Rib Buster. As she laced Carlos into it, Cher recounted how she'd broken a rib as a baby queen. She felt something pop as her friend tightened the reins, but commanded, "Keep going!" The pain was excruciating, but she'd spent three hours on makeup and was already tucked. So she chased 1,000 milligrams of ibuprofen with Red Bull and vodka, performed for hours, and ended the night with an ER doctor wrapping her black and blue torso in a brace.

"How am I supposed to *move*?" Carmen asked, bug-eyed and breathless, when Cher finished lacing her up.

"Pain is beauty!" Cher proclaimed. She felt qualified to paraphrase God since she'd gone to Hebrew school. "Y'all know what Yahweh says: *Pain is beauty; beauty, pain!* Especially you Gentiles. I mean look at Christ's abs on the cross!" *Pain is beauty; beauty, pain!* became a Feng Sisters mantra as they bent their penises backwards and duct-taped them between their butt cheeks, squeezed and taped their pecs into cleavage, and shoved their size-16 feet into six-inch heels two sizes too small. When the audience's rapt eyes and raucous laughter absorbed their pain, they were Beauty. Their pleasure was not a performance; its fullness obliterated the pain. Well, that and a lot of alcohol. They took pride in that transmutation. They believed in the amplification of the self. They were large; they contained multitudes! Pain was grace was beauty was Divinity.

Carmen started out wearing three pairs of Capezio tights, The Rib Buster, and a bra stuffed with socks. But after her first couple of weeks at Lucky Feng's, Cher took her aside and said, "Darling, it's time you learned about pads."

The following Friday, Carlos arrived two hours early to Lucky Feng's dressing room to receive Max's teaching. He was ready to *werk* but felt uneasy about the tuck.

Max tossed his head back and laughed. "Tucking is an artform that separates the men from the boys. Don't worry. The penis is a gymnast; those backbends get easier!" Max swigged whiskey from his flask and passed it to Carlos. He explained the tape and gaff methods and the necessity of shaving. Max used spray adhesive on top of duct tape and went through four razors a week.

Carlos swigged, started to hand the flask back, then took another swig. Wary as he was, he relished being let in on this intricate secret. Ever since his adolescent thespian days, he'd loved the backstage rituals, makeup, costumes, and hair. Drag was all of that magnified.

After the tuck, Max "layered the body" with 11 strata of shapers, spandex, pads, and tights. Carlos then tied him into his corset. Over all of that, he tugged on a shaper leotard like a bunny suit; a matching bra and panty set; and finally, his costume.

"Wow." Carlos looked multi-layered Max/Cher Noble up and down. "You look stunning, but that's a *lot*."

"Well, the bigger your pads," Max put his hands on his hip-pads, "the more layers you need to smooth out the foam. During the warmer months,

I skip the tights and spray tan my legs. But that means lots of shaving and oils to keep my skin glowing. Oh and spray glitter, because what's a queen without glitter?"

"I do like glitter." Carlos grinned.

"But for winter, it's layers and layers of tights, oh my!" Max plucked at his tights.

"Yes, Mommie Dearest," Carlos said just to hear Max protest in his old screenstar voice, *"DON'T* call me Mother!"

Carlos cackled. The show he liked best was this dressing room repartee. He liked playing the role of the Shocked Baby Queen to her Unphased Elders—vexing, wheedling, and backtalking his way into the Lucky Feng's family.

The Sisters would get to Lucky Feng's at 8 and wouldn't untuck until 3 a.m. They sucked it up if they had to pee.

"Really, you all do this?" Carlos looked wide-eyed around the dressing room.

"Mmm-hmm," the Sisters affirmed in chorus as Bama Dee Light blended her wigline, Lady Bangcock yanked Juana Bang into her corset, and Helluva Bottom Carter tugged on her eighth pair of tights.

Max insouciantly confided that he'd had four UTIs and saw his doctor weekly, which he considered part of the basic upkeep of a Busy Drag Queen.

Carlos squinted at Max in disbelief.

Max laughed long and loud, until the corner of Carlos' mouth quirked up. Carlos loved how Max laughed in the face of pain. He couldn't imagine Cher or any of the Sisters crying over some video in the Brooklyn Museum.

Carlos layered up, longing to be that invincible. Still his preparations were comparatively minimal, so he became the dressing room helper, making sure everyone's hair was glued down, corsets tied tight, and pads well-placed before he dressed. When it got close to showtime, Bama would say, "Enough child, get ready. Let me help you."

If they didn't do a late-late show, and sometimes if they did, the Sisters changed into their boy clothes and descended upon Katz Deli, where they performed for themselves and the hot things who sliced pastrami. Except for the five-pound corned beef sandwiches, it was just like lunch with the drama kids of San Jacinto High. The best banter, sing-a-longs, and choreography happened at Katz. The Sisters laughed over latkes with old Jewish men and NYU kids at that hour when everyone was drunk, tired, and wired enough to coexist. Carlos leaned back in his chair and watched, relishing their larger-than-life show.

"Whaddya think this is, kid, a peep show?" Carter (Helluva) would tease. "This pastrami's not free!"

"I told you, I'm *vegetarian!*" Carlos would say, walking right into a slew of jokes about what kind of meat he *did* eat.

When Carlos and Max trailed off into a side conversation about *Giovanni's Room*, Tony (Juana Bang) tumbled face down into Mike's (Lady Bangcock's) crotch and started snoring. Carlos took their teasing as a sign of affection. He liked being pulled back into the bawdy Katz Act, a cathartic holiday after the exhausting self-consciousness of Columbia.

One of the rare times the Fengs grew serious was when they talked about Dr. Yoon. "Dr. Yoon!" They sighed wistfully. "God, I miss him."

Carlos was mostly content to let their allusions to people and stories from their shared past slide by, but he couldn't help but lean in and ask, "Who's Dr. Yoon?"

"Dr. Yoon is our Drag Glamma," Lamont (Bama) said. "A First Lady of Lucky Feng's, there from the very beginning."

Drag was hard on the body and Carlos assumed that Dr. Yoon had retired, but that didn't explain the "Doctor" part. "Dr. Yoon was her drag name?" he asked.

"Dr. Yoon is always Dr. Yoon," Mike said. He explained that Dr. Yoon had been raised by his grandmother, who'd been a healer and taught him most of what she knew.

Carlos listened as the Sisters talked of Dr. Yoon curing them of ailments of the body and soul, feeling as if some current was passed to him through their stories. Dr. Yoon had recently completed a Doctor of Acupuncture degree, going to school during the day and performing drag at night. He'd celebrated his accreditation by traveling to Korea to search for his mother, who'd left him with his grandmother when he was four.

Carlos was struck by the parallels in their lives—mothers who'd left them with their grandmothers in another country, grandmothers who identified as healers. "When is he coming back?" he asked.

"We don't know," Tony said.

The Sisters shook their heads and stared off into the distance.

"Oh my god, did you just eat that *whole* sandwich?" Carter asked Max, dispelling the sadness that had settled over their table. "Where does it go?!"

"I'm a growing boy!" Max said, though Cher's hair and heels were the biggest things about his scrawny five-foot-seven self.

Tony, Mike, and Carter shared an apartment in Alphabet City, Lamont lived alone in Chinatown, and Max lived in Astoria with roommates from Tisch. Carlos no longer felt the need to carry a switchblade because the Sisters made sure that no one took public transportation in drag alone. Cher and Carmen would crash with Juana, Kim, and Helluva in Alphabet City or with each other if they didn't have money for a cab. Max's heat was out, so he and Carlos would spoon for warmth, sometimes falling asleep in their makeup. The possibility of sex was between them, but Carlos was embarrassed by his virginity and unsure if he wanted Max to be the first.

Sometimes Bama accompanied them home for extra safety. Six-foot-nine in heels, she suffered no sass. The Feng Sisters took care of each other, but that wasn't something that Carlos could tell Abuela. She felt bad that she didn't have the money to fly him home for Christmas.

"Will you be okay, mijo?"

"Honestly Abuela, it's safer." Border patrol didn't need probable cause to interrogate you within 15 miles of Mexico.

"I know, but will you go to church?"

Carlos stifled a sigh. "I'll try. Will you have your orphans' dinner?"

"Por supuesto. Everybody will miss you."

"I'll miss them, too."

Carlos sent her a modern take on a huipil blouse that he'd found in a vintage store and would have bought for himself if they'd had his size. Abuela sent him an early Christmas gift of two button-down church shirts and a pocket Saint Nicholas for protection, which Carlos tucked inside his makeup case.

Carlos didn't go to church, but he did partake in a ritual that Bama called Sanctuary. Because getting into drag wasn't easy and they didn't have a lot of free time, the Lucky Feng's Sisters tried at least once a week to arrive a couple of hours before they dressed to share dinner, kiki, and breathe. They'd order Indian, Thai, or pizza (Carlos couldn't stomach what passed for Mexican food in New York), bring a bottle of wine, and a blanket. Sleepless between their day jobs and midnight performances, they'd nap after dinner, spooned together on the blanket. When Max wrapped his arms around Carlos, he remembered Pilar enfolding his bruised body after prom. The pain that had come of their beauty that night. Their beauty in the wake of that pain.

Pilar had called Carlos a couple of times, once when he was dressing for a show and again when he was sleeping through the afternoon. He'd been working so many shows that he hadn't had a chance to call her back, but he'd bought her a hand-painted scarf with ocean-like washes of deep blue, green, and aquamarine at the Union Square Holiday Market. One only needed to look at Pilar's fashion choices to see what guilt did to a person. She just needed a pop of color. Pilar had had more fun when he'd dressed her. She'd been a different person in the sequin skirt. Carlos felt sure that her life would be lighter in the ocean scarf. It was more than he could afford, but fuck it, he'd eat all of his meals in the dining hall when school resumed.

Ringing Mother of Sorrows' rusted iron bell the first Saturday morning of Christmas break felt mystical. Carlos would have seen Pilar in creased jeans and a white T-shirt, weighed down by an overstuffed backpack and worn dufflebag. But Carlos couldn't feel the tingle of possibility that she felt along her spine.

MJ insisted on carrying her bag. "I wish we could have flown you home, but that blasted vow of poverty."

"I usually dread Christmas—just carols on the grocery store Muzak nauseate me. But this year feels different."

"I was never a big fan of 'Rockin' Around the Christmas Tree'," MJ said.

Pilar laughed. "Yeah, I *never* got that sentimental feeling."

"We'll skip that one, I promise," MJ said. "We're excited to have you for a whole month."

As they made their way to the Visiting Room, MJ said, "It's too bad the Daughter House has gone neglected for so long, or you could have a whole dorm to yourself."

"The Daughter House?"

"Those of us who joined in the 50s and 60s stayed there. Then we tried a three-month live-in for recruits in the 70s." Young women interested in becoming nuns could move into an east wing dormitory and take part in their daily practice before committing. "None of them lasted, and we've just had Letitia and Soledad join in the last three decades." MJ set Pilar's bag down in the Visiting Room, looked out the window. "I sometimes wonder if the whole nun thing will die out."

"Or maybe people will just become nuns online?" Pilar waited for MJ to turn and raised one eyebrow.

MJ smiled lopsidedly and shrugged.

Pilar thought again of her saying she felt the call to Mother of Sorrows like people fall in love. "Could I see the Daughter House?"

MJ cocked her head and fell silent.

"I promise I won't throw a party," Pilar said.

MJ laughed. "I'm curious myself, honestly. I can only imagine the state it's in."

She grabbed a silver swallow keychain from the rack beside Project Luz's bookshelves. Pilar followed her up a narrow spiral staircase to a low-ceilinged hallway. MJ fiddled with the lock and heaved open the jammed door. A massive spiderweb hung in the corner and it smelled musty. Ten plywood doors ran down either side of the hall.

MJ opened the first to reveal a twin bed covered by a black bedspread, a battered wardrobe, and a desk covered in dust. The only adornment was a stark wooden cross at the head of the bed. "It's such a shame—" She sneezed. "All this wasted space." She doubled over and sneezed repeatedly into the crook of her elbow.

Pilar couldn't bless her fast enough.

"Big Guy's no match for my allergies," MJ said, bleary-eyed. "But you have a look." She handed Pilar the key and stumbled out, sneezing.

Pilar closed her fist around the key and stood very still before she walked down the hall, quietly, as if she might disturb someone. She opened and peered into each small, bare, dusty room, until she got to the last one. She wrote her name in the dust covering the desk. She sat on the bed, ran her hands over the rough bedspread, and looked out the window—LA a toy city in the distance.

Now she knew what to give the Sisters for Christmas.

Mother of Sorrows' youth programs, including Pilar's workshop, continued through the holidays. Pilar guided her students from responding to authors to emulating them to pushing into their own voices. A revelatory thing for most. But Ceci had been writing little things since she was a child. She'd never shown anyone. She would discuss the authors they read in class, but she hadn't shared her own writing. Pilar stayed after class with her for an hour or so until her mother could pick her up. Her mother didn't want her walking the streets alone.

Ceci stayed after the first workshop of Christmas break and wrote while Pilar commented on student work. Pilar would glance up to see her staring into space, fingering the red ribbon she'd woven through her braid, and then scribbling away. She didn't think she'd ever written so freely.

Seeing her pause, Pilar sat beside her. "How's it going?"

"I think I finished a poem." Ceci shyly pushed it toward her, played with the end of her braid while Pilar read.

Sometimes I hate you for missing so much,
for making Mamá work your job and hers
and another to recover what you stole
If you showed up, I'd spit in your face
Other times, I'd let you in
if you just
came home
I tell myself if I pray, make that goal, "A", you will
On the other side of every blood-red "A"
is the scrape of you not knowing
The best moments are when I go up for a jumpshot
and there is just my body

Pilar took a deep breath. She knew that tangle of anger and want like an underwater sound. "Wow."

Ceci looked down. "You like it?"

"I *love* it." Pilar talked about its rawness and rhythm. "I like that you left yourself, and the reader, suspended."

Ceci smiled with her eyes before her mouth. She looked closer to 11 than 14—all those large feelings tumbling around her skin-and-bones body.

"My mother left when I was a baby," Pilar said. "I used to write her letters."

Ceci searched her eyes.

Pilar saw her child-self, eyes too old for her face. "I know you don't want to share it with the class, but would you show it to your mom? I think she'd be proud."

Ceci shook her head. "She never talks about my dad. She just says he's not a good man."

"That's okay. It can be just for you. I meant it when I said you're safe here." Pilar had the feeling she'd often had—of saying something as much for herself as for her students.

"Can I show you one of my favorite poems?" Pilar asked.

Ceci nodded.

Pilar pulled Mary Oliver's *Dream Work* from her backpack and read her "Wild Geese".

"My mom and I used to feed the geese in Echo Park Lake," Ceci said. "She takes the kids she nannies for now."

Pilar remembered a V of wild geese flying over the resaca, tilting her face toward the sky with her father. "I read it again and again. I'm still learning it. Do you want to take it home?"

"Are you sure?" Ceci asked.

Pilar looked up to see Ceci's mother, Flor—five feet, if that, round-faced with a purple scar beneath her right eye—watching them from the doorway. She felt, and understood, her distrust. She tried to put her at ease, gushing about Ceci's talent while Ceci gathered her things.

"Thank you for staying with her," Flor said.

A Mayan from Guatemala, Flor's first language was Maya. They spoke a mix of Spanish and English, but Flor never spoke much. She came to Sunday Mass, but didn't talk with people afterwards.

"It's really my pleasure." Pilar grinned at Ceci and she smiled back. "Oh, don't forget..." She zipped *Dream Work* into Ceci's backpack. "I want to hear what you think."

"I'll start reading tonight," Ceci said.

"Keep it for as long as you want," Pilar said.

Flor brushed Ceci's hair back from her forehead, pulled her into her body, and whispered something into her hair.

Pilar stood in the classroom doorway and watched them leave, Flor's hand on the back of Ceci's neck in a way that reminded her, painfully, of her father.

By the time Pilar got to dinner, the Sisters had already prayed and started eating. Soledad had everyone in stitches over all the mishaps during Nativity play rehearsals. Robin motioned for Pilar to sit next to her.

Pilar laughed as Soledad described how one of the wise men had tripped over the donkey, fallen on the crib, and knocked the baby Jesus (a sharpied cantaloupe until they could find a doll) out with sufficient force that it rolled off the stage.

Pilar served herself a hearty portion of spinach lasagna, garlic bread, and salad, and bowed her head. She thanked God for Margarita's cooking and for a place to spend Christmas. She prayed for her father's health (she reminded herself to call him), and for Ceci and Flor. Praying over meals was new and she still felt self-conscious, but when she lifted her head, she felt clearer.

Robin put her hand on her shoulder. "How was workshop?"

"Good. Ceci stayed after and wrote the most beautiful poem."

"I taught her Sunday school class a few years ago," Soledad said. "She's wonderful."

"She really is," Pilar said. "Is it just her and her mom? How long have they been at Mother of Sorrows?"

The Sisters looked at MJ.

"I found Flor passed out on Mother of Sorrows' doorstep 15 years ago. She'd walked through the desert to get here. She was very sick. She stayed in the Daughter House for a week and I did what I could before La Placita took her in."

"Do you know anything about Ceci's father?" Pilar asked.

MJ hesitated. "Flor's very private, but he's not involved."

"Did she tell you why she left Guatemala?"

"The army carried out a Mayan genocide during the Civil War, but she's never talked about it."

"With the help of the US," Soledad said.

MJ inhaled and slowly let out her breath. "With the help of the US."

Pilar didn't know anything about the Guatemalan Civil War, but remembered her father saying that her mother led women from Guatemala across the Rio Grande. The sadness in Flor's eyes made her think she didn't want to know.

"La Placita is Padre Bob's church?" she asked.

MJ nodded. "Have you met Padre yet?"

"No, but I was planning to go to his legal clinic."

"You should. La Placita does amazing work." MJ's face lit up. She talked excitedly about La Placita giving sanctuary to refugees of the Central American crisis and how their programs helped people navigate the immigration system. "They were the first church to join the New Sanctuary Movement and they're building an apartment for an immigrant family—"

Mother Connie bustled in and MJ fell silent. Connie hated it when the Sisters were late to things, but she was free to come and go on her own schedule. "Everyone have a productive day?" she trilled. She looked around the table with a rubbery smile.

The other Sisters offered mumbles of assent. Pilar watched MJ's jaw tighten.

Mother Connie sat at the head of the table and prayed over her food.

Everyone stopped eating until she lifted her head. Silence pooled outward from her like liquid glass hardening. There was just the sound of forks scraping plates for the remainder of dinner.

Pilar imagined climbing onto the table and fiddling with the light fixture, saying pointedly to Mother Connie, "Just checking the light. For some reason it goes out whenever you walk in."

MJ excused herself early, saying she was going to wash up before Vespers. Pilar and the other Sisters stayed until Mother Connie was done shoveling lasagna into her sour prune mouth.

Beyond teaching her workshop and helping with Project Luz, Pilar was free to come and go as she pleased, join the Sisters' rituals or not. She begged off Vespers, wanting a physical sort of prayer. She changed into a T-shirt and shorts, pulled her fine, wheat-colored hair into a bun. She took the silver swallow key from its rack and carried a broom, mop, and bucket of cleaning supplies up the spiral staircase to the Daughter House. She jiggled the key in the lock and heaved open the door. She admired the intricate work of the spider web. "Sorry, Charlotte," she said before destroying it with the broom.

She swept up and down the long hall. She'd heard that people shed over 100 pounds of skin in a lifetime, that dust was mostly skin. We got a new body every seven years. Seven years ago, she'd been Ceci's age. She didn't like those feelings flooding back. She held the full dustpan beneath the light, imagined its gray clumps and glittering granules as all that hunger and anger, and emptied it into a trash bag.

When she was done sweeping, she found the bathroom and filled the bucket. The water ran rust, brown, yellow, clear. The repetitive motion of mopping and sharp scent of lemon made her remember running through the citrus grove. That was the exhaustion she was after.

She opened the first bedroom. Its musty smell hit her in the face. She climbed onto the desk and pried open the window above it, stuck her head out and gulped the air. She wiped the thick layer of dust from all the surfaces. She swept under the bed as best she could.

This was the church she'd known growing up. She and her father had cleaned the house on Sundays with his scratchy records playing. She'd hated giving up swimming, reading, or later, Carlos, but when she gave herself over to the work, she became absorbed in its details—in making the stove, sinks, and faucets shine. If her father had a coughing fit, she'd sit him down at the kitchen table with lemon, honey, and ginger tea. He'd listen to his beautiful, brokenheart songs until his coughing subsided. Moving through the rooms together, it was as if they were scrubbing away that longing. Home looked different when they finished. They had everything they needed and all of it shone.

Pilar cleaned two more rooms, working until 1 a.m., until she didn't feel anything but the ache in her muscles. She had 17 rooms left to clean over the next eight days, but she'd finish in time for Christmas.

She took a shower in the small bathroom connected to the Visiting Room. She stood for a long time under the scalding water, watching grime stream from her arms and legs until her skin steamed pink. She shook out the folded white sheet MJ had left her and sank into a deep, dreamless sleep.

The Sisters had insisted that Pilar sit up in the choir with them if she came to Sunday Mass. She overslept and arrived six minutes late, which hardly counted. She'd thrown on a black T-shirt dress with a white pattern like a blurred x-ray. Its built-in bra made it her go-to outfit when she was rushed but had to wear something nicer than jeans. She wouldn't have minded wearing Mother Connie's roomy brown tunic. Mother Connie probably wore a girdle for kicks, but Pilar figured you could go commando under there. She'd pulled her hair into a ponytail without brushing it, but felt some satisfaction over having brushed her teeth.

When she entered, Mother Connie, who sat at the end of the first pew, turned around and clucked her tongue.

"Sorry," Pilar whispered, resenting her. Did she have to be such a caricature?

Pilar slid into the second pew next to Sister Letitia, who ran the community garden.

"Welcome," Letitia warmly whispered and Pilar felt guilty for detesting Mother Connie. As she prayed and sang, kneeled and stood, she asked God to make her more generous. But her mind kept wandering back to MJ. Volunteering at Project Luz, she'd seen MJ impatient and frustrated. She'd seen her use that heat to push through inhuman bureaucracies. But at dinner she'd seen bitter resentment on her face. Pilar kept stealing glances at MJ, who sat at the other end of her pew. Immersed in the service, MJ didn't notice, but Robin, who sat beside MJ, caught Pilar's eye and gave her a slow, unsure smile.

"Come in!" Robin called when Pilar knocked on the phone room door after Mass.

Pilar waited for Robin to finish scribbling on a prayer request form.

"Hello, dear." Smiling up from her worn armchair, Robin looked frail, though she was nearly as tall as Pilar. "Did you sleep alright? That Visiting Room couch is almost as old as I am."

"What was that all about at dinner?" Pilar asked.

"There's some history there." Robin sighed. "You'll want to pull in a chair."

Pilar pulled a folding chair in from the Visiting Room. Robin waited for her to sit, then locked the door. Who was she worried might come in?

"I told you how exciting the Church's movement into the world was for me," Robin said. "But for Mother Connie, that collision with the world was an assault."

Pilar nodded and leaned toward Robin, though their knees nearly touched in the tight room. She smelled of Pond's Cold Cream and beneath it, something grassy.

"MJ rode into Mother of Sorrows on the wave of Vatican II," Robin continued. "She charged into the world, pulling us along behind her, while Mother Connie tried to rein us back in. They have vastly different ways of expressing their faith and strong personalities. There was bound to be conflict."

"That doesn't surprise me," Pilar said. "I've just never seen MJ go silent like that."

"She chooses her battles," Robin said. "When churches across the nation banded together to offer sanctuary to refugees of the Central American crisis, MJ pushed for Mother of Sorrows to join the movement. Mother

Connie said the Sanctuary Movement defied the Carmelite charism of solitary, contemplative prayer. When 16 Sanctuary workers were indicted for harboring fugitives in 1985, Mother said that God had spoken.

"MJ talked about La Placita giving sanctuary to refugees of the Central American crisis. What she didn't mention was that Padre Bob was charged with conspiracy and given 5 years' probation. Mother Connie seized that as proof of God's condemnation. Padre and other Sanctuary workers fought until the government granted the refugees temporary protection. While that fight was going on, the refugees needed a safe place to stay. MJ made it known that she believed it was a crime against God for us to keep the Daughter House empty when 100 people who'd seen their loved ones murdered and homes destroyed had nowhere to go."

"She showed it to me yesterday," Pilar said. "She said all that wasted space was a shame, but I thought she was just talking about how nobody wants to be a nun anymore."

"I don't think that's at the top of MJ's concerns." Robin laughed. "Anyway, at the height of the whole conflict over the Sanctuary Movement, Mother Connie went 180 degrees in the opposite direction and decided to build hermitages so we could pray in solitude. At lunch, she passed around a sketch of these round stone huts with cone roofs."

"Like little hermit houses?"

"Exactly," Robin said. "She asked for our support in appealing to the Vatican for funding. MJ was sitting next to me, and I could feel her seething."

"Do you think Mother Connie did it to spite MJ?"

Robin narrowed her eyes. "I wouldn't put it past her. That said, I think Mother really believes in a contemplative practice. We all do. We wouldn't be Carmelite nuns if we didn't. She just takes it to extremes.

"Anyway, Mother went on about the hermitages until MJ demanded we use those funds to house La Placita's refugees. We'd pledged obedience when we became nuns, and none of us had ever defied Mother like that. The rest of us felt torn. We believed in the transformative power of prayer, and illegally harboring refugees would have endangered all the good we were doing through Project Luz.

Mother reminded MJ that harboring refugees was a federal offense, that we could lose the monastery.

"'We already have,' MJ said and stormed out."

"*That's* the MJ I know," Pilar said.

"Well, Mother looked like she'd been struck.

"After that, MJ threw herself into Project Luz with a ferocity that scared us. For a while, Mother Connie made the smallest step forward a battle of wills. MJ stopped asking her permission, knowing that she needed Project Luz to bring in parishioners.

"There was a period where MJ moved through our practice like a ghost— silent when we prayed, sang. I sometimes thought she would have been happier if she'd left. But she stayed. Over the years, she and Mother Connie have reached a sort of peace. What Mother wants most, after all, is to be left alone with her manuscripts."

The phone rang. Sister Robin smiled apologetically as she answered it.

Pilar folded her chair and carried it toward the door. "Wait," she said before she left.

Sister Robin asked the caller to hold.

"Do you still think MJ would have been happier if she'd left?"

Robin looked at the phone like the caller might have answers, or at least easier questions. "She's needed here and able to do a lot of good. Maybe that's as much as God grants us in this life." She looked up, clear-eyed, at Pilar. "We create *home* through what we give."

The only feeling Pilar could pin down was the desire to be out of that dim little room with its soapy, greasy smell. She headed outdoors, pried off her black ballet flats and left them on the doorstep. She wriggled her toes in the cool grass, scratched the tops of her feet. She listened to the trees breathing, birds singing, children playing. The bell chimed for the next Mass and she watched people file into the cathedral. She walked in

the opposite direction, questions crescendoing as the bell's reverbera-
tions dimmed.

She walked through the questions. She went back to what MJ made
her believe when she spoke to her class: that the broken parts of her
would become whole if she did work that was love. A calling rather than
a job. But maybe MJ's work was like any ordinary job, with its daily compromises and difficult bosses. (Her boss at Sprouts had had unruly nose
hair and refused to let her read when the register was slow.) Maybe MJ's
commitment to Mother of Sorrows was like any other love: at first you felt
the miracle, then you worked to keep it alive.

The wave of love Pilar felt when she met MJ was connected to her
openness, fearlessness, her deep, throaty laugh. Pilar thought MJ believed
in Project Luz and shared a real connection with her Sisters. But the way
she'd lit up when she talked about La Placita, against the strained anger
on her face when Mother Connie walked in, made Pilar wonder what kept
her at Mother of Sorrows.

Did MJ still love the work in a way that made the compromises worth it?
Carlos didn't understand why Pilar would take an hour-long bus to Mother
of Sorrows, why she couldn't volunteer, or if she *must*, go to church closer
to school. But it was *these* Sisters, *these* students who'd become hers. The
rituals of back and forth buses, overnight bags, and Visiting Room weekends made possible the high she felt after a good workshop or belly laugh
with the Sisters. And that high let her warmly greet the bus driver, calmly
study for an exam.

MJ would shake off the question of happiness. She had to be pragmatic
to do the work she did. Instead, Pilar asked if she could join the Sisters in
their morning rituals. If she wanted to know whether MJ still believed in
contemplative life, she needed to experience it for herself.

CHAPTER 11

The Sisters of Mother of Sorrows adhered to a strict schedule:

6: Wake
6:30 to 7:30: Centering Prayer
7:30 to 8: Breakfast
8 to 8:45: Morning Chapel/Silent Prayer
8:45 to 9:15: Singing of the Psalms
9:30 to 10:30: Mass
10:30 to 1: Work
1 to 2: Midday Meal
2 to 5: Work
5 to 6: Bathe
6 to 7: Evening Meal
7 to 8: Vespers
8 to 9: Compline
9 to 10: Private Contemplation
10: Lights Out

After the previous summer of waking early to make breakfast for her father, Pilar had fallen back into her night owl habit of going to sleep around 1 and waking around 9. Morning silence would be no problem—

she had trouble speaking for an hour after she woke, but waking at 6 was another thing. She'd asked MJ if she could join her for centering prayer partly because she'd never wake up otherwise, and partly because she'd never meditated. Centering prayer was essentially meditation. "Don't overthink it," MJ had said. "You look at God and God looks at you." Pilar overthought it and still wasn't sure what that meant. People looking at her made her self-conscious. Was God going to look at her for a whole hour?

She fell asleep some time after 1 Sunday night/Monday morning, woke late, threw a pair of jeans on under the T-shirt she'd slept in, ran up the stairs to the Sisters' dormitory, and arrived at MJ's cell breathless and 15 minutes late. Pushing her hair out of her face as she ran, she realized that the rubberband she always wore around her wrist was missing. When she pushed open MJ's door, she sat crosslegged in bed, her wide brown skirt spread over her knees, her back against the plain wooden cross at its head, eyes closed. There was no corpus on the cross because the Sisters were supposed to take Christ's place. MJ had pulled the wooden chair out from her desk, so that it faced her. She slowly opened her eyes, wordlessly motioned for Pilar to sit, then closed her eyes again.

Pilar sat in the hard-backed chair facing MJ and closed her eyes. She took deep breaths and tried to let the adrenaline drain. The back of her neck was damp and her hair, which she never wore down, was distracting. She ran her tongue over her teeth and wished she'd brushed them. She opened her eyes and searched for a clock, but there wasn't one. MJ wasn't wearing a watch. How would she know when an hour was up? Pilar's stomach growled. Why an hour of centering prayer and a half-hour for breakfast?

She closed her eyes and tried to look at God. She saw the sunset at La Llanura—stripes of magenta, violet, pink, and twilight blue piling up from the horizon; felt herself rocking on the porch with her father. She saw a dented brown Chevette driving away from the house, down the long dirt road. She smiled at the idea of God as The Bitch, driving her to a drag pageant. She thought MJ might laugh at that. And then she thought of her father waiting for her to come home and was flooded with worry.

Worries about her father's health and status spiraled into worries about Carlos walking alone at night, drunk in drag, spiraled into worries about Ceci and Flor, spiraled into anxiety about what she would do when she graduated. She hadn't applied to any jobs because she didn't want a job, she wanted a calling. She opened her eyes and looked at MJ, her eyes closed, back straight, breaths even. Was she still in love?

She couldn't even keep her eyes closed. She closed them again, took a deep breath, and sank into darkness.

She didn't know how long she'd been asleep when MJ gently shook her.

"Sorry," she blurted, breaking silence.

MJ smiled, mirth in her eyes.

Pilar rubbed the back of her neck as she stood. Her tailbone hurt, too.

All down the hall, the Sisters were emerging from their cells, looking peaceful and freshfaced in their Brownie uniforms. Pilar had never been a Brownie; she'd envied the colorful badges on their vests. The Sisters smiled encouragingly, put a hand on her shoulder as they made their way to breakfast. Was it obvious that she'd failed to earn her meditation badge? She sleepily ate Grape-Nuts with bananas and honey and thought that breakfast in silence was golden. The Sisters ate quickly, filed into a line to put their bowls in the dishwasher, then made their way to morning chapel.

Sandwiched in a chapel pew between the wrinkled serenity of Sister Robin and Marie Therese, the oldest at 91, Pilar felt like a teenager—all raw skin and gangly ache. The words of the Divine Office ran together, and she prayed, over and over in her head with her eyes squeezed shut, that her father would get citizenship before he died. It felt more like an OCD tic than prayer.

Her throat ached when the Sisters sang, in voices plaintive and off-key, Psalm 69: *I am worn out calling for help; my throat is parched.*

At Mass, they stuck out their tongues to receive the body of Christ. It was hard to believe The Body of Christ wanted anything to do with her tongue when she hadn't brushed it.

At lunch, the Sisters chattered around her, but Pilar remained silent. Her avocado sandwich tasted like mush. MJ gave her a long look and said quietly, "I promise it gets better. A relationship with God is like any other. Some days, it's ecstatic. Others, I wonder how I ended up here. We can't control whether Holy shows up with roses or skunk cabbage, but if you clear a space in the morning, you've done your part."

It got better. Tuesday morning, Pilar got to MJ's cell just two minutes late, having brushed her teeth and hair! As the days passed, her mind spun less and breathed more. There was less questioning, worrying, meaning-making. Less language and more imagery.

She sat in MJ's hard-backed chair, but moved through the mines. She felt her way through tunnels that snaked and narrowed, rose and dipped. She stumbled and picked herself up, ran her palms over cool rock walls. The passages tightened as she went deeper. She listened for silver in the stake's ring—a vibration spreading outwards through her body. The mine's vein became the body's became the brain's. Darkness hurtled toward her, had no end. She ran into its bend and wind, breathed it in— *forever and ever, Amen.*

Less imagery and more space. The cell walls fell away and she breathed in time with all eight Sisters and even Mother Connie. Their chests rose and fell in a single continuous wave. When she opened her eyes, the world was colored pale blue by belief.

After morning rituals, Pilar helped with classes, paperwork, and calls at Project Luz. She called her father after dinner. He marveled over a rare roseate spoonbill sighting, described a sunset or lightning storm. His breathing was even and he coughed less. Pilar would talk about her students or what Margarita had made for dinner. She encouraged him to go to Carlos' grandmother's orphans' dinner. He said he'd try, but she knew all those people would make him nervous. He'd be happier spending Christmas with La Llanura.

After talking to her father, she cleaned the Daughter House. The physicality of it complemented the morning stillness, the movement a counter to the immovable bureaucracies she dealt with at Project Luz—hours of phone holds and transfers between administrative departments ending in a dropped call. Centering prayer helped her to ride the ups and downs with more detachment. Each night, she moved through the rooms of the Daughter House, cleaning out decades of dust. When she finished cleaning a room, she left its window open to the night air so that it breathed proud and bare.

Everything was opening—sentences, prayers completing each other. *Before a word is on my tongue, you, Lord, know it completely*, she sang. She came to distinguish the particular notes of each Sister's song. She stopped praying so hard, trying so hard. God had a plan. She was meant to spend Christmas with the Sisters, growing strong enough in her faith to save her father. The days when they'd spun freedom from darkness returned.

On Christmas Eve morning, the Sisters woke an hour later so they'd make it through Midnight Mass. Pilar chanted with them in Latin. She kneeled and prostrated her face to the floor with the Sisters as they spoke of God becoming flesh. Her self-consciousness dissolved into their pools of brown polyester, hairy moles, double chins, turkey necks, and jiggling underarms—bathed by the blue-stained light into one eternal body.

The children performed their Nativity play at a 4 p.m. Vigil Mass. The Baby Jesus cantaloupe had been replaced with a doll, which a covetous toddler in a sheep pinafore stole from its crib and ran into the congregation with. Mother Mary ran after her, but only Sheep Julie's actual mother, in an impressive interception, managed to wrest the Baby Jesus from her grasp, return Him to His crib, and hold onto her protesting sheep for the shaky duration of the play. The Sisters laughed uproariously as they re-enacted this warmly received fiasco over dinner.

After dinner, Pilar called her father and they opened their gifts to each other. It was their tradition to open a gift on Christmas Eve. Her father always wrapped hers in the funny papers, more for the color than the jokes, which fell flat when they read them. Pilar's eyes filled when she opened his shoebox full of cinnamon buñuelos wrapped in *Peanuts* and *Garfield* strips and read the Spanish card meant for a younger daughter, a worn 20-dollar bill tucked inside.

"I'm sorry it's not more," he said.

"Do you know how much I've been craving these?" Pilar sniffled. "I'll have to share them with the Sisters or I'll eat them all. Thank you, Papá."

Her father flipped through the book on the birds of south Texas. He described a perfect V of wild geese swooping low, gliding across and landing on the resaca.

A sign, Pilar thought.

Before Midnight Mass, Carlos texted, "Merry Christmas Eve!" and sent a photo of the Sisters Feng after their Christmas Eve Extravaganza wearing sexy Santa and green sequin elf dresses, which is what Carmen wore with dramatic green eye makeup and tinsel lashes.

"You look divine," Pilar texted.

"Abuela might use a different word, but we were," Carlos wrote.

They'd gotten each other's packages and made plans to talk on Christmas. "I've got dim sum with the Sisters, so it'll probably be later in the day."

"Perfect. Good luck with the dim sum!" Pilar texted, thinking it was some kind of drag show.

As throngs of families filed into Midnight Mass, the Sisters sang "Silent Night", "The First Noel", and "What Child Is This?". Pilar stood beside MJ, freed by her joyful, inharmonious voice.

"I told you we'd skip 'Rockin Around the Christmas Tree'," she said.

"Thank God," Pilar said.

She finished cleaning the Daughter House after Midnight Mass and tumbled into the nearest bed. She dreamed of the swallow her father had rescued from the mine. In the story her father told, Roberto had carried the swallow out of the mine. But in her dream, her father, wrinkled and coughing, opened Roberto's red bandana and freed the bird. Its bright blue wings spread over the graveyard.

The Sisters woke on their own time Christmas morning and enjoyed a leisurely, garrulous breakfast of pastries that Margarita had made with citrus fruit from the garden. Mother Connie left them to their celebrations, choosing to honor the Lord's birthday in solitude. After a 10:30 Mass, they chatted with parishioners, then opened gifts.

The Sunday schoolers had decorated a kumquat tree in the community garden with red bows and homemade ornaments. The Sisters packed a picnic and spread a blanket beneath this Christmas kumquat. They ate egg salad and cheddar, avocado, and tomato sandwiches. They raved about her father's buñuelos.

"Do you miss him?" Robin asked.

"Normally I'd worry about him, but we've been talking every day and... I've been worrying less." Pilar smiled and shrugged.

"That's the centering prayer," MJ said and the Sisters nodded deeply.

Margarita had sewn the Sisters' MoS-monogrammed tote bags and an overnight bag for Pilar, Letitia had painted them watercolors of the community garden, and Robin had gotten them used books. MJ had made wooden bookends engraved with Ecclesiastes 3:1-8 (*For everything there is a season*), leaves falling around the verses.

Pilar shared some of her religion paper and told the Sisters how she'd come to appreciate, through them, her solitary childhood, but she didn't talk about her father's status. Robin stared at her in that intent way she had, and Pilar looked away—at the leaves flickering in the early afternoon light.

She was smiling when she turned back to the Sisters. "I have something to show you," she said. "I just need the key to the Daughter House."

The Sisters looked at each other.

"I guess we should give you this, then." MJ handed her a small wooden box. "From all of us."

Pilar opened the hinged lid and found the Daughter House key on its swallow keyring. She worried that the Sisters had found out her surprise.

"It's a work in progress," Robin said. "But we've drawn up a chore chart and it'll be ready by the New Year. Then you can stay there whenever, sleep in a different room every time! No one uses it, so you can leave things, make it your own."

"It may be ready sooner." Pilar smiled through tears as she pulled on her tennis shoes. She motioned for the Sisters to join her as she headed back to the monastery. She let them climb the spiral staircase ahead of her, supporting Marie Therese by the elbow.

Pilar unlocked the hall and watched the Sisters file in, exclamations of, *Holy moly! How long has it been?* ensuing. She'd left all the doors and windows open. Light poured in and the air smelled of lemons.

The Sisters found the rooms they'd lived in as novices. Pilar stood in the doorway of Sister Robin's old room as she sat on the bed, ran her hand over the pilled blanket. "I had this recurring dream when I slept here." Her voice drifted into the softer realm of memory. "Of floating on my back in a luminous sea."

"I had a dream of my house being consumed by flames," Letitia said from the room across the hall. "I watched, utterly at peace."

MJ stood in the doorway of the last room and put her fingers to her lips.

"Was it yours?" Pilar asked.

MJ shook her head slowly. "Flor's." Her eyes were shiny when she turned to Pilar. She blinked them clear and looked at her with wonder. "Where did you come from?" she asked.

"Where Texas ends, and the fun begins!" Pilar said loud enough for Robin to hear.

Robin let out a musical tumble of laughter.

Marie Therese, who was very deaf, somewhat senile, and rarely spoke, wandered out of her old dorm room into the hall. Her thin lips spread into a grin, folds of skin engulfing her sharp blue eyes. "I had a lover, a soldier returned from the war," she announced in a quavering voice. "We made love in the top balcony pew. It was the closest to God I've ever been."

The Sisters widened their eyes at this small, wrinkled woman and exchanged glances.

"Good for you!" MJ cried and they all burst into laughter.

"I smoked on the roof!" Robin said.

"I'd blast Sérgio Mendes in the kitchen," Margarita said. "*Never gonna let you go / Gonna hold your body close to mine!*" she belted.

"I made margaritas," Soledad said.

And then they all looked at Pilar and said, "Don't tell Mother Connie."

Pilar zipped her lips.

The Sisters had a couple of hours to call family, pray, nap, or stroll the grounds before they helped Margarita with Christmas dinner. Pilar moved her things into the Daughter House. She was drawn to the last room, the one that had been Flor's. She sat on the bed and opened Carlos' gift—a scarf painted like an ocean. Washes of deep blue, green, turquoise, and aquamarine bled into one another on delicate silk. It was extravagantly beautiful, expensive looking. It felt out of place in her plain room with its bare walls, scratchy brown wool blanket, and scuffed furniture. Pilar felt a rush of love when she turned over the "About the Artist" card to read: *An ocean of love. Always, Carlos*, but it seemed a waste that he'd spent so much on her. She wasn't a scarf wearer, especially now. The Sisters had their uniform and she had hers—white shirts and jeans laid out the night before so that she could dress without thought for morning rituals.

It made her feel distant from Carlos. She imagined telling him about what she'd experienced over the past week—that she understood her father as she never had, that she was happy. Carlos would make light of it or worry about her. This new life she was carrying inside was real. If Carlos couldn't understand it, could they know each other? Love each other?

———————————

Drunk and exhausted after their Christmas Eve Extravaganza, the Sisters Feng went home in drag. Carlos and Max slept over at Tony, Mike, and Carter's Alphabet City apartment. They had a reservation for Christmas dim sum at 1 the next afternoon and gifts for each other tucked in their roller suitcases. They ordered pizza and freed themselves from their corsets, electric tape, spanks, silver tinsel lashes, wigs, and heels. Tony and Carter fought over the bathroom, Mike washed his face at the kitchen sink, and Carlos and Max fell asleep in their makeup on an air mattress in the living room.

Carlos wished Abuela Merry Christmas while waiting for the bathroom the next morning (morning in Texas anyway). She'd been up cooking for her orphans' dinner for hours. Carlos' head was throbbing and he wished she'd stop clanging pans. He washed two aspirin down with coffee. Abuela told him she'd made the cream cheese and jalapeño tamales he loved (and pretended were vegetarian even though they were made with lard). She was planning to wear the blouse he'd given her. He told her to wear it with the dangly silver and turquoise earrings he'd helped her pick out at a street fair.

"I know the ones."

Carlos told her he was headed out for his own orphans' celebration.

"I'm glad you have people to celebrate with, mijo. Take the Santo!"

"Always," Carlos said.

Tony, Mike, Carter, Max, and Carlos started out walking the mile and a half to Chinatown. Though they'd seen every part of each other, Carlos had never been out with any of them besides Max in boy clothes in daylight. In skinny jeans, sweaters, coats, hats, scarves, gloves, and boots, they were a band of brothers, careening together to avoid a truck's splash. The light was bright, but it was freezing. Max hooked his arm through Carlos' and huddled close as the wind whipped around them.

"That's *it*!" Max's arm shot up as a cab approached. "I'm totally gonna be one of those Jews who retires to Boca," he said as the five of them scrambled into the taxi, Carlos on Max's lap and Carter in the front seat.

The driver looked at Carter with a long face and shook his head. The legal passenger limit was four.

"But it's *Christmas*!" Carter protested.

The driver resignedly stepped on the gas.

The Brothers cheered and pooled their cash to tip him well.

Christmas dim sum had become a Feng Brothers tradition after a turkey disaster two Christmases ago. Lamont met them at Jin Fong, and the host led the six of them through the capacious red-hued banquet hall to their table in the round. Servers wheeled metal food carts trailing mouthwatering aromas through the hall and patrons called out for their favorites.

Carlos went pescatarian. His brothers told him which of the dumplings, buns, rolls, puffs, and tarts had meat in them, but Carlos didn't ask for much guidance beyond that. He liked the surprise of not knowing whether a dish would be sweet or savory, or what the texture would be like.

After they'd eaten, they exchanged gift certificates for taxis, makeup, and beauty treatments. Carlos had made each of his Feng brothers a personalized mixed CD. He'd written the songs—alluding to private jokes, shared experiences, or wishes for the new year—in a spiral of red and green swirling outward from the CD hole. Tony, Mike, and Carter gave Carlos a key to their apartment wrapped up in a gift box. "We think you'll be doing a lot more shows after you graduate, and we don't want your sweet babydrag self going home to Brooklyn alone," Tony said. Mike and Carter seconded this sentiment with deep nods and Carlos' eyes filled.

Max gave everyone gift certificates for his favorite stylists, except for Carlos, whom he gave a book of Alvin Baltrop's photos of the underground gay culture along the Hudson in the 70s. They'd seen and loved an exhibit of Baltrop's work at the Museum of the City of New York.

Carlos looked up from languid photos of men sunbathing nude on the derelict piers, cruising in crumbling warehouses, to catch Max watching him with raw want—all his pomp and padding fallen away to reveal this hungry, vulnerable boy. Like a painting you'd passed a million times and never looked at until some collision of mood and circumstance made you stop. And then you couldn't stop looking; you stepped closer to take in its light and shadow.

The Brothers Feng exchanged glances, but Carlos and Max were in a world of their own.

Carlos put his hand on Max's thigh beneath the table and whispered, "I love it," beneath the clatter of food carts.

"Come to Christmas dinner with my family," Max said. An art book, a family dinner—he knew how to play to his audience. Carlos appreciated the tailored seduction.

"I thought you were Jewish." Carlos had never met anyone Jewish until he got to Columbia and he was still learning about the wideranging spectrum of Judaism.

"*Ish*," Max said. "We always do pizza and sushi."

"A veritable festival of starches!" Carlos grinned. "Count me in."

Carlos headed home after dim sum, where his full belly, hangover, and shoddy night's sleep induced a coma-like nap. He pressed his snooze button too many times, then took too long deciding on appropriate attire for his first Jewish Christmas. He put on the blue-checked button-down that Abuela had given him, then changed into a skintight maroon T-shirt and metallic mesh sweater with a slant neckline and bell sleeves to impress Max, then changed back into the church shirt to impress Max's parents. He couldn't decide who he wanted to woo. Then he remembered that Max's parents were revolutionaries back in the day. By the time he arrived at the compromise of the metallic sweater over the blue-checked shirt (collar askew), black skinny jeans, and faux red-suede Chelsea boots, he was running a half-hour late, and that was without the subway's holiday service changes. Carlos texted Max, hoping the Goldsteins leaned toward Valley time, where gatherings didn't start until an hour past start time. Max said not to worry; sushi and pizza night was a casual affair. His family lived at 122nd Street. It would be Carlos' first return to Columbiaville since school let out. He tucked Pilar's gift, which looked like a book of some sort wrapped in brown parcel paper and tied with red ribbon, into his tote bag. He ran to the subway, though his boots weren't made for walking, much less running.

Carlos sat at the end of a mostly empty subway car and opened Pilar's gift. He'd introduced her to Laurie Anderson, but he hadn't known about *Night Life*. Pilar had out-cultured him; he beamed with cool older brother pride. She'd bookmarked two drawings: one of four women on a couch floating down a river in the fog. The caption read: "I'm not sure whether they're people I know or people from paintings. I really wish I could go with them but there's no room on the couch. I shout but they don't seem to hear me." Another of figures sock-skating in a boardroom, their arms thrown back like wings, captioned: "The meeting with the production company is really awkward. To lighten the mood, I pretend to skate—sliding my feet and spinning. Humming ice skating music. Some people think this is a ridiculous interruption. Others begin to give it a try."

She'd inscribed the title page: *If anyone can sock-skate in a boardroom, it's you. And I'll always make room on the couch. Wishing you a year of wild, sweet, wondrous dreams realized. Love, Pilar*

He flipped through the drawings. The book was everything wonderful about Pilar: obsessively thoughtful, beautiful, strange, and a bit dark. He stared at the drawing of the women drifting out in the boat. He looked up at the blue subway tunnel lights cast over a scrawl of graffiti—as if the words were moving through water—and remembered nights of drifting through the resaca with Pilar. He hadn't felt that peaceful in a long time.

He texted her when he got out at 116th Street: *I love NIGHT LIFE—and you! On my way to dinner, but I'll call you tonight. Xxx*

I'm so glad, Pilar texted back. *I loved the scarf—thank you! Enjoy dinner, looking forward to hearing about it. xo*

Carlos bought poinsettias on his way, deliberating over their appropriateness for a Jewish Christmas. Oh, who cared? They were pretty.

He climbed the steps to the Goldsteins' brownstone, took off his hat, and ran his fingers through his shoulder-length hair before ringing their doorbell.

Max's mom, Susanna, tried to open the door, but a lanky-legged goldendoodle bounded toward Carlos, barking excitedly.

"Who is *this*?" Carlos set the poinsettias down and crouched to nuzzle the golden muppet. He loved dogs and dogs loved him.

"That's Ralph Jr.," Susanna said.

"As in Nader," Max said. "My parents got him to woo voters during his 2000 campaign."

"Ralph's a highly persuasive canvasser," Susanna scratched Ralph's head, "but he's on sabbatical until the next election."

Carlos tore himself away from Ralph and handed Susanna the flowers.

"Poinsettias, how festive, thank you!" A small woman with long, wavy dark hair, a red scarf headband, matching red lipstick, and sparkling brown eyes, Susanna warmly hugged Carlos. She felt the dry dirt in the poinsettia pot and carried the plant into the kitchen to water it.

Max led Carlos down a bowling alley of a hallway lined with eclectic art. He stopped to admire paintings and photographs, and Max told him about the family friends who'd made them. They passed a library with wall to wall, built-in bookshelves and a sliding ladder; walked through a living room of overstuffed couches, faded oriental rugs, and more art; and entered the dining room, where Max's dad, Stu, was laying out a copious spread of pizza and sushi and glistening bottles of wine on a natural wood table.

"The guest of honor!" Stu heartily shook Carlos' hand. He was built like Max, about five foot, seven inches and slight, with a handsome, chiseled face and stylishly cut silver hair.

"Hannah, sushi's on!" Max called.

In wandered Max's fraternal twin in snug vintage overalls and a red-and-white striped shirt. A dark brown swing bob framed a face at once delicate and playful.

"My vegetarian comrade!" She high-fived Carlos. She'd made sure that they had plenty of veggie pizza and avocado and sweet potato rolls.

They filled their plates and glasses and dove into the food and conversation. Susanna and Stu were youthful, talkative, and funny. They and Hannah were all so curious about Carlos—asking about what it was like to go from Texas to New York, his classes, Mask and Wig. Every question led to another question. They laughed at Carlos' jokes and seemed only mildly disappointed that he wasn't more politically engaged.

"Max is the same way," Susanna said. "We dragged him to one too many protests as a child."

Carlos found himself dramatically recounting the Metamorphosis. He wasn't sure why at first, beyond the fact that Max kept refilling his wine glass. As his political/apolitical *This I Believe* statement? Then he skirted around the details that made him look ungenerous and knew exactly why.

"So much of the language around gender and sexuality is new," Stu said. "Max teaches us things all the time. Language is always changing, culture's always changing, and you guys are on the frontlines, pushing and pulling and shaping the future. That push and pull, the struggle to understand one another, is messy, but the important thing is to engage. You're making it up in the dark, and it should be exciting as well as terrifying. You're not just asking the big questions; you're rewriting the questions. It's incredibly brave." He beamed at Carlos and Max.

Carlos had never imagined talking so freely about being queer with parental figures, much less this silver-haired father telling him he was brave. A wave of euphoria rolled through him.

"This is why his students love him." Max smiled at his dad, then turned accusatorily to Carlos. "Why haven't I heard this story?"

"Well, we had so much else to cover," Carlos said with a twinkle in his eye.

They moved on to tales of Max's childhood performances. "He'd write these elaborate solo shows where he played *all* of the parts," Hannah said. "I'd beg to be in them, and he'd begrudgingly allow me to be his dresser."

"A queen from the beginning." Carlos shook his head.

"*Guilty!*" Max cackled. "There was room for only one star in the family! Poor Hannah had to settle for being a cancer researcher." Max rolled down his bottom lip and wiped a single imaginary tear.

Max and Hannah's repartee made Carlos miss Pilar. He checked his phone and saw that it was 11:30; she'd probably go to bed soon. "I'm sorry," he said, pushing back from the table. "I have to call my... family."

Max offered his bedroom. "Second door on the right."

It was easy to find with its posters of James Dean, *Hedwig and the Angry Inch*, and Judy Garland. Carlos closed the door, sat on the bed, and called Pilar.

"Hi... Merry Christmas," she said somewhat absently.

"Merry Christmas! Sorry for calling so late, I lost track of time. I'm having the BEST Jewish Christmas." Carlos had holiday cheer for the both of them. He filled Pilar's silence with idolizing stories about Max's family, to which she offered little response.

"Are you okay?" he finally asked, miffed by her refusal to join in his joy.

"I'm okay," Pilar said. "I was just meditating."

She wasn't upset, just out of it. "So you liked the scarf?" he prodded.

"It's beautiful."

Carlos excitedly told her about the artist who'd sold it to him and all the ways she could wear it—as a loop, a pretzel, a knot, a necktie, a twisted necklace, a head wrap—all just with a white shirt. "Anyway, I just thought you could use a little flair!"

"Thank you," Pilar said flatly. There was a long pause. "Did you have a chance to look at *Night Life*? Isn't it like Anderson's this wonderfully honest friend with an eye for the absurd walking you though the creative process?"

Hurt by her failure to gush over the scarf, Carlos said coolly, "I flipped through it on the subway. I don't know how she remembered her dreams so vividly. I never remember mine. Thanks to the whisky, I guess."

Pilar never laughed when he joked about drinking; he knew it made her worry. "You're not, like, blacking out, are you?" she asked.

Carlos didn't care for her judgement. "I don't remember!" He laughed. "So is all this talk about the creative process your way of telling me you're writing poetry again?!"

"I'm creating other things," Pilar said defensively.

"Like what?" Carlos asked.

Pilar always tensed up when he asked if she was writing. He changed the subject. "Speaking of art, Max gave me the best gift." He talked about Baltrop's photographs, describing his favorites.

"Are you guys dating?" Pilar asked hesitantly.

"No. We're just... friends." If he described Max's and his movement into something more, Pilar would be overly excited. And he didn't want to get ahead of himself.

She went quiet again.

"What did the Holy Ladies give you?" Carlos asked.

Pilar told him about the Sisters' gifts and cleaning the Daughter House for them.

"You're cleaning their convent for free?" Carlos couldn't stop his voice from rising an octave. It sounded culty. He worried that Pilar's naivety was being taken advantage of.

"It wouldn't hurt you to serve something greater than yourself," Pilar said. She added more softly, "It was kind of a gift to myself, too, since they're letting me stay here whenever I want."

"Mmm." Even more culty. Pilar's deepening obsession with the Church could lead nowhere good, but Carlos didn't know what he could say that would make a difference.

"How did the dim—what did you say it was—go?" Pilar asked.

Carlos described the massive banquet hall, food carts, endless steamer baskets of bite-sized food, and the Feng gift exchange.

"That sounds nice," Pilar said.

Carlos knew she thought they were superficial. "I should get back to dinner," he said. "You would so love this family, Pilar."

"Okay, have fun," Pilar said, but sounded hurt. "Merry Christmas," she added.

"You, too," Carlos said. It seemed like she was waiting for something more, but he couldn't bring himself to say, "I love you."

Carlos stood at the window after ending the call. Snow had begun to fall, muffling everything. Loneliness washed over him. He rubbed the coin on his mother's necklace.

The door creaked open and Ralph Jr. nosed his way in, sat on Carlos' feet, and looked up at him with soulful eyes. Carlos gave him a good long belly rub, until his tail thumped the floor. They returned to the dining room together.

"I see Ralph's delivered you back to us," Stu said. Ralph trotted over to Stu, who patted his head and whispered, "Good work."

"I wasn't sure if you were still hungry, but I saved the last avocado roll for you," Hannah said.

"Thank you, I'm stuffed," Carlos said.

Max gave him a questioning look. "Good call?"

Carlos smiled weakly.

Susanna looked out the window at the snow. "It's really coming down out there!" She turned to Carlos. "I don't want you going home in that. Why don't you spend the night?"

Carlos looked from Susanna to Max, who said, "Yeah, you should stay."

Carlos looked down at his faux red-suede Chelsea boots. "Well, these boots weren't really made for snow."

"Good, it's settled." Stu clasped his hands and stood up from the table. "Everybody stays!"

It was a three-bedroom apartment. Carlos and Max got his old room with its double bed.

"I can make up the couch if that bed's too small." Susanna stood in the doorway looking between Max and Carlos, who sat on Max's childhood bed like teenagers who'd just hidden the pot they'd been smoking.

"I think we'll just fit." Max smirked.

"Okay, goodnight then," Susanna said, mirth in her eyes before she shut the door.

Max flopped backwards onto the bed. "She totally knows," he said, staring up at the ceiling.

"Knows what?" Carlos grinned and Max playfully shoved him.

"Your family's great." Carlos propped himself up on his elbow, facing Max.

"*Most* of the time, my family's great. Everybody loves pizza and sushi night—except for when Hannah brought that boyfriend we all hated. Was your call with your family okay? You looked upset."

"It was actually my friend Pilar. We grew up together. She's like a sister." Carlos looked away, scrunched up his face. "I just— I don't know. I just feel like we don't understand each other anymore."

"I feel shitty when something comes between Hannah and me," Max said. "We had our own twin language when we were little."

Carlos' eyes filled.

"Maybe text her? You don't want to sleep on bad feelings."

Carlos thought about it for a minute before texting, *It was good talking. So glad you had a good Christmas. xo* There was a bitter taste in his mouth as he sent it. He powered off his phone because he didn't want to read her response, which would be equally sweet—and distant. He didn't want to worry about her.

He turned back to Max, who slung his leg around Carlos' back. "Feel better?"

"Starting to," Carlos said.

Max looked in his eyes, all the confidence with which he stared out an audience laser-focused on his audience of one: *You are what I want and you want this, too.*

Again the pleasurable tingle of surprise, this face Carlos had watched transform a hundred times, transformed again. How many times had they seen each other naked? Still the air between them sharpened. How many times had he tied Max into his corset, and yet it was exciting to slip his hands under his T-shirt, run them over his stomach and chest. Exciting, too, that it was happening inside family life—sanctioned and slightly illicit. Carlos liked this shift into something else—Max's hand on the back of his neck, sudden ravenous pressure of those lips he'd studied as Max painted them. The sexiness of this unbuttoning, unzipping, untucking, re-seeing—someone known becoming unknown and then known again.

CHAPTER 12

Padre Bob was hardly the inspirational speaker Pilar had imagined. He wore lay clothes and was a large man in his 50s with close-cropped gray hair, a ruddy face, heavy eyelids and jowls, and a fastidious demeanor. He spoke in English and Spanish and had a tendency to get caught up in the minutiae of immigration policy changes, staring into the distance. Returning to their clouded faces, he'd translate without the tangents. MJ, Robin, and Soledad stood in the back of the classroom since all of the seats were taken. Pilar had tried to give up her seat, but they wouldn't have it. The rows were filled with Latine and a few Asian people. Pilar recognized some of them from Mass. Padre Bob explained that they would learn what to do during four stages, which he wrote on the chalkboard:

1.) INTAKE
2.) TIMELINE
3.) DOCUMENT GATHERING
4.) CREATING A CASE PLAN

Pilar's mind wandered during the dry, informational talk. She pulled her father's last postcard, of a pelican, from her bag. It wasn't Christmas until the pelicans came. Whoever saw them first would pull the other onto the porch and they'd watch them paddle, preen, and bob, dipping their long, pouched bills into the water, transfixed by their languid water ballet. *They didn't bother to come without you here*, her father had written. *Next year! Love, Papá*

She put the postcard away and took slow, deep breaths the way she did during centering prayer. She felt the people around her—the mother to her right, stilling the kicking legs of her daughter; the man her father's age to her left, whispering to his wife. Some, like Pilar, were alone, taking notes on the back of the informational sheet that Padre Bob had distributed. But she didn't feel alone. She felt connected to everyone there—a current moving through them.

She re-focused, leaned forward, and wrote everything down. Padre Bob did conclude in an inspirational, if somewhat bumperstickerish, way, saying, "No one understands your case better than you. You are your own greatest defender." There was a Q&A session, after which MJ, Robin, and Soledad ushered people out through the reception area, and a handful of people lined up to talk with Padre Bob. Pilar waited until he'd finished talking to the last person. Watching him light up over babies and laugh with people he knew from La Placita, she saw that he was a softy beneath his hard-boiled exterior.

Approaching Padre Bob after everyone had left felt fated, as if her whole life had led her to this. Pilar introduced herself, told him about volunteering at Project Luz. Talk from the reception area drifted into the classroom. Pilar glanced at the open door. "Would it be alright if we spoke in private?"

"Of course." Padre Bob closed the door and pulled two chairs to the front of the room. He motioned for Pilar to sit.

She felt like pacing but forced herself to sit. She wiped her sweaty palms on her jeans and shifted uncomfortably. She remembered her father sitting in a child's chair in Mrs. Guerra's classroom after she'd gotten in trouble for sticking out her tongue. Her tongue was a calcified lump now. It wasn't just that she hadn't told anyone besides Carlos. It hurt to hope so hard.

"I'm sorry." She shook her head.

"Take your time, my child." Padre Bob sat back in his chair, folded his hands in his lap.

Pilar closed her eyes and visualized her father getting papers that legalized his life, finding a job with benefits, seeing a specialist, making friends. Living without fear.

She opened her eyes and asked for these things. Her words had been so long buried that they sounded foreign: "My father came here from Bolivia in 1984 and he's been living without papers since then. I was born here and I want to know if I can petition for his green card."

Not in the business of creating false hope, Padre Bob answered quickly. "The only way would be for him to return to Bolivia for 10 years and come back."

"I thought— He can't— There must be something I can—" There was no path.

Padre filled her silence with legal talk. "Unfortunately, I have to tell people this all the time. If your father had arrived a few years earlier, he would've gotten amnesty under Reagan. But the waiver he'd need now can only come through a spouse or a parent, not a child."

His words washed over Pilar.

"I'm sorry, my child. I wish I had something more hopeful to tell you." He rose and laid a hand on her shoulder. "I'm going to let you take a moment." He left her alone in the classroom, closing the door behind him.

Pilar sat motionless in the chair. Before, so much energy had coursed through her that she'd had trouble sitting. She had a different body now: heavy, empty. It seemed pointless to stand. Her knees would buckle. She stared, unmoving, as chalk ghost-words about claiming your life became line after line of, *I will not stick out my tongue.*

When she finally left Project Luz, it was dark and everyone was gone. The Sisters were all in private contemplation, the monastery heavy with silence. She walked without thinking through shadowy corridors emptied of belief.

She'd been dreaming her life. Now she'd woken and none of it mattered. She didn't turn on the lights, but moved blindly through the dark. The sound of her footsteps, echoing—its insistence that she was a body moving through space—startled her. Then moved outside of her, into the dark.

She walked outside, no different from inside. Pointless to move, all places the same. She didn't belong here. She didn't belong anywhere.

There was nothing she could do. No path. She walked into the garden and stood before the kumquat tree where she'd opened gifts with the Sisters. Where she'd been blessed. That place—light through glossy green leaves—no longer existed.

An afterlife now. She'd just come to see what remained. She took off her shoes and walked barefoot through the dark, stumbled over roots and felt nothing. No pain, path, ground to break or hold her.

She started when a shadow beside the vegetable garden moved. As she got closer, she made out a body sitting, rumpled plaid pajama bottoms spread out in the grass.

"*Pilar?*"

It took a moment to come out of herself, make out the shape of this other life. Pilar squinted at Sister Letitia, who ran the garden. She didn't ask why Pilar was wandering through it in the dark, but talked up at her from the dirt, filling her silence.

"I was meditating, trying to focus on my breathing, but the smell of the holy basil on my windowsill got to be overpowering. It was crying to be let out of its little pot!"

It was absurd—and grounding somehow—that while she was wandering through what felt like the end of her life, this night prowler nun was planting holy basil beneath the moon.

"The roots take better hold at night," Letitia said.

Pilar nodded.

Interpreting her silence as judgement, Letitia confessed, "The truth is I'm out here a lot when we're supposed to be in our cells. I spent so much of my life in little rooms where people were dying. I feel closer to God with the crickets chirping." Letitia had been a nurse at St. Vincent's Hospital in Greenwich Village at the height of the AIDS epidemic.

Pilar nodded. She didn't hear crickets.

"The immigration clinic was tonight, wasn't it? How did it go?"

Pilar told her what had happened, like it had happened to someone else.

Letitia stood and put her hand on Pilar's back. "I'm so sorry." She stood still with her for a long time.

The warmth of Letitia's hand between her shoulder blades opened a hollow in her lungs. Her eyes stung. "I wanted it for him—us—so much." Pilar closed her eyes, let the tears spill.

"I'm glad you're out here," Letitia said. "Will you plant it?" She gestured at the small pot of holy basil at the edge of the garden.

Together they kneeled in the dirt. Pilar dug a hole with her hands. She thought of her father digging graves at night. Letitia unpotted the holy basil and handed her the seedling. The air filled with the smell of mint and lemon and the sound of crickets—rhythmic as a heart. Pilar pressed the plant's roots into the cool soil and covered them over.

Pilar slept through morning rituals and Mass the next day. She was just waking when MJ knocked on her door. Padre Bob hadn't told MJ what they'd talked about, just that she might check in. Telling Letitia, her voice had become a part of the soil, stars, crickets. Not less sad, but less consuming.

Telling MJ made it real, but also less heavy. This 64-year-old woman with her own sorrows, sitting beside her on her bed, was also real. MJ sat with her in her sadness, didn't push her to move beyond it. "I'm sorry," she said. She didn't talk about God. "Take the day to rest, walk... be," she said.

In the past, Pilar would have talked to Carlos. His anger would have stampeded over her sadness, but she would have felt him as a balance, his absence of hope leveling her excess. She would have felt better because he was the person she told these things, the person who'd known when no one else knew, who understood. But something had shifted. Their conversation on Christmas had left a bruise, still tender to the touch. He'd warned her not to get her hopes up. She'd imagined telling him after she'd begun filing the petition. No matter what he said now, it would be hard not to hear, *I told you so.* She needed to be in a better place to tell him.

She packed a sandwich, her notebook, and *Dream Work*, which Ceci had returned, in her backpack. She walked and sat beneath the trees. She didn't feel like writing, but looked at things with that attention. She watched a mother with her toddler daughter, the glee on the child's face as she wobbled a few bowlegged steps, then fell; the stunned space before she opened her mouth and howled. She noticed where Ceci had dog-eared pages of *Dream Work*—the trace of her young life through the pages.

Robin found her outside, not because MJ had told her, but because Pilar hadn't come to lunch. Pilar told Robin, too. It was becoming easier to speak it. Robin didn't offer advice, tell her how to feel. She didn't try to make it better, because she couldn't. She sat beneath an oak tree with Pilar as she ate her sandwich. The Sisters had faith in stillness.

Mother of Sorrows was a place that would wait, as long as she needed. The endless, empty stretch of time had been unbearable in high school. She'd needed Carlos, then—screech of guitars to rupture that silence. But the slow, patient listening of this place was what she needed now.

Pilar walked through the community garden and Letitia brought her freshly picked clementines, cradled in her shirt. She remembered gathering bruised oranges in her shirt as a child and hurling them at trucks on the days her mother did not come. She thanked Letitia, put the clementines in her backpack.

She brought them to her students the next day. Their sharp, sweet smell filled the air as she said, "My father's undocumented and I thought I could petition for his green card. But I can't. When I was little, he told me not to tell anyone. I'm telling you now because I want you to write about something you've never told anyone. You don't have to share it with the class, but I want you to know that you're safe here."

She let them move their desks out of the circle. They pushed into a solitary corner or sat on the floor and leaned against the wall with their eyes closed. At first they guardedly hunched over their notebooks, all elbows and furtive glances, but gradually the motion of their pens across the page, of the story they were telling, overtook their self-consciousness, and the knots of their bodies unraveled. Pilar was surprised by how they threw themselves into the writing, as if they'd been waiting to be asked.

Pilar didn't ask them to read it or turn it in. But Ceci shyly handed what she'd written to Pilar after the other students left. Pilar convinced her to share it with the other students in the next class.

The next Saturday, Pilar moved the desks back into a circle. Ceci stood in the center with her notebook. Her voice was shaky at first, but grew stronger. "What my mom wants most for me is a good education. She took a third job to send me to Catholic school when I started junior high. I don't have a dad and already my mom cleaned hotel rooms in the mornings and worked as a nanny in the afternoons. When I started Catholic school, she took a night job. She told me she was cleaning offices. There was no one to kiss me goodnight. My mom was gone until morning, when I saw her beautiful, tired face telling me to wake up for school. I missed her. I gave her my piggy bank. I told her I wanted to go to regular school, but she said I needed a good education so I wouldn't have to work three jobs like her.

"One night I couldn't sleep. I heard Mom getting ready for work. I got dressed and followed her outside. I was shocked to see her digging through our neighbor's trash for cans, wearing rubber gloves and raggedy old pants and pushing a shopping cart. My mother was a can collector. All those nights, I'd thought she was off in some skyscraper when she was wandering around my neighborhood. I joined her that night. I rode around on my scooter while Mom went from trash can to trash can looking for cans that we could sell for five cents. Soon, I had my own shopping

cart, gloves, and bags. I became a can collector, covering one side of a
block, while my mother covered the other. We were the only ones in the
street and everything was quiet, as if we shared a secret. Now I tell you
the secret." Ceci pushed her braid over her shoulder. The class held its
breath for a beat before cries of *¡Adelante!* and poetry snaps broke the
silence. When she sat down, the girl next to her gave her a hug.

Other students volunteered to read: A girl read about waking at dawn
to wait with her little brothers in a bread line; a boy about the summer
his family lived out of their car; another girl about the night her father
tried to strangle her mother, how they'd left in the middle of the night
and driven across the country to LA. They somehow found language for
these experiences that was raw and pulsing. Still the power was not in
the words, but the ruptured silence. Their voices went from shaky to sure;
their shoulders straightened. You could feel the heaviness, separateness
lifting from the air. Pilar felt a part of the circle and something beyond it.
She felt lighter.

"You built something today," she said. "You felt it, right?" They nodded.
"What if we built it bigger?" She proposed an open mic night where they
could share their writing. They balked at the idea at first. Pilar asked what
they'd felt after they read and when they listened to their classmates and
they talked about feeling less alone. "You could give that to people," Pilar
said. Soon they were spouting ideas for the open mic night—not just writing but music and dance—Pilar scrambling to list them all on the board.

MJ, Robin, and Letitia were happy to see Pilar so animated as she proposed the open mic night over dinner. Robin got the go-ahead from Mother Connie, who was fine with it as long as she didn't have to be involved,
and they set a date for a Saturday night a month away. Pilar returned to
SAU that Monday, but lived for weekend rehearsals with her students.
Saturdays, they worked on their readings, but on Sundays they practiced
other talents. They pulled her outside of herself. Albert, who always wore
Hawaiian shirts and cargo shorts, worked on a yo-yo act choreographed

to De La Soul's "Me, Myself, and I"; Lily, who sang in the church choir, sang "Beautiful" by Christina Aguilera; Sebastian, who wore square red glasses, played a mildly off-key but singalong worthy "Lean on Me" on his trumpet; and Lexi, Desiree, and Amanda performed a dance routine to Beyonce's "Déjà Vu".

Pilar didn't participate in morning rituals or attend Mass. She and God were taking a break. It was too simplistic to say she felt that God had let her down, like they'd had some binding contract. She didn't believe that, but there was pain around praying, an ache around the word *God*. Prying into it hurt, so she let it be. She channeled that energy into her students, helping them excerpt, workshop, revise, and perform six minutes of their strongest work. When she couldn't sleep, she pulled her laptop into bed and responded to their work. Hovering over her students' words in the dark felt like prayer.

Each student practiced their reading inside the circle of desks. Their classmates developed an ear for what needed flesh and what could be cut. They wanted not only for their six minutes to shine, but for the whole of open mic night to blaze. They insisted that those 120 minutes and the linebreaks, verbs, pauses, and gestures leading up to them mattered. Pilar lived inside their belief. Her chest swelled when a student practiced their reading again and again and finally nailed it. The child self that hadn't fit in anywhere, that she'd mostly wanted to leave, made sense inside this circle of desks.

Pilar and Carlos had kept in touch by text since Christmas. Neither of them wanted to hear the disconnect in each other's voices. Pilar texted Carlos about how rehearsals for open mic night were going and Carlos texted her about school or sent a photo from a Lucky Feng's show. Carmen would be in Cher's lap with her heels crossed in the air, or Cher would have her arms locked around Carmen from behind, but Carlos still had said nothing about their dating. Pilar hadn't told Carlos about her talk with Padre, but then he hadn't asked.

The weekend after Christmas, Carlos made the mistake of assuming he'd go home with Max after their Lucky Feng's show. Max, Carlos, Tony, Mike, and Carter walked up 1st Avenue together before the Aphabet City crew turned east. When Max went to hug them goodbye, Carlos did, too.

"Aren't you going with them?" Max asked.

"Oh." Carlos unfurrowed his brow into neutral, casual, cool. "I can."

"Tonight's no good. A friend is coming over."

Carlos imagined another boy the object of Max's spotlight stare.

Tony, Mike, and Carter exchanged knowing glances.

"Spend the night with us!" Tony said. "We'll do brunch tomorrow."

"Done!" Carlos pecked Max on the cheek and headed off with the Alphabet City boys, forcing himself not to glance back.

From then on, he was clear on the terms of their arrangement. He told himself it was for the best. He had no time for romance once school resumed. His Senior Design course, in which he was working with a team to create an automated bike kickstand, swallowed most of his time. When he wasn't studying, he halfheartedly applied for engineering jobs, sending out a standard cover letter he didn't bother to personalize. Hoping to save enough for a summer of freedom before he started some job he hated, he took on more tutoring. He only had time to work Lucky Feng's Saturday night show. Max returned to his whirlwind schedule of performing, teaching, nannying, and commission work.

They'd get to Lucky Feng's an hour and a half before everyone else and hook up in the dressing room. If they didn't hook up before the show, it didn't happen. It took too long to get out of drag, and they were exhausted by the end of the night. The sex was good and got better the more comfortable Carlos got. Afterwards, he'd lay on the blanket they'd thrown over the floor, dazed and sated, and Max would say, "I'm gonna get a drink from the bar, you want something?" Their friendship wasn't secondary to the benefits—Max would ask about Pilar, Carlos about Max's family—and there was real affection in the care with which they helped each other dress. Susanna and Stu paid Carlos generously to walk Ralph, Jr. in Riverside Park and invited him to dinner so often that he ended up giving Max updates on his parents.

Lucky Feng's shine had begun to wane. Last Saturday, a bachelorette had thrown up all over the bathroom and Bama, in six-inch ruby heels, had slipped in the vomit, tearing her dress and pulling her hamstring. Another night, they'd been serenading a birthday girl who'd drunkenly clambered up on stage and pulled off Cher's expensively styled wig. Cher snatched back her wig and got up in Miss Birthday's face, lowering her voice so that Nathaniel, who watched from the back of the restaurant, couldn't hear. "I don't care if it *is* your birthday. You don't get to come up on stage and touch a queen."

Lucky Feng's Galentine's Day show was their usual act plus red and pink eyeshadow, heart tiaras and balloons. Carlos was meeting Max beforehand for their usual act, plus a bag of Hershey's kisses he bought at a bodega on the walk from the subway. Carlos paused outside of Lucky Feng's to watch couples enter the French bistro next door, and felt a momentary longing for a relationship with dinner reservations.

Which wasn't to say he wasn't looking forward to dressing room sex with Max. Unfortunately, their Valentine's hookup was just heating up when they were interrupted by a brisk knock on the locked door. As they tugged on their jeans, Nathaniel called, "Carmen! Cher! I've got news!" Of course everyone knew that Carlos and Max were hooking up, but Carlos hadn't realized that Nathaniel knew too. He gave Max a concerned look as he unlocked the door, but Max shrugged.

"Hellooo, lovebirds!" Nathaniel bustled in and perched on the makeup counter, swinging his distressed leather ankle boots. "Virgo that I am, I've been thinking ahead to our summer lineup. Bob and I had a talk after his unfortunate vomit mishap. Drag, as you know, takes its toll on the body, and Bob's been doing it since the 80s. He'd like to do fewer shows, and he suggested that *you*," Nathaniel looked intently at Carlos, "might take up the slack."

Max opened his mouth wide and baby-clapped at Carlos.

"Oh, wow..." Carlos molded his mouth into a smile. Why the sinking feeling? Was he in a funk because he and Max had torn themselves apart just as things were getting good? Or tired after a long week, with an even longer night ahead? Wasn't this what he'd been working for?

"I know you're swamped with school, but if we start working on your act this spring, I think you'll be ready to perform solo by summer," Nathaniel continued. "You know I like for girls to put in at least a year before they go solo, and by summer you'll have been here a year! Which is *perfect* timing because that's when we amp up our schedule."

Carlos pushed past the gnawing in his stomach. "I'm definitely up for performing solo this summer."

"Fabulous!" Nathaniel excitedly proposed a flamenco number to Madonna's "La Isla Bonita" while Max chimed in with ideas for costume updates.

"Wasn't Carmen Miranda Brazilian?" Carlos asked.

"Who *cares*?" Nathaniel did two flamenco snaps over his head. "Madonna was an Italian from Michigan, but she put on her red flamenco dress in that video and batted her eyes at the hot hombres!"

Nathaniel and Max continued brainstorming for his Carmen Madonna act. As Carlos looked between them—their hands sculpting his future in the air—the questions in his head crescendoed. Why wasn't he more excited? If he *werked*, he could turn his Lucky Feng's solo into a professional drag career, but did he want Max's life of shaving, tucking, padding, plucking, and self-promoting only to pour the money into his next costume? And if he didn't want that, what *did* he want? And if he didn't know what he wanted, shouldn't he become an engineer and give Abuela her dream? Was he wrong to want more? Would he spend his life working his ass off for things he no longer wanted when he achieved them?

Pilar was in her Daughter House cell trying to sleep, but final preparations for tomorrow's open mic night kept popping into her head. She switched on the lamp and was jotting down details about everything from the lineup to the pep talk she wanted to give her students when Carlos sent her a photo of the Feng Sisters in heart tiaras captioned, *Happy Galentine's Day!*

Mini quiches in oven at 5, Pilar added to her list, then texted, *Happy Galentine's Day! How'd the show go?* She would've forgotten about Valentine's Day if the Sunday schoolers hadn't decorated Project Luz with scripture valentines. Her eyes had filled when she'd read a heart decorated with Psalm 85:10: *Love & truth will meet; justice & peace will kiss,* a Hershey's kiss taped beneath it. She hadn't read any of the the others.

Hoping that Pilar's excitement for him would overtake his ennui, Carlos texted that Nathaniel was going to let him perform solo after he graduated.

Congratulations! Does this mean El Ojo's making a comeback?

Desafortunadamente, no. Nathaniel's cooked up a Carmen Miranda/ Madonna hybrid I'm calling Carmen Madonna. A flamenco number to 'La Isla Bonita'. After a second, he added: *But he's letting me sing! All the other girls lip-sync.*

Pilar felt Carlos' need for her affirmation. El Ojo hadn't needed anyone's approval. *That's wonderful,* she texted. *You have such an amazing voice.* Too amazing for cheesy Madonna covers, she thought. *Do you still feel like Carmen and Carla would never be friends?*

Pilar was not making him feel better.

Who knows? he shot back. *There've been unlikelier pairs.*

A few months ago, Pilar might have read it as a celebration of their improbable friendship, but now she absorbed its sourness like a sucker punch. Her thumbs hovered over the keys.

We're headed to Katz and I have GOT to get out of this corset, but I'll text you tomorrow, okay?

Have fun, Pilar wrote. She was hurt that Carlos didn't seem to remember that open mic night was the next day. She told herself he'd wish her luck tomorrow. Though she was staunchly opposed to multiple punctuation marks, she pushed through her resistance to finish with three deliberate, emphatic exclamation marks. *Congratulations again!!!*

But Carlos didn't read her text because the Sisters were spilling into the dressing room, turning up the volume and singing along to Stevie Wonder's "Uptight (Everything's Alright)".

The next afternoon, MJ helped Pilar set up for open mic night in the big classroom, where they'd held the immigration clinic. Pilar saw Carlos' text while setting up folding chairs.

So, you got my life update. I need the Pilar Salomé Reinfeld 411 please!

Nine students emailed me last minute changes to their readings, Pilar texted. *They're all so nervous.*

All Pilar had talked about for the last month was the open mic. After a sleepover and brunch, Carlos was back in Brooklyn, alone with his self-pitying hangover and envious of her small, easy fulfillment. He wanted to poke holes in it. He wanted her to want more. *Not your students. YOU. I don't even know if you're applying for jobs or what???*

Pilar set her phone on the table. She still didn't know what she was going to do when she graduated. When she looked at job listings, her breath caught in her chest; the words blurred. There was fear around wanting something, reaching for it. The safe, obsessive little world she was building in that classroom dissolved. Again she was sitting across from Padre, asking for something she'd wanted before she'd known it was a thing she could want.

MJ returned with a platter of fruit in one hand and cheese and crackers in the other. Pilar realized she was staring blankly at the chalkboard, her hands shaking. She relieved MJ of the platters and texted Carlos. *I've got to finish setting up and shower before the kids arrive. Talk later!*

"SHIT," Carlos said aloud. The open mic night was that night. *Pilar, I'm so sorry I forgot. I feel like an asshole,* he frantically typed. He paused before sending it. He re-read his last text, cringing but thinking it wasn't obvious he'd forgotten. Admitting it would just hurt her more. He deleted his apology and texted, *It's going to be AMAZING!! You've worked so hard.*

Try not to worry, just enjoy it. I'll be pulling for you and all of your students. Big love! BREAK A LEG!!!

But Pilar had left her phone facedown on the table and gone to put the mini quiches in the oven.

Pilar showered and dressed and hurried down to Project Luz to greet the early arrivals. She hugged parents she knew from Mass, met the few she didn't, and handed them programs she'd spent too long making. She'd encouraged her students to dress up and even Albert wore ironed khakis with his Hawaiian shirt. Seeing Ceci in black slacks and a pink blouse, she could imagine her running for office someday.

"Thank God this day has come because Sebastian's been driving us crazy with that trumpet!" his dad whispered to Pilar while Sebastian piled cookies on his plate.

Pilar laughed. "I can't wait!"

"Lily made us late changing clothes *three* times," her mother complained.

Lily clicked her tongue, shook her head, and made her way toward her friends.

"Well, she looks beautiful, *no matter what we say*," Pilar said.

"Thank you, miss," Lily said defiantly over her shoulder, and Pilar and her mother exchanged smiles.

Even Pilar had worn a sleeveless black dress and turquoise drop earrings. After reading Carlos' text, she'd put on his scarf as a headband. She'd send him a photo with her students.

All of the Sisters came, except for Marie Therese, who was too deaf to enjoy it. Even Padre Bob came. While Padre talked with Flor and the Sisters mingled with the other parents in the reception area, Pilar circled up her students in the classroom.

"I want you all to know how much I've loved watching you grow these past five months. Tonight's about celebrating that growth. Don't worry about being perfect. Just be you and know, no matter what, how proud of you I am." She looked around the circle at her students—smiling, fidgeting, chewing their bottom lip. "Okay, group hug before I cry!" They put their arms around each other and squeezed into a huddle.

Pilar caught Ceci's large, anxious eyes as the circle dispersed. *"You do not have to be good,"* she said softly.

Pilar made sure that Flor sat up front. Padre Bob sat beside her.

And then her students' voices filled the room where belief had left her. Pilar had interspersed heavier readings with lighter ones or a performance. When Lily sang "Beautiful", Pilar loved Christina Aguilera as she never had. A curly-haired boy named Miguel who'd procrastinated all through rehearsals wowed everyone with a spoken word performance of his poem. When Sofia hesitated, her classmates filled her silence with snaps and calls of, *You got this!*, parents joining in. Sofia looked out at them, took a deep breath, and went on. They made paths—of words and linebreaks, heartbreaks and beats, breaths and gestures, dance moves and yo-yo tricks.

Ceci was the last to read. The class had workshopped her essay about collecting cans with her mom, and she'd painted the streets, filled the night air with sounds. But all of that was just color around the true thing at its center—Ceci and her mother moving through darkness together, her mother covering one side of the street and Ceci covering the other.

Pilar sat on the edge of her seat and leaned into that love. Ceci didn't stumble once.

When Ceci finished, she looked up and found her mother's eyes. Her hesitant smile spread into a grin. Only then did Pilar turn from her to look at Flor, who sat across the aisle in the front row, eyes filling with her daughter's.

The night ended with Sebastian's performance of "Lean on Me". Pilar had put the lyrics in the program so that everybody could sing along. Sebastian played a little off key and the audience swayed in their seats and sang a little off key, but the brokenness was part of the beauty.

Pilar brought the class up for a bow when it was over. The Sisters and her students' families gave them a standing ovation. Pilar got Robin, who'd been the first to leap to her feet, to take their photo. She told each student what she'd loved about their performance before they left.

Flor thanked Pilar, her eyes shiny, as she and Ceci made their way out.

"You've raised an incredible daughter," Pilar said. "All I want to know is when she's going to take over the world."

After all of the students and their families had left, Sister Letitia put her arm around Pilar and said, "We wanted to talk to you." They pulled chairs up to the front of the room. Pilar sat in a circle with the seven Sisters and they said words—about how proud of her they were—that were uncannily close to the ones she'd said to her students. Pilar thanked them for trusting her to start a writing program, letting her do work she loved. She hoped the Sisters would return to their cells for similar pep talks from God.

"We wanted to offer you room and board and a small stipend for a year to keep doing this work after you graduate," MJ said.

Pilar hadn't seen this coming—that the next step might be given to her, she wouldn't have to fight. She waited to hear the rest before she let herself feel anything.

"I talked to Mother Connie about the vital work you're doing, and she's in support of your staying on," Robin said.

Pilar raised her eyebrows.

Robin nodded reassuringly. "She knows the youth need more structure come summer. We were thinking you could lead a daily workshop. The idea is that you continue to teach and help with Project Luz, and use the rest of your time as you wish. You're under no obligation to take part in our religious life."

Still on unsure terms with God, Pilar was relieved that the Sisters had no delusions about her becoming a nun. That wasn't what this was about.

Letitia sat next to Pilar, smelling of citrus and earth. "We know you've gone through a lot recently. We wanted to give you time to gather yourself—reflect on next steps, research jobs or graduate school, write."

"This way the students wouldn't have to lose you, and we wouldn't either," Robin said.

Pilar looked around the circle at these wise, warm, wrinkled seekers—each wild in their funny way.

It was nothing so dramatic as a call. But for the first time since her talk with Padre, she felt the calm she'd experienced after morning rituals, quiet joy of the first notes of the psalms breaking morning silence. A sense that her voice was held, even before she opened her mouth.

She was still unsure what, or how, to sing, but if she could just hold the voices around her until she found her own, that was something. If she worried less about what she believed and just followed that ring in her body.

The Sisters waited for her answer. All those days of waiting for her mother, and now these mothers waited for her.

Yes, she nodded, then said, "I don't want to lose you, either."

"I'm proud of you," her father said when she told him about open mic night.

"You taught me to tell stories," she said.

"I guess I'm guilty of that." Her father laughed, then coughed a little.

"Papá, the Sisters offered me a year to keep teaching and working at Project Luz." She took a deep breath. "I said yes. I'm not ready to leave. I need time to figure things out. My students, the Sisters—they're teaching me things."

"Are you really okay, mija?"

Her eyes filled. Her father always felt the things beneath her words. It was hard not to hear in his voice the loss of the life she'd wanted for him. The line of that dream vibrating, dying between them.

Her father waited, like the Sisters. His gravelly breath held her silence. She felt it in her lungs.

"Yes," she said. She was letting yo-yos, Beyoncé grooves, and off-key trumpets move through the loss. She was planting things in the dark.

"You know you can always come home."

"I know. Thank you, Papá. I'm coming home next Christmas, hopefully sooner." She would take on more work-study hours to save money for the flight, maybe tutor like Carlos.

"One of your canoe benches rotted, so I built a new one. For when you come down. I know you love that canoe."

"I do. And I love you." She'd started saying it more. He'd been surprised at first, but now they always said it.

"I love you, too, mija," he said, though he'd already said it when he repaired the canoe.

Her father's labored breath was the truth. We were all dying. But he was alive now. He talked about mending the porch; a conversation he'd had with Padre Oscar, the priest who'd given him his job. "He arrives as I leave. Always up early. Not like you."

Pilar laughed.

"He remembered you coming to Mass last summer. I told him you were teaching at a church in LA. He remembers you as a baby, sleeping on my chest as I walked through the graveyard."

"That's sweet." She was glad Padre Oscar was looking out for her father.

"I bought a hammock," he said.

"What?" She laughed. It was so unexpected.

"At that place you and Carlos bought the canoe."

"Was the woman still there? With the Coke-bottle glasses and rat's nest hair?"

"Still there," her father said. "I strung it up between palm trees by the resaca. I was going to clean on Sunday, but I laid down in the hammock, closed my eyes, listened to the water, and fell asleep. I can't remember it, but I had the most beautiful dream."

She pictured her father asleep in the hammock, cradled between trees, the sun and breeze on his weathered face, the lost dream and the sound, in the sky, of wings.

Pilar called Carlos when she got back to SAU. When she sent him the photo with her students, he'd texted, *You wore the scarf!! You look beautiful.*
CONGRATULATIONS—I want every detail!!! Her Sunday night return to
her dorm room after the high of open mic night felt a little lonely, though
there was less anxiety around everything now that she had a path.

Carlos gushed as she described her students' performances, bringing
back the euphoria she'd felt. She leaned into it, gathered strength to tell
him about her talk with Padre.

"I'm so sorry, Pilar," Carlos said with real feeling. "Why didn't you tell me?"

"I guess because you told me not to get my hopes up." Her voice
cracked. "I *really* got my hopes up."

"I know. I love that about you. I also worry about you."

"I was really struggling for awhile, but teaching lifted me out of it. You
asked if I was applying for jobs—"

"Yeah, I don't know why I asked," Carlos cut in. "No one's figured that
out yet, including me."

"Well, I've got next year figured out at least."

"Woah, so much news! This three-act play needs an intermission. Le'me
just dab my brow. Okay, ready."

Pilar told Carlos the plan.

Carlos was silent for a beat. "You're going to live there?"

"Just for a year until I figure out next steps."

"Are they, like, grooming you to become a nun?"

"*No,*" Pilar said, annoyed. She recommitted to being generous, lowered her voice. "They know it's been a tough winter and they're offering
me time."

"You just found out your father can't become a citizen. You don't have to
rush into anything. People are just starting to apply for jobs."

"I'd just be applying for teaching jobs, and I have a teaching job I love.
I'm not ready to leave these kids or the Sisters. I understand why you don't
trust the Church, but I trust these women."

Carlos sighed. He didn't understand why these sexless old shut-ins were her only friends, why she was holing up in a monastery after she graduated. He did understand why she'd let teaching replace creating: Pilar was afraid to write because she was afraid to feel. "Sweetie, you've just gotten a gut-punch confirmation of how few fucks this country gives about us. Have you gotten angry as hell yet? Because that's your next step, and I don't see you taking it in a nunnery."

Was she angry at God? Was that why they weren't speaking? "Anger's part of what I feel and I think I *can* work through my emotions, in my own way and time, at Mother of Sorrows. I talked to the Sisters about it. I told my students. It's just a place that won't let anger burn down everything."

"It just seems like you're walling yourself off from the world."

"Isn't anger a way of walling yourself off, so you don't have to feel anything else?"

"I'm not just talking about feelings, Pilar. We're supposed to be diving into life, taking risks, making mistakes."

She heard clearly, undeniably, what she'd read into his text yesterday. He saw her life as small, less real than his. Her body tensed. "Is that what you're doing?" she asked sharply. She stopped herself from saying, *with your Carmen Madonna flamenco routine.*

Self-righteousness, that was how Pilar walled herself off. Still it stung. "Carmen Madonna may not be my dream act, but I'm putting myself out there. I'm not hiding in a convent praying my life away."

"Is it really *you* you're putting out there?" Pilar shot back.

"What does that even mean? You think you know me better than I know myself?"

Pilar thought of El Ojo. "Sometimes," she said softly.

"Sometimes I think we don't understand each other anymore," Carlos said and immediately regretted it.

Pilar's eyes filled. Why did it hurt to hear it aloud? She'd imagined telling Carlos about her father fixing the canoe for them, buying a hammock from the woman with rat's nest hair. She'd imagined reminiscing about those nights when they were the world.

"I'm sorry," Carlos said. "I don't understand, but I love you and I want to try."

"No, I'm sorry." She swallowed her hurt and dug for the love. "You're the most talented person I know. I want the world to see what I see."

But they'd made each other small, and it felt too late for largeness.

CHAPTER 13

The Sisters had wanted to attend Pilar's graduation, but she had no interest in walking the stage if her father couldn't be there. *I'm so proud of you, mija*, he'd written on a postcard of a Buff-bellied Hummingbird. She moved against the grain, lugging her roller suitcase, backpack, and MoS-monogrammed overnight bag past families and students thronging toward the Sunken Garden, where commencement would be held. People hugged, bickered, and smiled for photographs beneath banners strung between blossoming jacaranda trees congratulating the Class of 2007. Mothers absently glanced up at this long-limbed girl in her faded jeans and white T-shirt as they pinned their daughters' graduation caps. Boys looked past her as they bellowed each other's names across Alumni Mall.

She stopped in front of the senior apartments and looked up at the third-floor balcony from which Buster had called to her. Her eyes filled. She shook her head to clear them, thanked the pain for the light it led her to, and walked on. She did not look back at the mall a-swish with graduation gowns, but strode purposefully toward the parking lot where MJ waited in the white 1995 Volkswagen station wagon that was the Sisters' sole vehicle. MJ went back with Pilar to her dorm room to collect what was left—bedding, a bathroom caddie, a microwave, books. Then it was two, soon to be nine, moving together against the grain.

MJ's laugh as they wrestled everything into the trunk, smog colored by wonder as they drove from west to east LA, Leonard Cohen singing "Hallelujah" as they pulled through Mother of Sorrows' peacock gate was The Commencement. "Hallelujah" played in Pilar's head as MJ helped her carry her things into the monastery, down the long stone corridor past the courtyard and up the narrow spiral staircase that led to the Daughter House, reaching its climax as she stepped into her spare, sun dappled room.

The only thing that Abuela was deathly afraid of was flying. When planes took off in movies, she'd squeeze Carlos' arm and hide her eyes. Carlos had told her it wasn't worth it to come to his graduation and promised to send photos. She would have stayed in his room. He would have had to hide Carmen, Carla, and all of his drag accoutrements.

Graduation was an unappreciated referendum on where he was in life. Though he was graduating with honors from his dream school and launching a drag career in New York City, he felt stuck at some rusty gas station between Texas ghost towns. The disjunction between what he'd achieved and what he felt only heightened his malaise. *Disjunction Junction, what's your FUNCTION?*, he sang to himself as he paired the red-plaid church shirt Abuela had given him with mariachi pants embroidered with red flowers and white vines and the red pleather platform boots left over from his Ziggy Stardust days. He'd put so little effort into applying for engineering jobs that he'd only been offered a government job, which required a full background check. He was relieved to have an explanation for Abuela as to why he'd turned it down. He'd told her he'd keep searching while performing "cabaret."

Graduation was at 10 a.m. on a Sunday. The Fengs had all performed the night before and Carlos didn't expect them to wake up early and hightail it an hour uptown to watch him walk the stage sans heels and strut. It was Susanna and Stu who jumped out of their seats to clap and whoop and take photos as he accepted his diploma, a preppy-nonconformist centaur beneath his graduation gown.

The Goldsteins hugged and congratulated him after the ceremony.

"I LOVE this look!" Susanna exclaimed when he unzipped his graduation gown.

Carlos thanked her, then asked if she could take a few photos—gown on and waist up—for Abuela.

As he chatted with Sue and Stu, he looked out across Low Plaza at all the students clustered with their families, some of whom he recognized. Carlos was grateful to have his own cluster.

"Wasn't Max supposed to come?" Stu asked.

Max had said he'd come, but Carlos knew he wouldn't. "He was out all night at a show," he said.

Jyoti from US Lesbian and Gay History came over and hugged him. "Are these your parents?—Oh my God, our class *loved* your son!—He's the most amazing person," she run-on gushed at Susanna and Stu before Carlos could correct her.

"We know." Susanna winked at Carlos.

Stu put his arm around Carlos. "We couldn't be more proud."

Jyoti's idolatry was bittersweet as the bravery and vulnerability of their final class was missing from his life. Carlos put his arm around Susanna. Sandwiched between the Goldsteins, he said, "Honey, you know it took *all* of us to turn that class around! Jyoti was my annotation soulmate," he told Susanna and Stu. "We always underlined the same things." He asked Jyoti what was next, and she said she was going to work with refugees in Jordan through the IRC.

"Wow, *that's* amazing," Carlos said.

Susanna and Stu asked Jyoti a half-dozen questions about the work she'd be doing. Carlos listened, admiring her sense of purpose and feeling mildly jealous of the Goldsteins' enthrallment.

"What about you?" Jyoti asked.

"I'll keep doing drag, see where it leads."

"Don't be modest," Susanna chided. "He starts singing solo this summer."

"That's wonderful," Jyoti said. "People need to hear your story."

She must have thought he'd be performing some heartfelt monologue. Carlos tried to imagine bringing that rawness into Lucky Feng's and couldn't. He thanked Jyoti, his cheeks rubbery and sore from fake-smiling.

After she left, the Goldsteins invited him to lunch. He turned them down to walk alone through Riverside Park. Though the cherry blossoms of early May had replaced the swirling dead leaves of late November, it felt like that walk through the park after his Brooklyn Museum breakdown. How could he have experienced so much only to loop back to the same lost feeling? Only now he felt too numb to cry.

It was Ralph he wanted, sitting wordlessly beside him, lifting his face to the breeze coming off the river, licking his nose and then Carlos. The Goldsteins were only blocks away and he considered asking if he could walk Ralph, but he couldn't think of a nice way to say, *I don't want your company, just your dog's.* What he would have told Ralph, who would have listened without judgement, was that even though Pilar was moving into a monastery with a bunch of sexless old ladies, he was the one who felt hopelessly old.

Carmen Madonna sold. Lucky Feng's audience loved her "La Isla Bonita" solo, which involved a lot of flamenco hands, tossing a rosary around audience members, and molesting a banana pulled from her fruit turban as she sang, *When a girl loves a boy, and a boy loves a girl.* It culminated with Carmen tearing away her gold-lamé skirt to do a seductive rosary dance in gold-lamé hotpants. Carlos asked to no avail if Carmen could strip out of her fruit turban, too, which was so heavy it gave him a headache. "Pain is beauty!" Nathaniel snapped.

Canned as the choreography was, Carlos' talent was undeniable. His facial expressions, comic timing, and the spontaneities he smuggled into his act gave "La Isla Bonita" a serrated edge. Once Carmen became a beloved staple at Lucky Feng's, she entered an open drag competition judged by established queens. *10-minute slot—show us what you got!*, the website call read. Carlos added some standup to the Carmen Madonna number and rosary-shimmied his way up the drag ladder.

Max continued to school Carlos, both in and out of drag. As they dressed, Cher scolded Carmen for getting sloppy with her costume and care regimens. "When the love comes too easy, darling," she batted her freshly applied eyelashes, "it's meaningless."

"What do you know about love?" Carmen had intended it as flirtatious repartee, but it came out sounding bitter.

Though Max was disappointed in Carlos' slouch and a little jealous of his easy success, he taught him which venues offered equal and respectful pay and helped him book shows, negotiate with management, facilitate contracts, create a photo-blog, and post fliers. Soon Carmen had a loyal following and regular gigs at both historic venues like the Stonewall Inn and more improvised spaces like Bottoms Up, where the dressing room was a kitchen and girls stuffed the ovens with costumes and shoes.

The gap between Carlos' success and the hollowness he felt grew. The more he performed the same shtick, the more impossible it seemed to create anything real. The deader he felt inside, the meaner his Abuela jokes got, and vice versa. He avoided talking to her because she always asked whether he'd heard anything about engineering jobs. The more he avoided her, the easier it was to flatten the blur of love, anger, guilt, resentment, and need he felt into lifeless parody. The emptier his performances became, the more he needed his audience's validation and felt scorn for how easily they gave it. It was one big vicious cycle.

Weekend nights, when he had back-to-back shows on opposite sides of town, were hell. He'd lug two roller suitcases—one containing Carmen's wig and fruit turban on blocks and her accessories, and another containing her costume and shoes—onto a crowded Saturday night subway car. There was never anywhere to sit so he'd struggle to corral his unruly roller suitcases while holding onto a pole as the train swerved. Carmen would have her first show at 8, leave at 8:45 for a 9:30 performance at the next venue, then hightail it to a third venue for an 11 p.m. performance that ended at 2 a.m. She had to ride the subway in costume to her second and third shows, which meant lighter suitcases but more curses and stares. If the subways were slow, Carmen had to run on stage without so much as reapplying her lipstick.

Now that Carmen was an established queen, she looked out for the baby queens like her Feng Sisters had looked out for her. Carlos was the first person to travel with a new girl to her show. If she took the subway home in drag, he'd accompany her before he went home. For awhile, Carmen and her baby queens endured nothing worse than slurs and swears that died down when they moved to the other end of the subway car.

The next time she had a three-gig night, Carmen dressed at home so that she wouldn't have to lug two suitcases, just a backpack with boy clothes that she could throw her costume in at the end of the night. Her first show was near Times Square. She took the subway to Atlantic Avenue and transferred, turning up the volume on the iPod shuffle clipped to her bicep-tutu to block out commentary. Carlos had always loved music, but now it was a forcefield. Carmen found a seat on the N train and settled in for the ride to midtown, relieved to have nothing more than her backpack to hold onto.

Carlos had downloaded *Horses*, which he hadn't listened to since high school. From the first words of "Gloria", he knew why. Patti Smith's voice—not a vocalist's, but a prophet's—clawed at some painful part of him that he hadn't spoken to in a long time. That burning desire to sing in whatever voice emerged. El Ojo strode through his brain, all elbows and knees. He envied that past self with a greenness that could bring bad juju for years if he didn't touch it.

It hurt to touch it. He felt himself cracking open, a tingling along the raw nerve edge as he drew close to something submerged, unreadable and straddling the line between life and death like the tags scrawled on the tunnel walls, flashing beneath blue lights then gone. He felt himself canoeing through that sorrowful juju to some pulsing beginning. Patti sang softly to that fragile egg of a self and Carlos sang with her, an underground lullaby lulling him into a dream state. His eyes filled.

Carmen didn't notice the man striding toward her until he was hovering over her. He gripped a pole and leaned toward her, spit misting the air between them as he screamed that she was *a sin, a perversion, an abomination, the Devil*. As if the rawness invited the attack. Had he watched her face soften, eyes go shiny? Was that what jerked him out of his seat?

A few people looked up, but most kept their heads down, burrowed into their own bubbles of music, books, or parenting.

Carlos looked at the watchers and they looked away. He remembered the boys who'd watched that night at prom; the girls who'd cried for Alfonso to stop, for their dates to make him stop. From the circle's edge they'd cried and screamed because girls were allowed to cry and scream, their emotional displays tolerated, if not heard. They'd screamed for their boyfriends to use their weight and muscle to save them from having to witness this violence.

But the boys couldn't hear the girls above the machinelike pistons pummeling the soft thing inside, outside, inside, until one eye shut by force, the other by surrender, until the soft thing's (its, her, his, their, our) mouth shut, went silent, went dead. They'd killed it a thousand times before, those boys who loved their mothers and grandmothers, held the door, said *God bless you* and *yes, ma'am*, sang praise songs in the Fellowship of Christian Athletes; those fists had held roses, birthed calves, bathed pigs they told their secrets—who else could they tell?—then sent to slaughter. It was that sweetness they tried to kill, the way they'd been taught to gun down the silver shiver of sinew and breath through the brush, made to exchange that beauty for a glassy-eyed head on the wall, made to chew and swallow the killing so that this crying whatever-in-a-dress was just one more softness to kill.

This stranger screamed at Carmen on a New York City subway, but Carmen was Carla back in that Echo Hotel parking lot, inside and outside of the circle, one eye closed by Alfonso's fist, the other by despair. When both eyes closed, it was Pilar who reached her, in blindness, in darkness, in blood; her long body shielding Carla's. Carlos wanted to be a body like that, a body like Pilar, like Patti—long, lean androgynous shield. A body thinking nothing of her body, her absence of fear animal, a blood pumping fist against the machine.

A soft body slaying.

Pilar was not someone to follow rules, submit to safety, and that was why he didn't understand her binding up her body in the Church's rules. She'd been the one to say, *We're getting out of here*, so that even in darkness he could see the set of her jaw. She meant it. They meant it. Together they made it happen. He needed her to be brave so that he could be brave. And she'd left him, abandoned him for a Bible-bound, shut-in life. That was not what they'd promised each other the night they'd said, *We're getting out*. They'd meant, *we're not going to close the other eye, surrender to fear and silence*. They'd promised each other and they'd broken that promise.

This man yelling in his face on the subway was just another piston thrusting, another part of the machine. He'd moved on to hellfire and damnation, but hell was here, hell was fear, and Carlos knew what this stranger, not a stranger, was afraid of because it scared him, too.

Carmen turned up her music. She kept her head down, fists clenched, eyes on the dirty subway floor as the man yelled, but the music spoke to her, told her to look up. *I won't give up, won't give up, don't let me give up...*

This man could scream his religion of sin, rigidity, masculinity, righteous division and all-swallowing Fear, but Carmen and Carlos were rising out of their seat, beads, earrings, and bracelets jangling, to scream back the religion that clawed El Ojo into being—religion of rawness, strut, rage, sorrow, beauty, wonder, elasticity; religion of the future, of the now, of expansion, light, space.

As the subway pulled into Times Square, Carmen hiked up her gold lamé slit skirt to her knees and spread her legs wide to surf the stop. She held one cherry-nailed, pinky-ringed hand up to witness, and the other to her ear to receive Patti's *telegram to the new breed*. Carlos still remembered the words, screamed them as he moved toward the doors, something animal, fetal, bloody birthed as he rose above this man's Land of Fear to watch it die from the endless stretched-out sky. *"I couldn't hear them before, but I hear 'em now, / ...Moving in like black ships, they were moving in, streams of them, / And he put up his hands and he said, 'It's me, it's me.'"*

Carmen darted off the train and the man followed her, yelling, helling. She tightened her backpack straps, yanked her skirt up again, and bounded up the stairs as best she could in her platform heels. She pushed through the crowds in the station, watermelon earrings whirling like propellers as she wove around and bumped into people. "Hey!" they cried, but she did not look back.

She hurried out of the station and into Times Square's hordes of tourists. Never had she been so grateful for them. Still she ran and wove, checking over her shoulder. She got gridlocked behind a school group, but by then, she was sure she'd lost the man.

As she slowed, the adrenaline drained and the shock, the full danger of what had happened, set in. She realized that her whole body was shaking, bangles clanging, her feet worn red and raw from running in heels. She yanked her skirt down and limped slowly behind the school group until her bangles stilled.

Somehow Carmen got through her show, though she couldn't remember any of it. When it was over, she stood numbly inside the roar of applause. She canceled her next two shows, saying she'd come down with something, changed into boy clothes, scrubbed off her makeup, and took a taxi home.

At home, Carlos sat with his feet soaking in the tub, a drink in one hand, and his phone in the other. He called Pilar and told her what had happened.

Her voice spiked with worry. "Oh Carlos, I'm so sorry, that sounds *terrifying*. Are you okay? How in the world did you perform afterwards?"

"I can do Carmen Madonna blind." Carlos sighed. "I *have* to half the time when eyelashes get in my eyes."

"I wish I could have been there. I don't know what I could have done, but—"

"You were," Carlos said. "I remembered prom. I don't know if I ever told you how brave you were—"

"*You* were brave."

"No. *We* were. I want to be brave like that again. I want to do something I can't do blind. I don't know what that is yet, but—"

"You don't always have to know. That's what I'm learning," Pilar said. "And you can't be brave all the time. You need to take care of yourself. It's okay to take time. To heal, be."

Carlos took a deep breath. "Yeah... When was the last time I *be'd*?"

Pilar laughed. "It doesn't mean you're not creating. I've been thinking about how writing's not just writing, it's also attention. You know, looking with the right eyes."

"Oh Pilar, I missed you," Carlos said.

"I missed us," she said.

When he told them about The Subway Heller, the Alphabet City boys insisted that Carlos spend weekends with them.

"It's why we gave you a key!" Carter scolded.

"Come Friday, bring your suitcases, we'll get ready together, and we'll make sure you get to your next gig safely," Mike said.

"We are *not* above paying for your cab," Tony said.

Carlos did start spending weekends in Alphabet City, but it was his roommate Timon who solved the problem of traveling quickly and cheaply between venues. Timon biked everywhere and told Carlos that biking could cut his commute time in half. Carlos hadn't ridden a bike since he was a kid, but he liked the idea of whipping past onlookers instead of being trapped in a subway car with them. Timon helped him find a used bike on Craig's List. He put a rack on the back so that Carlos could transport, in pannier bags, the parts of Carmen that he couldn't bike in.

On a bike, Carlos felt fast and powerful, above and outside of it all. On a bike, no one could catch him. Carmen biked between back-to-back shows in her gold halter, hotpants, bicep tutus, and platform heels, her turban replaced by a watermelon bike helmet. When men catcalled, she flashed a glossy red grin and was gone. Biking through the city in drag was like being on a parade float, only Carmen en la Bicicleta whipped by gawkers so quickly that she must have seemed like a mirage.

Carlos got into a routine of spending weekends with the Fengs then biking home Sunday night to spend the week in Brooklyn. Biking home along the Hudson River was the perfect transition from the frenzy of three-gig nights and weekend-long sleepovers. Listening to a softer soundtrack, he became a melodic bubble of sound drifting over the Manhattan skyline with the moon. Timon had mostly moved in with his girlfriend, but held onto the apartment because it was rent-stabilized. He kept Carlos' rent low because he felt safer with him there—collecting mail, watering the plants, and keeping an eye out for the threatening notices their corrupt management company had begun to slip under neighbors' doors. Timon had started spinning mellow beats at a yoga studio across the street and played this music in the apartment when he was home. The two of them would float through it, dreaming their dreams, occasionally colliding in the kitchen.

Max joined the Alphabet City sleepovers when he wasn't meeting other "friends." The sex was still sweltering, but what Carlos came to appreciate more was Max as a sounding board for hazy artistic aspirations. Max was so sure of his own aesthetic that he took no offense when Carlos confessed that Carmen Madonna wasn't really him. Max had known, of course, but been kind enough to wait for Carlos to say it.

One rainy Sunday afternoon, the Sisters Feng swapped costumes, turned up the music, and danced. They knew each other well enough to lovingly, hilariously caricature each other's moves and facial expressions.

There was something freeing and true about their merry-go-round of a persona-swap. Carlos absorbed the scene as if he were painting it from the street—bright strokes of color and motion, bodies brushing, converging through the rain-streaked windows.

"THIS," he said to Max, his arms spread wide. "This is what I want in my art." He meant this rainy Sunday masquerade, but also their vogue showdowns, biting reality TV commentary, battles over the bathroom and stolen makeup; their snoring, fucking, masturbating, and meditation mantras drifting through the thin walls; their catfighting, forgiving, and nursing one another through colds, flus, crabs, and gonorrhea, praying there wouldn't be worse. He meant this knowing each other by their most intimate birthmarks and tattoos; loving each other like soldiers who'd fought wars together, like the fiercest of families—the family you chose.

Carlos continued to perform Carmen, but felt most himself shedding wig, glitter, and lashes as he biked between drag venues, Brooklyn and Manhattan, Carmen and Carlos. He stuffed parts of Carmen in his pannier bags, kept parts of her on his body, and became the revolution of legs in between. Biking brought back the dream space of driving in Texas, especially when he listened to his idols—Laurie Anderson, Lou Reed, David Bowie, Arthur Russell, and of course Patti Smith. The Sisters thought he was crazy, but Carlos loved nothing more than biking from his apartment to Lucky Feng's over the Pepto-Bismol-pink Williamsburg Bridge with its tangled graffiti. Tattooed cyclists with chain locks slung across their torsos zipped past. The whole world—skin and streets—was a canvas. He looked with old, new El Ojo eyes and the city cracked open.

CHAPTER 14

Pilar's open mic night was such a success that they made it a monthly event. Her students' friends, siblings, and cousins came. By summer, many of them joined Pilar's writing program. Three days a week, she taught a morning workshop for middle school students and an afternoon workshop for her old high school students, including Ceci. The other two days, she taught a new group of high school students.

At first, the extroversion of teaching five days a week was exhausting. Come Friday night, Pilar would tumble into bed at 8 and sleep for 12 hours. In particular, her class of 20 middle schoolers had a lot of energy and needed a lot of supervision. Pilar pictured herself as a frenzied bee buzzing between students, dying in a petunia as soon as class was over. Gradually she instilled a drafting process and they became more independent. It was a steep learning curve for both parties. Pilar would say something too abstract and the quiet ones would look at her blankly; the outspoken ones would cock their heads and ask, "What do you mean?" She'd try to explain and they still wouldn't understand. She'd try again, carve a bright red door into a poem instead of a shadowy gray one. Eventually they'd step into the poem together and plod around in a way that made a new poem. Some things got lost in translation, but some things held. She was learning to celebrate that rickety bridge.

It was a whirlwind of teaching, reading, and lesson planning, but she liked the structure, immersion, and purpose of it. She joined the Sisters' rituals when she could, but skipped them if she'd stayed up late reading students' writing or needed to prep for class. If she arrived late for the Singing of the Psalms, Mother Connie might scowl, but the Sisters were happy to see her come and go as she pleased. She took meals with them on Tuesdays, Thursdays, and weekends. They talked about the ups and downs of their work, and all of it—gardening, teaching, cooking, answering prayer requests, Project Luz—felt connected. Pilar believed in the world they were building.

She started talking to God like a friend. Thinking of prayer as attention, gratitude, presence.

She talked with her father a couple of times a week.

"When I come home, we're going out in the canoe together," she said.

"I don't trust that thing." Her father laughed. "I'll watch from the hammock."

Carlos would call and tell her about his ideas for performances. He liked working out raw ideas in dialogue. Pilar kept hers close to her chest, but she did tell him that she'd started keeping a journal. She wrote down images, phrases, and ideas—fragments that didn't have to become anything.

Her Monday, Wednesday, Friday afternoon workshop ended at 5, and Flor came to pick Ceci up around 6. Pilar loved this hour with Ceci. She'd bring a snack from the kitchen and Ceci would talk to her about school, her friends, or what she was reading. Pilar was usually too self-conscious to write with anyone else in the room, but something about Ceci's quiet, humming energy as she read and wrote let her.

One Friday in June, Flor was late. By 7, Ceci waited anxiously in the reception area, staring out the window. She hadn't touched the spaghetti that Pilar had brought her. Pilar called Flor's work numbers from the classroom. The mother Flor nannied for said she hadn't shown up that afternoon and hadn't answered when she called. Pilar called the hotel.

The manager got on the phone and said that ICE had raided the hotel and taken Flor, along with 60 others, to the San Pedro Detention Center.

Pilar's stomach churned. She was nine again—praying in her father's truck. "I don't understand." She lowered her voice so that Ceci wouldn't hear. "Flor told me she has a green card."

The manager said that many of the people they'd detained supposedly had green cards, that he didn't have more information. "We called the emergency number Flor gave us, but it was out of service," he said.

Pilar wondered if that number had ever worked.

She called the detention center and got an automated message saying that detainees couldn't receive calls. She hesitantly left a message for Flor saying she'd look after Ceci and talk to Padre Bob about getting her out.

First she needed to take care of Ceci, who looked as if she was about to cry.

"There's been some mistake with your mom's papers and they've taken her into detention," Pilar said as calmly as she could.

Ceci's mouth wobbled.

Strands of hair had slipped from her braid. Pilar pushed them out of her eyes. "Don't worry." She started to say, *Everything will be alright*, but stopped herself. She wanted to be truthful, because that's what she would have wanted. "You can stay with us tonight and I'll do everything I can to get your mom out."

Not wanting to involve Mother Connie, Pilar waited until Compline was over. She led Ceci up to MJ's cell during private contemplation, whispering that they had to be very quiet. She checked the hall before pushing MJ's door open. MJ motioned Pilar and Ceci in. She was sitting by the open window, wearing a white shirt that hung to her knees, the Bible open in her lap.

"Flor's been detained," Pilar whispered.

Ceci's shoulders started to shake and MJ wrapped her arms around her. "We're going to get your mom released," she said firmly. "And we're going to take good care of you."

They got fresh sheets and made up the bed in the room next to Pilar's. They made sure that Ceci had everything she needed and tucked her in.

"Do you have something to read?" Pilar asked.

Ceci pulled *The House on Mango Street* from her backpack.

Pilar smiled. She and MJ hugged Ceci goodnight. "I'll leave my door open in case you need *anything*," Pilar said.

As soon as they were out of earshot, MJ said, "We need to talk." She led Pilar to a back staircase that went up to the roof. They heaved open an oak door and stepped into the summer night, the air thick with honeysuckle. They stood in the center of four turrets and looked out across the houses of the surrounding neighborhoods.

MJ stared up at the scattered stars and said, "Lord God, that woman has suffered enough."

"Visitation hours start at 8," Pilar said. "If I stay with Ceci, could you go?"

MJ took a deep breath and exhaled slowly. "I can't."

"But you took Flor in. She needs you. Is this because of the conflict with Mother Connie over the Sanctuary Movement?"

"Who told you?"

"Sister Robin."

"Robin doesn't know the whole story. No one but Mother Connie knows. Sit down."

Pilar sat and pulled her knees to her chest. She felt small beneath the night sky. MJ's words tumbled out. She paced, her voice drifting in and out. Pilar listened without stopping her.

"When Mother Connie chose to build hermitages instead of saving 100 refugees, I felt deeply at odds with the Church. I wanted to leave, but I was terrified of returning to my Lost Days. Though I already had. I moved through the monastery's corridors like I'd moved across glaciers—lost and angry and alone. When the anger drained, I felt numb.

"Six years passed in that numbness and then I found Flor on Mother of Sorrows' doorstep. She was unconscious, not even 100 pounds. Sister

Soledad and I carried her up to the Daughter House, to your room. She slept and slept and hardly ate. She slept in this way that broke my heart—her knees curled to her chest, hands balled into fists.

"Mother Connie announced that Flor could stay no longer than a week. We stared each other down. It was one thing to refuse 100 refugees and another to boot one sick woman—whom God had delivered into our care—onto the street. Still, something held me silent.

"I talked to Padre Bob and La Placita took Flor in. I kept talking to Flor. It had been a couple of weeks and she was regaining her strength when Padre Bob showed up at Project Luz. He interrupted my class. I got someone to take over and led him into a conference room. 'Not here,' he said.

"We drove to a McDonald's and sat at the back. Padre was sweating and said, 'I'm going to ask for your help. Regardless of what you decide, promise you'll never repeat this.' I promised. He told me that he'd heard Flor's confession that morning. The coyote she'd paid to guide her to the US had raped her, and now she was pregnant with his child.

"Flor had confessed to Padre that she'd been praying for the child's death, that she couldn't stand it growing inside her. That she would never be able to look at it, much less love it. He asked if I would take Flor for an abortion if he got the money. 'No one can know I was involved,' he said. 'Not even Flor. You'll have to get her to tell you herself. She can't know I told you about her confession.' I knew that if I was found out, I'd be excommunicated. I said I'd do it.

"Flor didn't want to tell me whose child she was pregnant with, but I told her about the others. Women who'd come to Project Luz who'd been raped by coyotes, soldiers, drivers who'd given them rides. 'God understands if you can't have this child,' I said. A week later, I took Flor to Planned Parenthood. I wrote Mother of Sorrows' phone number on the form. I fantasized about Planned Parenthood calling and Mother Connie picking up. About being forced out.

"Finally a nurse called Flor's name. I helped her climb into the bed. She looked so fragile with her feet in the metal stirrups. When the doctor came in, she started shaking. She shook her head, tears running down her face. 'No puedo,' she said. I held her hand and said, 'God understands.' Flor climbed down from the bed and stood shaking before the doctor in her paper robe. 'I can't,' she told him. She wouldn't say more. She was silent on the taxi ride back to La Placita.

"I didn't leave Mother of Sorrows, but waded through our rituals in a fog. I forgot that I'd put Mother of Sorrows' phone number on Flor's forms until Planned Parenthood followed up. Mother Connie answered the phone. She pieced together what they didn't tell her.

"Soon after she got the call, Mother Connie cornered me. She said what I'd done was cause for excommunication. She threatened to report me to the bishop. She let me squirm, then asked, 'What will you do with your life?' I remembered snow-shoeing through white forests, how it was the cold inside that burned. I remembered pushing my way through fog toward the sound of the ocean. Standing on the edge of a cliff and screaming until my voice went hoarse to convince myself that I was alive.

"I stepped back from that cliff. I looked at Mother Connie with tears in my eyes. She needed me to run Project Luz, but this way she could keep me under her thumb. 'The important thing is that you didn't go through with it,' she said.

"I was forced to withdraw from Flor. Padre let me know how she was doing. La Placita saw her through her pregnancy, then helped her find work and an apartment. Against all odds, her life moved forward. And mine did, too."

MJ stopped pacing. "I still feel connected to Flor. Seeing her with Ceci at your open mic night made me very happy. But it's in her best interest that I keep my distance. The old war with Mother Connie surfaces whenever I mention Flor. Mother Connie's never told anyone about my transgression, but she holds the threat over me. If I get involved in Flor's case, I could lose my life here. And I no longer know who I am outside of this life." There was a plaintiveness in her voice that Pilar had never heard.

Pilar stood and squinted at her. She looked ghostly, standing at the roof's edge, white shirt billowing around her knees.

She remembered the poem that Ceci had written about her father and vomit rose into her mouth. She moved toward MJ. "How could you lie to Ceci? You said you'd get Flor released. You lied to me, too. You said a community built by Teresa had to be fearless. You talked about moving through the world in ceaseless prayer—*knee-deep* in the world's sorrows. You said you felt the call like love." How many times had she returned to those words when she thought about who she wanted to be? She was sick of people lying about love. "I'm here because I believed you."

MJ nodded, absorbing all of this. She took a deep breath. "Some days all of that is true," she said slowly. "But no world is without compromise. What's true now is that I can't get involved in Flor's case." She stepped closer to Pilar and searched her eyes. "Can you see how all of those things can be true?" she asked softly.

Pilar couldn't hear the softer questions. Heat spread through her body. She saw now the tangle of lies—about Roberto, her mother, love, America, God—that led her here. She knew her anger was larger than MJ. She'd let it speak once and her father had screamed, ¡*Cállate!* and slapped her. Her father, who loved her more than anyone, could not love that part of her. Her father had slapped her, her mother had left her, and she could not hold the anger alone.

She fired certainties automatic rifle-style at MJ: "You're hiding here because you don't know who you are. You're afraid of change, afraid of the world, afraid to do what's right. You're living a lie."

MJ stopped trying to respond. She shut up, held out her empty hands in the dark.

Still Pilar's anger burned. MJ's silence was the silence of God, unanswering.

MJ let her hands fall to her sides. Her voice returned to its characteristic pragmatism. "Call Padre Bob. He has the resources to get Flor released. As to Ceci, Mother Connie is more likely to be compassionate if I'm not involved. Talk to her after the Singing of the Psalms; don't break morning silence. You can let Ceci sleep until then."

Some unflown bird hung between them before MJ said, "I'll head down first. Wait a few minutes before coming in."

Pilar watched her leave. She stood numbly at the roof's edge and stared out at the wobbling world. Belief lifted like a muzzle and beneath it was boundless, burning rage. Her body shook with it.

She wanted to jump into its flames but thought of Ceci and called Padre. Though it was late, he picked up after one ring.

"Padre Bob here." He sounded at once distracted and alert. His voice softened when Pilar told him that Flor had been detained.

"I need to be here for Ceci," she said. "Could you visit Flor in the morning?"

"I'll go first thing. I should be able to get her released since she's Ceci's sole caretaker. I'll text as soon as I have news."

Pilar thanked him and hurried downstairs to check on Ceci.

As soon as she cracked open Ceci's door, Ceci closed *The House on Mango Street* and asked, "Can you get my mom released?"

"Padre thinks he can." Pilar sat on the end of her bed. "He'll go first thing tomorrow."

Ceci chewed the corner of her lip, then her nails.

"Can't sleep?" Pilar asked.

Ceci shook her head. She'd unbraided her hair and it hung in beautiful waves down her back.

Everything had unraveled, even beauty. Pilar couldn't find words, so reached for those of others. "Want me to read to you?"

Ceci handed her the book. "I'm at 'Minerva Writes Poems'."

Pilar read nearly to the end before Ceci's eyelids started to droop, but it was a line from the beginning that rang in her brain as she tucked Ceci in, about being *sad like a house on fire*.

She threw open the monastery's heavy oak door and waited until she was beyond the courtyard's echoing corridors to call Carlos. She needed air and didn't want anyone to hear. She stopped beneath the shelter of a thick old oak to call.

Carlos had just gotten out of drag after the last Lucky Feng's performance. "Hold on, okay?" he said amidst the Sisters' dressing room commotion. "Le'me just get outside."

He headed north on 1st Avenue, drunk people stumbling around him, as Pilar unfurled the whole convoluted story.

Pilar couldn't walk and tell the story at the same time. She ran her hand over the rough grain of the oak's trunk, words pouring out numbly. Then Carlos would gasp, *My God*, or say softly, *Oh, Pilar*, and her eyes would fill. She pressed her forehead to the bark and choked back a sob as she spoke of Flor's rape, Ceci not knowing who her father was, and then her tears mounted into fury.

"I don't understand how MJ can choose this fucked up Church over helping them. Carlos, I believed she was *happy*. She talked about being fearless, being *love*, when all she is is a *lie*." She stripped leaves from a branch as she yelled. "She made me believe I'd be happy here, but it's just more of the lies I grew up with!"

Carlos had never heard her this angry. He'd seen it in her face, determination, but she never screamed, swore. He was worried about her, but also had a sense that this had been a *long* time coming; this was necessary if she was going to move forward.

"Oh sweetie, I'm so sorry, but I'm *so* glad you called. You must be reeling." He turned on East 10th Street, made his way into Tompkins Square Park, and found a bench where he could sit and listen, away from the bars and traffic.

Pilar walked in long, reckless strides away from the monastery. There was only the half-light of the moon. She stumbled over tree roots, pitching forward in the dark. "I'm so *angry* at everyone who's ever lied to me," she screamed through gritted teeth. "Why couldn't my father ever talk to me about his brother's death, all that pain buried in all those stories, all that speaking about it without speaking about it? And he was so *angry* when

I asked how he died, he *hated* me for asking, *hated* me for knowing my mother left us." She cradled her flip-phone with her left hand, flung her right hand at the sky.

"He was *furious* and then just— *silent*." Her knees buckled and she collapsed into the grass. She sat with her legs splayed out like a rag doll, hands limp beside them, phone lifelessly cupped in her palm in the grass.

"Pilar, sweetie, are you still there?" Carlos asked worriedly. "Where are you right now?"

"I'm lost, Carlos!" She spoke softly, hoarsely. "We were silent because we were never allowed to be angry. We're supposed to be *so* grateful for this wasteland, keep our heads down and carry it on our backs. Papá *never* asked for more. He couldn't talk to me about being undocumented because he was ashamed and afraid when this country should be ashamed, stealing our blood, breath, sweat and giving back nothing but fear. What Flor went through to come here and they took her for *working*; they took Ceci's mother, her *everything*."

She scrambled up and walked until the crosses topping the monastery's turrets receded into the darkness. "I prayed—before I knew what prayer was—that they wouldn't take my father; they didn't take him all at once, they're taking him slowly, painfully, and he will *die* having given his life to this graveyard of a country!" Her throat raw, she stopped yelling and big, ugly sobs shook loose.

Carlos struggled to understand her. The only time she'd cried like this was after that fucker, Buster... Pilar had always been so contained, but he'd known, deep down, that *she* was the fragile one, that when she finally cracked, it was going to be bad. And then, possibly, okay. If he could just get her to catch sight of *okay* in the distance.

"Pilar, my love, listen to me," he said firmly.

But she raised her voice and choked out these words, sobbing, "I can pray until my tongue turns blue, but *no one* is listening. Not my mother, not God. My father lied about my mother and then I lied to myself, waiting in the sugarcane, waiting on my knees for God. Oh my God, *Ceci*." She sucked back tears, wiped her nose with her shirt. She tripped over a root and flew forward, scraping her hands and knees. "*Fuck!*" Her phone flew out of her hand and arced into the grass.

"*Pilar?!*" Carlos cried. An unhoused man approached and asked for money. *Sorry*, he mouthed, dazedly shaking his head. Carlos walked away through the park, frantically yelling, "*Pilar*, are you okay?"

Pilar crawled on scraped hands and knees toward the muffled alarm of Carlos' voice. She found her phone, stood, and kept walking, yelling into the phone, into the dark. "I wanted so *badly* for there to be something large enough to hold all of it because I can't hold it alone, it's too heavy, but the truth is we're all just talking to ourselves and lying to each other. We're all so afraid of the truth, when believing and losing that belief hurts more."

She walked until she got to the tall stone wall at the edge of the property. Her voice gone, she whispered, "We never tell each other who we are, so we don't know anyone, we end up alone with the lies, protecting them, hiding them, when we can't protect *anyone*." She felt her way along the wall like a child learning to ice skate. "I came to this place where I thought the silence wasn't hiding anything, I thought the silence was love, *God*, light, but it's just more lies and now MJ's made me a part of the lie and I don't know what I'm doing here. I'm *so lost*—" Her voice cracked. She slid down the wall and sat with her head leaned back against it, tears rolling down her face. There was just the sound of her own breath, fast and uneven, and then quieting. She felt hollowed out, lighter.

"Pilar, my love," Carlos said softly, "I've never heard you like this, you've never let yourself go. It's terrifying, I know. Letting go of yourself, everything. But I want you to think of it as a beginning."

He waited and heard her breathing steady. "As long as I've known you, you've been on this quest—searching for Truth, God, Love, Meaning. You were always searching for something larger than yourself in books, your parents' stories, the Church... And sweetie, you are *right*. There's heartbreak at the end of that quest.

"What if there's no truth to search for? Face it, no mother, father, Sister, God would be enough. You don't *want* a simple answer. Because really, all there is is your love, anger, sadness, belief, fear, questions and what you make of them. Maybe that's only sad until we stop mourning and start *making* our truth."

Pilar thought about it. "The answer *is* Ceci's poem," she said slowly, "what she made from that darkness."

"*Yes*," Carlos said. "What if life is just a great gaping hole and how you choose to—"

"Tunnel through it?" Pilar sniffled.

"I was going to say *make love to it*," Carlos laughed, "but same, same! Now that all the lies are out, you get to decide what you believe. Who do you want to be, Pilar Salomé Reinfeld?"

"I don't know," she said helplessly.

"But not knowing is a beginning. Anger is a beginning. Fuck, anger got us scholarships to college, remember? *Use* the anger to get out of there."

He said the thing he'd wanted to say for a long time: "Come here. You can live with me. Timon is moving in with his girlfriend at the end of August, but he says I can still sublet the apartment. You can have his room, and I'll help you find work."

"Oh, Carlos, I don't know, I can't think straight right now—"

"Take some time, but will you think about it?"

There was a long silence. "Yes," Pilar finally said. "*Thank you.*"

"You can do this, Pilar. I know how strong you are. I know you."

Pilar dreamed that she was her mother crossing the Rio Grande, losing to the undertow. Eyes squeezed shut against that maquiladora acid bath, she thrashed only to be yanked backwards by the remolinos, shot up for breath only to find herself further from shore. Only when she let the river pull her under, felt her limbs go limp, the departure of breath and blood, did she realize how much she wanted what she'd let go: sand beneath her fingernails as she clawed her way to shore, gasp of polluted sky.

She overslept and rushed to dress for the Singing of the Psalms. She ran up to the chapel and stepped into the line of Sisters behind Mother Connie, who brought up the rear. She sat with Mother Connie in the back pew, glad that she didn't have to make eye contact with the Sisters. She tried to sing, cringing at Mother Connie's high-pitched warble. She thought of Ceci's poem: *On the other side of every blood-red "A" / is the scrape of you not knowing...*

As soon as the singing ended, she told Mother Connie about Flor's detention and Ceci spending the night.

"I must be notified of all overnight guests," Mother Connie said, her face pinched.

"This all happened very late, and we..."

"*We?* Was a Sister involved?"

"I didn't want to wake you." Pilar tried to ignore the angry twitching around Mother Connie's mouth. "Padre Bob thinks he can get Flor released, but Ceci needs someone to look after her until then."

"Go look after her, then, instead of making me late for Mass."

Pilar hurried out.

"See that you don't create any more disturbances!" Mother Connie called after her.

The Sisters turned to watch her go, but Pilar didn't look back. She checked her phone, but there was still no word from Padre.

She found Ceci showered, dressed, and reading, her hair wet and slicked back in a ponytail.

She cooked her a breakfast of eggs and pancakes. Pilar sat across from her at the center of the long table for twelve. When Ceci bowed her head to pray, Pilar squeezed her eyes shut and prayed for Flor's release because she didn't want Ceci praying alone.

Ceci held her back very straight and pushed food around on her plate.

Pilar kept glancing at her, smiling when Ceci caught her. She forced herself to chew rubbery bites of pancake.

She kept checking her phone, willing good news, until Padre Bob finally texted, *got Flor released on our way.*

Ceci's eyes filled when Pilar told her.

Pilar jumped up to hug her and then, glancing down the length of the table, said, "Stupid table," and awkwardly reached across it to squeeze Ceci's hands.

Pilar and Ceci waited on the bench outside of Mother of Sorrows' gate. Ceci's worried grimace held until her mother walked toward her, her eyes sunken, scar darker in the morning light. She and Ceci cried as they moved toward each other. Padre Bob smiled as they embraced.

Pilar asked Flor how she was and she told them about the raid and her detention. How 12 officers had gone through the hotel with guns and rounded up all of the workers—maids, kitchen staff, bellmen—and taken them out to the parking lot. They'd lined 100 of them up against the wall. "Like the Kaibiles do before they kill you," Flor said. "'Citizens to the left, aliens to the right,' they'd yelled. I told myself I was legal. I lined up with the citizens." The other immigrants who'd been working with Flor since the 90s lined up with the citizens, too. They showed the officers what they believed were green cards. The officers handcuffed them along with the aliens. They marched 60 workers single-file into a bus and nine SUVs. "Women were crying, screaming that they were legal. I was shaking, but I did not cry.

"They put all of us, men and women, in a holding cell. It was hot and crowded and they kept shoving more people in. There was one toilet—no toilet paper, no privacy. People were sleeping on the concrete floor, crying." They waited in this cell for hours until their documents were processed. One by one, officers handcuffed people and took them out. They asked them questions and took their fingerprints and photos.

"I told them I had a child, but they wouldn't let me go." That night, they put Flor in a room with 30 women in three-high bunk beds. Ten beds, three women stacked on top of each other. They gave them white sheets to cover the mattress stains. Flor lay awake, worrying about Ceci, listening to women crying. "They threw our food at us. It made me gag. I didn't eat or sleep. I almost fainted when I saw Padre."

Ceci was still holding onto her mother. Not knowing what to say, Pilar moved into their embrace.

Pilar paid for a taxi to take Flor and Ceci home. She made sure they had Padre's and her numbers. Padre told Flor he'd be in touch.

Pilar sat down on the bench with Padre Bob. She asked why Flor had been detained and he answered in a rapid grumble, spitting out words like bullets. She realized that he was angry, too.

He explained that La Placita had tried to get Flor to apply for asylum, but she hadn't been able to talk about her past. The more they pushed, the more she withdrew. She'd seen a corrupt notario who'd made up Flor's asylum application and told her that her work permit was a green card. Padre went on to relay a longwinded series of missteps on the part of this notario, closing his eyes and huffing and puffing out legal acronyms like a big benevolent wolf. He paused and opened his eyes to make sure that Pilar understood.

Pilar nodded, though her sleep-deprived mind was swimming. Before she could make sense of it all, Padre started in with more details. Pilar wondered how much of her situation Flor understood. What Pilar understood was that Flor was going to be deported unless she talked about what she'd experienced in Guatemala.

"La Placita's interviewing sanctuary candidates. I know what Flor went through to get here—" he paused for the first time, "and I think I can convince the committee that Flor and Ceci are worthy candidates. But I need your help." Padre Bob locked eyes with Pilar. "I can get Flor a new asylum interview, but you've got to get her to talk about what happened in Guatemala."

Pilar shifted away, squinted at Padre. "Why would Flor talk to me?"

"I see the bond you have with Ceci—who's the most important thing in the world to her. And you understand what Flor's citizenship would mean for them." Padre Bob looked intently at Pilar.

Pilar shook her head. "I can't go through that again."

"This is not like your father. I believe Flor can get asylum if she tells her story. Take today to think about it and call me tomorrow."

Pilar did what she always did when she had to make a decision. She withdrew—from the Sisters and Carlos—and tunneled into herself. She walked the perimeter of the monastery grounds the way she used to walk the perimeter of her junior high schoolyard, sandwich in one hand and dog-eared copy of George Oppen's *Primitive* in the other. She walked and ate, peanutbutter and poetry: *the poem begins / neither in word / nor meaning but the small / selves haunting / us...* She imagined herself walking New York City streets with Carlos, laughing, red and yellow leaves falling. She'd never seen fall.

As she passed the garden, Letitia saw her and came out to ask if everything was okay.

"Everything's okay." Pilar smiled a tight-lipped smile.

Letitia searched her eyes in that way that used to comfort her.

Pilar looked away.

"Okay, come help me weed if you want." Letitia smiled. "Tempting, I know."

"Thanks, but I have a lot of papers to get through," she said.

Pilar kept walking, the smell of citrus trailing her. She remembered the orange on the floor after the man in the black car left, fear taut in her body as she picked it up and peeled it for her father. That fear unfolding as she pushed her fingers into the packed soil of the garden, handed clementines to her students.

She couldn't leave Ceci. She had to try to help with Flor's asylum application. But who was she to do that? A recent graduate who still hadn't figured out what to do with her life. She was barely figuring out how to teach poetry to adolescents—not quite the same stakes. She was angry that there wasn't someone more capable. She hadn't understood half of what Padre said. It wasn't fair to Flor. And then she was angry at MJ again, talking about what a hero Padre Bob was for fighting the battles she wouldn't. MJ blaming Mother Connie for her own cowardice.

She glimpsed the path that led through the woods to the hermitages, which hadn't been used in years. She shuddered and kept moving, thinking, reading, walking in circles.

MJ gave Pilar space, but Robin came to her cell after she missed dinner. She asked if everything was alright, and Pilar again said she just had a lot of papers to get through.

She fell asleep no closer to a decision. In the middle of the night, she shot up in bed from some nightmare she couldn't remember. She put on shoes, descended the stairs, and walked toward what scared her. She felt her way along the path through the woods, arms outstretched, pushing branches back and stumbling over roots and rocks.

Five hermitages stood in a row. She could see by the light of the moon that their roofs had collapsed. Vines grew through their broken windows. A bad feeling filled her bones but she pushed through it, opened the splintered door of the first, and ducked under the low threshold. Cobwebs clung to her face. The air smelled mildewy. She closed the door. The bench creaked when she sat. She ran her hands over the warped wood.

Voices filled her head, prayers that were not about peace.

She threw the door open and stumbled out. The moon swelled and branches wrapped around her throat. She felt Buster's weight, his hand pinning her shoulder as he unbuckled his belt. She thrust his body off of hers and her breath came back, sharp and jagged.

She ran back to her cell, blood pounding in her ears. She opened her notebook. Poems poured out in the shape of confessional boxes:

Flor:

>   his boot in me before his dick no difference his animal
>   hands and the desert rubbing me raw his body thrusting
>   and the buzzards circling no difference after you're dead
>   *forgive me God* I dream I drag his body through red des-
>   ert sand I dream I feed it part by part I dream I uncircle
>   the buzzards

MJ:

>   life does not begin when the man meant to guide her
>   binds her wrists guides his fist inside her mouth foreplay
>   for a louder silence she has paid this *coyote* to claw
>   through wire and now she carries his bastard seed inside
>   her for forty nights your light has died her body shrivel-
>   ing like the desert while the hole grows inside her *forgive
>   me father* what devil calls this life she was dead when
>   she came to me I did not ask how many months I took
>   her to a doctor who would not turn away we could not
>   close the hole but we could see the ugly ways in which
>   the flesh tried to grow back

Maybe those words, inside and outside of her, running through her veins and onto the page were God.

She called Carlos and told him that she would stay at Mother of Sorrows until her students returned to school and then move to New York.

Carlos squealed and she smiled. Telling him made it real.

She said she'd continue teaching and do all she could to help with Flor's asylum application until then.

"Are you sure you're up for that?"

"I'll hate myself if I don't try."

"Okay, but I want you to call me anytime. I'll be checking in on you. When do the kids go back to school?"

"August 20th."

"Great. August 20th. I'm buying you a ticket so you can't back out. If you need to come earlier, we'll change it. But I want you to have an end in sight."

Pilar protested about his paying for the ticket, but it was no use. She'd made her decision, and Carlos had made his.

"I need to tell you something else." Her voice cracked. She could feel Carlos listening—the taut line between them.

"You were the only person I talked to after—"

"I know, sweetie. You don't have to say it."

"Yes, I do. You were the only person I talked to after Buster raped me." The words pushed through her skin, outside of her.

Carlos' love absorbed them the way the caña absorbed bodies.

CHAPTER 15

If Carlos performed Carmen Madonna one more time, he'd vomit in her fruit turban. Encouraged by his Family Feng, he marched into the back office, where Nathaniel was tallying up the night's earnings, and demanded to perform a song of his choice in a costume of his design.

"Absolutely not," Nathaniel said without looking up. "You've just started doing Carmen and everybody loves her."

"Except me," Carlos said. "Shouldn't that matter?"

Nathaniel finished tallying a few more receipts before he looked up at Carlos over his chartreuse reading glasses. He puffed air through his lips and the receipts rustled. He swizzled his chair around to examine the NYC Firefighters calendar on the wall. "How's Thursday?" He swizzled back around and italicized his checkmate with a raised eyebrow.

Carlos gulped. "*This* Thursday?"

"I assume you wouldn't have asked if you weren't ready, and I'm not going to let you launch your little experiment on a Saturday. Thursday's my final offer and it can't be any longer than your Carmen Madonna act. And it's *your* tips if the bachelorettes don't get it."

Carlos took a deep breath and said, "Deal."

He spent the next few days strutting around his apartment to "Gloria", bounding onto his desk chair and singing it into a hairbrush. Thursday night, he buzzed around Lucky Feng's dressing room in shorts and a T-shirt, helping the Sisters dress. He planned to wait until they were gone to slip on the eagle's wings dress. He wanted a moment alone with it, and he wanted to surprise them.

"What are you doing?" Cher shooed him away. "Get ready!"

"I'm not wearing anything under my dress and I'm just doing a little makeup," Carlos said. He also wasn't wearing a wig. He'd been growing his hair since he started working at Lucky Feng's. It was glossy black and wavy and fell past his shoulders.

"No tights, no pads... no *tuck*?" Cher pursed her sparkling purple lips and Carlos felt her holding her tongue. "Okay, okay, free and easy like. It's very Brooklyn of you, very avant garde. At least let us see the dress, though."

Carlos shook his head. "Not yet."

"Aw, not before the wedding," Juana said.

The Sisters' cooing over Baby Carlitos before his big night was arrested by a small Korean woman in a gauzy white shift walking into the dressing room, parting the haze of Aqua Net and glitter.

The Sisters turned toward her with unbridled smiles like a flock of geese changing course. "Dr. Yoon!" they cried and lined up to hug her like she was the Dalai Lama.

So this was the legendary Dr. Yoon. Carlos craned his neck around the Sisters' barrage of big hair to get a good look. She was the subtlest queen he'd ever seen. Her luminous skin made it difficult to tell her age. Something about her made Carlos think of the resaca when it was very still.

Nathaniel popped his head in to see what all the commotion was about. "Sweet Jesus, the Prodigal returneth!" He threw his hands up in the air before enfolding Dr. Yoon in a deep embrace.

"Baby Carlitos, meet Dr. Yoon, our Drag Glamma," Bama said.

Dr. Yoon smiled at Carlos and his chest cavity opened like clouds parting.

"How was Korea?" the Sisters asked. "Did you find your mother?"

Dr. Yoon shook her head, a wisp of dark hair slipping from her bun. "No, but I learned Salpuri from the masters."

"I've had that soup!" Cher cried.

Dr. Yoon laughed, crow's feet crinkling around her deep-set eyes. "It's an ancient Korean healing dance. I've made it my own. You'll see tonight, I hope..." She looked at Nathaniel.

"We'll put you on before Carlos," Nathaniel said slyly.

Cher gasped. Juana's eyes grew wide. Kim chewed her bottom lip.

Seeing Nathaniel's smug smile before he left the dressing room, Carlos understood, with a Cyclone drop in his stomach, that he'd just been sabotaged.

Nathaniel introduced Dr. Yoon with none of his usual innuendo: "A woman of wisdom and grace, a healer of wounds. Let's hear it for Dr. Yoon!" Her only props were a tall metal standing fan and a projection screen. She wore a white silk dress made of draping folds of fabric and held a white scarf. When she walked on stage, the audience stopped talking, the waitresses stopped serving, and Joey stopped twisting balloons into ménage à trois configurations.

An elegiac flutter of piano keys began tentatively, like a memory surfacing. Carla recognized it as Philip Glass' "Mad Rush", which she'd walked around listening to for days after she first heard it, feeling expansive and dramatic and like everything was connected.

Dr. Yoon began a slow, stilted turning, drawing the white scarf through the air, ushering morning light into the dim bar. Carla remembered egrets lifting from the resaca as she pulled up to Pilar's house.

The melody repeated, gathering force. Dr. Yoon's turning shifted from broken to fluid. She crossed her arms over her chest and became a dervish, the scarf's shadow whirling across the screen.

She curled into herself, kneeling, tightening into a knot. She hung down from her waist like a rag doll, fingers brushing the floor, slowly sweeping from side to side like a clock pendulum, swinging faster as she whooshed upward. She stretched her lithe body skyward, swayed the spread tips of her fingers like windblown branches.

The audience's, Sisters', and even Nathaniel's eyes were transfixed.

Dr. Yoon bent toward the fan. Wisps of hair slipped from her bun and lifted into the air like thoughts departing the body. She lay on the stage, rolling her body like waves. Carla held her breath, then breathed deep as Dr. Yoon changed the tides.

The notes accelerated and tumbled into each other, crescendoing and colliding, opening and dying. Dr. Yoon's movements became frantic, bipolar. She leapt across the stage, then crumpled like she'd been stabbed; pirouetted wildly, then froze. She walked a tightrope between dancing and falling. She was barbed wire and open road. Cliff edge and crescent moon. Fireflies and razed field.

The music slowed and broke down. Dr. Yoon ran toward the audience, arms outstretched, then stopped abruptly, her head and body jerking backwards like she'd crashed into a wall. She tried again, tiptoeing slowly, tentatively toward them and crashed again. The fluid motions of her arms broke down like some dying machine. She collapsed in a heap at the edge of the stage, her eyes drifting over the audience and landing on Carla. She held her at the border between sadness and light, opened her mouth and called her by some soundless name.

Dr. Yoon rose up like a redwood breaking through cables, tunnels, sewers, and concrete to grow in that cramped East Village bar. Her roots entangled with a mycelium network swimming through the audience's bones, brains, and marrow.

She stretched out her arms, her hands reaching, straining, pulling Carla toward her. The under of her spoke to the under of Carla. This was the egg drawn over her skin and cracked; this was the spotted yolk. The stumble out of faith, into faith. Carla hadn't realized she'd lost it, hadn't realized there was more to believe. She stood mute, broken, lost in the nameless darkness beneath a beginning. Tears rolled down her cheeks.

Nathaniel's introduction was a distant, underwater sound: "Every queen has a diva, and Carla's is Patti Smith..."

Carla jumped when Cher put her hand on her shoulder and exhaled a ragged breath. "Are you ready, sweetie?" she asked dazedly, tear tracks trailing through her foundation.

Carla shook her head, open-mouthed, unable to speak.

"Yes, you are, honey." Cher wiped Carla's tears. "Head up, shoulders back," she demonstrated, "like the Queen you are. Show them what you're made of."

Carla no longer knew what she was made of. She stared out at the audience—newborn, blurry-eyed, primed to absorb everything. And she was supposed to perform another old, wornout act. An old, wornout self. She closed her eyes and imagined herself listening to "Gloria" in the car in high school, tried to feel the wind and speed of driving toward the border, the queens of 10th Avenue tilting toward El Ojo like sunflowers. But that air lodged in her throat. The song she heard in her head was a dull-edged ventriloquism.

Nathaniel waited at the microphone, his face pinched.

Carla breathed deep, fingering the gardenia tucked behind her ear.

Feeling generous after Dr. Yoon's performance, a bachelorette started chanting, *Carla!* The chant spread through the tables of bachelorettes and tourists—*Carla! Carla!*—growing louder, but it was a dull roar in Carla's ears.

The sound of the audience dimmed and the insistent pulse of her heart beneath those frayed gray wings answered, *No. No. No.*

Carla walked slowly up to the stage. She was a child walking through the redwood forest the bar had become, wandering alone through those endless giants, feeling, knowing her smallness in the universe.

Nathaniel shoved the microphone into her hand.

The bartender who doubled as DJ put on "Gloria".

As the opening chords played, Carla looked out at her Sisters, who'd stopped waiting tables and stood frozen, watching her with worried faces. She wanted to tell them that there was nothing to worry about, nothing to fear.

"You can do this," Cher mouthed slowly.

Sweet Max, Carla thought. She felt such overwhelming affection for him in that moment that it was painful. She shook her head, smiled slowly.

She looked at the DJ and drew her fingers across her throat.

He cut the music and the bar fell silent.

"I can't do this anymore," she said and felt the exhilaration of freefall surrounded by a soft cloud of zen. Was this what a skydiver felt when they lay back into the fall and threw out their arms?

Dr. Yoon smiled at her from the back of the bar. She nodded at Carla, as if her work here was done, and left. Carla stared out at the audience, the Sisters, and even Nathaniel, who'd cried during Dr. Yoon's performance so that she saw the bullied freckles-and-braces boy beneath his facelift.

"You were all so beautiful tonight," she said. She put her right hand over her wings like a pledge of allegiance and said what seemed like the only words we needed: "I'm sorry... Thank you."

Nathaniel rushed back up to the stage, grabbed the mic, and shoved Carla out of the way. He ran a hand through his coiffed silver hair and announced, with a tight smile, that the show would resume after a brief intermission.

Carla lifted her dress and floated down the steps leading offstage.

"Sweetie, what happened, are you okay?" Cher asked when she got to the back of the bar. The Sisters gathered around her, worried.

"I'm really okay." Carla squeezed Cher's arm, smiled at the Sisters. "I'll call you," she said a little dazedly and made her way to the dressing room.

In the dressing room, Carla slipped the eagle's wings dress over her head, carefully hung it in her garment bag, and changed into her boy clothes.

The Sisters were singing their emergency backup number, "Girls Just Want to Have Fun", as Carlos left. It was a lame followup to Dr. Yoon, but they performed with all of their usual zeal, showgirls to the core.

As he wove through Lucky Feng's tables toward the door, Carlos remembered something Susanna had told him as they walked Ralph in Riverside Park. She'd said that the dirt path they were on was a desire line—a path made by people who wanted a path where there wasn't one.

Carlos biked west toward the Hudson River. He rode through Washington Square Park, looping three times around the fountain while listening to "Mad Rush", taking in the kaleidoscopic whirl of students, couples, musicians, chess players, skateboarders, and cops. He took Gay Street to Christopher Street, passing the Oscar Wilde Memorial Bookshop, the Stonewall Inn, the Big Gay Ice Cream Shop, dreaming himself into that desire line. As he approached the river, he caught his breath at the full yellow moon sailing over the glittering skyline.

He stopped at Christopher Street Pier, where he saw a circle of Black and Latine teenagers near its end. The circle parted and he caught sight of shadows slicing the downtown skyline. He hadn't known that vogue battles still happened on the piers. He'd learned in his queer history class about activists from the ballroom scene creating Kiki Houses for queer youth, many of whom had been rejected from their families and faced homelessness, joblessness, or HIV. Each "house" had a "mother," "father," and "children" who competed in balls, vying for prizes in runway competitions and performance-art battles, the most well known of which was voguing.

He locked up his bike and walked toward the circle. House music pulsed on a boombox, a song with a circular, rising beat, its boom moving into his solar plexus as he got closer. He moved his shoulder in time with the music as he edged through the crowd toward the circle's center. He dropped his body as the beat escalated, locked eyes with a muscled boy in a tank top as he rose.

He joined in the watchers' cries of awe and affirmation as voguers flailed their arms, twirled, pranced, spun, duck-walked, breakdanced, did the splits, rolled, twisted, backwalked, high-kicked, dipped precariously, then rose. Neon nails and braids, metallic sneakers and laceup boots flew through the air. An MC chanted rhymes as bodies of all kinds carved themselves out against the night, carved out space for their beauty— defiant and railing, flailing, scrawling their stories against the sharp-lit windows of skyscrapers behind them. He thought about how the circle protected, enabled, the center. He thought about voguing as survival, preservation, celebration. A motion of making your self, your circle. A dance between love and rage, rawness and ferocity, being eyed and staring back—sharp arms controlling, framing the gaze. Carlos watched, open-mouthed, woken and held by the beauty of this fight/dance beneath the moon, by the river, that fluid border, the water rising, sloshing against the pier, the circle, center of them screaming, kicking into the night.

He watched for a long time before biking south along the water, mind on fire. He didn't understand how yet, but felt that Dr. Yoon's and the Kikis' dances answered each other. One ethereal, transcendent, other-worldly; the other raw, visceral, unscripted. One brokenness churned into love, the other rage and sadness exploded into celebration.

What was the desire line between them? Did it look like moonlight scattered over the Hudson? That heartbreaking beauty in this hardhearted city?

Max texted: *Let me know you got home safe.*

When he got home, Carlos unzipped the eagle's wings dress from its garment bag. Moonlight slanted through his uncurtained window as he stripped off his boy clothes and slipped on the dress as he had that first time. There'd been no mirrors, just Carla surfacing from a sea of discarded things and Pilar saying, *It's you.*

She wore the dress like that castoff skin. She slipped her sparkly purple toenails into flipflops, tucked her wallet into a canvas grocery bag, and walked out into the summer night. Carlos hadn't walked through his neighborhood in a dress since the night of the Subway Heller.

Carla reclaimed the late-night markets where Carlos grabbed essentials on his way home from shows. She wandered the vegetable market on Nostrand. The pretty Jamaican woman who worked the cashier late at night and called everybody *Honey* bantered with a man who'd come in to flirt. Carlos didn't really need anything, but bought honey, cinnamon, and collard greens just to hold them in Carla's hands. She felt the cashier staring as she pulled bills from her wallet. The woman's head was still cocked when Carla handed her the money.

"You reminded me I needed honey, Honey."

The woman laughed softly, and then as Carla's lips spread into a sly smile, more freely.

Carla wandered over to the 24-hour green market on Franklin, examining things with her manicured hands and settling on salted milk-chocolate almonds. She knew the late-night cashier here, too, a 16- or 17-year-old Asian boy with spiky hair the color of psychedelic grass who'd ask, "Is this good?" as he rang up people's items.

"Beautiful dress." The boy reached out to touch—as if he couldn't help it—the frayed edges of the wings over Carla's collarbone.

"Thank you," Carla said. She saw herself in his wonder and chutzpah, curiosity and desire to charm.

"Where'd you get it?" the boy asked.

Carla painted the landscape of the Ropa Usada, foothills of castoff lives waiting to be reclaimed.

The boy listened with his chin propped in his hands. "Wow," he said.

The story swam in the charged air between them. "Can I take this pen?" Carla asked as she signed the receipt. "And do you have paper?"

"Totally!" the boy said. He ducked behind the counter and pulled a notebook from his backpack. He tore out three sheets. "Is this enough?"

"Perfect, thank you." Carla smiled dazedly and headed for the door.

"Hey, you forgot—" the boy called after her, holding up the almonds.

"Keep them," Carla called without turning around. "Thanks for the pen and paper!"

Carla walked past the restaurants, bars, and bodegas on Franklin Avenue to the Eastern Parkway Mall. She found a bench beneath a street lamp and started writing the desire line between Dr. Yoon and the Kikis. She had no idea what shape it would take, but not knowing was a beginning.

For now, it looked like a list of scattered moments, songs, and ideas.

It looked like the stream of cars, flashing like fire through the trees.

CHAPTER 16

The original sanctuary movement moved in secret. Refugees were hidden because they were fleeing civil wars created or funded by the US. In the new movement, families took sanctuary openly and churches publicized their stories. "As long as the family is public and in the legal process, we're not breaking any laws," Padre said. He met with La Placita's Sanctuary Committee and told them about the raid that had caused Flor to lose her job. He told them, in confidence, that Flor had been raped and impregnated by her coyote and kept the child, a daughter who was now 14 and whom she was raising alone. He told them that she was Mayan and Guatemalan and that the tortures she'd fled were so horrific that she hadn't been able to speak about them in her asylum interview. He said that over the next couple of months, Flor would struggle to unearth that story for a new asylum application. He said she was in danger of losing her apartment, that she and Ceci needed a safe place to stay, and that she needed help with Ceci's Catholic school tuition. The committee voted unanimously to offer Flor and Ceci sanctuary and volunteers from La Placita helped them move. Padre Bob got a press release to the *LA Times*.

The Sisters pored over the article at midday meal.

"Thank God," MJ said.

The Sisters who knew Flor echoed her relief.

Pilar narrowed her eyes at MJ, angry at her for pretending she cared, but said nothing. She'd told Padre Bob that she would help with Flor's asylum application, but she hadn't told any of the Sisters. She didn't know if she could trust them.

"Flor is Ceci's mother?" Letitia asked, remembering Ceci from open mic night.

"What's this about Flor?" Mother Connie asked sharply as she entered the dining room.

Robin explained that Flor had taken sanctuary at La Placita.

Mother Connie snatched the newspaper from the table and propped her reading glasses, which hung from a chain around her neck, on the tip of her nose. She puffed air through her thin lips as she read about Padre Bob's activist history. "They write about him like he's a hero when he's violating the sanctity of the Church. Five years' probation wasn't enough?"

MJ shot a sideways glance at Pilar.

Pilar looked away. They were not allies.

"I know that those of you at Project Luz are close to Flor, but let me make clear," Mother Connie's sunken gray eyes bore into Pilar and MJ, "in case you have any inkling of involving yourself in Flor's case, that that kind of political entanglement is utterly in conflict with Carmelite life."

Pilar's chest tightened. She widened her eyes at Sister Robin and Letitia, but their faces remained placid.

Mother Connie saw and fixed on her like a hawk. "Though my work keeps me from being as present as one might like, rest assured that within these walls, God and I make the rules." Her voice was low and cool except for sudden, startling emphases, like a ruler rapping knuckles. "You are here because *I* have allowed you to be here, and we are not a political order. Our work is in prayer and service. *Your* work is teaching and you must be *very* clear on the fact that Mother of Sorrows will *not* be housing any political dissidents."

Pilar stared back icily.

"Let us pray that we remain true to our mission." Mother Connie bowed her head and the Sisters followed suit.

Pilar did not close her eyes. She stared straight ahead, words gathering in her throat.

She'd planned to tell Robin and Letitia that she was leaving before announcing it, but now she blurted it out defiantly almost as soon as the Sisters opened their eyes: "I've realized that this isn't the right place for me." Her heart raced, her armpits grew damp, and her voice was higher than she would have liked. She kept her eyes on Mother Connie, afraid to look at the Sisters. "I'll teach until my students return to school and then I'm moving to New York." New York was a place she'd seen only in movies, but when she spoke its name, it was as if the Statue of Liberty herself rose up through the center of that long table of nuns and opened her arms.

Pilar let her guard down and looked at MJ.

MJ's eyes shone briefly before she smiled. "We absolutely support your decision. We want you to be happy." She held Pilar's eyes and said it with such uncomplicated good will that something broke inside her.

Luckily Mother Connie rushed in with a tart, "Well, we're sorry to see you go, but then few of us are made for Carmelite life." She smiled knowingly around the table.

The Sisters, to their credit, ignored her.

"Of course, we completely understand," Letitia jumped in, "and we're so grateful for the work you've done here."

Then Robin, her eyes brimming unabashedly: "What you've achieved with the youth is remarkable. Mother of Sorrows won't be the same without you."

The other Sisters chimed in with their own thanks and blessings.

Their softness, when she needed to remain hard and separate, hurt. She remembered planting holy basil in the dark with Sister Letitia and her body loosened. She felt the loss of these women, what they'd been to her, what she'd believed them to be. Her nose stung and there was a burning in the back of her eyes.

Robin gave her a worried look.

She would not cry. She straightened her back, looked Letitia, Robin, and even MJ in the eyes, and thanked them. Her voice was soft, but she kept herself bordered. "I'm grateful for my time here. I've learned a lot."

She politely excused herself, saying she had to prepare for class.

What hurt more was when Robin, and then Letitia, came to her cell afterwards.

"I just wanted to say again how much we'll—*I'll*—miss you." Robin stood in her doorway.

Pilar turned from her desk, smiled and thanked her.

"Is it okay if I come in?"

Pilar nodded, not knowing how to say no.

She felt queasy when Robin plopped onto her bed, leaned toward her, and said too brightly, "Tell me about your plans for New York!"

"I don't really have plans, just a friend I can stay with."

"Is that the friend you used to canoe with?"

Pilar nodded uneasily. She'd forgotten that she'd mentioned Carlos to Robin. It was impossible to talk about home without talking about him. She had to start walling things off.

Her cell felt cramped and airless, the pathway between bed, desk, and wardrobe, between Robin and her, all sharp edges.

Letitia said she was happy for her. "It was such a sad time when I was at St. Vincent's, but I loved that city. I used to walk along the river at night. I talked to it sometimes. The river or God—who knows?" She laughed.

Pilar smiled with her mouth, but not her eyes.

"I know teaching keeps you busy, but come take a break in the garden from time to time, okay?"

Pilar nodded—wanting that so badly that she could feel the sun on her shoulders, her hands in the soil—knowing that those days were over.

The double grille came down and they could not touch.

At first it was painful to sit down to meals like a family and feel their separateness, to bow her head and hear nothing. And then gradually the sharpness of the lie dulled and became part of her—a limp she no longer noticed.

Was that how it was for MJ? Was that how it was for her father?

In workshop, Ceci stared into space as the other students wrote. Pilar squatted beside her and asked how she was. Ceci shook her head. She'd believed the card her mother carried everywhere could keep them safe. She'd arranged her books and trophies on the shelves of her room at La Placita, but there was no sanctuary.

"Do you want to just read?" Pilar asked.

Ceci nodded and pulled the battered copy of *The House on Mango Street* from her backpack.

Pilar noticed for the first time that it was a library book. She would buy her a copy before the next class.

Padre picked up Ceci after class. Because they'd publicized Flor's sanctuary, she could be apprehended if she left La Placita. Pilar talked with Padre about when she would meet with Flor. They decided that one night a week was enough—anything more would be too intense—and planned for him to pick Pilar up at 9, outside the gate, after the Sisters were in private contemplation.

La Placita was just a mile and a half from Mother of Sorrows, in Echo Park. It was an old church, its offices and conference rooms along narrow, windowless hallways. Pilar met with Flor in a conference room. Padre unlocked the room. He set a file with Flor's old asylum application and two copies of the blank application form in Spanish on the table. He showed the old applicaton to Flor and said, "You can see that the notario made this up." He left to work in his office down the hall.

Flor looked at the photo of herself attached to the old application. "That was so long ago," she said. "My eyes were dead then." She put the photo back, closed the file.

Flor had told Ceci only that her family had been killed in Guatemala's Civil War. She would have to decide how much more to tell her, how much of her story she wanted to make public. Pilar imagined she hadn't told anyone about the coyote raping her besides Padre and MJ. She didn't know that MJ had told Pilar. Because Padre had sworn MJ to secrecy, Flor didn't know that he'd given MJ the money for her abortion. She didn't know that Padre had told the Sanctuary Committee that her coyote had raped her and that that story was part of the committee choosing her and Ceci over dozens of other applicants.

The web of secrets they were tangled in made Pilar anxious. She felt tightly wound, angry for Flor. Constructing a story amidst so many hidden things was at once familiar and impossible—like tiptoeing around Roberto's death to find the words that would save her father. She had the same sense that all the silences were connected, that one secret would unlock another.

She and Flor sat across a table from each other, staring at the application. Pilar read the questions aloud as if she were reading an assignment to her class. She knew that these metallic words were the wrong way to begin.

When answering the following questions about your asylum or other protection claim (withholding of removal under 241(b)(3) of the INA or withholding of removal under the Convention Against Torture), you must provide a detailed and specific account of the basis of your claim to asylum or other protection. To the best of your ability, provide specific dates, places, and descriptions about each event or action described. You must attach documents evidencing the general conditions in the country from which you are seeking asylum or other protection and the specific facts on which you are relying to support your claim.

Flor's expression shifted from confusion to anger as Pilar read. She folded her arms over her chest.

"You have every right to be angry," Pilar said.

The question was followed by a narrow box. Padre believed that Flor had the kind of case that fit in this box, which is to say the kind of case that could never fit in this box. And what about people who hadn't fled government torture? Wasn't it enough for your father and brother to die in the mines, for your town to have an average lifespan of 40, for everyone you knew to have died? Where did that circle in which survival equaled death fit? Why wasn't it enough, for that matter, to have made a life and a family here, to do work that was needed, to look out like a lover each morning upon the small, dry patch of America you'd struggled to make your own against their power to take it from you at any moment?

Pilar wanted to crumple the application into a ball. She realized she was making a fist.

Flor was silent for a long time before she said, "They don't care what happened. I'm here out of respect for Padre and you, but I don't believe this will change anything."

"Padre thinks he can get you asylum if you'll talk about what happened in Guatemala. You don't believe him?"

"I believe what I saw. Six men came into the lunchroom with guns. A bunch of women eating—lunch the only time we're more than machines. They rounded us up like animals. Fifteen years in this country, working three jobs, paying taxes, carrying that stupid card, and they do this to me? To *these* people I'm going to speak what I've never spoken?"

Flor unfolded her arms, her body, and began to pace. The room was the too small box.

"I told them I was a citizen, and they put me in jail. I begged them to let me go for Ceci—it was the only time I cried—and they kept me overnight. My story does not matter to them."

"It's not just for them," Pilar said. "Padre says stories like yours change laws. You're telling your story for all the people who've sacrificed everything to come here and still live in fear. For Ceci, so she can know the strength she came from."

Flor's eyes went opaque. "That story is dead. I don't want Ceci to know."

Pilar said nothing for awhile. "Did Ceci tell you my father's undocumented?"

Flor's face softened. "Ceci told me there's no hope for him. I'm sorry."

"I grew up afraid to speak about it. Papá told me not to tell anyone, that if I misbehaved he'd be deported. An officer came to the house when I was nine. I'd gotten in trouble at school, and I was sure he'd be deported. His father and brother died in the mines in Bolivia, and we never spoke about that, either. We never had people over. My father still lives with that fear. I still live with that fear. But you could pass a different story to Ceci."

Pilar and Flor stared at each other from across the room for a long time until Flor began to nod—tentatively and then fiercely.

Flor pushed the file with her old application away as she sat next to Pilar. "I'm not that woman anymore," she said. "I'm stronger now."

Pilar saw that she was ready. All she had to do was listen, be a body to remind Flor as she told that story, *You're not there; you're here*. She knew how to sit in darkness and listen.

They'd begun sitting across from each other. Now they sat shoulder to shoulder.

They circled the wound. Flor could only remember the afterward. "I remember leaving what had been my village—dead after what I saw." Her body knew only to move, to let the air in. The wind breathed for her—the grit of it in her teeth. Her body walked out of the mountains and got on a bus. Her body became the bus—rusted metal and worn tires churning through dust, air whistling through the cracked windows.

"I returned to the family I worked for in Guatemala City. I said nothing of what I'd seen. My lips moved only to say, 'Sí, señora,' but I listened to everything they said. Their language was ugly, like their lives. But I knew I would need it to leave. I had learned enough Spanish to get by in my first year with them, but now I repeated phrases to myself as I worked. I had the children read to me. I watched their fingers move over the letters as they sounded out the words. I pored over their books late into the night. I copied words, learned to read signs.

"I wanted so much more for Ceci. That's why I cried when she read her writing. I never thought I would have a child. My body was dead for so long."

For 10 years, she worked. Her body moved to erase the past—footprints, crumbs, dust. "I tucked every bill I earned under my mattress. I lay awake with hunger, repeating phrases in the dark, until it was late enough to sneak food from their kitchen.

"I saved for 10 years. Every cent I gave to that coyote. I can still see his slimy smile as he counted the bills. Jorge no last name, Jorge not really his first name. He guided me north through Mexico, then through the desert toward the border. We heard la migra's Jeep when we crossed. We hid behind rocks until it passed. We continued walking through the desert. My shoes were soft and the nopal pricked my feet. I hardly felt the pricks or heat. I crossed the border a ghost.

"There were so many of us. Olvidados. We did not speak." They had no words for what they'd seen, what they'd sold. There were so many— washing dishes, making beds, erasing the leavings of las canches' lives. "Invisible, but we didn't care. It hurt to be seen."

Pilar looked at Flor and Flor looked back, but there was something absent in her eyes. They made her think of her father's eyes.

"MJ told me what the coyote did," she blurted and immediately hated herself for it.

"She shouldn't have told you." Flor's eyes flashed. She pushed back from the table, moved toward the door.

Pilar remembered how angry her father had been when she'd asked as a child how Roberto had died. "I'm sorry." She held Flor's gaze. "She only told me to protect you from..." The Mother Connie saga was too much to go into. "You're right; it wasn't theirs to tell. I shouldn't have—I'm sorry."

Pilar thought about how hard it was to speak that pain, how as best you could you built another life, tried to find meaning and joy. How hard it was to dredge up that past life in language, how you had to feel it to speak it. You'd moved on, you were living in another country, breathing different air, and you had to drag that darkness into it, admit you'd never left it.

And in that moment when you asked someone to help you hold it, it was so raw and pulsing and desperate that it was *all* of you, so that you could barely survive it before someone—she was so lucky her someone was Carlos—accepted it. Flor was being forced to do that for a near-stranger.

Flor stood by the door.

"I'm so sorry," Pilar said again, standing to look her in the eyes. "I think you should try to get a good night's sleep. We'll meet next week."

Flor tipped up her chin, narrowed her eyes. "Did MJ tell you I was saved?"

Pilar shook her head, not knowing what she meant.

"After days of walking through the desert, muscles cramping, heart racing like I'd faint, I thought, *After everything, I am going to die.* I was too angry to die. I fought with the coyote, who'd told me it would take only a day. And yes, he beat and raped me. He said he would leave me to die. Buzzards circled above me.

"But I didn't die," Flor said defiantly. She described a woman walking out of the horizon, quick and silent, the light so bright it blacked her out, until she stood behind the coyote. A shadow against the sun, small with a mass of curly black hair, she raised a scythe like Santa Muerte and brought it down on the coyote's neck as he thrust into Flor. "Blood gushed into my mouth. When I next woke, MJ stood over me at Mother of Sorrows. I thought I'd dreamed the woman, but others have stories. They call her Luz."

The hair on the back of Pilar's neck stood.

"They say she smuggles immigrants through tunnels."

Pilar thought of how her father had prayed to El Tio, who went where God wouldn't.

"Have you heard of Luz?" Pilar asked Padre Bob as he drove her back to Mother of Sorrows.

His eyes flicked left then right. "A myth the immigrants believe in," he said without looking at her. "Santeria, that's all."

"What if we drag Flor through this process and they don't give her asylum?" Pilar asked.

"The stories from Guatemala—from that time—are horrific. My gut says Flor's got a clear asylum claim."

"Your gut?"

"You aren't backing out, are you?"

Pilar stared out the window at the world rushing by.

"I'm not letting you back out," Padre grumbled. "My gut says you need to see this through."

The next time they met, Flor walked to the edge of the story. "At 15, I left my village in the highlands and took a job as a maid in Guatemala City," she said. "My father was sick, and my family needed the money. I worked and saved for a year. When I heard that the army had burned my village, I returned home. I walked through a blackened field, burnt husks beneath my feet, ash in the air. At the edge of the field was a cow carcass, its head cut from its body. Its eyes looked at me, flies buzzing around them. The buzzing filled my chest."

Flor stopped.

Pilar stared out at that blackened field with her in silence.

"She needs more time," Pilar said to Padre Bob on the drive back to Mother of Sorrows.

Padre Bob nodded. He was quiet, worn down by his own troubles. The road was deserted, darkness hurtling toward them.

"I'm tired of being trapped inside," Flor said the next time they met. La Placita had involved her in its English, yoga, and meditation classes;

fellowship groups; and choir, but she had not been outside of its walls for a month. Even if they filed a strong asylum case, it could be many months before Flor's case was heard. Flor paced with her hands clasped on her head. "It gives you too much stress. I feel nauseous. Like I can't breathe."

"I used to run before I came to Mother of Sorrows," Pilar said. "If I was sad or scared, I ran through it. I could push my body into a different place. Sometimes I ran in the dark, when I shouldn't have been running alone."

Flor and Pilar stared at each other, the same question in their eyes.

"If I could just walk outside," Flor said. "Just breathe the air."

"We'd just be two women walking," Pilar said. "Why would they stop us?"

Flor leaving Sanctuary, the two of them walking the streets at night, was dangerous. But they needed night to hold darkness. They walked through empty blue streets hatched by the egg-shaped moon. They became Senoras de las Sombras: in their country, there were no secrets, shame, borders. They walked through the neighborhoods surrounding La Placita, up and down hills past condos, warehouses, parks, and houses— the downtown skyline in the distance.

When they'd walked awhile, Flor said, "I remember..." then shook her head, the memory dispersed in the thick summer night. The air held their silence. They kept walking. Silence became a thing they could pass through.

"I started running after I was raped," Pilar said. "It was nothing like what you— It was just someone I knew. Thought I knew. Someone who said he loved me. I fought, but it didn't matter." She hated that her voice still broke.

She took long strides uphill, looking in the windows of the houses, focusing on the shifting scenery, insisting: *You're not there. You're here.*

Flor reached for her hand, tugged her backwards, still. She hugged her like a mother. Pilar's five-foot-ten-inches sank into Flor's not quite five-foot embrace. It felt like she'd walked for days—years—through a desert to be held, soft and warm and fierce, like this. Her anger, anxiety, aloneness melted and left sadness like a bruise in her throat.

Flor didn't pull away until she did. They faced each other at the top of the hill.

"For a long time, I stopped fighting," Pilar said. "I wasn't talking to Papá, but I felt his fear. I ran to take back my body. This is worth fighting for, Flor."

They looked out at the sprawl of houses and hills, the city lit in the distance. "You and Ceci belong here."

As they descended the hill, the sky cracked open and it began to rain. The drops picked up speed until it was pouring. They ducked into a crumbling stone tunnel in a park. Boxes were flattened over the ground. Rain fell slantwise at the openings. A car drove past and soft red light illuminated graffiti at the far end of the tunnel.

Flor saw it before Pilar. She walked toward it: *LUZ* in shadow letters. "Una señal," she said. A sign. She ran her hand over the letters, and then the car was gone and the tunnel went dark.

Flor's words rushed out before Pilar's eyes could adjust to the darkness so that they seemed to emanate from the tunnel. "My body walked to the well, drawn to all those other bodies. I could smell them. The Kaibiles had filled the well—tangled arms and legs, eyes and mouths all the way down. I'll never forget the eyes of the children. I had lived to look in their eyes." Flor's voice echoed, mixing with the rain, dissolving into shadow.

"They'd burned the houses down. I sifted the ashes of my home through my fingers. They'd tried to burn the church down, but the fire had left the back wall—splattered with blood. The fire had left the charred remains of bodies, their limbs amputated, heads bludgeoned. The women's bodies were naked and splayed. Pregnant women's bellies had been cut open. Girls bore the marks of hands around their necks.

"My nine-year-old sister Ariché's body was at the top of the pit—naked, violated. I kneeled in the dirt and heaved, my stomach empty."

Pilar could barely make out Flor's silhouette. Her voice carved out that 16-year-old girl, heaving in the dirt. In darkness, there were no skins—one body bleeding into another. Flor's voice became the air around Pilar. The tunnel an ear canal that held her words.

"I buried my sister. Her body had gone stiff. I was afraid I wouldn't be able to lift her, but my strength was superhuman. I carried her into the forest where we used to play and buried her there."

Pilar felt her way along the damp wall of the tunnel. She moved toward Flor's voice. She folded herself over this five-foot woman, who felt so much larger—that dark story coursing through her veins—and the tunnel folded around them. They stood, two shadows staring into the darkness, for a long time before they walked back to La Placita in the rain.

Pilar walked Flor to the sanctuary apartment. Ceci was asleep. Flor had not cried. She seemed in shock. She said she just needed sleep. Pilar made her tea while she changed out of her wet clothes. She sat with her until she was sure she was okay. She wrapped her arms around her. "You're going to get asylum," she said.

She found Padre Bob bent over papers in his office. In spite of his large-ness, he looked fragile, his silver hair shorn too short. He didn't notice her until she shut the door. Pilar sank into the chair across from him and let the tears fall.

"Flor's going to get asylum," Padre said.

Pilar wiped her eyes with her fist and nodded, the bones in her face sharp as knives.

CHAPTER 17

Carlos called all of the venues where he did drag and canceled his shows. He excitedly told the Fengs that he was writing a solo show called *Desire Lines*. He set a goal to finish before Pilar moved to New York.

"How's *Desire Lines* going?" the Sisters now asked.

"Meh," Carlos grumbled and asked about their lives.

Lamont had started teaching dance, Carter was applying to fashion school, and Max was moving to Paris to apprentice at the Comédie-Française. His brothers were courageously forging their own desire lines—Max across an ocean—while his own life was an unbudging cursor.

Beneath the title, he'd typed the list of ideas from the night Carla claimed Crown Heights. He'd added some things to the list. But he hadn't actually written anything. He'd squeezed a desk into the narrow space between his bed and the wall, but writing there reminded him of all the times Abuela had sent him to his room as a child, punishing him for painting his nails or making a necklace of magazine beads. He tried writing on the living room couch, but the pigeons were distracting. Dozens of them lined up along the roof ledge of the building next door. They lifted their heads, opened their wings, and dove. All. Day. Long. Carlos shuddered at the whoosh of their wings. His pigeon phobia was worse than Abuela's fear of flying. He hated their grimy, putrid, rat-scavenging ways. You could dodge a rat, but swarms of pigeons would descend on you the minute some idiot kid threw bread. *Desire Lines* was a scattered trail of stale breadcrumbs gobbled up by the pigeons.

Why had he pushed Pilar to write poetry? The most physically grinding job was healthier. He texted her often to check in. Flor had told her story, but Pilar would say only that it was unimaginably heartbreaking. He worried about her, but he also had faith in her. Pilar was good in a crisis, as long as it wasn't her own. She was proud of him for leaving Lucky Feng's and excited about *Desire Lines*. She told him that Mary Oliver wrote while walking, suggested he try something like that. She insisted that he was brave, but the urgency of what she was doing only highlighted the frivolity of what he was doing.

Max suggested more structure. "I always get more done when I'm busy." He said that Dr. Yoon was looking for an assistant for his acupuncture clinic.

Carlos hardly knew what acupuncture was, but he met with Dr. Yoon. All he knew was that her Lucky Feng's performance had opened a space in him that he had no idea how to fill. If he could just return to that moment—when he'd known beneath knowing—that there was nothing to fear.

One of the Psalms the Sisters sang was Psalm 139:16: *All the days ordained for me were written in your book before one of them came to be.* Pilar no longer believed that. She wanted to believe that we could write our lives.

Ceci hadn't written since her mother's detention. She read while the other students wrote.

Pilar crouched beside her in class. "I know this past month has been hard, but I miss your writing. The class misses your writing." She stopped herself, backtracked. "Who cares about us? We're just your biggest fans."

Ceci gave a small smile.

"Write for yourself. Write your *sanctuary*—whatever that means to you."

Pilar looked at Ceci until she looked back. In that moment, she saw Flor's face—the shadow of it shifting to the surface as Ceci nodded, tentatively and then fiercely.

She walked Ceci home to La Placita after class. They found Flor making a Mayan soup called kak'ik. The smell of coriander, annatto, and chile filled the small sanctuary apartment. Flor invited Pilar to stay. Ceci went to her room while dinner was cooking. "There's something I need to write," she said.

Pilar tried to smile.

"Have you talked to her?" Pilar asked Flor after Ceci had shut her door. Flor wanted to share her story on La Placita's website to spread the sanctuary movement. She'd finished writing it with Pilar the week before, but they wouldn't post it until Flor had talked to Ceci.

Flor shook her head. "Not yet."

It was too quiet as they ate, the air dense with worry, spoons scraping bowls. Flor hardly ate.

"What is it, Mamá?" Ceci asked.

Flor shook her head. "Eat, mija."

Ceci started to clear the table after they finished. Pilar got up to help her.

"Leave it," Flor said to Ceci. "I need to tell you something." She pushed herself up from the table. "Not here." She stared up at the low ceiling. "These walls push in on me. Come to the cathedral."

"I'll clean up," Pilar said.

"Come." Flor's eyes pleaded.

It was easier to breathe in the cathedral—the arched bones of its ceiling a colossal rib cage opening. The air felt different. Flor, then Ceci, then Pilar slid into a center pew. They were flanked by rows of stained-glass windows depicting the lives of the saints. Saints who'd been skinned alive, shot through with arrows, beheaded, burned at the stake. Christ was suspended in his agony on the cross before them. Flor told Ceci about the saints in her family and village, added those dark shards to the gold, green, and blue. Ceci reached for her mother's hand.

Pilar remembered walking to the SAU cathedral in the midst of a panic attack, how everything had slowed and deepened inside, how the air held her.

The flesh, blood, and bones of this religion, all those stained saints in the windows, enfolded Flor's story into their history of pain and light. Made space to rise out of it.

Flor did not tell Ceci about the coyote raping her. She told her their salvation story. That the coyote had abandoned her in the desert to die, and that Luz had saved her. Saved *them*. She told this story so that it spoke loudest. Here, in the surety of Flor telling her daughter, *We are a miracle*, was the making of that miracle. Pilar witnessed it in Ceci's eyes: the circling buzzards dispersed and a desert sky opened—a blank page on which to write themselves.

Ceci curled her knees into her body and laid her head in her mother's lap.

The pink and orange sky as Pilar walked back to Mother of Sorrows made her think of watching sunsets on the porch with her father. They hadn't spoken since MJ's confession—her anger at MJ tangled up with her anger at him, guilt for feeling it. The desire to talk to him came to her like hunger.

He was washing up after dinner when he answered the phone. Pots and pans clanged, then stopped. Pilar could picture him cradling the phone between his chin and shoulder, the light in his gray-blue eyes as he said, "Good to hear from you, mija."

Love and guilt washed over her. She told him that she was moving to New York, that she'd stay with Carlos.

He was silent for a long time. She steeled herself for his disapproval. He'd never liked Carlos.

"Is this what you want?" he asked softly.

Her eyes filled. "Yes," she said.

"You can always come home."

"I know," she said. "I'm coming for Christmas, Papá."

She'd told him about Ceci and now she told him about helping Flor apply for asylum. "They make me want to know about my mother. You told me she led women from Guatemala and El Salvador across the river."

"It's very sad, what happened in Guatemala. And what happens to the women crossing. Your mother—" he started.

Pilar waited in the sugarcane, the stalks over her head. Their sharp brush made the hair on her arms stand.

"Flor said a woman named Luz saved her."

Her father began coughing, gasping for breath in a way that alarmed her.

"Papá, you sound terrible. Promise me you'll go to the clinic tomorrow."

His coughing subsided, but his breathing was labored. "I'm fine, mija."

"*Promise* me."

"Okay. I'll go."

She felt she'd caused his coughing fit. She didn't ask about her mother again. "I'll call tomorrow to check in," she said.

"I don't want you to worry," he said.

"I love you," she said.

"Love you, too, mija."

She got his answering machine when she called the next day.

She couldn't help him from 1,600 miles away. She would find a way to fly down sooner. For now, she'd focus on what she could do.

She threw herself into working on Flor's asylum application. She woke as night and day pulled together and wrote what Flor had told her. She researched the Mayan genocide. In an attempt to end the guerrilla insurgency, the Guatemalan army employed a uniform system of torture on the Maya from 1980 to 1983. What they did to Flor's village, they did to 626 Mayan villages. Soldiers separated children from parents and killed them. They raped women, cut open their pregnant wombs; beheaded and impaled men. The government instituted a Scorched Earth policy—burning buildings and crops, slaughtering livestock, fouling water supplies, violating sacred places and symbols, and eradicating villages. The US funded, trained, and supplied munitions to the army to carry out the genocide. According to the 1999 UN Truth Commission report titled "Guatemala: Memory of Silence," the army killed or disappeared over 180,000 people and displaced an additional 1.5 million. None of the soldiers and leaders who'd carried out the genocide had been held accountable.

After working on Flor's asylum application, she prepared for her classes. Her mind would leave her in the middle of grading, teaching. *Where are you?* she'd ask. Who was she asking? She continued work on Flor's application late into the night. She stared out the windows of the computer lab. The darkness stretched on for miles and it felt as if she were the only person in the world.

Once MJ saw that Padre and Pilar were taking care of Flor, she withdrew into the endless work of running Project Luz. What Pilar had seen as a remarkable presence to whatever task was at hand, she now saw as MJ's means of burying her past. She avoided Sister Robin and Letitia. She called her father and got his answering machine again. She prayed for him, because that was what she could do from LA, but she still didn't believe that anyone was listening.

Her loneliness was a palpable thing—a buzzing in her head and around her body. In life she felt separate, but when she slept, she dreamed herself into everyone. She was Flor burying her sister, Luz killing the coyote, MJ screaming on a cliff. She woke to her own screaming, her face wet.

The electricity of the dreams still running through her, she wound down the Daughter House stairs to the computer lab and emailed Carlos. She wrote him about things she'd read that were too heavy to hold alone. He asked the questions he'd asked after her rape—whether she was eating, sleeping. Pilar said she was eating, but not sleeping, because of the dreams. He said she should do what Laurie Anderson did: write them. He asked what she was doing on her last day of class. "You should celebrate all you've created together over the last year."

Pilar took his advice. She shot up in bed, her skin damp, mouth dry. She switched on her lamp, reached for her notebook, and wrote:

I am cleaning the Daughter House with my father,
sweeping out years of silence and dust
His Sunday records croon a beautiful sorrow
We clean until everything is bright and bare
But a dust storm billows,
blows in through the windows
I rush to close them,
while the storm gathers in his lungs,
his cough a record scratch
I wait at the window
For the storm to pass
Dust sweeps through my mind like a warm, dry wind
The sky quiets
I look down and
my hands and feet have turned to dust,
my bones a swirl of glinting motes

With Sister Letitia's help, she started planning a class garden, which her students would plant on the final day of class. They looked into what could be planted in summer and mapped out a bed big enough for all 60 students to plant something. Letitia drove Pilar to a nursery in the Sisters' old station wagon and they bought a variety of fruit, vegetable, herb, and ornamental seeds and transplants. The mixed tape that had played when MJ drove Pilar to Mother of Sorrows on graduation day was still in the tape deck. Leonard Cohen crooned "Hallelujah" as Letitia told Pilar about how she'd started growing herbs for cooking or healing in little pots on her windowsill when she was a nurse at St. Vincent's. "Almost all of my patients were dying of AIDS. It was the smallest gesture, those little pots of life in my studio apartment. I named them after my patients, prayed as I watered them. My favorite was the air plant, which doesn't need soil. You give it a weekly soak, and it grows on air." They stopped at a light and

Letitia dug through one of the nursery bags in the backseat. She handed Pilar a tiny, spiky plant.

Pilar held it in the palm of her hand, smiling. "It's so perky," she marveled.

"Precisely," Letitia said.

Pilar couldn't help but let Letitia in. At lunchtime, they dug the bed in 80-degree heat under a mandarin tree, which would protect the plants from direct light. Those afternoons of sun and dirt and sweat saved her. Letitia promised that she would keep the garden going after Pilar left. Imagining her students caring for it after she was gone was comforting.

Pilar asked her students to pick a piece of writing to share in their final class. On the last day, they went out to the garden, chose what they wanted to grow, and planted it. They gave their plants names and wrote them on little wooden stakes. Albert the yo-yo pro named his melon plant Edwin II, because his pet turtle was Edwin I. Ceci chose to plant a fern "because they've been around since before the dinosaurs." She named it Esperanza.

Pilar laid a sheet down over the grass. Her students all sat in a circle and shared their writing. Most of them read pieces that they'd performed at one of the open mics, but Ceci, who shyly volunteered near the end, said, "I just wrote this." She looked up from her notebook, wrinkled her nose, and said, "It's really short."

"Best kind of poem," Pilar said.

A breeze rustled the leaves of the mandarin tree as Ceci read, her voice soft but sure.

I find my mother standing at the window
Morning light so bright that we squint,
close our eyes and pull close
I lean my head back on her chest
the rise and fall of her breath the sea
She wraps her arms around me

and I can feel the sun

The class didn't know that Ceci's mother couldn't walk out into the world she watched at the window, but they didn't need to. Her poem had its own light.

Pilar had told Padre that she would get Flor's asylum application to him the next day. After class ended and she'd walked Ceci to La Placita, she worked on it late into the night, until she was too tired to think straight.

Too tired to work, but too wired to sleep, she walked out into the night. She slipped off her tennis shoes and walked barefoot through the grass, thinking, *help me I am of that people the grass blades touch*. Only they didn't. She walked into the cathedral, hoping to feel the old loosening. She lowered herself onto a kneeler and prayed for Flor and Ceci. She tried to believe.

She opened her eyes and stared up at the wax cast of Saint Vibiana, or her bones, enshrined above the altar. The sleeping wax girl dressed in white silk hung above a gold reliquary that contained her tongue, blood, teeth, and jawbone in glass vials. When her tomb, inscribed with the laurel wreath symbolizing martyrdom, was unearthed in Rome in 1853, they found her body reduced to dust and bones. But her tongue was whole and wet as it had been in life. This was seen as a sign that she died for speaking God's truth. Pilar read it as a promise that truths would out, even beyond the grave.

That night she had one of those dreams that went on and on, one dream running into another. She felt as if she was still inside the dream as she wrote:

I walk up the long cathedral aisle to stand before Saint Vibiana. I wait for a sign from the sleeping wax girl. I listen hard, but her tongue will not speak. I unlock the reliquary and take out the glass relic jar containing her tongue— black and hard as a pumice stone.

I raise the relic jar high and shatter it. Glass shards glint on the marble floor. Mother Connie's heavy hand lifts from my back. I fish the tongue from the shards of glass, rub its coarse, grainy surface between my fingers.

I run with Saint Vibiana's tongue clenched in my fist, into the wide, strange world. Flor runs with me. We are in the Freddy Gonzales Elementary parking lot, where my father told me never to stick out my tongue. He told me inside those white lines that he was illegal, those lines inside us now. We run but the lines become the boxes on the asylum application.

The grid stretches toward a tall green sugarcane field. If we can just get there, we will be safe. We realize that we left Ceci in school with that teacher, writing, "I will not stick out my tongue" on the chalkboard. We try to get back to her. The parking lot grows as we run. The grid—the sadness—expands.

It is an ocean. We scream into the wind, sea, calling for Ceci.

CHAPTER 18

Carlos worked at Dr. Yoon's clinic from 12 to 8, so he had his mornings free to write. He'd gotten some good scenes down, but was avoiding the painful stuff. It was summer, the city alive with outdoor concerts, salsa, barbecues, and fireworks; the streets a kaleidoscopic, scantily clad party. That high-adrenaline heat was in his writing, a manic summer sweep past the trauma to the transformation.

He looked forward to biking to the clinic, which was in Dr. Yoon's China-town apartment. He stopped at the top of the Manhattan Bridge and took a photo for Pilar of the light ricocheting off the river and skyscrapers, which he'd email to her with the caption, *Hope your last day of class dazzles!*

Dr. Yoon lived on the third floor of a five-floor red brick walkup on Bowery and Hester. Carlos locked up his bike outside. Garbage bags were piled near the mailboxes and the walls of the first floor were dingy, but Dr. Yoon's apartment was always spotless. Carlos walked up the three flights of lopsided stairs and rang his bell. Dr. Yoon answered wearing an olive-green Shaolin-style long gown shirt, blowsy short-pants made of the same cotton, and square pinewood glasses. This was his work uniform, which he had in an assortment of rich earth tones. He'd shaved his head since peforming at Lucky Feng's to mark his passage from drag queen to full-time healer. He wore no makeup, but paired different glasses with different colored robes.

"Our first client's not til one," Dr. Yoon said. "How about some lunch?" Dr. Yoon tried to keep his mornings free. He did a walking meditation along the East River most days.

"Yes, please," Carlos said emphatically.

He led Carlos down his wide entryway hall lined with pictures of relatives, some of the photos black and white and in Korea; on through the living room he'd transformed into a waiting room with a large reception desk, where Carlos usually worked; and into his cozy kitchen.

They made fried egg, avocado, and tomato sandwiches. As they ate, Dr. Yoon asked how the writing had gone. He always asked, even when they were rushed. He was less concerned with Carlos' highs and lows, and more with his "faithfulness to the practice." He insisted that if he'd cleared a space in the morning, he'd done his part.

Dr. Yoon listened attentively, pushing up the bridge of his pinewood glasses as he bit into his sandwich. Carlos felt a rush of gratitude to be working for someone who knew and encouraged this side of him. He still had no idea how he'd arrived in this life, which was like nothing he'd envisioned for himself and everything he needed.

Some of Dr. Yoon's patients were from the LGBTQ+ community, some were longtime residents of Chinatown, and some came all the way from Long Island's Koreatown. Either they or their parents had come to Dr. Yoon's grandmother when she was alive. Dr. Yoon spoke broken Korean and had picked up some Cantonese. He asked his patients about their ailments, but sometimes even they didn't know—described pain and meant sadness. He read their bodies.

His office was in a small room in the back of the apartment. The white walls were papered with acupunctural maps of the body and a chart of the five elements of traditional Korean medicine—wood, fire, earth, metal, and water. Each element was associated with sounds, senses, emotions, directions. It seemed a language unattached to anything in the city, in which the borders of feminine and masculine, what's seen and what's felt, might merge.

There was a single window, a massage table, a rolling stool, a Mayo stand, and a narrow table with acupuncture needles and supplies. Patient after patient lay down in this white room and Dr. Yoon gave himself over to them, as if he, she, or zhe was the only person in the world. For the whole of their appointment, they were. They came in for cancer, HIV, depression, arthritis. They had to lie still, for up to 90 minutes, with needles in the correspondent pressure points.

Carlos didn't know how they laid still, in total silence, for an hour and a half. He avoided Dr. Yoon's silent white room, preferring to answer the phone, schedule appointments, do accounting, and bike to get supplies. When Dr. Yoon called him in with patients, Carlos popped his head in and declined with a smile. "Your desk girl is busy."

"Leave the phone," Dr. Yoon said. "I need you." He'd ask Carlos to chart patients' medical history, prepare a foot soak of hot water and tea, or worse, to apply ointments. Carlos cringed as Dr. Yoon inserted needles in patients' stomachs, feet, shins, knees, skulls, shoulders, jaws, and jugulars, rocking the needles back and forth to get the qi moving. When patients lay on their backs, he avoided their eyes.

Still, Dr. Yoon kept calling Carlos in, saying, "I need you," meaning, *You need this.*

That afternoon, there was an unnerving hum beneath the silence of Dr. Yoon's white room as Carlos handed him needles. He fidgeted in the narrow space between the patient and the table and knocked an open gallon of rubbing alcohol onto the floor. He dove to mop it up with paper towels, cried, "I'll buy some more!" and dashed out of the room before Dr. Yoon could respond.

He took the stairs two at a time. Soon he was flying on his bike through the sizzling heat and blaring traffic, gulping the glorious carbon-monoxide air.

When he got back to the office, he wordlessly set the gallon of alcohol on the Mayo stand as Dr. Yoon inserted needles around a patient's ear. He returned to the reception desk and spent the rest of the day checking in patients and doing accounting.

When the last patient had left, Carlos proudly showed Dr. Yoon his flawless Excel sheets. "I took Finite Math for an easy A."

Dr. Yoon gave him a quiet, knowing smile. "Experiencing acupuncture might help you to let go of your fear," he said softly. "Would you consent to treatment?"

Dr. Yoon wasn't going to fire him if he refused. He could go on answering the phone and making Excel charts. Carlos pictured desire lines—meridians—running through a map of the body and resolutely agreed. "Let's get that qi moving," he said with a swizzle of his hips.

Dr. Yoon asked him to lie face down on the massage table, gave him a folded white sheet to cover himself, and left him to undress.

Carlos climbed onto the massage table, pulled the sheet over himself, and pressed his face into the donut headrest. Dr. Yoon put on music in the waiting room—slow, arrythmic drumbeats leading into a ghostly keening of voices and strings. Carlos stared through the donut hole at the woodgrain of the floor and longed for the silence that had preceded the keening.

He was relieved when Dr. Yoon returned—as a *she* in a high-waisted, hoop-skirt dress that looked very old; the stiff, white fabric yellowed; the hem frayed.

"This is Salpuri music, and *this*," Dr. Yoon ran her hands over the hoop skirt, "was my grandmother's Salpuri hanbok."

The Salpuri's keening ebbed and flowed. "Let yourself feel whatever you feel," Dr. Yoon said as she inserted needles along Carlos' spine, from his tailbone to the base of his neck. If she was going deep, she'd instruct him to take a deep breath and insert the needle as he exhaled. It didn't hurt; there was just slight pressure, a current between the needles.

"My mother was one of many people my grandmother lost," Dr. Yoon said as she worked. "She had family in North Korea she never saw again. Memories came to her when snow whorled at the windows. She would dance Salpuri until the pain moved into the whiteness outside. I would dance with her. The air was different afterwards—the heaviness gone."

When she'd inserted the last needle, Dr. Yoon said, "Qi flows like rivers through the body. Acupuncture restores that flow when it's blocked. Try to lie still." She gently cupped the back of Carlos' head before leaving him alone in the white room.

The window was open. A breeze rippled along the trail of needles down his spine. He felt nothing but the wind on the surface of his skin, but there was a slight twinge of nerves along his spine. How strange to bypass the surface and pull at what was underneath. Carlos remembered Abuela's egg ritual, saw the dark line through the yolk. *You draw the ojo de chicas y chicos, confuse the ojo. Ojo that doesn't know what it wants is the worst kind.* The Salpuri drums swelled, the bowing sharpening, the woman's voice vibrating between moan and shriek, rising into a howl. Then that cacophony dissipated into quiet echoes.

Carlos' body released the fear. Tears came in a flood. He let himself cry until the sobbing eased. He closed his eyes and remembered staring across the Rio Grande, imagining his mother. He thought of the drawing in *Night Life* with the four women on a couch floating down a river in the fog. People—even the ones you loved—appeared and disappeared. Even ourselves.

He remembered driving with Pilar, the wind and light of his life stretching into the unknown. Diving into the Ropa Usada piles—all those possible selves—and coming up with the eagle's wings dress. He saw the cracked egg become whole, his grandmother's wrinkled hand close over it.

Carlos hadn't realized that so much time had passed until he felt Dr. Yoon above him, removing the needles. When she'd plucked the last of them from Carlos' spine, she had him roll onto his back. She looked in his eyes. "It's time for you to return to your grandmother."

Carlos nodded, too sleepy to take this in. The nervous energy had drained from his body, his muscles loose, his mind empty.

"Stay as long as you like," Dr. Yoon said. "I'll bring you a blanket."

Carlos reached for Dr. Yoon's hand. "Thank you."

Dr. Yoon's intent stare broke into a slow smile.

When she returned with a blanket, Carlos was already asleep.

Carlos slept a deep, dreamless sleep and didn't wake until late the next morning. Dr. Yoon had left a note: *Off for my walk. Help yourself to breakfast.* But El Ojo wasn't hungry.

Chinatown was abuzz when they stepped into the street. El Ojo was an Eye taking it all in—seeing, accepting, and letting it pass through them. El Ojo eyed neon signs for palm readers, healers, magic jewelry; Buddha shops, pawn shops, and windows hung with chicken carcasses—all of it connected. Dark puddles dribbled out from fish markets and soaked their shoes. This would have bothered Carlos, but it was as if irritation, anxiety, pain had been pulled from El Ojo's body.

The crowd moved for them. El Ojo walked north without thinking, into the Lower East Side. They walked into a hair salon full of tattooed stylists. A stylist with an electric blue mullet and combat boots sat them down, pulled their hair out of its ponytail, and asked what they wanted. El Ojo ran their fingers through the hair they'd been growing since they started working at Lucky Feng's. It was dark, thick, and wavy and fell to their shoulder blades. *Ojo that doesn't know what it wants is the worst kind.* They knew what they wanted.

"Shave the left side of my head," they said fiercely.

It was frightening, watching half a head of hair fall to the floor. And freeing. The half-sheared head staring back at El Ojo from the mirror a question mark: *Who do you want to be?* Showing them that it was possible to return, again and again, to that early question, which only died when you stopped asking.

El Ojo followed that question into a piercing parlor, where they pierced the ear on the shaved side of their head with seven steel studs; then into an overpriced Ropa Usada. They searched for Dr. Yoon's bald beauty, that unspeakable language of fire and metal. They emerged from the vintage store wearing an angular cut shirt of black and white eyes drifting through a turquoise background, a roomy A-line skirt in a black and white geometric pattern, a chunky black beaded necklace, and purple patent leather lace-up boots. In a nearby makeup store, they added turquoise eyeshadow, cat-eyes, and purple lipstick with a glitter gloss. They tossed back their half-head of hair to reveal a stubbled jaw that only made their full lips more sensuous.

On their bike ride home, El Ojo drew a different kind of stare. They watched faces shift from confusion to admiration, or from curiosity to aversion, and knew that they'd forced others to reckon with the cracked egg question of being.

———

Pilar completed the narrative components of Flor's asylum application. Saturday night, she met with Padre Bob and Flor in Padre's office to finalize the paperwork. If all went smoothly, it would be two to three months before Flor's Master Calendar Hearing, at which Padre hoped the judge would grant her asylum. If there were holes, the judge would adjourn to a Merits Date, a full-blown hearing on the merits of Flor's case including evidence, witnesses, and expert testimony. He promised to keep Pilar posted.

Padre asked if she wanted a ride back to Mother of Sorrows. She shook her head. She wanted to walk off the unease that she always felt in transitions. Padre wasn't a hugger, but before she left his office, he laid a hand on her shoulder and said, "You've done God's work."

Pilar walked with Flor back to the sanctuary apartment to say goodbye to Ceci.

"How do you feel?" Pilar asked her.

Flor squinted down the long, dim hallway and said, "Like my life's in motion again."

Pilar imagined seeing Carlos in New York, nodded deeply and smiled.

She gave Ceci an air plant. They teared up when they hugged. Pilar wiped her eyes. "We'll email. Better yet, we'll snail mail. I want you to send me your writing."

She embraced Flor. Remembering how Flor had held her at the top of the hill, she hugged her tighter. Flor didn't let go until she did.

Pilar texted Carlos that they'd finished the application. "I'm so proud of you," he texted back. But as she left La Placita in the dark, she thought of her walk with Flor. She saw the well filled with bodies, the eyes of those children. She shook the image from her head, crossed the street without looking. A car blared its horn—an angry smear of glass and metal—and then the street was deserted. She felt angry and empty like that. Now that there was nothing to do but wait, she didn't know what to do with her anger.

The Sisters were in Compline when she got back to Mother of Sorrows. Her footsteps echoed through the empty corridors. She would pack to-morrow; she didn't have much. It felt strange not to be working on Flor's application or reading students' writing. She felt unmoored.

She wandered into the library and sat down at the long mahogany table covered in newspapers. She flipped through that day's *LA Times* and stopped at the headline, "Mexican Border City Gripped by Tale of Avenger Luz Oscura". "Like a character from a graphic novel, a five-foot woman, dressed in black, kills bus drivers who sexually assault women," the article began. "In a place like Ciudad Juarez, known for its years of brutal killings of women, the story has inexorable appeal. But how much of it is true?"

The hair on Pilar's forearms prickled as it had when her father began to speak of her mother. She followed this vigilante mother, who went where her father wouldn't.

She read about the investigation into the murders of two bus drivers. A woman hailed the bus, climbed the steps, pulled a gun, and shot the driver. The killer, witnesses said, was a small, middle-aged woman dressed in black, with dark curly hair. Nobody saw how she escaped. Or at least nobody would say.

The second murder happened 24 hours later, on the same route. A woman boarded the bus and requested a stop a few blocks later. She walked towards the exit, motioned as if she were looking for bus fare, but instead drew her gun. "¡Ustedes se creen muy chingones!" she spat into the driver's ear before she shot him twice in the head and fled the scene.

Two bullets to the head, in both cases.

The next day, an email showed up at a local newspaper, claiming to be from someone called Luz Oscura (Dark Light):

You think we, the women of Juárez, are weak, but we are strong. And if we don't get respect, we will take it with our own hands. Though a lot of people know we've suffered, no one protects us. We will no longer be silent.

"We cannot be sure that the email was written by the killer or killers of the bus drivers, whether Luz Oscura really exists," Gustavo de la Rosa, a human rights activist in Juarez, told the *Los Angeles Times*, "but in the city's imagination, she is real."

The article continued: "Hundreds of women, many of them maquiladora workers, have been killed or have gone missing in Ciudad Juarez. Some disappeared after boarding buses, their bodies found in the desert, abandoned lots, or mass graves. Families have endlessly protested the lack of justice for their daughters, sisters, and mothers. 'I have no way of knowing if this is true,' Imelda Marrufo, coordinator of a network of women's organizations, said. 'But we are probably talking about a victim, someone who was raped and has lived with such a lack of justice that she has no hope that whoever did that to her would ever pay for the crime.'"

Pilar tore the article out of the paper and carried it up to her cell. She woke at 3 a.m. from a dream of Luz Oscura. When she opened her eyes, that dark savior was the truest truth she could see—sharp as a knife, loud as a gun. She opened her notebook, but it was no longer enough to write the dream. To follow that mother. She needed to become her.

She dressed in black jeans and a black T-shirt and tucked her hair into a black cap. She carried a flashlight and wore the runner's belt, phone and switchblade zipped inside, that she'd worn after Buster raped her. She wound down the Daughter House stairs and through Mother of Sorrow's dark corridors. She walked quickly across the monastery grounds and slipped through the bars of the peacock gate.

She descended the hill: a pilgrimage in reverse, away from the Church. She needed dark to hold darkness—deserted blue streets, the bellow of a drunk stumbling by, the infant-like cries of stray cats. A skinny boy in baggy jeans with his cap pulled low over his eyes stood guard on a stoop, his neck too thin, hands shoved deep in his pockets.

She circled the Echo Park Lake until it became the resaca, the well. Until that wound became an oil-black mouth.

She boarded the bus as Luz Oscura. She looked at the tired faces of the scattered passengers, backlit by stark light. She felt connected to them as the bus pulled through the darkness, like she had to the people in the pews at Sunday Mass, waiting with bent heads for some motion beyond themselves.

She looked for a sign and saw *LUZ* everywhere—etched in the bus window, on the underbellies of bridges, on tenements hunched in the shadows of high rises. She trailed that buried light—sought the vein.

She returned to the tunnel where Flor spoke of what happened in Guatemala. A thick-muscled man in a cap and baggy shorts watched her as she entered the tunnel, but she went in anyway. She shone her flashlight over the scrawl of graffiti on the walls until she'd found the tag of *LUZ*. Only now it was *LUZ O*—the O a shadowed hole—an all-swallowing, all-creating nothing. Pilar moved toward it as she'd moved toward the hole in the sugarcane.

She ran her fingers over the coarse mouth of the O, then over her lips.

The hair on the back of her neck rose before she heard footsteps. The footsteps quickened and she turned to see the thick-muscled man running toward her.

She took out the switchblade and ran with it clenched in her fist. Lightning cracked in her lungs as she pushed forward harder—her long legs flying, aching. Two syncopated sets of footsteps echoed through the tunnel.

She thought she heard the man's footsteps slow behind her, then stop, but she did not look back. Her sneakers slapped the concrete, her feet vibrating. She could see the end of the tunnel, the lamplit park beyond. It was like swimming through darkness—those long, breathless strides under the resaca, her father waiting at the dock with a towel.

She started when her phone rang but kept running. It rang and rang, an alarm ricocheting as she sprinted out of the tunnel, into the park.

She surfaced, gasped for air. She turned back to see the silhouette of the man hunched over, breathing hard, near the opposite end of the tunnel.

She breathlessly answered the phone, her whole body shaking as she walked through the park to the street that bordered it, gracefully full of cars even at 4 a.m., because this was LA and film sets were waking. She held the phone in her left hand, clenched the switchblade in her right.

"Mija," her father said in a raspy whisper. "Lo siento—" He struggled to catch his breath.

Her eyes filled. She wanted to be the kind of woman who could outrun this, but her legs felt like they would buckle.

He told her he was in the hospital. He was very sick. She should come soon.

When El Ojo woke, they stood at the window and watched the pigeons dive. Carlos would have shuddered, cursed them. But El Ojo saw their beauty—the way they circled in the sky, high above everything, then lined up like soldiers, their necks and wings tucked into fists. They lined up on the ledge and dove in a single swoop—a parabola of shadows darting over brick. El Ojo opened the windows and listened as they fell, the beating of their wings some great sweeping out. They dove again and again—something of breath in the cyclic motion. Their wings opened, spread wide, fell. *Life was diving*, the pigeons said. Again and again.

El Ojo turned on "Because the Night". They blasted it, the sound trailing out of the windows. They went up to the roof and stood in piles of beer cans, under low-slung wires. Patti Smith's twang drifted beneath the buzz of electrical boxes. The pigeons lined up along the ledge of the adjacent building unfolded their wings. El Ojo stripped off their shirt, closed their eyes, and waited for them to dive—the wind of dozens swooping past. Wings beat around El Ojo—not soft, but fierce. The stubbled half of their scalp prickled; their long hair blew across their face. El Ojo did not want soft beauty. They stood bared inside the dirty current of those winged rats, their body humming with some strange conduction. When the chorus rose from their windows, they sang: *Take me now baby here as I am.*

When that waking overcame them, the person they wanted to tell was Pilar. It was too early in LA to call her, so they turned down the music and spoke into their tape recorder. They pictured her listening, leaning forward, her gray-blue grandmother eyes absorbing everything, and the words poured out.

Pilar called them as if she'd heard.

"Pilar..." they said breathlessly. They struggled to find words and then heard, in her silence, that something was wrong. "What is it, love?"

"Papá's in the hospital," Pilar said. "He may die." Her voice was quiet but uninflected, as if she were relaying something happening to someone else. "I'm going home. Come with me?"

"Of course," they said, though nothing scared them more than returning to the Valley.

Mother of Sorrows looked different when Pilar slipped back through the wide rungs of its peacock gate. What good were its tall stone walls when you could slip through the gate? The outline of its towers, turrets, crosses, and steeple receded into the darkness. She knew its insides now—human and dying.

There was no Tio in the Valley. There was Santa Muerte, a skeleton in a hooded robe, a scythe in one bony hand, the globe in the other. Her scythe was said to cut a silver thread at the moment of death. Pilar felt that fragile silver seam running through everything.

She forgave the Sisters. It would take longer to forgive herself.

She told Letitia, then Robin, then MJ that her father was in the hospital, that he might die, that she was going home instead of to New York. They hugged her with real force. It was such a relief to be held.

MJ offered to drive her to the airport, but her flight was at 6 a.m. She said she'd take a taxi.

MJ woke early the next morning to unlock the gate for her. It was still dark when she walked Pilar, for the last time, through the echoing corridors of Mother of Sorrows' courtyard, her suitcase wheels clattering over its stone floors.

Pilar remembered the first time she'd heard her talk—about moving through the world in ceaseless prayer. She prayed the words of the George Oppen poem she'd returned to after MJ's confession. They walked through the grass and she felt every blade, MJ's white nightgown and the tree boughs billowing.

The taxi was waiting. MJ helped Pilar heave her suitcase into the trunk and hugged her tight.

As they embraced, Pilar saw her walking through a snow-covered forest, white particles whirling around her body. She felt the burn of the cold inside.

CHAPTER 19

Pilar's flight got into Harlingen just before Carlos'. She went straight to his gate, wanting to be there when he stepped off the plane. She'd slept on the three-hour flight from LA to Dallas, her stupor sharpening into thick-knotted anxiety as she walked through the Dallas airport. A few minutes before Carlos' flight arrived, she realized, shaking with hunger, that she hadn't eaten anything all day. She made her way to a café a few gates away, keeping an eye on Carlos' gate as she scavenged the menu for vegetarian fare. Passengers started to file off of his plane as she bought hummus and veggie trays for Carlos and herself. She shoved carrots into her mouth as she speedwalked back to his gate.

The slow-shuffling crowd of beef-fed faces and bellies slumped over tooled leather belts parted and she saw him—a streak of lightning setting a prairie afire. When she'd last seen him over Christmas break of their junior year, he'd worn T-shirts and jeans and his hair was short. Now he wore a sleeveless, zebra-patterned shift and strappy purple platforms. One side of his head was shaved and his side-swept hair fell long, thick, and wavy past his shoulder.

So much had happened since they'd seen each other. They'd lost and found and lost themselves again, but they hadn't lost each other. They were changed, and still themselves, all of it born out of those piles of discarded clothes and the dark O of the resaca. Who else could understand?

Seeing Carlos, she felt the bright line of her life crackling, connected to his. She ran toward him.

El Ojo saw this pale, too-thin, five-foot-ten swish of ponytail and legs sprinting toward them, a deli-container in each hand, and couldn't help but think, in spite of the horrible circumstances, in spite of the fact that they'd always envisioned Javier Bardem as their romantic co-star; in spite of the fact that roses, rather than Mediterranean plates, would have been the traditional prop; that *this* was their Airport Scene.

"*PILAR!*" they called out, laughing, crying, and ran toward her, platforms blistering their feet, zebra-print satchel flapping against their hip. They threw open their arms. She tossed the hummus plates onto a chair and threw herself into them.

El Ojo hugged Pilar for a long time. They let her pull away first.

"You look *amazing*," Pilar said. She smoothed her ponytail, knowing she looked more the ghost-pale waif than ever.

El Ojo tossed back their half-head of hair to reveal the stubbled line of their jaw and sang, *I've changed my hair so many times, I don't even recognize myself.*

Pilar laughed in gratitude. "What do you want me to call you?" she asked.

El Ojo felt too performative, like they were trying to upstage Pilar's pain. It would definitely be too much for Abuela. They would dress like they wanted and people would see what they wanted. *They* would become *We*. *We* was large enough to hold Pilar's, Abuela's, their own pain. *We* contained multitudes. "You call and I'll answer," We said. "I'm here for you."

"Is it okay if I call you Carla?" Pilar asked. Carla reminded her of the day at the Ropa Usada—diving into sordid remains and finding something beautiful.

Carla nodded, proud of the history her name held.

Pilar and Carla held each other's gaze as they had six years before in the San Jacinto High library. Theirs was a recognition that held the seismic shifts of their lives since then, that made sense of the Valley's sameness.

Carla walked quickly with her head down past the four border guards standing sentinel at TSA. The crowd of people waiting outside of security parted for her. Heads turned to stare. It was a different stare than in New York, which expects the unexpected, which quickly becomes the expected, and leaves everyone expecting something stranger. Here there was space to stand aside, time to gape. When kids at Columbia had asked Carlos whether everyone in his town was a cowboy, he'd told them that the Valley was more Mexico than Texas. But watching cowboy hats, boots, and big hair drift past steakhouse advertisements featuring massive hunks of dripping meat, Carla was struck by how Texas the Valley was. How quickly she'd forgotten where she came from. When she stared back, people swiftly turned away. Fathers put their arms around their wives and children and moved, in tightly huddled pods, toward the baggage claim. A kind of loneliness that she never felt in New York descended upon her.

Pilar slipped her hand into Carla's. She rented their car and did not put Carla down as a driver. The border guards lined up at TSA had been reminder aplenty. Though she hadn't driven since high school, she drove, scanning the road for cops.

She drove straight to the hospital. Carla asked if she wanted her to come into Marin's room or if she should stay in the waiting room.

"I'm afraid he won't say what he needs to with you there." Pilar both hoped and was afraid her father would say what he had left to say.

Carla nodded. She and Marin had made peace, but they'd never understood each other. "I'll bring you food, but I won't stay. If you change your mind and want me there, just have the nurse come get me."

"Thank you." Pilar squeezed Carla's hand.

She told her that she could find her father's room on her own, but she had to ask three staff members for directions.

Her father was sleeping. He was blue-skinned, emaciated, and hooked up to oxygen and feeding tubes. He'd lost so much weight that the oxygen tube seemed to cut into his cheekbones. His doctor told her that he'd waited too long to seek care and his silicosis had become complicated by severe scarring—progressive massive fibrosis. In the year since she'd seen him, he'd aged ten years. She covered her mouth, breathing in the sharp antiseptic smell until she could stop crying.

Marin's eyes fluttered open, then closed. He did not seem to recognize her. His breathing was rapid and labored. Pilar held his hand, ran her thumb over his swollen blue fingertips and cracked nails. She watched his chest rise and fall. Her thoughts, the blood in her veins, were moving too fast for this slow-swimming hospital room. She felt like pacing, but sat beside her father until the nurse came in to ready him for bed. After the nurse left, she ran her fingers along the vein in his wrist, began the story of the mines: *Buscamos la vena.* But the story would not come.

There was a reclining chair, but she didn't recline. She didn't sleep that night. She was conscious of every sound. The sound of a gurney in the hall made her jump. She listened for shifts in her father's breath. She breathed in time with him. It felt like rocking on the porch together.

His breath became the clock. One day ran into another, the window looking out on the parking lot darkening and filling with light. Carla slept in the waiting room. She came to check on Pilar and brought her food, but didn't stay. Marin slept, occasionally opening his hollowed blue eyes. Pilar was able to hold his gaze—a private sky between them. Her father's cracked breath was a landscape like the Valley—barren, dusty, stretching on forever.

The third night, she dozed off and his voice woke her. "Mija." His eyes were lucid.

She raised his bed, helped him sit up. "Do you know that I love you?" There was a heat in his voice that had never been there. "That I'm proud of you?"

Pilar nodded, thankful that they'd started saying those words, wishing they'd said them more. "I love you, too, Papá."

He wanted, though he had no breath for it, to tell stories. He spoke in halting sentences, his words hovering like moths, eyes distant with memory. He was on morphine and his stories moved in and out of time, trailed off.

Again they moved through the tunnels, but now Pilar saw the slit throats of the llamas sacrificed to feed El Tio, buckets of their blood tossed over the mouth of the mine. She kicked that cruel God in the balls. She ran with Roberto through caving passages, felt his hand slip from hers. She rolled out of the mine just before the entrance collapsed, opened her eyes to see Roberto gone, opened her mouth to gasp for air—sucked in the gravelly breath of her grandfather, father, death. She kicked and kicked at the boulders sealing the mine, until the blood turned to rust.

Roberto was gone, so they took the night shift in the Big Mine. They moved through the tunnels with hundreds of men. Their bodies disappeared into that massive body, dynamite explosions, dust billowing. The boss led them to the bottom where the masters drilled in 100-degree heat, masks covering their mouths. Dust filled their mouths. The boss led them out of the mine, but they couldn't stop coughing. "You'll get used to it," he said. They stared down at the graveyard in the valley. The boss offered them the night shift and they took it. They took death into their lungs. They gave up light. They thought if they slept during the day, the nightmares would stop. Every night, they dreamed of Roberto's death. Every night they failed to save him.

They dreamed of Roberto until they dreamed of Luz. They followed her, weaving through la caña behind the women. The cane looked soft but was sharp. They wanted to touch the halo of curls around Luz's face, but she raised her switchblade. They fell in love before she loved them back. She was slow to trust. Because of what the women had told her.

They crouched in the brush on the US side of the river and watched Luz walk across the water. She didn't need them, but they needed to see her cross safely. A priest took the women from Luz and she walked back across the river to Mexico. She was angry when she caught them squatting in the brush. She told them to stop following her. They told her they couldn't: They loved her.

The farmers burned the cane one night. Flames rose into the black sky. They thought they'd lost her. They shone their high beams across the river, though la migra could have seen. They searched the cane and saw a ripple, quick as wind, ahead of the flames. Luz running—faster than fire. The cane was taller than the women, but you could see the line of them in the ripple of stalks, almost out. They stopped themselves from calling Luz's name. She wouldn't have answered.

Her father sat up in bed. Light entered his eyes. His blue hands shaped his words. "When the women came out of la caña, I turned off my lights. I watched their shadows wade into the river and cried. I did not hide, but waited at the river's edge. Luz passed the women off to the priest and climbed into my truck, dripping. Her kiss tasted of burnt sugar. She came home with me and slipped out of her wet clothes. I told her again that I loved her. That night she said it back. Being with her was like fire spreading through the cane."

Pilar hadn't thought words would ever rush like that from her father's mouth. His unstoppered talk felt like a dream.

"Is she really dead?" Her voice shook.

"I don't know."

"You said she died giving birth to me."

"I wanted to tell you." His face was rutted with pain. "And I didn't want you to know. She left you. She left us. To help the women."

"I don't understand."

He gestured under his bed and the pulse oximeter came off of his swollen blue finger. The machine beeped frantically. Pilar put it back on, the beep slowed, and her father's eyes closed. She didn't know if he'd been having a morphine dream, but she felt a shift in the air, a weight lifted.

Marin was asleep when a nurse came in to check on him. She put a hand on Pilar's shoulder and said, "You haven't moved for three days."

Pilar looked blankly at her, still sifting through the dream. Had it been three days?

The nurse asked if she wanted to use their shower.

"I'm afraid he'll— and I won't be here."

"They choose, honey," the nurse said kindly. "They choose when they want to go. Why don't you do this for yourself?"

Pilar was suddenly conscious of her sour, sleepless smell. Her father still had will; he'd never talked so much in all his life. Still, she showered quickly and hurried back to his room, hair dripping.

His skin was waxy and drained of color, his face slack, mouth open—a crevice—the sound of his breath gone. His bluish hands lay on top of the sheet. The nurse had closed his eyes. It was as if the sky was gone.

"I'm so sorry," the nurse said quietly.

The slow unfurling of time in the Valley, the flat fields stretching on forever, had made Pilar think there might still be time. She'd imagined taking her father home, cooking for him, staying with him until he got better. Being the daughter she hadn't been.

She kissed his papery cheek, bent his stiffened fingers around hers. She wished he'd let her be there for him when he took his final breath. He'd left the world the way he lived—quietly, without ceremony, alone. He'd spared her.

"Do you want me to call anyone?" the nurse asked.

"Will you get Carla?" Pilar's voice cracked.

Pilar didn't cry until Carla hugged her. Pilar held her tighter, afraid of the aloneness that waited when she let go. Carla was her only family now.

She called Padre Oscar, the priest who'd given her father his job in the cemetery. There was no one else to call. Padre Oscar came, hugged Pilar, prayed over Marin's body.

When he left, there were only white walls and the hum of machines. The story of her father gliding her through the resaca was dead, and with it, her kick. The hope that he would be rocking on the porch when she returned had made her running possible. As if her life had been a thing he was dreaming.

Carla helped her fill out the papers to have Marin cremated. He'd told her once, as they ate breakfast on the porch after his long night at the cemetery, that he didn't want to be buried where he worked. "Scatter my ashes here." He'd stared out at La Llanura. "This is what I work for."

Carla led her through the labyrinthine hospital halls and out to the parking lot. The silent rows of glinting cars swept Pilar back to her elementary school parking lot, her father saying, "I am illegal." She stood at its edge—afraid to wade into that memory.

She was too shaky to drive, so Carla drove them back to Marin's house. She drove carefully, scanning the roads for cops. La Llanura's long gravel drive was overgrown with brush. They didn't need the key that Marin kept hidden in the porch boards; the door was unlocked. The house smelled rancid. There were pots on the stove caked with beans, dishes piled in the sink. A fresh wave of guilt washed over Pilar. "I don't know if I can sleep here," she said.

Carla looked around, nodding, and took a deep breath. "I think Abuela will let us stay with her," she said, though she wasn't sure. She wore a sleeveless purple shirt with zebra capris and her purple platform sandals. Abuela might yell, *You show up after a year and a half looking like this?* and slam the door.

Carla drove, but the car seemed to move of its own volition down the familiar dark road. She summoned the largeness she'd felt in Dr. Yoon's white room, let the broken white lane divider stitch her past and present. She thought about how bewildered Abuela must have been to receive a five-year-old in her 50s, a changeling who'd forced her to reckon with the changing times. How hard it must have been to raise another child who'd leave her.

"Did you tell her you were coming?" Pilar asked.

"No, I'm here with you," Carla said resolutely. "It'll be a surprise." She waved her fingers like a sparkler.

Pilar raised her eyebrows, but felt like the flat, empty landscape pulling past her window. She turned back to it, relieved to be moving away from her father's house, to be swept up in someone else's drama.

The house was smaller than Carla remembered, its gray paint peeling.

Abuela gasped when she opened the door. She let them in, but clasped her hand over her heart, sank into the couch, and said, "Ay, Dios mío, I knew Nueva York would do this to you." She looked at Carla again, snapped her head away like it hurt. "My heart, Dios mío, my heart."

Pilar stared Abuela down with her arms folded over her chest while Carla sat close to her on the couch. She reluctantly sat when Carla motioned for her to join them.

Abuela looked at Pilar for the first time—her hair pulled into a tight ponytail, pale face, dark circles under her eyes. "You look worse than he does."

"Pilar's father died, Abuela. That's why we're here."

Abuela's eyes clouded. "Lo siento mucho, mija." She touched Pilar's arm.

"Thank you," Pilar said.

"He was a very nice man," she said. "A little strange, but..." She waved her hand.

Behind her, Carla shook her head at Abuela's incorrigibility. "I've missed you, Abuela," she said.

Abuela raised her eyebrows, but let Carla take her hand.

Carla ran her fingers along the inside of her arm, feeling her heart and lungs as Dr. Yoon had shown her. She felt Abuela's fear. She held her liver-spotted hand and felt bones, yellow, cold.

"Abuela—" Carla looked her in the eyes and said the thing under all of their conversations. "I'm going to be okay. I haven't forgotten what you taught me." She did not say: You taught me how to slip into other skins.

Abuela heated up menudo for them. Carla and Pilar ate it, picking around the meat.

She'd kept Carla's room clean and unchanged. As they climbed into bed, Pilar remembered the night of prom. How it had changed everything and nothing.

Carla turned on Patti Smith, soft and low.

Pilar turned on her side and Carla held her.

Abuela had already left for the panadería when they woke, but she'd left them papas con huevo tacos. Pilar wasn't ready to pack up the house she'd grown up in. She wasn't ready to tell Carla that her mother might be alive. Telling Carla would make it real. And there was something else—anger. Buried. She couldn't be angry at her father when he was dead.

They drove around with "Mad Rush" blasting. Sun-dried fields and strip malls of signs with missing letters rushed past their windows. They drove down the dry banks of the canals. The water was very low. They drove past tall fields of sunflowers and undulating golden grass beneath a perfect blue sky. Pilar thought of her father's ice-blue eyes and cried silently, staring out the window.

Carla reached for her hand. "Mad Rush" made her think of Dr. Yoon. *You don't have to say anything*, Dr. Yoon had told her. *Just be with her.*

They returned to the river and watched the bright red ball of the sun sink into the horizon.

Days passed before Pilar was ready to return to La Llanura. Carla drove her, stopping to pick up boxes. Dust ghosts rose on the dirt road that led to the house. Pilar had her window down, to suck in the air. But as Carla drove past the resaca, she shuddered and raised it. The rustle of palms whispered some unfinished thing. The resaca's dark mouth pulsed like a heart.

Carla parked. She went to open her door and Pilar stopped her. "I can't," she said. The air outside breathed Marin's cracked breath. She bent forward and put her hands over her ears.

Carla told her Dr. Yoon's story about dancing Salpuri with his grandmother until the air cleared of ghosts. She didn't know if she believed in Salpuri, but she knew this much: Get into motion and the motion would open things.

Carla got out and opened her door. She took Pilar's hand.

Pilar let Carla pull her out of the car into the vast nothingness of La Llanura. "I'm so glad you're here," she said.

"How about I tackle the kitchen and you take your room?" Carla asked when they got inside.

Pilar still hadn't been in her room. She threw open the door and then the windows. Wind blew the dust around. She sneezed and began to box up her old books, trophies, knickknacks. It felt right to move through grief—to hold it, then box it up. It was how her father had moved. She found and set aside her old composition notebook, in which she'd tried to record his stories of the mines. She did not read it, but kept moving.

Carla came to check on her. She helped Pilar box up the last of her things. They dropped the boxes off at Goodwill. Pilar looked back at the house as they drove away, until it was a speck in the distance. She imagined it weathering until it was swallowed by brush. And then they were driving through the miles of emptiness that came before town—the sun setting orange over brown fields and hay bales.

As they drove back through a thick syrup of night, Pilar told Carla that her mother might be alive.

They hadn't gone in her father's bedroom. Pushing open his door, Pilar thought about how rarely she'd gone in his room growing up. Even after the man in the black car came, even with her father gone every night, she'd never snooped. Crossing his threshold felt like crossing a border.

His room was dusty, but the bed was made and everything was in its place. His comb was on his nightstand. Pilar held it to her nose and her eyes filled. It smelled of his hair oil.

Pilar and Carla kneeled on opposite sides of the bed. They slithered under it until their fingers touched. Carla was the first to touch the metal box. Cocooned in dust, she held it out to Pilar.

Pilar sat with the clasped box in her lap. Had it always been here? *I wanted to tell you. And I didn't want you to know.* She remembered the ease of slipping through Mother of Sorrows' gate.

She took a deep breath and unclasped the box. Inside, she found Roberto's threadbare red bandanna, the metal ore eyes of El Tio, burnt sugarcane, a rock threaded with silver, and a picture of her in her high school graduation gown. Beneath those things was a photograph of a small, plump woman with a mass of dark curly hair and a crooked smile. She wore jeans and a T-shirt and squinted into the sun, shielding her eyes.

Pilar squinted back. Those years of waiting in the sugarcane had nothing to do with this woman.

Pilar showed the photograph to Carla. "Do I look like her?" she asked.

Carla looked between Pilar and the woman. "You squint into the sun like that."

Pilar got her old notebook and tucked the photograph inside. She stood on the porch and stared out at La Llanura as her father had, watched snowy egrets rise from the resaca as if for the first time. The world he'd made for her was so beautiful.

Her father had made a love that walked on water and ran through fire. Made it with his seeing, believing.

Seeing was not believing, but a hole, shapeless, opening. Maybe that was why she'd never looked for photos of her mother.

Carla stood beside her, was there when she answered herself. "There should be fire."

Pilar told Carla her idea: To build a pyre of sugarcane in the canoe, light it, and swim back to shore. To let the fire carry her father's ashes into the sky.

Carla could see what she wanted, the flames rising into a black bowl of sky. "I'll get gasoline and one of those torch lighters," she said. Without gasoline, the fire would smolder. The canoe wouldn't burn. "We'll have to swim fast..."

Pilar nodded.

"Can you cut the cane?" Carla asked, knowing that this, too, was part of the ceremony.

Pilar hugged her—for her understanding of the mechanics of beauty, her belief that it was worth danger, even if seen only by them.

Pilar watched Carla drive off. Though it was 90 degrees outside, she put on a hooded rugby shirt and jeans to protect her skin from the sugarcane. She found a machete and gardening gloves in the shed. Light fell over the tall stalks. She moved into the cane and swung at the stalks a few inches from the ground, careful not to damage the roots. It took several swings before she hit hard enough. The wind blew a hole in the cane. Pilar cut a path toward it, and the hole closed over. It was exhausting, and the exhaustion felt good. When she finished, she stood still inside the stalks towering over her head and cried.

When Carla returned, she was waiting on the porch with two large bundles of sugarcane. At sunset, they piled the belly of the canoe high with it.

They climbed into the canoe, the sugarcane pyre, gasoline, and urn filled with Marin's ashes between them. They paddled to the center of the resaca, lay the oars in the canoe, and watched in silence as the sun sank into the horizon, streaking the water pink and red. Pilar felt the calm she'd felt in the sugarcane. Here, all the parts of her life converged: her father teaching her to swim, the night she and Carla cut themselves free, and this homecoming that came too late. The sky was softer, rounder now. Time ran backwards and forwards, the resaca a wound they would pass through again and again.

Pilar scattered half of Marin's ashes into the water as the sky darkened. She cried silently. Carla sang a Spanish lullaby that her mother had sung to her. It came to her slowly—was maybe her first memory. Pilar scattered the rest of the ashes into the sugarcane pyre. Carla poured gasoline over the cane. Then she stripped off her tank top and jean shorts, tossed them into the pyre, and dove into the water. The stripping was improvised, but Carla was right: They needed to dive naked into the wound.

Carla told her to swim to shore. She swam underwater, tunneled for minutes through that submerged silence before she broke the surface and sucked in air. She turned to see the canoe burst into flames, followed by the explosion of the gasoline can. She didn't see Carla and fear shot through her. But soon her sleek seal head popped out of the water, not far from her. Carla smiled.

If Marin was in Pilar's submerged tunneling, Luz was in her shoring. When Pilar rose out of the water, she knew what her mother felt, rising out of the river with the women, the fire behind them. She knew the blood and severance of birth.

Pilar and Carla sat naked at the edge of the resaca, hugging their knees, and watched the canoe burn. The fire rose high into the black sky, smoke billowing amidst the stars.

CHAPTER 20

From the minute she stepped off the plane at LaGuardia Airport, Pilar felt she'd made a mistake in coming to New York. As she and Carla waited in the endless taxi line, people and cars jostled for space, horns blaring. Anxiety hovered around her like the muggy, acrid air. Carla wrapped her arms around Pilar and the buzzing quieted.

As their taxi sped along the BQE, Carla again felt the blood pulsing through her veins. She'd felt so heavy in the Valley. Staring out the window at the glittering Manhattan skyline, she felt the rising tide of exhilaration one feels upon returning to a lover. "That old whore." She shook her head. "She makes everyone think she shines just for them."

They drove through Hasidic Williamsburg with its bearded men in black 19th-century frock coats and tall fur hats and mothers in 1920s-style wool dresses and glossy wigs pushing strollers.

"Where *are* we?" Pilar asked.

"It's an Orthodox Jewish community. Kind of like the Menonos, I guess. I'll bike through this neighborhood at 2 a.m. on a Friday night when they're all coming back from Shabbat, pushing their baby buggies through the dark, and it's like sailing through some sepia-toned dream."

Pilar's brow furrowed. "How do they survive here?"

Carla shrugged. "Everyone fights to survive here."

Pilar didn't feel she had the fight in her.

They traveled forward in time to gentrified Williamsburg with its organic markets, street art murals, and artfully curated fashion. Their taxi driver drove like an ADHD adolescent, flooring the gas then slamming on the brake, weaving wildly around cars. Pilar lowered her window, feeling like she might be sick.

Carla thought she was reacting to Williamsburg. "It's a bit much, even for me," she said.

As they rounded Grand Army Plaza, Carla pointed out Prospect Park. Cyclists in Italian Lycra on racer-thin bikes wove through groups of runners wearing race bibs and medals exiting the park. A saxophonist in the stone gazebo at the park entrance competed with a salsa party on the Brooklyn Public Library patio across the street.

"You're going to love running here," Carla said. "Of course, Central Park has its charm—*if* you don't mind dodging tourists, cars, and horseshit." They passed the library. On the doors were bronze panels of literary heroes—Moby Dick, Tom Sawyer, Edgar Allen Poe's raven, and Brooklyn's own Walt Whitman. "They'll hold books you reserve on shelves under your name. Imagine your favorite poets sandwiched between erotica, self-help, and breadbaking manuals. If that isn't popular democracy, what is?" They continued down Eastern Parkway past the Brooklyn Botanic Gardens. "You can smell *all* of the roses in summer and vacation in the tropics in winter." Next to the BBG was the Brooklyn Museum. Three years before, they'd built a modernist glass entrance pavilion and bleachers that looked like a spaceship had crashed into the original Beaux-Arts-style building. "Every first Saturday of the month is free," Carla said. "Their dance parties are my favorite."

Carla belonged here. She was like a proud bird, chest puffed out and peacock feathers fanned iridescent blue, as she introduced her city. She was trying in her way to help, to draw Pilar outside of herself. But she also wanted Pilar to love it.

And Pilar did not love it. Everyone was performing and no one was watching. Melodramatic bursts of color exploded against the dingy, bricked in sky, then disappeared. The fireworks were overwhelming, too loud and too bright so that no one's one story meant anything. She just needed one story to hold still, come to its end. How could she make sense of her father's, mother's, her own unfinished stories here? There was no space, no patience for it. She felt worlds away from Carla, and their separation brought back this fresh wound:

She was alone.

Her breath quickened and all of it blurred. She squeezed her eyes shut to keep from crying.

She wanted to love her best friend's love. She opened her eyes to a gray stone building with a turquoise steeple and a wide arch cloistered walkway on the corner of Bedford and St. John's. "What's that?" she asked.

"Oh my God, I meant to tell you. It was a Carmelite monastery until 10 years ago—like a super extreme order. The nuns never came out and depended on parishioners to send in food. The last of them moved to Highland Park, and now it's an old folks' home."

"Now it's a home for dying people," Pilar said quietly and the tears came in a flood. "Sorry, I don't know why that—"

Carla again wrapped her arms around her. "You're going to be okay," she said with such surety.

Their taxi pulled to a stop in front of a six-floor red brick building with one scraggly tree out front. "This is home." Carla propped her chin on Pilar's shoulder. "You're going to love it here. Just give it time."

After they'd lugged Pilar's suitcase up the five flights of stairs to the apartment, Carla took her to get pumpkin roti at Gloria's. The soft roti skin—the food equivalent of being swaddled in a warm blanket—reminded Pilar of her father's tortillas. The memory of him hungrily watching her eat flooded back. Her eyes filled.

Carla reached for her hand.

"It's just so good." Pilar laughed and took another enormous bite. Roti was the first thing she loved about New York.

Dr. Yoon paid Carla well. She could afford to keep the apartment when Timon moved out to live with his girlfriend. She kept the lease in Timon's name, afraid a background check might uncover her undocumented status. She could afford to take care of Pilar until she found her footing. She helped her set up Timon's old room. She showed her the grocery store, drugstore, laundromat, bank. She spent mornings with her before heading into the clinic. She was okay with stepping back from the writing. Returning to the Valley, seeing Abuela, the fear she'd felt passing the airport border guards, Pilar's father dying without citizenship—there was deeper work to do there. She watched the pigeons dive as she made coffee.

Pilar opened her eyes when light seeped into her room, then closed them and lay in bed listening to the sound of the pigeons diving—breathing for her. Carla would get her out of bed with rocket fuel coffee and they'd make breakfast. They tried making Abuela's papas con huevo tacos, but the potatoes didn't fry all the way and their tortillas were too thick. They made faces as they chewed the half-raw potatoes.

"Abuela would tell us straight up how disgusting these are," Carla said.

"She totally would," Pilar said.

They laughed and went for roti.

Pilar was Carla's audience as she assembled her lewk—pink satin shorts with an eyelet lace poet shirt and a puffed sleeve blue blazer; a long white shirt dress with a yellow and green striped wide tie and green hightops; or a leopard-print unitard, black bowler hat, and strappy purple platforms. Carla blasted music, catwalked, and tossed her half-head of hair. She did goofy dances to make Pilar laugh.

Pilar laughed harder than she ever had, gasping for breath. She could never choose one outfit over another. She loved them all. Carla's color, sass, laugh, and strut felt like life. She sashay-shanteed in front of the living room windows, her edges outlined in sharp light. Pilar loved her so much it hurt.

Dr. Yoon let Carla move her hours around so that she could do things with Pilar in the evenings. Carla took her to see Pedro Amoldovar's *Talk to Her* at Film Forum, a piano and cello duet of Schubert's dark love songs performed in a friend's living room, and a Buddhist talk on impermanence in Greenwood Cemetery's chapel. Those moments of beauty exploded the fog. Pilar sat on the edge of her chair, her heart racing.

But when Carla left for work, the emptiness set in. Pilar stood at the window and watched her ride off in her watermelon bike helmet. As soon as she was out of sight, she felt heavy and tired. The pigeons dove. The day stretched endlessly before her. Padre Bob had given her the numbers of people in the New York Sanctuary Movement; he'd suggested translation work. She was going to call them, but her brain felt slow. The lilt of Spanish made her sad. She didn't trust herself not to cry in an interview.

Carla encouraged her to go to the park, library, or botanic garden while she was at work. When she did go out, it felt like the city was racing past her. She wound through a drugstore's aisles only to forget what she'd come for.

She started riding the subway to get in motion. It was a relief to descend below ground. The air in the tunnel was hot and muggy, but cool air enveloped her when she stepped on the train. On weekday afternoons in Brooklyn, there were just a few scattered passengers in the cars. She held fast to a steel pole and thought of her father leading Roberto through the mines after their father's death.

The cars filled as the train entered Manhattan. People clung to the pole with Pilar, hands carefully spaced apart. They listened to separate songs, enveloped in bubbles of sound. They stared past each other with faces like gravestones. Blue lights lined the tunnels—everyone bathed in their ocean.

An express train hovered across from Pilar's for a moment. She peered at the people across the tracks—so close, their every detail illuminated in the car's stark light. They crowded around the same steel poles, watched each other through the windows, a skewed reflection.

Pilar searched the face of a girl in office clothes on that other train. She was reading, her dark hair pulled too tightly into a ponytail. She turned a page and the express train pulled away, its windows flashing, all those split-second lives there and gone.

Pilar turned to look at the people behind her. They stared at the passing express train, their eyes flitting left and right, the way our eyes move when we dream. She wanted to dream something unbroken.

She looked for a tag of *Luz*.

How could my mother have left me? she asked that river of drowned light.

How could you have left your father? the electric blue moons answered.

A blur of writing on the tunnel walls flashed past the windows like flipping pages—an underground diary of black words scrawled on white panels. Pilar made out *LUCKY ME* and *ATLANTIC CITY*. She imagined writing her poems on buried walls, a different kind of publication, audience. Someone had risked their life, crawled through rat nests and cesspools, to write those words.

She pushed backwards through the train, trying to read more. She kept pushing through the people huddled around steel poles, until she got to the door between cars. She pulled the lever. The doors slid open and a rush of hot wind blew her hair back. She stepped into it, stood on the platform between cars, the roar filling her ears.

She pushed through the next car, and then the next. Still, she couldn't make out the words. As she neared the end of the train, the cars became less crowded and she could run. It felt good to run. Her body became the train, tunneling through that blue-black wound. She ran until she got to the final car. She was too late. She kneeled on the last seat, pressed her palm to the glass, and watched the pages pull into the distance.

Pilar Googled "graffiti diary on the 3 line" and learned that it belonged to a graffiti artist named Revs. The words, about gambling, didn't speak to her, but the act did. Revs had inspired a generation of street artists in the 90s, covering overpasses, walls, and roofs with his tag. Then he spent six years writing his autobiography on the walls of subway tunnels. He painted and wrote on five-by-seven-foot pages in the dark spaces between platforms. 235 pages were hidden inside the tunnels.

Through Revs, she found a photographer named Julia Solis who'd documented the city's subterranean labyrinth—from the bowels of Grand Central to the cathedral-like inner sanctums of the Brooklyn Bridge to the gang tunnels under Chinatown—in her book *New York Underground: Anatomy of a City*. She photographed decomposing theatres, theme parks, asylums, and prisons, talking about the intimacy of decay: "Something reveals its essence most truthfully when it's in a state of decay." Pilar thought of her father revealing everything as he died.

Before emptiness engulfed her again, she wrote an email to Julia Solis, asking for an interview.

When she heard Carla coming up the stairs, she signed off with her phone number and hurriedly hit send. It felt impulsive and slightly deranged. Why in the world would this woman respond to her?

"How's it going?" Carla asked. She assumed that Pilar was writing and was glad to see her in motion.

"Okay." Pilar closed her laptop. Her heart raced and her armpits were damp. She didn't know what she was hiding, but the hiding was instinctive.

Carla waited to see if she wanted to say more, but clearly, she wasn't ready. Pilar had only ever shown her a few poems, after they'd been workshopped and revised. Carla didn't read poetry and wasn't sure she'd understood them. She hadn't known how to respond, beyond saying that they were beautiful.

Carla talked about her day at the clinic. She said that the point of acupuncture was to get the qi or energy circulating, that sickness was the result of a blockage of the qi. A stoppage of motion.

Blue tunnels mixed with veins in Pilar's mind. She knew that emailing Julia Solis was just the beginning. What she needed was deeper. Not proximity, but experience. Not words, but action. She needed to be brave like that—to trespass borders, walk through walls, tunnel through and out of death.

If she was going to survive her life, she had to reclaim it. Remake it.

The more gender non-conforming Carla's presentation became, the more she felt herself, the uglier people's attacks were. People called her a *faggot, tranny, he-she, hairy piece of shit.* They muttered under their breath when they passed her stopped at a light on her bike. They stopped eating or shopping to stare, laugh, point, and call out, *Look! That's a man in a dress!* Even the admirers got old, following her with a camera, taking photos without asking.

She asked Dr. Yoon to call her Carla and use she/her pronouns. She was leaning into her femme side. *Carla* was a comfortable placeholder until she found a name that held her history and future. When she told Dr. Yoon about being harassed, he welcomed her to change clothes at the clinic, which she did most days. Bringing a change of clothes had the added benefit of ensuring she didn't get sweaty and wrinkled on the bike there. Some patients gave her compliments and some gave her looks, but Dr. Yoon ensured that she was always respected.

When Carla did leave her apartment in full gender-fuckery fabulousness, she steeled herself. She carried her tape recorder and kept an audio diary. Some days she stared back at her assailants, coolly documenting their slurs on her tape recorder: *Boy in sadass pleated khakis taunts those of superior fashion and imagination.* Some days she turned up the music on her headphones and drowned her harassers out. Some days, her recordings were a run-on catharsis of rage and pain. And some days she channeled El Ojo. She detached from her own pain and felt her harassers' entrapment. She envisioned a street scene in which everyone was free from gender norms.

She moved deeper into Dr. Yoon's white room, closer to sickness's smells, sags, and scars. She learned how much bodies spoke. She learned to sit with silence and pain and hear the things under them. She began to feel patients' fears and desires as a vibration that pulsed. And gradually, to distinguish the varying pitches of each patient. Each emotion. And then, faintly, to hear her own pain. In time, she made out the harmony between her own pain and the patients'. Many of them were undocumented. They didn't have to say. She recognized that unspoken self, saw how its burial bent the body.

After a long week, she came out to Dr. Yoon as undocumented. She still hadn't told anyone but Pilar, Mrs. Bonura, and Mr. Cancino. That identity wasn't one she'd chosen and she'd tried to leave it behind. She talked to Dr. Yoon about Pilar's father's death, how he'd lived his whole life in fear.

"I used to hate him, not just for separating Pilar and me, but for being so helpless." Her eyes filled. They were standing in the white room after the last patient had left. Carla had spent the whole day there. She felt raw, porous, helpless. "How can you live here your whole life and do everything right and there's no path and no one cares enough to change that?"

Dr. Yoon sat Carla down at the little table in his kitchen and poured her a glass of iced green tea. He sat in silence, let her gather herself. Then he told her about volunteering at an immigrant advocacy organization called Make the Road. They looked up the website and saw that there was, among other events, a Trans Latinx March, Monday at 4.

"Why don't you go?" Dr. Yoon asked. "It could be good to be around people who care enough to try to change things."

Carla read the Antonio Machado quote on the home page: *Caminante, no hay camino. Se hace el camino al andar.* Searcher, there is no road. We make the road by walking.

"Like a desire line," she said.

"Yes." Dr. Yoon grinned.

Carla knew that Pilar would have loved to join the march, but she wanted to immerse herself in the experience without having to look out for her.

Pilar seemed to be doing better. Carla woke Sunday morning to find her making coffee. She told Pilar that she wanted to spend the day writing.

"Great, me, too," Pilar said.

"I'm glad you're at it again." Carla read her to see if she really was okay. A pen was wedged in her ponytail and she'd written something on her palm.

"Trying." Pilar shrugged and handed Carla coffee, just the way she liked it, with half and half, honey, and cinnamon.

Carla spent the day making a black steel-studded *Undocuqueer and Unafraid!* T-shirt. She paired the T-shirt with a stretchy rose metallic mini-skirt, purple knee-high socks, and zebra-striped Converse hightops. She trimmed a weekend's worth of stubble into the perfect five o'clock shadow and wore frosted pink lipstick, turquoise nails, dangly turquoise beehive earrings, and her mother's necklace. She grinned at herself in the mirror. She looked like freedom she'd fashioned with her own hands.

Pilar did look back at some old poems and change a word here or a line break there, but she spent most of that Sunday researching urban exploring sites.

Steel-studded, Carla moved through the streets of Jackson Heights with a throng of trans folk, mostly women, many of them undocumented immigrants; activists, nonprofit workers, and all manner of queer folk. She pictured Dr. Yoon's bodily map of meridians, felt those bright lines branching out through the marchers' bodies, voices, the streets. She imagined the meridians as strings that could be plucked, bowed, their symphony vibrating electric in the humid air as they screamed, "We're here! We're queer! We're fabulous; don't fuck with us!"

The hyper-feminine trans-Latinas didn't mind Carla's gender-questioning presentation. They clasped and raised their long-nailed hands with hers outside of the donut shop where their sisters had been arrested for eating donuts while trans. Together, they yelled, "¿Qué queremos? ¡Jus-

ticia! ¿Cuando? ¡Ahora!" They marched to demand an end to police bru-
tality and work, healthcare, and housing discrimination. Carla screamed
with them until her voice went hoarse.

———————————

The instructions Pilar found for exploring the Freedom Tunnel were hard
to follow, but she eventually found her way up the railway embankment
at 125th Street and through the gap in the fence. It was 4 on a bright
Monday afternoon as she walked along the raised tracks that led to the
tunnel's opening.

The Freedom Tunnel was a three-mile active Amtrak train tunnel under
Riverside Park that ran from 122nd to 72nd Street. The tunnel was named
for graffiti artist Chris "Freedom" Pape, whose recreation of Francisco
Goya's *The Third of May*, Salvador Dali's melting clocks, chiaroscuro study
of the *Venus de Milo*, mural *There's No Way Like the American Way*, and
self-portrait depicting his head as a spraypaint can lined the walls. Trains
had stopped running through the tunnel from 1980 to 1991, years in which
it drew New York's biggest graffiti artists. The tunnel had also been home
to the Mole People, a colony of squatters who constructed a labyrinthine
village from scavenged materials inside. They were evicted in 1992,
when trains began running through the tunnel again, their shantytown
bulldozed, the tunnel chained off. Still people continued to live in the
Freedom Tunnel, graffiti artists to tag, urban explorers to explore.

Pilar stood at the mouth of the tunnel—aswarm with brightly colored
tags—and stared at the double tracks curving into the darkness. Light
from the tunnel's opening glinted off the tracks. She felt that light along
her spine. She remembered outrunning the man in the tunnel in LA, ran
her fingers over her switchblade. Her skin prickled as she stepped into the
tunnel.

Inside, the sweltering air cooled and stilled. She moved through a deep
quiet. She walked along the tracks, two at a time. She felt both held and
as if she were the only soul in the world. Grates on the tunnel's ceiling

opened to the park above and slats of light, followed by dark patches, fell over the tracks. The ghostly laughter of children drifted down from the park. Who she was and what she was after were a world away.

A mile in, the tracks vibrated. Her spine snapped to attention. She turned to see a train's light boring through the tunnel. Its horn exploded the silence.

———————

Vendors stared warily as the Trans Latine March moved through the streets of Jackson Heights. Teenagers gawked. Men spit on the sidewalk. But the women behind a bakery window raised their fists in solidarity. A woman selling churros clapped and cheered. They stood outside a diner that had refused to serve some of the trans women and yelled "¡Jackson Heights, escucha! ¡Estamos en la lucha!" Carla thought of Dr. Yoon saying that qi—the life force—flowed like rivers through the body. She thought of the rivers running through the bodies in the march, all flowing into a single river sweeping through the streets of Jackson Heights.

She thought of parking by the Rio Grande with Pilar, how that place on the riverbank, her sweaty body in a silk dress, let them tell each other what they'd never told anyone. Everything ran back to that beautiful, filthy river—always in motion, always changing, always a constant in her life. It held her hopes and losses, past and future. When it rained, the border shifted. Carla wanted to move like that.

She reached back to her origins for a rebirth at once feminine and masculine, old and new, borrowed and blue. She submerged herself in the river of chanting marchers and baptized herself *Río*.

———————

Pilar covered her ears as the high-speed train barreled toward her, horn blaring. She stepped off the tracks and pressed her back to the wall.

The train whooshed past, a roar of noise and light. It blew up dust and debris, blew her hair back. She stared up at its brightly lit cars, the people inside so clear. Could they see her? When the last car roared past, she stepped back onto the tracks and watched the train snake into the shadows. A sound rose from her belly to her throat. She called out her name: *Pilar Salomé Reinfeld*. It fractured into ghostly echoes, then dissolved into silence.

Ahead, six shafts of light, stark as pillars, poured through a grate. They illuminated Freedom's *The Third of May 1992*. Pilar stood in the light, amidst whirling dust motes. She walked up to Freedom's mural and studied it. He'd altered Goya's depiction of the Spanish resistance to Napoleon's armies to represent the Mole People's eviction from the Freedom Tunnel. A line of soldiers fired at people kneeling, their arms raised in surrender, beside a bloody body. A single battered crutch and an overturned traffic cone leaned against the mural. Pilar had seen a photograph of the Mole People camped around a fire in front of it.

She walked further and found Freedom's dystopic comic-strip mural, *There's No Way Like the American Way*. He'd adapted Margaret Bourke-White's *Kentucky Flood,* a 1937 photograph of Black flood victims standing in front of a billboard declaring, "World's Highest Standard of Living: There's No Way Like the American Way" over an image of a smiling white family driving. Freedom's mural juxtaposed this image and slogan with an image of a policeman wrestling a gun from a man, shouting, *Drop the gun, Mole!* and a Coca-Cola logo. She couldn't find Freedom's Venus de Milo, but would come back for it.

Walking along the tracks through all that silence was meditative. She almost didn't notice the 72nd Street marker. There was supposed to be a gap in the fence through which to slip out of the tunnel and into the park at 72nd Street. Pilar combed the fence, but couldn't find the gap. Blood beat in her ears so that she couldn't think. She sat down in the dirt and took slow, deep breaths.

She noticed a bunch of paint buckets stacked by one of the concrete pillars that punctuated the chain link fence. Someone must have used them to climb onto the pillar and hop the fence. She added more paint buckets to the stack, climbed onto it, and pulled herself onto the pillar. It was a ten-foot leap down. She thought of the pigeons diving and jumped. The landing sent a shock through her feet.

The bright world of Riverside Park—families playing baseball and riding bikes—felt surreal. The light hurt her eyes, but she chose it. She walked through the park and into the city's bustling streets.

Río sat in the waiting room of Immigration Equality, an organization that offered free legal services that they'd learned about at the Trans Latine March. The march had inspired them to talk to a lawyer about their status. It was an open floor office in the financial district and the staff looked friendly but overworked, their desks piled with files, the phone at the front desk ringing off the hook. Río sat next to a Black trans woman, her Afro accented by a yellow silk scarf.

"I *love* your scarf," Río said.

"Thank you, darling. I love your lipstick," the woman said in a Jamaican accent and flashed a wide smile.

Río was wearing plum lipstick and pale-blue pantaloons swimming with green turtles. Across from them, a silver-haired man in a blazer clasped the nervously jiggling knee of a younger Latino man.

Next to "gender identity" on the intake form, there were boxes to check for "male," "female," and "non-binary." Where it said "other," Río wrote *Wake and make!*

Next to "preferred pronoun," Río hesitantly checked "they." The transformation that began after their acupuncture session with Dr. Yoon ran beneath language, and they resented having to nail it to this question-naire. Some of the speakers at the march press conference had used they/them pronouns. Río had worried about misgendering, or misconjugating, them. Now they worried about misgendering themselves. Maybe they should just claim the masculine or feminine pronoun that they felt most in the moment? They were trying to decide when the lawyer called them.

"Río Gomez?" It was the first time anyone had said it aloud. It was thrilling to rise from their seat and answer its call with a seductive, "Yes."

"Javier Gonzales." A young lawyer wearing a navy blazer extended his hand. Dark circles shadowed his eyes, but he was cute in a cleancut way. He looked a bit like Javier Bardem.

Río shook Javier's hand, their rebirth sealed by this handshake.

Javier's eyes lingered on Río. Río could feel their own magnetism.

They sat across from each other at Javier's crowded desk. Javier looked over Río's intake form.

"Sometimes I've wanted to move through the world as a man, sometimes as a woman, sometimes as both. Lately as neither." Río shrugged and leaned toward Javier, who had the thickest, longest natural eyelashes that they had ever seen on a man.

Javier reddened beneath Río's stare. His eyes grazed over Río's half-shaved, half-long hair and full, purple lips. He checked "non-binary" on the form.

"I always think about how straight folks don't have to go through a big drama of declaring themselves to the world." Río searched Javier's beautiful face, unsure whether he was straight, but he didn't look up. "I want to flow between genders. You know, like a river." Río gave Javier a full-watt grin signaling that they were fully aware of their cheesiness, but fabulous enough to pull it off.

Javier blushed again and Río realized that he had no idea how good looking he was. "I understand. It's just for the form."

By the time Javier had finished reviewing Río's intake information, he'd returned to practiced lawyer mode. He looked Río in the eye and said, "I'm not sure how much you know about IE, but we offer free legal services to LGBTQ+ and HIV-positive immigrants, including asylum seekers, bi-national families, detainees in immigration jail facilities, and undocumented people. Among other reforms, we're fighting for the end of the HIV travel ban and the passage of a comprehensive DREAM Act."

Río was reminded of Arvin, his crush from his Senior Design team—so hot until he opened his mouth and out gushed a torrent of programming jargon. Javier was the lawyer version, so a little smoother, but definitely in the same genre. Río guessed that he never dated, that his personal life was buried six feet under his work. Javier wasn't really their type; still, Río longed to crack his polished professional shell.

"I'm a DREAMer!" Río declared with mock-enthusiasm. They told Javier about their mother leaving them with Abuela when they were five and discovering that they were undocumented when they went to get their driver's license.

"Is your mother still a Mexican citizen?"

"She didn't keep in touch."

Javier's large brown eyes softened.

"I'm still close to my abuela, though. She believes New York's corrupted me."

Javier laughed.

Río smiled impishly. They didn't want Javier's sympathy. They'd found a way to get a license. They remembered the feeling of driving The Bitch for the first time. They felt like that again, being Río.

They locked eyes with Javier. Río watched him work through the surprise of his attraction to them—his eyes squinting slightly, then widening; one side of his mouth escaping into a half-smile. He reddened, looked down, then looked up at Río again. He stuck a finger in his collar.

Río was enjoying the effect they were having on Javier.

Javier collected himself and said, "So we've been fighting for a DREAM Act that would give you conditional residency and let you apply for permanent residency after six years. It includes driver's licenses, work permits, and in-state tuition. We're hopeful because there's strong bipartisan support for DREAMers. But as of now, there's no path. You'd have to return to Mexico for 10 years before applying to come back."

Río shut down the sinking feeling in their chest and called up the feeling of baptizing themselves Río. They refused to let the law piss out their fire. They straightened their spine and said, "That's what I thought."

"I'm sorry," Javier said. He looked at Río with sad golden retriever eyes.

Río repressed an urge to muss his hair. They stood, extended their hand, and, feeling confident enough to rename everyone, said, "Thanks for your help, Javi."

Javier blinked his long eyelashes and smiled a beautiful, unguarded smile. "No one calls me Javi but my mother." He started to shake Río's hand, then said, "Wait. We're meeting with Senator Clinton next Wednesday to hold her accountable to the immigrant community. You should talk to her about your experiences as a DREAMer."

"Good luck with that," Río said. "I just heard her opposing driver's licenses for undocumented people."

"She's got a mixed record on immigration, and she's definitely been reluctant to include LGBTQ+ people in her push for reform. That's why she needs to *see* the people she's impacting."

"You think Clinton will *see* me?" Río gestured to their turtle pantaloons, put a hand on their cocked hip.

One corner of Javi's mouth quirked upward. "I've seen it make a difference. And the community of people you'd meet would be a support."

Río put their hands on Javi's desk and leaned toward him. "And *you'd* get to see me again."

Javi's breath thickened.

Again, Río was a teenager with a new car, recklessly careening around hairpin turns. "You want change?" they whispered. "You and I could make change."

Javi reddened and swallowed. "What do you mean?"

"We could go out?" Río cocked their head, smiled.

Javi looked around to make sure no one was watching. Lowering his voice, he said, "I can't date clients."

"But there's no hope for me, so we're done here," Río said. "Unless you want to create a dream in the here and now."

The furrows in Javi's forehead arced into rainbow formation. He leaned toward Río, helplessly.

Río nodded at their intake form. "You have my number." They felt Javi's eyes on their back as they sauntered toward the door. They turned to look at him before they pushed out into the light.

When they got home, Río told Pilar that they'd met with an immigration lawyer and found out that nothing had changed.

Pilar remembered what it felt like to talk to Padre about her father. "I'm sorry." She hugged Río. "I'm so proud of you for trying."

"I'm totally okay." Río pulled away. "*Really*," they reassured Pilar, who looked like she might cry. "At least I know I've done what I can."

Pilar didn't understand how Río wasn't angry. She was angry for them.

"I'm making my own change," Río said. They told Pilar about becoming Río—baptizing themself in the river of marchers.

"Río. I love it! And the march sounds *amazing*."

Pilar's face lit up as they described the march and a wave of guilt washed over Río. "I'm sorry I didn't take you. It was last-minute and I went straight from work and Jackson Heights is a trek—"

"I totally get it," Pilar cut in. She remembered screaming her name in the Freedom Tunnel. "You needed to do this on your own. I *love* that you marched. Le'me see the shirt!"

She was actually beaming at them, not an ounce of bad feeling.

The relief on Río's face made Pilar conscious that she should tell them she'd walked the Freedom Tunnel. As Río went to get their shirt, she thought about how to explain it in a way that didn't sound crazy. Río wouldn't understand. Maybe no one needed to understand it—this dark self she was walking through. Its beauty belonged to her and she didn't want to translate.

Río came out wearing the shirt. Pilar effused over it and Río detailed how they'd made it.

"I put Río down on my intake form," they said. "When the lawyer called me, I had this, like, *electric* feeling. He was really cute... in that preppy, wholesome way that's usually not for me. But the way he looked at me? *Not* wholesome." Río cocked one brow and smiled. "He asked me to meet with Hillary, but I could tell he just wanted to see me again. So I asked him out." Río tossed their head back and laughed.

"What did he say?"

"He turned bright red. I think he blushes more than you."

"Shy could be good for you." Pilar laughed.

She hoped the shy lawyer would call. What was it that let people cross the space between an old self and a new one? She thought about passing through the silence and darkness of the Freedom Tunnel, that jarring feeling of stepping into the world.

There were days when Río couldn't shed the weight of Dr. Yoon's white room, when they biked furiously, recklessly home, weaving though traffic with their headphones blasting. A week after they'd met with Javi, Río was biking home from a long, sorrowful day. They'd stayed late to help with a patient and friend of Dr. Yoon's named Richard. Richard had AIDS and his health was rapidly declining. Shame had kept him from seeking treatment until it was too late. Río had assisted Dr. Yoon for the whole of Richard's two-hour acupuncture session. A silver-haired man with a dry wit and grace that Río admired, Richard had shed his gray tweed coat, maroon scarf, leather gloves, and large, round wooden glasses to reveal an emaciated body. Laid out on Dr. Yoon's massage table, there wasn't enough flesh between that body and death.

Río biked home over the Brooklyn Bridge. They needed to be held by its granite towers and steel cables—bones built to last. Biking across it was a rite of passage that washed off the day's sadness and flooded them with love for their city. Their chest opened as they biked beneath its massive limestone arches, headphones blaring. Suspended above the East River and the rush of traffic, they were a bird cradled in a glittering nest of sky-scrapers. They looked over their shoulder at the postcard of a downtown skyline. They inhaled the city, its ever-changing story stretching back to Whitman walking this same bridge. *It is not upon you alone the dark patches fall.*

And then their phone rang. Worried that something had happened to Richard on his way home—or Pilar—they pulled over and answered.

"Hi... It's Javier. *Javi,*" he corrected with a sputtered laugh. "From Immigration Equality?"

"Oh, hi Javi."

There was a long pause in which Río could feel Javi struggling. They'd put anxious people at ease all day at the clinic and here was another. "How'd the meeting with Hillary go?"

Javi groaned. "Not well. I knew she'd say it would be impossible to push immigration reform that included LGBTQ+ people through Congress, but I thought she'd give us a *remotely* human response."

As Javi anxiously, breathlessly rambled about the meeting, Río thought, *What did I get myself into?* After their long day, Javi's struggles just felt like another weight that they had to carry.

Javi took a breath, a quaver entering his voice. "We lost two asylum cases we should've won this month and I just feel like I'm at breaking point. Either I have to stop hoping or I've got to put some of my hope into something else. I've been thinking about what you said..."

"What I said?"

"About creating a dream in the here and now."

"I said that?" They'd been swept up in the newness of being Río—a child enamored with their power to move, control, wound. They felt guilty, then resentful of that guilt.

"You did. So I, uh, was wondering if you'd like to have that date?"

Río's body went rigid. They knew that Javi had never done anything like this before. There was something of those bones laid out on Dr. Yoon's massage table—needles along a rickety spine.

"Hey Javi, I was actually biking home when you called. I'm standing on the Brooklyn Bridge and it's really crowded. Can I get back to you?"

"Oh... sure. Of course." Javi tried too hard to sound casual. "Get home safe!"

Four days passed and Río still hadn't gotten back to Javi. They guiltily confessed to Pilar.

Pilar excoriated Río as they expected—and secretly wanted. "You led this guy on and he put himself out there and you can't even go on one date? Can you imagine what he's feeling?"

"It just feels like he's put so much weight around this one date."

"How do you know that?"

"Oh Pilar, he's *such* a virgin."

Pilar looked at Río with her disappointed grandmother eyes, knowing not to push.

Saturday night they were supposed to see Pina Bausch's *Café Müller* and *The Rite of Spring* with Dr. Yoon at the Brooklyn Academy of Music. Pilar had fallen in love with the *Café Müller* scene in the opening of *Talk to Her*. They'd nabbed nosebleed seats months in advance, just before the performance sold out. Dr. Yoon called that afternoon to tell Río that Richard had been hospitalized. He was with him and wouldn't make Pina. He believed that Richard would pull through. He insisted that Río find someone to take his ticket and tell him everything.

Río told Pilar that Dr. Yoon wouldn't make it. "How about I invite Mike?" Pilar had met all of the Fengs on this side of the Atlantic, and Mike was her favorite.

"Why don't you invite Javi?" Pilar suggested. "It'll be the three of us, so less pressure."

Río thought that Javi would probably have plans, but inviting him would at least assuage their guilt.

Javi picked up after one ring. He didn't have plans other than spending the night catching up on work. "I'd *love* to go. I'm a huge fan of the ballet, but I've actually never seen modern dance. I'm excited!" he added unnecessarily.

Río ended the call and looked at Pilar. "He's coming."

"Wonderful." Pilar's smile seemed, to Río, a little smug.

The night of the performance, Río scanned BAM's crowded lobby and spotted Javi, wearing a suit, across the room. Río had lately favored David Bowie-style unitards. Tonight's was a Jackson Pollock-print worn beneath a black leather skirt with red stiletto boots. Pilar wore a simple black dress with a turquoise necklace that Río had loaned her. Javi's face lit up when he saw Río. He walked toward them with a confident, measured stride. He was taller than Río remembered—six feet, maybe more—and broad-shouldered.

"Hi again," Javi said to Río, his full lips curving into a smile. Río was struck—*struck* was how it felt—by his beauty. He introduced himself as *Javier* to Pilar. "Río's the only one besides my mom who calls me *Javi*, but you can, too, if you like." His face flushed briefly. Still, Río couldn't connect the man who stood before them with his anxious voice on the phone. They recognized a fellow performer who'd had years of experience appearing strong in high-pressure situations, betraying nothing beneath the surface, which made Río want to delve beneath the surface.

Río tried to get Javi and Pilar talking, telling Javi that Pilar had helped a woman apply for asylum, before they left them to pick up the tickets. They were fumbling when Río left, but deep in conversation when Río returned—not about immigration law, but about books they loved. Javi was a voracious novel reader. "I love that there's space for people's lives to breathe." He leaned toward Pilar, spoke with his hands. "That the details of someone's day *are* the story."

"Sometimes literally—like *Mrs. Dalloway*," Pilar said.

"I *love* that book." Javi sighed.

"Have I read that one?" Río asked.

"I'm not sure," Pilar said, though Río had tried to read *Mrs. Dalloway* and told her it was a *snooze*. She turned back to Javi.

"I thought I'd be telling people's stories as an immigration lawyer. I'm so tired of choking the complexities of citizenship, race, and identity into bureaucratic boxes."

"Don't forget gender." Río stepped closer to Javi, noticing a boyish sourness mixed with sandalwood.

"Exactly." Javi barely glanced at Río before turning back to Pilar. "Sometimes the best part of my day is those 20 minutes on the subway when I'm absorbed in some character's life."

"I had nightmares about the asylum form." Pilar shook her head. "I don't know how you do it."

Javi and Pilar talked intimately, seamlessly, one picking up where the other left off, their hands carving shapes in the air—their conversation its own dance. They were too busy talking to notice the bell signaling that it was time to find their seats. "Come on, you two." Río inserted themself between Javi and Pilar, wrapped their arms around their shoulders, and ushered them into the theater.

The performance began with *Café Müller*, the piece in *Talk to Her*. Amid the plaintive swell of Henry Purcell's arias, a sleepwalking woman in a slip of a nightgown staggered barefoot, arms outstretched, through a dark, cramped restaurant. She crashed into chairs, slid down walls. A man entered. He rushed to clear chairs out of the woman's path, struggled— failed—to save her.

Pilar imagined her father gasping for air as he drove himself to the hospital.

Then there were two men: a sleepwalker running like a caged animal into chairs and walls, another lunging to clear his path. Pilar saw Río hungrily look at Javi. Javi sat between them, his beautiful face rapt, eyes shining, oblivious that Río was watching him.

Río wanted to turn Javi's dimpled chin toward them, to kiss his full lips. They forced themself to watch the performance.

Pilar watched Javi steal glances at Río, the flush that crept up his neck against his starched white collar. Río did not notice.

There was a repeated series in which a man in a suit arranged a sleep-walking couple into a kiss. He arranged them slowly at first, then faster and faster, frantically. He tilted their faces into a kiss, draped their arms into an embrace, and lifted the woman into the man's arms only to have him drop her. There was something about the way the man unconsciously let the woman fall—the gradual, inevitable unfurling of his arms against the weight of her body, the woman's slow slide from his grasp. She tumbled almost gently to the floor, but the heap of her body landed with a thump. She immediately leapt up and threw her arms around the man's neck. Faster and faster, the couple was shifted into position only to fall out of it.

The woman threw her arms around the man; the man let go. Río looked hungrily at Javi; Javi looked shyly at Río. Pilar saw it all. She knew that Javi talked to her about books because he was achingly drawn to Río. Terrified that his desire would surface, he submerged himself in the distraction of abstraction. Or tried to: secretly, he waited for Río to see him. He wanted that so badly that he missed it when it happened. Río couldn't understand not talking to the person you most wanted to talk to. They believed that they were being ignored, which made them want Javi's attention more. They were so different. In their difference was both the power to diminish one another and to make each other larger.

The sleepwalking woman removed her nightgown, sat in a chair, and laid her bare torso on a table, prone, arms outstretched, the curved notches of her spine facing the audience. The way the dancers moved—colliding, catching, falling—laced sorrow and hope. Pilar felt that knot in her chest. *Café Müller* was a dance about the ways we try and fail to love, the ways we disappoint each other. Was there something beyond that? Could we step outside of the patterns we thought of as ourselves?

When *Café Müller* ended, Javi pressed the heel of his hand to one eye and then the other. Pilar kept her eyes on the dancers bowing, two tears slowly trailing down her cheeks. "What am I going to do with you two?" Río asked.

"God, I needed that," Javi said during intermission. He stared down at the rows of people beneath them as he spoke, searching for words. "Even though the movements were repetitive, there were these subtle shifts that changed the story. Maybe those shifts are happening all the time, but we need things like this to make us see them."

"I read that Pina loved to dance because she was scared to speak," Pilar said to Javi. "She said when she was moving, she could feel."

Of course Pilar identified with this, Río thought. They looked past Javi and said to Pilar, "Dr. Yoon didn't speak 'til he was five. Salpuri let him speak." Río didn't explain who Dr. Yoon was. Now the conversation was between Pilar and them, with Javi on the outside. They glanced at Javi when they said, "I wish he could have come."

Pilar gave Río a look, but they didn't care. She hadn't even known who Pina was before they took her to see *Talk to Her*. It wasn't just that Javi was ignoring Río. It was that Pilar no longer talked to them like she talked to Javi. Río had been happy to give her space to grieve, but here she was talking a blue streak to someone she'd just met.

Rite of Spring arrested their attention, obliterating other thoughts. Sixteen women in flesh-toned slips wandered a dirt-covered stage. One woman slept on a red silk slip thrown over the dark earth. The others slowly moved into dance. Dazed by the red slip, they circled the sleeping woman. With the climaxing music, they transitioned from fluid to violent, staccato movements. One woman stood apart, thrashing.

Sixteen men entered. The interactions between the men and women transitioned from sinuous to warlike. Different women stood at the center, holding the red slip. The men circled the women—desirous, predatory. A woman put on the red slip. A man caressed, then seized her. The dance exploded into an animalistic carnival of fear and desire. In the end, the woman in the red slip stumbled, stricken, one breast bared. She beat her chest and covered her eyes in agony, then fell to the ground as a line of dancers stared.

There was something cathartic about watching this violence explode after being trapped in *Café Müller*'s melancholy patterns of inhibitions and misses. Javi and Pilar sat on the edge of their seats, awakenings washing over their faces.

When it ended, Pilar felt as if years had rushed by. She sat dazed, motionless, while Javi and Río shot out of their seats to give standing ovations. Pilar slowly rose to join them. The dancers came out for a second bow. Javi and Pilar looked at each other with wet eyes, took a deep breath, and turned back to the dancers. Dry-eyed, Río envied this exchange.

The three of them walked to the subway station together, hushed by awe. Before Pilar and Río parted ways with Javi, Río said, "I'm glad I could drag you away from the office on a Saturday night." They laughed a bit sourly.

Javi forced himself to look Río in the eyes. "Tonight gave me back things I didn't know were missing. I spend my days trying to legislate spaces for bodies outside of the law. I forget that those spaces already exist. I really can't thank you enough." Javi's tidal wave of sincerity drowned Río's resentment. Javi awkwardly hugged Río, then hugged Pilar more easily.

How Río wanted him as he disappeared down the stairs. Pilar wanted that for Río. She knew not to interfere anymore, not to try to arrange them into position. They would have to break out of their patterns to see each other. They would have to wake to embrace.

"You and Javi really seemed to hit it off," Río said on the subway home.

"I liked him," Pilar said benignly. Already her head was elsewhere—wisps of ideas drifting through her brain like cirrus clouds. If she didn't write them down, they'd dissolve into an empty blue. She looked through

Río, then saw that they were waiting for something more. "Javi would have talked to you if he didn't like you so much," she said.

"That doesn't make sense," Río said.

"Couldn't you tell when he said goodbye?"

"I thought he just loved Pina."

"*You* took him to Pina. He kept looking at you during the performance... when you weren't looking at him. Text him. You'll see."

Río cocked their head, considering Pilar's challenge for only a nanosecond. "Okay, I will." Just like that. This was the difference between them.

"Good." They got off at Franklin Avenue and walked home past people gathered outside bars, their laughter tangling with cigarette smoke.

As soon as they were in the apartment, she said, "Pina inspired me. I want to get some things down while they're fresh in my mind. Thank you for taking me." She hugged Río. And then she was gone, her door closed, Río shut out.

Río texted Javi, thanking him for coming on such short notice, wishing him luck with his work. This time there was no immediate response. They texted Dr. Yoon, who said the hospital would release Richard the next day. Still the apartment felt too quiet.

Río knocked on Pilar's door.

"Come in," she called. She sat on her bed with her notebook.

Río leaned against her doorframe. "How come you don't talk to me anymore like you talked to Javi?"

Pilar hated that she'd caused the hurt on Río's face. She thought for a moment and said, "You're always so sure about things... It's hard for me to figure out what I think if I talk to you first. I need time to work things out. But I'm always thinking about things you've said."

She'd been thinking about what the words *Dream Act* might mean outside of the law. About those words in relation to *Café Müller*'s sleepwalkers stumbling through the dark with outstretched arms, walking through silence with Flor, writing dreams on walls. She thought of the dancers exploding into motion. *Dream Act*, she'd written. *An act that bridges one's*

dreams and waking life, so outside of one's normal patterns that performing
it brings a new self into being.

She pushed against that long, strong instinct to hide herself and let
Río in.

––––––––––––––––

Pilar didn't tell Río where they were going the next day. She told them to
wear clothes they didn't mind getting dirty and comfortable shoes.

They rode the 3-train uptown, Río in a sleeveless purple and black
leopard-print unitard, purple headband and wristbands, and Converse;
and Pilar in running clothes.

As Pilar led Río up the trash-strewn railway embankment at 125th
Street, Río inhaled the dirty air and exclaimed, "So scenic!"

Pilar laughed and led Río through the gap in the fence to the tracks.

Río widened their eyes as they squeezed through but bit their tongue.

"I promise it's worth it," Pilar said. She led Río along the tracks. She felt
the frayed anxiety and excitement she'd felt when she submitted poems to
her writing workshop.

She caught her breath when they got to the Freedom Tunnel. They'd
whitewashed over the colorful tangle of tags that had surrounded its
mouth. She stopped and squinted, as if the tags might return. "There used
to be..." She waved her hand at the tunnel and wandered in.

Río stood in the arch of the tunnel. They understood that this tunnel
meant something to Pilar. They registered her devastation over its fresh
white paint. But as they peered into this shadowy wasteland at the glinting bend of double tracks, fear blared in their body like a parking garage
full of car alarms going off.

"Pilar! Wait!" they called.

Pilar didn't answer. She ran her fingers over the looping ghosts of letters showing through the white like she was tracing a lover's scar.

Río forced themself to enter the tunnel. They stood in a pillar of light
pouring down through a ceiling grate. "Are there rats in here? Or more

importantly, axe murderers? Or trains?" Their voice ricocheted through the tunnel. They shuddered.

A fog enveloped Pilar. "There used to be murals," she said. She turned from the whitewashed wall to face Río. "I wanted to show you the murals. I don't know if they're still here." She kept walking.

Río followed Pilar, stepping around broken glass, unwound cassettes, spray paint cans, condoms, syringes. They understood that this was her crazy way of walking through grief, but anger had overtaken their fear. Had she even thought about the fact that they were undocumented, what would happen if they were caught? Let her find out whether the murals were gone and then they were getting out of this hellhole.

Pilar's breath left her when she came to the place where *The Third of May 1992* had been. Its absence felt like a hole in the sky. She tried to explain what had been lost to Río.

Pilar rambled on like she had during her religious phase until Río cut her off. "It sounds beautiful. I know you wanted to show it to me, and I'm sorry it's gone. But listen, Pilar, we need to get out of here now. I don't know if you noticed, but I'm an undocumented brown man in a unitard."

Pilar heard her father's fear—*can't, can't, can't*—choking off every breath. She had been that daughter. She had been good. And what good had it done? "I just need to see if there's anything left. We're not going to get caught. People come here all the time."

"Clearly they're welcome." Río waved their hand at the whitewashed walls.

Pilar hurried through the tunnel, surveying the damage, searching for traces of what had been erased. *There's No Way Like the American Way* was gone except for a faded Coca-Cola logo. She found that they'd left Freedom's small, less political paintings—his self-portrait, Venus de Milo, David, and dripping clock.

Río stood behind her as she studied these remnants. "I'm serious, Pilar. I want out of here now and you're coming with me."

Pilar held up her hand. She realized how much the mystical quality of the Freedom Tunnel depended on its hallowed quiet.

"This is crazy, Pilar," Río kept saying. Their voice echoed through the tunnel, filling every hole.

Pilar whipped around to face them. "It was a mistake to bring you here."

"Agreed," Río said. "Now get us out."

"I thought you'd understand." Her voice cracked. "You taught me everything I know about rebellion. You did drag in *San Jacinto*."

"I don't do drag anymore. I care for people who are *dying* and have no choice about it." Río's mouth twisted with anger. "*You* have a choice and here you are trying to kill yourself."

"No, I'm trying to walk out of fear. You've never understood..." Pilar heard a rumble in the distance.

"I've never understood *what*?" Río snapped. "Hiding in a nunnery then hopscotching train tracks?"

"*Shh.*" Pilar listened.

"Don't shush me!"

The rumble grew until Pilar saw a light boring through the tunnel. She grabbed Río's hand and pulled them against the wall with her.

A silver train shuddered by, lifting dirt and debris. Río squeezed their eyes shut and screamed a shrill, piercing scream that lasted for the entirety of the train's seemingly endless passing. Before, the train's shimmering silver body passing hers had seemed magical. The people inside had pressed their palms to the glass in secret greeting. Now their mouths opened, as if in their own ugly, answering scream. Before, there was a moment after the train passed when the tunnel got very still and Pilar had that feeling of standing in the sugarcane. Now Río's scream echoed until the last of the train had snaked into the distance.

As soon as Río caught their breath, they snapped, "No more tunnel fun! Which way's quicker?"

Pilar pointed in the direction they were headed and Río took long, furious strides. "What's the nearest exit?" they yelled without looking back at her.

"72nd Street."

"How far is that?"

"I'm not sure," Pilar said.

"*How far?*" Río barked without stopping.

"A mile, I think."

"A *MILE!*" Río's exasperation ricocheted through the tunnel.

They walked the tunnel's remainder in a silence so tense that Pilar wished Río would complain.

Desperate to get out, Río used their phone light to find the gap in the fence at 72nd Street that had eluded Pilar. They blinked as they walked into the bright light of the park, but did not stop. They walked briskly, silently, through the ball field, out of Riverside Park, through the streets, and into the 72nd Street subway station. Pilar trailed behind, which was fine because Río could not look at her. When their train arrived, they sank into a seat with a long exhale.

It took Río four subway stops to collect these words: "I'm sorry, Pilar, but that was *crazy*. Never mind what could have happened if we were caught, we almost *died*. I get that you're grieving. I get that this has something to do with your father's stories. But your father gave you a different life. Promise me you won't do this anymore."

Río looked hard at Pilar. She saw herself through their—most anyone's—eyes. Río had given her everything. Why did she need to do this? Maybe she was crazy—the kind of woman no one could understand. Her mother's daughter.

She'd believed that their passage through the Freedom Tunnel would return them to that shared dream of gliding through the resaca at night, the shadows theirs to shape. She'd imagined it so clearly: the two of them closing their eyes and laughing as the train passed, the tunnel's dust on their tongues.

"Okay," she said finally. She swallowed the ache circling her windpipe and resolved to want less from Río. Need less.

CHAPTER 21

A week after they'd seen Pina, Río met Javi outside of his Cobble Hill apartment and the two of them walked to Red Hook past red brick rowhouses with leafy plants spilling out of window boxes. The leaves on the trees had just turned golden and there was a bite in the air. Río had gone for zany prep, pairing a joyful collision of primary colors and patterns with a red Mr. Rogers cardigan and matching lipstick.

"I love this time of year—that feeling of everything becoming something else." Río looked up at the trees, then at Javi.

"Me, too." Javi's shy smile spread into a full one.

They discovered that they'd been at Columbia at the same time—Javi in law school when Río was in college. Río asked how Javi had become an immigration activist and Javi told them that he was the child of Peruvian immigrants. His father fought to rise out of poverty and become a cardiologist in Peru, then fought to make a better life for his family in America. Because his visa was tied to practicing in a medically underserved area, their family had settled in rural Utah. *No wonder he's such a virgin*, Río thought when Javi said that his family had joined the Church of Latter-day Saints at the center of their new community. Javi turned to Río, shielding the setting sun from his eyes. "I never talk this much about myself. Something about you makes me—" He smiled lopsidedly. "What was it like growing up with your grandmother?"

Río told Javi how Abuela's criticism had made them a chameleon, how they'd channeled their hurt into acting. Only they didn't act with Javi, didn't parade out the comedic anecdotes. They told him about the first time they did drag, about reclaiming El Ojo. "That was when I got that we create ourselves."

Javi started to ask what they meant, then took in Río, with their deep red smile, half-shaved hair in a topknot. That freedom—Río a country of their own—was where he wanted to live. He slipped his hand through theirs.

Javi, much to Río's appreciation, had made a reservation at a cozy restaurant called The Good Fork. The cabinet-maker owner had designed the interior like the cabin of a sailboat. As they ate, Javi told Río that he hadn't come out to his parents. Río told Javi about seeing Abuela after Pilar's father died. Javi told Río about the panic attacks he'd had in law school. Río told Javi about Abe and Max. Javi told Río that he'd never been drunk, broken a law, fallen for anyone. Río knew that Javi was telling them things he hadn't told anyone. They felt increasingly drawn to Javi as they huddled together below deck, more and more unmoored.

———————————

Back at the apartment, Pilar took out the garbage and gagged on the rotting smell of her father's kitchen. She shoved the bag down the chute, but the guilt stayed. She dragged around big rotten bags of it.

———————————

After dinner, Río and Javi walked along the Red Hook waterfront. They walked to the end of piers and stared out at the full moon drifting through the steel necks of cranes; Lady Liberty rising, triumphant, against a violet sky. It was the perfect setting for a first kiss. That tension hung in the air like their breath.

Javi broke it. "Have you seen the trolley?"

Río shook their head.

Javi led Río to the three rusted, faded green and silver 1930s street cars
behind the Fairway Supermarket. He explained that they were the remnant of transit buff Bob Diamond's failed attempt to revive the Red Hook
trolley line.

Río peered in the windows, imagining the women who'd ridden the
trolley with their pinwave bobs, cloche hats, and laughing red mouths.

"Magical, isn't it?" Javi peered in, his face close to Río's. Río imagined
Javi turning their face toward his, but he looked at his watch and said,
"The music's starting at Sunny's. Should we go?"

They walked toward a desolate corner of the harbor. Three red letters—
BAR—beaconed through the darkness. This tarnished sign and owner
Sunny Balzano's old-timey turquoise truck were Sunny's sole markers.
It was crowded inside, the walls lined with antique signs, knick-knacks,
and musician figurines. Río could imagine bearded fishermen in rubber
waders and galoshes sitting at the bar. Its new patrons still favored fisher-
man beards.

Javi and Río pushed their way into a small back room, where a pianist
sat in the corner with a mandolinist, upright bassist, banjoists, fiddlers,
and guitarists of all ages circled around him. The musicians were mostly
white guys, though there were some women and the pianist was a young
Asian man. A couple of people left and Río nabbed their chairs, while Javi
went to the bar. The musicians started playing Woody Guthrie's "This Land
Is Your Land". Javi returned with a margarita for Río and a Moscow mule
for himself. He and Río swayed and bellowed the chorus with the audience.

When the song was over, a blond, lanky guitarist called out "Free Born
Man" and the musicians started playing it. The guitarist tossed his head
back and crooned.

"Folk's not really my thing, but this is pretty great," Río said. "Did you
grow up with this music?"

"I grew up singing Mormon hymns. But a few folk songs got passed
down from the pioneers. They were about the same things—unity, courage,
protest." Javi described gatherings of Mormon youth singing cross-legged

on shellacked gym floors, voices and hands raised. "There were all these rules: No alcohol, tobacco, hot drinks. No criticizing the leadership. No extramarital sex—*especially* with someone of the same gender. But the singing was a kind of freedom."

"Sitting cross-legged was against Abuela's rules," Río said. "Also playing house, drawing rainbows, and roller skating."

"Stricter than the Mormons!" Javi widened his eyes and laughed.

"I wasn't singing hymns, but music was a kind of religion." Río talked about driving nowhere at all with Pilar, the Smashing Pumpkins' "Tonight, Tonight" crackling through The Bitch's speakers. How scream-singing, *Believe in the resolute urgency of now!* into the wind filled the Valley's nothingness.

"When I'm burned out, I still go to Mormon services," Javi confessed. "Somehow I find them comforting even though they think I'll wind up in hell. Sunny's feels like church."

"A church for sailors and sinners!" Río grinned.

"Yes." Javi grinned back.

Different musicans called out songs and stepped into the center of the circle. Players dropped in and out, pushing tables back and trading guitars. When Río and Javi left around midnight, the music was still going strong. Coming out of the bar, they were struck, again, by the majesty of the Statue of Liberty rising out of the darkness. Río could have kissed Javi, but something—a newborn faith in things built over time—made them wait. Instead, as Javi walked Río to the subway in Cobble Hill, Río reached for his hand.

It was a half-hour walk to the subway, during which they were mostly quiet. The only other person Río had been so comfortable with in silence was Pilar. Río thought of them sitting on the resaca's shore after scattering her father's ashes.

They told Javi that they were worried about her. They told him about the tunnel. "Am I completely overreacting?" Río asked.

"No. She's trespassing on Amtrak property, which is a federal offense. If she's arrested, she could serve jail time. Getting arrested is one of the nicer things that could happen. She could be attacked or mugged and who would hear her scream?"

"Or hit by a train." Río exhaled and shook their head. "I just don't understand her."

"She's making sense of the senseless." Javi shrugged. The senseless was, newly, something he knew something about. Before Río, he'd been attracted to clean-cut straight men. Could you have a type when you didn't date? He didn't have time to date. He fought for other people's relationships. Then Río walked into his office with their refusal to fit on the form.

Javi could have said, *This is none of my business*. But he tried to understand, strategized with Río about how to help Pilar.

Río threw their arms around him when they said goodbye, his body just the right ratio of muscle to flesh, hard to soft.

Javi connected Pilar to a job at the New Sanctuary Coalition of New York. They needed someone to coordinate their immigration clinics; Accompaniment Program, through which volunteers accompanied immigrants in final removal proceedings to ICE check-ins and hearings; and interfaith network of congregations offering sanctuary.

She began spending her days in the basement offices of Judson Memorial Church organizing volunteer trainings, ensuring that immigrants had legal representation and communal support in the courtroom, and building Sanctuary networks. When it began to feel like secretarial work, she'd listen to Ravi Ragbir, the NSC Director, who was undocumented himself, talk at volunteer trainings. "Remember that our movement not only has widespread terrestrial backing. We have *celestial* backing!" he'd proclaim.

Pilar attended as many hearings as she could. The New York City Immigration Court was an imposing black building with tiny dark windows. Occasionally Pilar would translate, hand the judge papers, or busy the immigrants' children with games. But mostly she sat silently beside the immigrants and other volunteers on the hard wooden benches, struggling against the white fog of bureaucracy. When her mind wandered, she would call up the echo of Flor's voice inside of that rainy LA tunnel. She would try to listen like that.

She started leading a Saturday youth writing workshop at Make the Road. Many of her students were DREAMers. They were brave and generous with what they shared and she realized how much she'd missed teaching. A trans, undocumented youth organizer named Leo helped her lead the workshop. Leo had big hazel eyes, dimples, a sandy brown pompadour, a Mayan tattoo on his forearm, and wooden stretcher earrings. He was a spoken word poet and his speech was infused with poetry. When he spoke, people listened, and when he listened, people felt heard.

"Hold up," he said as students gathered their things to go after their first workshop. He had everyone stack their hands and yell, "¡Justicia! ¡Fortaleza! ¡LUZ!" If Pilar had done it, it would have been cheesy, but from Leo's mouth it was a spell. After that, they always ended class by circling up, stacking hands, and waiting for Leo's words.

She remembered her father's swollen blue hands on the hospital sheet and her students' hands blurred.

She lay down her hand and let her students cover it. She let their courage, Leo's spell, and Ravi's belief fill the emptiness. She stayed late at Judson Church and Make the Road, helping with whatever needed doing. Judson ran a daycare from 6 to 9 p.m. for immigrant families. There were usually around 20 children ranging in age from infancy to their early teens and barely enough volunteers to keep them entertained. Pilar stayed until the last weary parent came to pick up the last straggling child, grateful for those hours of noise and chaos and running around.

Afraid to be alone afterwards, she walked through Washington Square Park. A cellist started playing and a murder of crows lifted from the trees. She thought of her father watching birds lift from the resaca. She saw his sunken eyes before he died, their sharp light emptied.

The cold and dark rushed in and she was alone.

The trees turning yellow over the Eastern Parkway Mall set off a siren in her chest. Already, too much had changed. The idea of winter, which she'd never experienced, filled her with dread. She thought about her graveyard of a family tree. Would it make her feel more or less alone to find a mother who'd left her?

Pilar's job as New Sanctuary Coalition Coordinator didn't pay much, but gradually she was able to repay Río her half of the September and October rent, as well as rent for the months going forward. Río protested, but Pilar gave them her unbudging stare and said, "I can and *want* to do this."

When Río asked her about work, Pilar animatedly described the impromptu singalong of "Do-Re-Me" that broke out at Judson's daycare when five-year-old Rick began banging on the xylophone. A 50-something actress who always brought her guitar and rallied children to accompany her on toy instruments began singing *Doe, a deer, a female deer*, guiding Rick in striking the right bars. The volunteers all looked up from blocks and storybooks and sang along.

"Who needs God when there's Julie Andrews to unite you?" Río asked.

Pilar laughed and Río was convinced that she was doing better.

When she lay in bed at night, Pilar's lungs constricted with her father's gravelly, gasping breath. She couldn't unsee his open mouth—that dark hole—after he'd died.

The days grew shorter and the nights grew longer and Río walked deeper into fall with Javi. Together they walked over the Brooklyn Bridge, wind whipping through the steel cables and chapping their cheeks. Río remembered pulling over to answer Javi's call. Javi confessed how afraid he'd been, how hurt when Río hadn't called him back. He walked faster, not looking at Río, words tumbling out. "I'd forgotten what it was to want: Anything, anyone. And then you walked into my office in those ridiculous turtle pants and I no longer knew myself."

Río pulled Javi to a stop. "First of all, come here."

Javi stepped toward Río.

Río pulled him closer. They laid butterfly kisses on Javi's cold eyebrows, eyelashes, nose. And then, for a very long time, they kissed his beautiful mouth, warmth spreading through their body.

"Secondly," they laid their hand on Javi's stubbled jaw, "my turtle pants are *not* ridiculous."

They walked along the Brooklyn Heights Promenade when the downtown skyline was lit up across the harbor like a postcard. They went on Brooklyn Botanic Garden tours with titles that Javi might have written—"The Subtle Beauty of Deciduous Trees After They've Shed Their Leaves". Javi usually spent the night at Río's because Río wanted to keep an eye on Pilar. On Sunday mornings, they'd make breakfast tacos and sit around talking politics, medicine, art. Río talked about treating patients with HIV, and Javi talked about IE's fight to end the HIV travel ban. Javi loved hearing about the immediate impact Río had on patients' lives, while Javi's talk of Supreme Court decisions and Congressional bills offered respite from that immediacy, like a city seen from the air.

Javi missed nothing. He could listen to some longwinded political theory on WNYC as they cooked dinner and later summarize it in a sentence for Pilar. Río was occasionally annoyed by his sustained powers of focus for even the dullest of subjects, but mostly they marveled at his mind. In conversation, he listened intently to everything being said, deliberated before he responded. When he talked law, Río could see him fitting the pieces together to build a case, the blueprint becoming a house. Río would imagine him delivering a closing statement in court, pacing in a dark suit, the heads of rapt jurors following him like a tennis match, and it was all they could do not to drag him into the bedroom.

Río loved unbuttoning Javi's stiff collared shirt, unbuckling his leather belt, pulling him out of his lawyer suit. "Let me look at you," Javi would say and slowly run his eyes and hands over every inch of Río's skin. Río remembered Abuela sweeping an egg over their body. Javi healed that wound. He pulled Río to him. Legs and arms intertwined, Río's face buried in his neck, Javi pulled Río closer still. He closed his eyes and inhaled Río, kissed them hungrily. Such raw passion and need sprung from someone so contained was a revelation.

When Javi slept over on a weeknight, he would bring his suit in a garment bag, briefcase, and dopp kit. He'd wake up before Río, quietly dress, then bend over them in his suit to kiss them goodbye. Río would sit up, stretch, and yawn, their hair rumpled like the feathers of some crazy bird. Javi would grin at them as he backed out the door.

He'd leave Río alone to write by 7. Javi made Río more disciplined about their writing, and Río helped Javi to find balance. The solitude and vulnerability of writing was easier because Río wasn't alone. They were used to earning an audience's love, but Javi loved Río for their offstage, artless self. He grinned dopily as Río dumped piles of cinnamon into their coffee and tea, on fruit and peanutbutter sandwiches. When Río didn't want to fend off harassers, they dressed in black jeans and gray V-neck sweaters. At first, they felt self-conscious about Javi seeing them this way. But what Javi noticed was their ability to strike up a conversation with anyone—the bagel girl, the elderly woman they helped in the grocery store, old men sitting on stoops complaining about their kidney stones.

Though Río and Javi always invited Pilar to eat or watch movies with them, she sometimes stayed in her room. She felt lonely in their presence. With their burgeoning love, they were so much in the land of the living, whereas on her best days, she ferried between the living and the dead. She tried to write, but there was no feeling behind her words. She thought of lines from a WS Merwin poem: *my words are the garment of what I shall never be / Like the tucked sleeve of a one-armed boy.*

She sent work emails, read students' work, or wrote Ceci. Ceci was not only still writing, but editing her high school's literary magazine. She'd sent Pilar the latest issue, themed around borders.

Flor's Master Calendar hearing was scheduled for November 23rd. Pilar called every night during the week leading up to the hearing. When Flor called to tell her that she'd been granted asylum, the knots in her body uncoiled. Ceci had missed school to be at the hearing. Pilar cried as she described her mother telling her story in the courtroom, saying she'd lived so that her daughter could tell a different story.

When she got off the phone, she closed her eyes and her lips shaped these words: *Thank you, thank you, thank you.*

She opened her eyes and remembered returning to her father's hospital room after showering. His breath gone. The cold drip of her hair down her back.

Río finished a draft of *Desire Lines* and read it for Javi and Pilar in the living room. They read the monologue and played snippets of the songs, the performance of which they were still working on.

"We made roads from dust and motion and music," Río began. Their play moved between finding out that they were undocumented when they went to get their driver's license and confirming six years later that nothing had changed, becoming Carla at the Ropa Usada and reclaiming El Ojo amidst the pigeons, performing drag for the first time at 10th Avenue and their queer history class' Metamorphosis, being assaulted at prom and preaching "Birdland" to The Subway Heller, Abuela's egg cleansing and their first experience of acupuncture, singing "Because the Night" in the canoe and the funeral pyre for Pilar's father, leaving Lucky Feng's and moving into Dr. Yoon's white room, singing "We Have Always Been on Fire" at the Brooklyn Museum and joining the circle of Kikis voguing at Christopher Pier, a dueling duet between Carmen and Carla and a scene of baptizing themselves Río in the Trans-Latina March.

It was about the family you chose and the family that held you no matter how far you ran; the possibility in the space between people, how we
made each other brave or small, beautiful or ugly; and the way we sang
when our desire was larger than our fear. All of it woven through with the
idea of desire lines.

Pilar and Javi watched from the couch, laughing and crying, immersed
in the world that Río was spinning. Javi's arm brushed Pilar's as he wiped
his eyes, and they smiled at each other, tears trailing down their cheeks,
before turning back to Río.

It wasn't just Río's beauty that made Pilar cry. She—or a version of her—
was very much in the story: That girl who'd thrown her body over Carla's
against Alfonso's flying fists; who'd decided, *We're getting out of here*,
and through sheer ferocity of will, had made those words come true. The
woman who'd declared, after her father died, after she'd lost everything,
There should be fire.

"What was the desire line between vulnerability and defiance?" Río
looked her in the eye and asked. "Did it look like Pilar's long, lean body
shielding mine?"

Pilar cried because it was so good, but also because she was mourning
the death of that fierce, beautiful girl. How had she been that person?
How had she lost her? How would she find her again?

Javi gasped at the end. He and Pilar stared up at Río with tears in their
eyes, struggling to find words.

Río rambled to fill their silence: "Is it too confusing to cut between the
Valley and New York? Of course, I'll do a quick costume change. Did the
part where it was just the sound of me breathing during the acupuncture
scene go on for too long? Should I cut it?"

"No!" Pilar shook her head adamantly. "I loved that part."

Javi rose from the couch and moved toward Río. "I loved all of it. I love
you." It was the first time he'd said it.

"I love you, too." Río pulled Javi in for a kiss.

Pilar smiled at them. She walked over to the windows, letting them have their moment, gathering herself. She watched her filthy winged costars dive.

"Wait, can I put this in the play?" Río asked. "*In which our hero finds love with the lawyer who told them that citizenship was impossible!*"

Javi and Pilar laughed.

"I never said impossible," Javi corrected. "I said we have to fight for it."

"Oh, that's *good*." Río scribbled down Javi's words in their notebook. "I'm totally using that."

"You're easy to win over," Río said to Javi. "Pilar's the true test. What did you think, Pilar?"

"I *loved* it," she said, her eyes filling anew as she walked toward Río.

"Really?" Río's eyes filled.

"*Really.*" She threw her arms around Río. She was so proud of them.

She felt loved and held and still she wanted more. She knew, again, what it was to want. And she knew what she wanted. She wanted to be the woman whom Río had written.

She needed a Dream Act. That Sunday, while Río was at Javi's, Pilar dressed in black, tucked her hair into a black ski hat, and returned to the Freedom Tunnel. Edgy with guilt, she chewed off her fingernails as she rode the subway uptown.

She shed her guilt as she walked the tracks leading to the tunnel. She carried the switchblade and a backpack with spraypaint inside. She felt her father's fingers on her wrist; she felt her pulse.

Icicles hung from the tunnel's roof like stalactites. They glistened in the light streaming through the grates. Others had come before her; others had made the road. They'd covered the tunnel's walls in new tags—bright wires crackling through the white. Pilar thought about immigrants finding ways through the Wall. Of her mother running through fire.

She smelled smoke and turned to see smoke curling, as if from an invisible fire. Silhouettes of bodies shaped themselves from the smoke. The figures multiplied, one body forming from another, stretching backwards through the tunnel, into the darkness.

The tunnel filled with bodies and she was no longer alone.

They turned to face her. Waited.

She pulled the spray paint from her backpack, purple—the color Santa Muerte wears for opening passages—and black. Her "L" was shaky, but her hand grew steadier, the motion both her own and beyond her—connected to the bodies on the track, to the succession of fronterizos who'd claimed this vein as their own. She wrote *LUZ O* three times—a Trinity of dark light—until she'd perfected the shadowed O.

She didn't hear the train coming, didn't move against the wall until it was almost too late. Its horn filled the tunnel. In most places, there was a wide space between the tunnel walls and the tracks, but here the tunnel narrowed. She flattened herself against the wall and closed her eyes. Wind swept over her when the train's shuddering steel body passed hers. She saved, claimed her life.

The train disappeared and smoke silhouettes began to move along the track. They swam through a river of drowned light. They clasped hands—current of dreams running through. They moved through the tunnel like miners.

Pilar walked parallel to them along the opposite track. She envisioned a procession—stories passed from mouth to mouth like breath, the borders of each body dissolving in the darkness until they moved as one.

The hair on the back of her neck rose—a listening. She heard the voices of her father, Flor, and Río layered over Spanish Mass, churned into a chorus lifting like dust toward the ceiling grates, filling the dark cathedral of the Freedom Tunnel.

Walking out of the tunnel into Riverside Park, she resolved to bring this vision to life.

The air felt different, the light a part of her.

CHAPTER 22

Pilar trailed the smoke figures she'd seen in the Freedom Tunnel, listening for their voices. That drowned world pulled close, while the physical world—dim light of New York in December—ran on a parallel track. As she walked through the tunnel of skeleton trees along the Eastern Parkway Mall, she moved through the Freedom Tunnel's graffiti and shafts of light. Sometimes her father pulled her by the hand; sometimes she led him. The branches of the trees became her veins, the cars her pulse. *Red light! Green light!* the children at the Judson Church daycare cried, and she ran with them, as fast as they could before they were caught. Sometimes she was Luz Oscura keeping watch on the women in immigration hearings, staring down the judge like a woman with a pistol in her purse.

The people she passed on the street, strangers not strange, moved through the Freedom Tunnel with her, became the ghosts of everyone who'd passed through the tunnel, everyone who'd passed through her life. She moved from a circle of desks into a tighter circle, stacked her hand on top of theirs and cried, *Justicia! Fortaleza! LUZ!* She listened for the words beneath those words, scattering like birds when their hands flew. She listened for the sound of a train.

She stayed late at Make the Road and listened to Leo talk with three other youth organizers about wanting to organize a rally that brought together the queer and immigrant communities and combined spoken word and activism. The youth organizers sat around a long table, eating pizza. Pilar sat at the computer behind them, submitting next Saturday's lesson plan. The hair on the back of her neck rose as Leo spoke. She swiveled her chair around and watched how he captivated the other organizers, who nodded their approval, interjecting ideas between bites. If anyone could help her bring her vision to life, it was Leo.

Leo's back was to her, but Antonio, a friendly DREAMer whose family had emigrated from Mexico, offered her pizza. Realizing that she'd been staring, Pilar's face reddened. She thanked Antonio and took a slice of pizza that she didn't want. She turned back to the computer, but continued to listen.

Pilar and Leo were the only ones who took the 7-train home. As they walked to the station, Leo talked about their students. Pilar nodded and smiled, heart thudding. She wracked her brain for how to translate what she'd seen in the Freedom Tunnel. Words evaporated when she reached for them. Then she thought of Leo's chants: it wasn't about the words; it was about pulling people into a circle, laying down your hand so they could cover it with their own.

"I heard what you were saying," Pilar said after they'd ridden a few stops. "I've been wanting to do something like that."

"Awesome." Leo listened intently to her stories about her father, Río, Flor, her mother.

Within his belief, Pilar's ideas became more coherent. "I'm imagining a procession of stories like theirs and yours," she said.

Leo talked about the spoken word readings he'd participated in. "Immigrants, people of color, queer folx, artists, activists, teachers, social workers, *whoever* reclaim their lives and you feel how together we're so much larger. But no one's sitting on this subway thinking about how people in some community they're not a part of face similar struggles. They're just surviving."

"I didn't know what the DREAM Act was until Río told me," Pilar said. "It got me thinking about what those words might mean outside of the law. Like: an act that brings a new world into being."

"I love that!"

Leo was full of bright energy, and still his enthusiasm stunned her. Her armpits were damp. She kept talking as she tugged off her sweater, her voice muffled and then too loud. She looked at the passengers around her, but no one was paying attention.

And then the vision moved outside of her, into the space between them, Leo teeming with his own ideas. They went back and forth, laying one hand down and then another.

When she told Leo that she wanted the procession to happen in the Freedom Tunnel, it was hers again and very dim. She waited in the dark for Leo to tell her that she was crazy.

Leo's brow furrowed, like he was struggling to see it.

Pilar was honest about the risks, but also about it being urban exploring for beginners. "It's too risky for anyone undocumented. I want stories like my father's, Río's, and yours in the procession, but I haven't figured out the logistics."

Leo nodded, but said nothing.

Pilar stared at the trampled potato chips on the speckled black floor, a roar in her ears drowning out the conversations around her. She buried her fists under her thighs, pressed her nails into her palms.

"Hey." Leo put his hand on her shoulder. "Next stop's mine."

Pilar looked up, her face hot.

"I need to see this tunnel," Leo said.

"I don't think that's a good idea."

"Have you ever seen a cop?"

"No, but if we're caught, you could be deported."

"I risk my life every day just walking down the street as a trans man. I refuse to live in fear."

It was a version of what she'd said to Río. Hearing it said back to her, fleshed out as Leo's life at risk, her body hummed with fear. She wished she'd never spoken.

Leo stood as the train pulled into his stop. He didn't hold onto a pole, just widened his stance and rode the wave.

"Wait—" Pilar said as he stepped off the train.

"I'll text you," Leo said.

She nodded uncertainly before he slung his backpack over his shoulder and walked off with a bowlegged stride.

That night, she dreamed that she stood with Leo before the absence that had been Freedom's *The Third of May*. A row of broken crutches leaned against it like a fence. Milky sentences looped through the white, the letters crunched at the ends like the writer had fallen asleep. Pilar pulled closer and the words disappeared. She used to know what they said. She turned to Leo. "Can you see them?" Leo's face was as blank as the white-washed mural. *Your words are the garment of what you shall never be.* The Freedom Tunnel narrowed with each step. A policeman walked toward them from one end and a train barreled toward them from the other.

Pilar couldn't sleep all week and taught her Saturday workshop in a sleep-deprived haze. She hadn't heard from Leo and he didn't show up until after class. Pilar was trying to read her students' writing, but her mind kept circling back to the nightmare, dread flooding her body.

Leo pulled a desk up to Pilar's and sat down facing her. "Something's come up. I can't be your collaborator, but I'll help you get the word out."

Relief washed over Pilar. "Please just forget I said anything. The whole idea's crazy."

"A Dream Act has to be a little crazy." Leo grinned. He insisted on taking her to a meeting of the CUNY DREAMers.

Pilar protested, but Leo wouldn't let her back down. "Just put the idea out there and see if it speaks to people."

He convinced her to write a call to action. It wouldn't become real unless people were moved to join her.

Pilar spent Sunday sitting in bed with her laptop, working on a flier. The dull winter sun sank at her window; the pigeons dove and dove. She felt triumphant writing it, but as soon as she'd finished, doubt swallowed her.

JOIN A BEYOND THE SHADOWS MARCH THROUGH A TUNNEL THAT CLAIMS THE RIGHTS OF THE IMMIGRANT AND QUEER COMMUNITIES. EMAIL SUBTERRANEANSOLIDARITYMARCH@HOTMAIL.COM.

- *The Subterranean Solidarity March will be a Dream Act: an enactment of a dream of a country where everyone is entitled to civil liberties, democratic and economic inclusion, and human rights.*

- *The march will be a physical manifestation of past Coming Out of the Shadows rallies in which undocumented immigrants have declared themselves "undocumented and unafraid": We will walk through the shadows of the underground and rise into the light.*

- *We will cross borders, slip through fences, and hop walls to create a shared city.*

- *We will join our voices with the ghosts of the marginalized communities who've laid claim to the tunnel—legions of street artists and squatters.*

- *We will claim the city's body as our own—tattoo our nighest names upon its skin, pass through its dark birth canal to define ourselves as we dream fit.*

- *As we pass through this liminal space—through darkness, silence, shafts of light pouring in from the grates above—we will tell our stories. We will absorb others' stories as our own.*

- *In darkness, there are no edges. One body, story, becomes another. Our borders dissolve as we walk through the tunnel, until we move as one body.*

- *Until we are one dream, rising into the light.*

Leo wasn't able to come to the CUNY DREAMers meeting, but he'd made sure that the sponsor allowed Pilar to speak. There were about 40 students in the classroom, the majority of them Latine, with a few Asian, Arab, and Black students. Members were running for office. Pilar sat in the back and listened to their speeches. Some of them were DREAMers and some were allies—social justice activists, international students, first generation Americans. And then the votes were cast, the officers elected, and the sponsor introduced her.

Nine years after she'd tried to tell her seventh grade Texas History class who she was, she tried again. She looked out at the waiting students. She'd dressed like Patti Smith on the cover of *Horses*—white shirt, black ribbon, black jeans and jacket—a spin on her seventh-grade Catholic school girl attire. She was glad for the jacket because her shirt was soaked under her arms. She'd pulled her hair back in a tight ponytail. Her face grew hot, her tongue thick and dry as a cottonball. Her notes fluttered in her shaking hand.

Carlos had saved her in seventh grade. And then Carlos had become Río, and she had become... *Who did she think she was?*

She took a deep breath, looked out at the students, and spoke plainly about her parents, Río, and Flor. Río was in her story, just as she was in theirs. She let her love for the people she spoke about overtake her fear. "All of that led me to dream up a march where we could hear others' stories as our own."

She spoke in a kind of trance, like when she spoke to her students about a poem she loved, so that she wasn't sure of what she'd said when she finished. A few students smiled, but there were a lot of blank, confused faces. Pilar handed stacks of fliers to the people sitting at the end of each row of desks, her hands still shaking. She'd done her best. The pigeons would dive for her; she'd watch through the window. She thought of their endless gray swoop and her face cooled.

A bright-eyed redhead with a half-shaved head like Río's approached her holding the flier and said, "This is awesome!" Her name was Fatima.

She spoke quickly and enthusiastically, saying that her parents had emigrated from Egypt and that she was involved in a bunch of immigrant advocacy organizations. She was a political science and media major whose thesis was a podcast of interviews with LGBTQ+ immigrants. Then came Angelina and Diego, who'd co-organized Know Your Rights nights for immigrants at their Catholic church. Diego was gay and they wanted to organize an LGBTQ+ inclusive event. Angelina was a first generation Mexican-American student who was all business and detail. She wore a button-down black and white dress and carried a matching purse. Diego was a graphic design student with a sweet, round face and wire-frame glasses. "I'm all in as long as I don't have to walk through any tunnels!" He tossed his head back and laughed. "Tunnels freak me out." Pilar assured Diego that the procession through the tunnel was a small part of the Dream Act: she needed help organizing, publicizing, and documenting the march. "I'm definitely more interested in the organizing part," Angelina said. They set a meeting for New Year's Day.

Pilar walked, grinning into space, for 20 blocks in the bright cold until she could no longer ignore her frozen fingers and toes and finally looked for the subway. Riding the train back to Brooklyn, she imagined the tunnel she passed through leading to the pale blue tunnels she'd walked with her father, to the tunnels that Luz smuggled immigrants through, to the tunnel where Flor told her story, until she came to the Freedom Tunnel. She imagined walking through and out of loneliness.

Río was spending Christmas through New Year's with Abuela. They'd invited Pilar, but she hadn't wanted to spend Christmas in the Valley without her father. She'd volunteered to help with a Christmas dinner that the New Sanctuary Coalition was hosting for immigrants who were away from their families. Pilar and Río exchanged gifts before Río left. Pilar gave Río an ex-library first edition of James Baldwin's *The Price of the Ticket*. Río gave her air plants held by four figures carved from pinewood. The figures had bendable joints and you could arrange them in poses on magnetic stands. Together, they arranged the figures like Pina's dancers—sleep-walking with outstretched arms, falling, running, leaping.

Río decided it was too much to ask Abuela to use "elle" instead of "él" (Río's Spanish was rusty and it was difficult for them, too), but insisted that she call them *Río*. This led to Bible thumping, followed by an all-out fight, followed by the silent treatment. Still Río went to midnight Mass with her on Christmas Eve and helped her cook an enormous meal on Christmas day for all of the huérfanas from her panadería and church.

When Yole, the first huérfana to arrive, kissed Río on the cheek and exclaimed, "Carlitos!" Río looked at Abuela, half pleading, half giving up.

Abuela hesitated, her lips parting, mole quivering. "Carlos goes by Río now," she said quickly before thanking Yole for the tamales she'd brought and carrying them into the kitchen.

"I made lots of the cream cheese and jalapeño tamales for you," Yole said. She and the others seemed relieved to name what they'd always known.

One of the younger women complimented Río's Frida Kahlo-inspired ensemble of a bright-flowered huipil, ropelike gold necklace, and high-waisted pants.

"I wore blouses like that as a girl," Abuela said. She looked at Río and said proudly, "Río gets his beauty from me."

Javi texted Río sweet messages from Utah. After everyone was asleep, they called each other to vent and laugh. Río checked in on Pilar, too, and her spirits were surprisingly bright. After the NSC Christmas dinner, there'd been a dance party. One of the volunteers taught everyone a new version of "Little Drummer Boy": *Come they told me / Barack Obama! / A new born king to see / Barack Obama!* They'd sung it all through the cleanup.

As Pilar watched children unwrap gifts, she remembered her father's cinnamon buñuelos wrapped in funny papers and felt like she'd been punched in the throat. She pinched the bridge of her nose to keep from crying.

She thought of Fatima, Angelina, and Diego and what they would create together.

The four of them met at a café on New Year's Day. As they talked about their hopes for the march, Pilar marveled at their motley crew: Fatima with her off-kilter spontaneity, Angelina with her buttoned-up order, Diego with his ready laugh. Angelina and Diego with their religious affinities, Fatima with her anarchist leanings. Pilar felt an upwelling of love for these dreamers careening through the tunnels with her.

"What do you think, Pilar?" Angelina called her back to the bricks of the world they were building.

"What do I think about—"

"We need a band name!" Diego cried.

"What about 'The Dream Team'?" Pilar asked.

They set a march date for May third, worked backwards to create an organizing timeline that included publicity and town hall meetings, and divided up responsibilities. Pilar would write a press release and build partnerships, Angelina would create and manage their social media, and Diego and Fatima would design a website. They brainstormed domain names and settled on www.LuzOscura.net.

Everyone agreed that the tunnel aspect would make it difficult to get the backing of any organization, which would make it difficult to rally a critical mass. "I don't want anyone undocumented walking the tunnel," Pilar said. "I was thinking the march could continue aboveground?"

They agreed to meet weekly and come to the next meeting with ideas.

"Hold up," Pilar said as everyone gathered their things. She had them stack their hands and chanted, "Justicia! Fortaleza! LUZ!"

As she cooked dinner with Río and Javi that night, it was as if they waded through the same pool of light. Each with their own love, mysterious and unknowable. Not telling them about the march didn't feel like a lie. Like any early love, Pilar's was still too tentative to tell anyone.

She hummed to herself as she chopped vegetables and stirred pots. Río and Javi exchanged glances.

"I bet she's got a crush on some passionate revolutionary," Javi said to Río that night. They lay in bed facing each other, the tips of their noses almost touching.

"That would be her type," Río said.

"Probably they're just exchanging furtive glances, trembling when their arms brush."

Río laughed. "You've been reading too many Russian novels."

"She'll tell us when she's ready," Javi said. "Don't pry."

"Me, pry?" Río pulled Javi close. "I would *never.*"

Over the next two months, Pilar spoke about the march at rallies and activist meetings. Angelina, Diego, and Fatima joined her when they could, but none of them loved public speaking and Pilar wanted them to do what excited them.

She learned to tell stories that left space for others to come in: her mother leading women across the Rio Grande, the line of them holding hands like crosses; her father leading Roberto by the hand when his headlamp went out. She connected those stories to the march, asked people to bring their own. She submerged herself in the story she was telling and her heart slowed. She learned to look people in the eyes and fill a room with feeling. She looked for people riding trains on parallel tracks. They'd cross the platform to join her, wrap their hand around the same pole. Through all of the ups and downs, she was healed by the Dream Team's faith. Even if the world never accepted their dream, its beauty breathed in their solidarity.

By the two-month mark, it seemed that everything might come together. Established citizens would carry the stories of undocumented immigrants through the tunnel and into the light. They would emerge from the tunnel at 72nd Street and the march would continue aboveground, through Riverside Park and down Broadway. Diego had secured a protest permit for the aboveground portion, which meant that they could safely include undocumented immigrants and whoever else couldn't risk the tunnel; Angelina had found a venue for their town hall meetings; Make the Road, thanks to Leo's support, seemed receptive to backing at least the aboveground portion of the march; Fatima had recruited two filmmakers to document the tunnel procession; Pilar had found two journalists to write about it; and Ravi Ragbir had agreed to join the aboveground march and help them to rally a critical mass.

After meeting with the second journalist, a young woman who believed that the Dream Team was creating a movement, Pilar moved through a world that dazzled: children running along the Eastern Parkway Mall as the sinking sun glowed orange in the building windows, the dance of hands and scissors in a barber shop on Nostrand, neighbors' heads thrown back in laughter.

Javi had had the opposite sort of day. His knife clacked violently on the cutting board as he told Río and Pilar about taking a group of bi-national same-sex couples to meet with representatives about the Uniting American Families Act. "They all say the same thing: How can we talk about the rights of bi-national gay couples when we can't pass the Marriage Equality Act? We're supposed to hold our breath til the *Defensive* Marriage Act falls and god knows when that'll happen. We're not even having the same conversation. I'm so goddamn tired of asking people to bare their hearts to political machines. I'm tired of pretending it does any"—here a red bell pepper received two emphatic chops—"*damn good.*"

Río gently pried the knife from Javi's grip. "When Javi says *damn* twice, we know two things," they said to Pilar. "One: It's been a real fuckshow of a day. And two: He should not be wielding a knife."

Río brought Javi a glass of wine, massaged his shoulders.

"I think that's just it." Pilar turned down the heat on a curry and walked toward them. "You're *not* having the same conversation. What if we could create a space where people *felt* the connection between the queer and immigrant communities? It has to start with the people, with *us*"—she locked eyes with Javi and Río—"experiencing our connection on a gut lev- el so that we're moved to fight for each other's lives. If enough of us come together, we can stop asking and start *demanding* they represent us."

Río assumed that Pilar's TED Talk poise came of taking on a greater leadership role in the New Sanctuary Coalition, but this burst of opinion from her was not new. At San Jacinto High, she'd sit silent in a desk in the back row until midway through the semester when some topic they were studying intersected with some idea she'd been thinking about. She'd raise her hand and out would flood a torrent of words that no one fully understood. Pilar didn't care. Her gaze was on some point in the distance beyond their heads.

Her ability to see so clearly the world as it could be was what Río loved about her. It was what scared Río about her—that mix of wonder and con- viction when she'd gone on about that deathtrap of a tunnel. Río stopped massaging Javi's shoulders and waited—as if acupuncture needles had been inserted along their spine—for more.

Javi, who'd sat through plenty of these speeches from young activists, sipped his wine and said gently, "I understand that that's the thinking behind the Sanctuary Movement, but even they acknowledge that there's only so much that communal power can do."

"The Sanctuary Movement can't realize the true power of community because they insist that God's the source of it," Pilar said.

"I admire your idealism, Pilar, I do," Javi said. "But you haven't been in the trenches for as long as I have."

"Maybe you have to climb out of the trenches to see what's possible. What was it you said about Pina—that it made you see that it was possible to create spaces for people unseen by the law?"

"Something like that," Javi said vaguely.

"Maybe instead of holding our breath for the system's broken machinery to move, we start a movement that transforms how people see. My father's death changed how I saw everything. Experiences of birth and death transform us. Art transforms us. What if we combined all three?"

"What are you getting at, Pilar?" Río's voice rose.

"I'm getting at what was in my father's stories. What if that imagined experience of moving through a shared world was paired with a physical manifestation of oneness?"

"Like immersive theatre?" Javi asked.

"I could connect you to people," Río said. They'd started workshopping *Desire Lines* with a group of theatre artists.

Pilar sat down across from Javi. She took a deep breath. She imagined Río, Javi, Angelina, Diego, Fatima, and her gesturing over steaming plates of rice, beans, and tortillas—one family.

Río searched her face as she searched for words. "*Please* tell me that this has nothing to do with that tunnel."

Río's Freedom Tunnel scream tore through Pilar's imagined family scene.

She saw Río widen their eyes at Javi, who frowned almost imperceptibly before neutralizing his expression. From this split-second exchange, Pilar gathered that Río had told Javi their version of the story, in which she had a death wish. She imagined all of their kid-glove strategizing about how to handle their *grieving* friend.

It felt like the time she'd been looking at directions as she walked down the street and a man had slammed full-force into her. She woke to her own, the world's, borders. How had she thought she could tell them?

"*Pilar—*" Río searched her eyes, the light gone.

"It's nothing. Just ideas," Pilar said, that strain in her jaw. *You don't need to worry about me anymore*, she thought.

She stood up from the table and started to wash the dishes.

"She's definitely fallen in with some revolutionary type," Javi said to Río as they undressed that night.

"I hope that's all it is."

"It won't last. She'll need us when it's over."

"If I interfere, she'll withdraw."

"So we won't pry. We'll be present, supportive, nonjudgmental."

"Here when the shit hits the fan."

Organizing was diving. Pilar walked to the ledge and dove again and again. She built up a stamina for this go, do life, but was sometimes so drained by the end of the week that all she could be was the old quiet, withdrawn Pilar. She was grateful that Río and Javi asked nothing more of her, grateful to listen to Río talk about their patients, Javi about his clients, or the two of them talk about some movie they'd seen. She'd try to remember the last time she'd seen a movie and her mind would turn to all the work she could be doing. Río would sing, "Pila-ar! Yoo-hoo!" in their old Spanish teacher's voice. "Pilar está en otro mundo." Río and Pilar would laughingly recall their copying assembly line.

There had always been a schism between home and the world: La Llanura and the world outside. Her father asking if she was getting enough to eat, enough sleep, while she wrestled with questions of God and language.

She and Río shared the base of Maslow's hierarchy. She learned to want less from them, the way she'd learned to want less from her father. It was as if they'd worked out an exchange: She asked less of Río, and Río asked less of her. It was a generosity, she told herself—to not need Río to be her everything. Watching Javi feed Río a spoonful of arroz chaufa, an affection for their unlikely family would fill her chest. And then a wave of guilt would roll through her. She tamped down that nausea, pushed her betrayal to the back of her mind.

With one month left before the march, all of their planning fell apart. They lost their town hall venue. One of their filmmakers was leaving for a residency in Scandinavia; another was driven from New York by bedbugs and student loan debt. A journalist set to cover the march was sent on assignment to Afghanistan. Make the Road decided that the march was too controversial to back. On top of all of that, none of the urban explorers whom Pilar had asked to be safety marshals had responded.

The Dream Team struggled to find alternatives. Pilar met with people before work, on her lunch break, after work. She left before Río woke. On her way out, she touched the heads of the pinewood figures that Río had given her—sleepwalking, falling, running, leaping. She would stumble through the dark with outstretched arms until the march became real. When it did, she would tell Río.

But with each rejection, the dream became harder to believe in. Walking home through a gray rain with no umbrella, all the potholes glared. A black SUV stopped just short of hitting her as she crossed from Eastern Parkway to Nostrand. She pointed at the walk signal, but the windows were dark and the only response was the SUV spraying her with puddle water as it continued on its way.

She grimaced at Río and Javi by way of a greeting and went straight to her room.

"I think the love affair's over," Río said to Javi.

Pilar draped her wet clothes over her desk chair, toweled off, and changed into sweats and fluffy socks. She shuffled out of her bedroom with bedraggled wet hair.

"Tea?" Javi asked.

She nodded and thanked him and he fired up the teapot.

The three of them sat down with steaming mugs of green tea sprinkled with cinnamon. Pilar wrapped both hands around the mug and inhaled the steam. Gratitude and guilt filled her.

"What, no *Sound of Music* singalongs today?" Río asked. "*When the dog bites / When the bee stings / When I'm feeling saaad,*" they sang, bumping shoulders with Pilar. They looked to Javi for accompaniment.

"*I simply remember my favorite things / And then I don't feel so bad,*" Javi sang with Río.

"Come on, you know the words." Río put their arm around Pilar.

Pilar shook her head. Her eyes filled.

"It's okay, you don't have to sing," Río said. "Talk to us."

She ached to tell Río everything. Río, more than anyone, would understand what it took to fill a room with feeling, what it felt like when the room emptied.

Her head filled with Río's voice echoing through the Freedom Tunnel: *I've never understood* what? *Hiding in a nunnery then hopscotching train tracks?* It was hard enough to keep the faith without Río attaching her *Fall from Faith* to the march. She just had to keep stumbling through.

She stumbled over the words when she lied to Río. She looked off at some point in the distance and said she was upset that one of the women in the accompaniment program had gotten an order of deportation, which had happened, but they had a strong case for its appeal.

"You've got to maintain some detachment, Pilar." Río stood and wrapped their arms around her from behind.

Pilar worried that Río could feel her heart pounding.

"Want me to look over her case?" Javi asked.

"Her lawyer thinks she'll be okay. I'm just tired. Thank you, though." Pilar looked between Javi and Río. She told herself that she was protecting their friendship. She would not ask more until she'd made the march real.

"It's not about the deportation, is it?" Río asked Javi after Pilar had gone to bed.

"I'm sure that's part of it," Javi said. "Probably a bunch of things, including her revolutionary love, blew up at once."

"So what do we do?"

"Be present, supportive, nonjudgmental."

Pilar lay in bed, her body heavy with exhaustion, her brain ablaze with anxiety. She replayed her lie. She remembered how self-righteously she'd told her father that La Llanura was a lie, believing she could outrun it. She remembered returning to his hospital room—his wax slack face, mouth open, breath gone.

At the next Dream Team meeting, Angelina ran through a list of organizations that had turned them down or never responded. They'd contacted not just activist organizations but arts, theatre, and literary collectives that intersected with immigrant and LGBTQ+ advocacy.

"So on a logistical front, things look bleak. But on a personal front..." Angelina looked at Pilar, Fatima, and Diego. "If this march happens, I want to be in it. I want to tell my mother's story. *My* story."

Pilar grinned at Angelina. "I'd love that."

"If you're going in that freakin' tunnel, then damnit, I am, too!" Diego cried. He looked intently at Angelina. "You should read them what you wrote."

Angelina looked questioningly at Pilar and Fatima.

Pilar nodded emphatically, leaned in.

Fatima raised her fist and gave a rock concert cry of "*Yeah!*"

Angelina took a paper out of her purse, unfolded it, took a deep breath.

"You've got this," Diego said softly.

She read about being ashamed of her family in high school. "I held myself above them because I was born here."

Pilar remembered trailing mothers in the grocery store as a child, her frustration over her father's dependence on her, and swallowed hard.

A class called Latinos in the US had inspired Angelina to become an activist. "But the pain came too close with my mother, so I never asked about her crossing until yesterday." She read about her mother's struggles with diabetes. "I'm always nagging her to take better care of herself, but I don't know how much longer she'll be around. I wanted to know her story."

Her mother had crossed when she was 14. "She walked through the desert at night with a group of migrants. They crawled through a sewer, then hid from la migra inside an irrigation pipe for a night and a day, praying it wouldn't rain, until another nameless coyote came for them. They rode hunched over for miles in the back of his van, the coyote yelling, *Get down!* La Aduana didn't catch them, but the police stopped their driver to check whether the van was stolen. They shone their flashlights into the back and saw 20 migrants bent over, muttering prayers. One of the cops called them pollos. My brave mother sat up and yelled, *Tu madre.* The police let them go. They pretended it was an act of mercy. Really they needed them to work the fields.

"I am no longer whitewashed. I see it all in color—my mother crawling through the sewer, telling off the police." Angelina's voice broke. "I want to speak that truth."

Pilar's eyes filled. "That's everything I want from this march."

She looked from Angelina to Diego (wiping his tears with a napkin) to Fatima (her bright eyes shiny). "I have something to tell you, too." Pilar told them about keeping the march from Río and Javi. "I can't ask hundreds of strangers to enter our dream and shut out my family. I'm going to tell them."

"Would they try to stop the march?" Fatima asked.

"I don't know." Pilar shook her head. "But I can't march for oneness and live a double life."

"No, you can't," Angelina said with conviction.

"What if we walked the tunnel now?" Pilar's question rolled out on the electric tide between them. "Then even if it doesn't happen, it'll happen for us."

"*Now?*" Diego's voice crept up an octave.

"We are, right now, engaged in the Dream Act. *As it was in the beginning, is now, and ever shall be, world without end.*" Pilar looked at Diego, Angelina, and Fatima.

Fatima jumped out of her chair and screamed like Victor Frankenstein, "Our dream is alive, *ALIIIIIIVE!*"

The tension broke and Angelina and Diego laughed. They nodded slowly at each other and then at Pilar.

Diego threw his head back, cackling maniacally, and the Dream Team followed him out of the café with outstretched arms.

They stopped at Diego's for flashlights, then rode the subway uptown, a giddy band of runaways.

"It's a full moon," Fatima said, pointing up as they exited at 125th. "That's when all the weirdos come out," she sang, shifting her pointing finger to Pilar, Angelina, and Diego.

Pilar had never walked the Freedom Tunnel in the dark. Everything held the charge of night: scrambling up the railway embankment in the shadows, slipping through the gap in the fence. Every step along the raised tracks that led to the Freedom Tunnel felt destined, as if the full moon pulled them.

When they reached the tunnel, Pilar shone her flashlight up at the colorful jigsaw of tags around its mouth. There was so much new graffiti since she'd tagged—a neon spring rite of turquoise, yellow, green, and orange letters tumbling into each other. Angelina and Diego stared up at the arch while Fatima snapped photos from different angles, her flash sparking.

Angelina peered anxiously into the tunnel. "There have to be rats in there."

"Big ones," Diego said and grabbed a stick to defend himself.

Still Angelina was the first to step inside. "I can't believe I'm doing this," she said in disgust and awe.

Inside the air was cool and still. Dense with dust and history. They heard themselves breathing.

"So this is it." Diego laughed nervously and the tunnel threw back the sound in ghostly echoes.

The tracks glinted beneath their flashlights, curving into the darkness. They could only see a few feet in front of them. They moved into the tunnel's history and made it theirs.

They shone their flashlights over fresh tags and art. An artist had incorporated a portrait of Robert Moses with the Coca-Cola sign that remained from Freedom's *There's No Way Like the American Way* mural. Fatima drew close, searching for remnants of the old mural.

Pilar felt the darkness filling with color as her life. She showed the Dream Team her Trinity of Luzes. Angelina had heard about the Luz who smuggled immigrants through tunnels. Fatima wanted to know about the woman in Juarez who shot bus drivers. Diego wanted to tag.

They moved as one, and as themselves.

Diego pointed out the different fonts of the tags with his stick.

Fatima crouched to photograph the debris littering the tracks—zooming in on shards of glass, rusted spray paint cans, condoms, pill bottles, syringes. Her flash split the darkness; its light hung in their minds after the dark returned.

Fiery tags flickered through the space where Freedom's recreation of *The Third of May* had been. Pilar told Angelina and Diego about it.

"May third is the march date!" Angelina said.

Pilar didn't realize it until she said it. She turned from the wall to face Angelina, Diego, and Fatima. "It's meant to be," she said.

She pressed her palm to the mural's space, then motioned for Fatima, Diego, and Angelina to lay their hands over hers. The heat of their hands pressed together over the damp cool of the wall felt electric.

"*LUZ!*" they chanted three times and lifted their hands.

Their voices ricocheted off the walls and returned to them holy. They woke to the protest of their existence. They went quiet, their footfall the only sound. Moonlight fell through the ceiling grates, striping the tracks. Their silence felt full. They walked until they could see their dream shining in the darkness, their four bodies becoming a hundred.

"Wait," Pilar said when they reached the exit. The red rage and sadness of that long suppressed *I want* clawed at her throat. She tilted her head toward the moon shining through the bars of the ceiling grate and let out a long, wild wolf howl.

"*All* the weirdos." Fatima laughed and let out her own riotous howl.

Diego howled, laughed, howled.

"This one's for mamá!" Angelina let out an elegant, mournful howl.

The Dream Team filled the dark cathedral of the Freedom Tunnel with their wild wolf call. The supernatural echo of it sang backwards though the shadowy passage of the tunnel as if it were an extension of their throats and their howl would go on traveling its storied entrails long after their bodies passed into dust. They howled until their voices went hoarse, until the red rage and sadness of *I want* became the silver sovereignty of *WE WANT*.

Pilar got home after midnight. She flipped on the light and saw that Río and Javi had left a note:

> *Ciao Bella!*
> *Eggplant parm in the fridge—help yourself.*
> *Buona notte, sweet dreams!*
> *xo, Río and Javi*

Nausea overtook her euphoria. She was starving but couldn't eat the food they'd left her. She undressed and lay in bed staring at a crack in the ceiling.

She slept for a couple of hours, then jolted awake before sunrise, edgy with adrenaline. She had two hours before Javi woke, hours she knew she wouldn't spend sleeping. Though Río had encouraged her to start running again after her father died, she'd been too depressed, and then too consumed. She hadn't run since the summer after her rape.

She dug her running shoes out of the back of her closet and ran through the dark to Río's and her music—"Because the Night", "Some Kinda Love", "Tonight, Tonight". She remembered driving with Río, shaping themselves from wind and song.

Her limbs loosened as she ran west through the brownstone-lined blocks of Park Slope, warehouses of Gowanus, and shops of Cobble Hill. She ran toward the Brooklyn Bridge.

Ascending the bridge, she marveled at the cathedral-like arches of
the stone tower at its center and glittering skyscrapers floating in a deep
purple sky. She noticed for the first time the American flag on top of the
tower—a scrap of cloth tossing in the wind. The flag disappeared from
view as she neared the tower, the wire suspension cables slanting upward,
the spaces between them widening. Her chest opened.

She stopped at the base of the vertiginous tower and gazed up at its
Gothic arches. She turned off her music and breathed in. She felt at once
tiny and expansive. She straightened her shoulders, imagining a back-
bone of steel and stone. The sky lightened, deep purple becoming pale
blue like a fading bruise.

She looked at what she'd been running from—she could not have both
her dream and Río. She saw it through their eyes: She wasn't just risking
her life, she was jeopardizing others' lives, and in the name of what, a
march no one would see? Río would not understand and she would lose
the only family she had. Did she want this Dream Act at the cost of what
was real?

Who was she without Río, who'd believed in the girlhood ghost of
her wandering the dusty lunch yard of South Junior High? Who was she
without Río to drive down the highway with, without wind and speed and
sound filling up the miles of nothingness? Who was she without Río to
talk-and-laugh-and-cry-and-defy-and-dance-and-canoe-and-grow-and-re-
member-and-rise-and-fall-and-be-still with?

Your words are the garment of what you shall never be. She'd asked people to risk their lives and what had she risked?

She imagined life without Río. She walked to the railing and peered
down at the East River, which would go on breathing long after her. She
watched the silver shudder of a train across the Manhattan Bridge until it
was gone. Her eyes filled. Her breath came in knife-like gasps.

She swallowed the knife and ran into a city of steel and glass. Her
muscles ached, but it felt good to propel her body through space. She ran
until her breath regained its rhythm. Until the hyphens down the center of

that Texas highway disappeared and it was just her driving alone down an empty gray road.

Pilar emerged from her room, showered and dressed, as Javi wandered into the kitchen in a pinstripe shirt and slacks. They often ate breakfast together while Río wrote. Javi sat down with coffee and cereal.

"Will you get Río?" Pilar asked.

Javi's spoon paused midway to mouth. "Everything okay?"

Pilar's body tightened. "I need to talk to you both."

Javi got Río, who stumbled into the kitchen with their hair sticking up and a worried look on their face. Pilar handed them coffee. Río and Javi sat on the couch and Pilar sat in the armchair facing them.

She looked at Río. "Remember when you told me that all there is is what we feel and what we make of it?" she asked softly. "That life is just this great gaping hole and how we choose to tunnel through it?"

"I didn't mean that *literally*—" Río's voice rose.

Pilar held up her hand. "Let me finish." She tried to tell them about the march in the generous way she'd rehearsed. She said she'd never have found the courage to organize something like this if she hadn't collided with Río in the SJH library six years ago. She didn't get very far in her explanation of the tunnel procession before Río shot up off the couch.

"You're organizing a march *where?*" Río yelled.

Javi put his hand on Río's arm. "Couldn't you just stage it in a theater?" he asked.

Pilar had attached so much meaning to the Freedom Tunnel, invested so much into making others see its beauty that she couldn't imagine the march as separate from it. She shakily stood. "We want it to be more than art."

"Art *and* a death squad—how novel!" Río exclaimed. "I can't believe you did all of this behind our backs. We thought," they laughed bitterly, "you were in love. Here we were cooking for you, helping you find work."

Javi stayed seated. "Look, Pilar, it's a beautiful idea—I'll give you that."

"I just don't understand," Río said. "You're doing good work, Pilar. Why isn't that *enough* for you?"

Javi nodded. "Why do you need to be this extreme to make your point?" he asked quietly.

"The Undocumented and Unafraid movement is about defying the fear forced on us," Pilar said.

Javi narrowed his eyes. "I've never really bought the whole *Give me liberty or give me death!* thing."

Pilar told them that the bulk of the march would happen aboveground and they had a permit for that, that the tunnel portion would include no more than 100 secure citizens. They were able to take the risk and would be accompanied by safety marshals.

"You're still walking through an active train tunnel, Pilar," Javi said.

"What do you know about being undocumented and unafraid?" Río demanded.

"Nothing." Pilar's jaw tightened. "My father *died* of fear."

"I can't believe this." Río ran their hands through their bed-head cockatoo hair and paced. They knocked their shin on the edge of the coffee table. "*Fuck!*" They felt knocked off center. "You're like one of those cult leaders passing out cyanide in little Dixie cups." They squinted at Pilar. "You know, all I'd have to do to stop this is tip off Amtrak." And then they were pacing again, hands flailing. "I don't even know you anymore. Who *are* you?"

Even now, hands and hair in the air, Río filled the room as they always had, with motion, color, beauty. "Do you know what I fear most?" Pilar's voice shook. "Losing you." Saying it aloud, her heart raced.

"The crazy thing is," Pilar stepped close to Río, "I understand you better than I ever did. What you always told me, *showed* me, about *doing*, stepping into another self before you understand it. It's killed me not to be able to tell you because I know... I used to know you'd understand better than anyone."

"I'm sorry, Pilar, I *don't* understand. We fought so hard just to be here." Río walked to the window and looked out at the people drinking coffee on the patio of the community health center, the 24-hour barber shops, unventilated nail salons, roti shops, bodegas, and filthy-winged soldiers plunging through blue sky. They turned back to Pilar. "If you don't kill yourself or someone else, you could go to jail. I bet you think you'd be fine as long as you had a book. Trust me, prison's not as nice as Mother of Sorrows. You can fight to make this march happen, but *I'm* fighting for *you*." Río's voice broke.

"I couldn't make you see what I saw in the Freedom Tunnel." Pilar searched Río's eyes. The memory she did not like to think about surfaced. She remembered crying to Río, Río the only one she told. "When did we stop seeing each other?"

Río looked in Pilar's eyes, bloodshot with the strain not to cry, and said softly, "If I mattered to you, you wouldn't do this. It's *selfish*, Pilar."

"You taught me this. Watching you as El Ojo, thrusting that wild self into the world. Maybe all I ever wanted was to create something as defiant and beautiful as you. You inspired everything that this march is..."

Pilar turned, stared out the window. "And you hate it," she said, as if to herself. "I always accepted you and I want you to accept me, this dream. I didn't think it would be possible without you in it. I never wanted—what does it matter what I want? Why should I want so much from you?" She'd thought that if Río didn't understand, no one would. "I found other people who understand. Who *need* this. I owe it to the people who put their trust in me to make this march happen. I owe it to myself."

"You owe *more* to yourself." Río raised their voice. "You owe more to your father. *Me*. More to the people who've tried to keep you—I brought you here because I was *worried* for you, Pilar. Worried you'd do something—You *are* doing something crazy."

Pilar continued to stare out the window, already gone.

"Tell her, Javi," Río pleaded. "Tell her how *insane* this is."

Javi shook his head and sighed. "I'm late." He retreated to their bedroom.

Río knew that Javi could still hear them hurling half-truths at each other, but Río couldn't stop yelling. Their body shook. Pilar had always listened to Río, *needed* them. She'd left the convent, come to New York because Río had told her to. Even when she didn't agree with them, she'd always taken Río's feelings, friendship into account. She'd seen how terrified Río had been in that tunnel, and she didn't care. She'd promised Río she wouldn't return, then spent months organizing this march behind their back. The full weight of her betrayal rolled through Río's body.

But it wasn't just the betrayal. With Pilar, Río had always been the makeover artist. And now she'd become this whole other person without them. Not only did she re-create herself, she created this huge thing with a whole new cadre of collaborators. Río felt abandoned—lost to Pilar and themself.

Pilar turned to face Río. "Are you going to contact Amtrak?" she asked quietly.

Río looked at her for a long time, took a deep breath. "I don't know. I need some space to think. You and I are just too—" They waved their hand as if to clear something.

Pilar nodded. Río's eyes filled and hers echoed.

"I'll stay at Javi's for awhile," Río said.

"No, I'll go."

They looked at each other in a way that held the whole of what they would lose.

CHAPTER 23

Carla painted Pilar's lips and then her own a deep red and drove her toward the border, Patti Smith crooning. She parked The Bitch in the old lot of brush and rusted cars by the Rio Grande and led Pilar along railroad tracks. She lifted her eagle's wings dress and Pilar tugged down her turquoise sequin mini-skirt as they stepped from track to track.

"Where are we going?" Pilar asked anxiously.

"We're crossing."

The tracks led into a tunnel that ran under the river. Pilar didn't want to go in. "My father—"

"Trust me," Carla said. "I cross all the time."

"Isn't it illegal?"

"*I'm* illegal." Carla pulled Pilar into the tunnel.

As they moved through the darkness, Pilar's fear lifted. She noticed things that Carla never had—shadows, tags, broken glass. She ran her fingers over a tangle of tags. She said they meant something. She looked at them the way she'd looked at El Ojo.

"It's just graffiti, Pilar."

They felt a rumble at their feet, a wind, and then there was a blast of light. A train hurtled toward them through the narrow tunnel—thunder and grind of metal. Carla tried to pull Pilar into an alcove, but she pulled away.

"I can almost make out what they say." She traced the tags.

Río grabbed her.

Pilar jerked away and fell onto the tracks.

Río tried to scream her name but couldn't.

Out came a lock-jawed mewling, which they were oblivious to until Javi laid his hand on their chest.

Río shot up in bed.

"You were making this noise like a kitten being slaughtered." Javi squeezed their shoulder.

Río looked hollow-eyed at Javi, then disorientedly around his bedroom. Dazedly they described the dream. "Then I wake up and the reality's worse."

"You are not responsible for this." Javi made Río look in his eyes.

Río nodded slowly.

"Can you go back to sleep?"

Río shook their cockatoo hair.

"Breakfast tacos?"

Pilar told Fatima that she'd come out to Río and it had not gone well. Fatima generously offered her couch. There was no longer any division between home and the world. Pilar and Fatima breathlessly talked about the march over improvised meals of hummus and vegetables. Her apartment was cheerfully chaotic with the comings and goings of her three roommates and now Pilar. Even the plants were in motion. They kept the windows open and leafy hanging plants swayed in the cross-currents of spring breezes dueling with a floor fan.

Late at night, when the talk, laughter, and commotion of five women in a small apartment came to an end, Pilar lay in the dark staring up at the swinging plants, replaying her fight with Río. *I don't even know you anymore. Who are you?* She swung between self-excoriation and anger, sadness and self-righteousness. She felt guilty for waiting so long to tell Río, but she'd told them now. Río could report the march to Amtrak, but for her, for the Dream Team, it was already real.

They moved through the final month of organizing with wolf-pack swiftness. For Pilar, it was the swiftness of freefall. There was nothing left to fear. No's slinked off their bristly coats like rain and they ran on. The dream lived in the pistons of their hearts and legs, the nightshine of their eyes. They howled into the world and it echoed back.

Pilar called Flor and asked her if she'd tell her story in the Freedom Tunnel procession. She'd started working as a community organizer for the Coalition for Humane Immigrant Rights of LA. In front of audiences of 300, she talked about what had happened to her village, her detainment, taking Sanctuary, and applying for asylum. She said that she would come to the march and bring as many people as she could.

After Flor, Pilar talked to MJ, then Padre Bob, feeling like the different parts of her life might come together. That she could choose to be a part of, rather than apart.

———————————

Río broke down at work and told Dr. Yoon everything. They waited for commiseration, running their hand over the stubble of their half-shaved head, but Dr. Yoon said nothing.

"Please say something."

Dr. Yoon squinted at Río as if considering what they were ready to hear. "Rites of passage break with one life to create another, and that *break* often involves danger. But the danger's circumscribed by rules and community that make order of chaos. Sometimes people need to destroy an old self to create a new one. In the absence of ritual, people find their own ways to destroy themselves. Pilar's created a rite of passage that lets people walk together through destruction into creation. I think it's beautiful."

Río looked hard at Dr. Yoon. "Dr. Yoon, I say this with love: I'm not in the mood for your New Age bullshit."

"Do you think I was always this person?" Dr. Yoon narrowed his eyes at Río. "I lost count of the times the Sisters held my hair back while I puked into some piss-laden toilet, the mornings I woke up in some stranger's bed and stumbled home to sleep off my hangover just so I could wake up and do it again. That's why people come to me with their STIs and suicide scars. That's why *you* came to me.

"I can heal people because I had to heal myself. That trip to Korea? I'd hit bottom. I wasn't just searching for my mother. I was searching for a reason to live. You met me after I'd come out on the other side, but I never wanted to be your god. No one is pure, not me or anyone else. No one is one thing and not another.

"You invent a new self, name it, become it, and never look back. Pilar looks back; she gets stuck.

"I've watched you learn how to be still with patients. How to stay in a relationship. While you were moving inward, Pilar was moving outward. She has your old need for an audience to bring her dream to life. You've switched places and you don't understand each other anymore. But neither of you would have changed without the other. Your past with Pilar isn't one you can just cut yourself off from." Dr. Yoon held Río's eyes. "I don't need to be a doctor to tell you that you might as well cut off your leg, because you will both limp through the rest of your lives."

Río let out a long sigh. "So what am I supposed to do?"

"Like I said, I never wanted to be your god. I can't tell you what to do, but I can give you the day off to think. You're clearly in no state to work."

Río left their bike locked up outside of Dr. Yoon's office, walked to East River Park, and sat on a bench by the river. It was a bright, crisp day and they longed to be one of the bikers whipping along the water, wind in their hair. They couldn't remember the last time they'd sat alone. They felt as if all of the people passing by were off to something better.

They watched the light reflecting off of the river's surface and gradually sank into their thoughts. The East River with its view of the downtown skyline receded and memories of another river surfaced. They sat on the sunwarmed hood of The Bitch with Pilar, watching the sun set over the Rio Grande.

Río stayed until sunset, watching the layers of pink, orange, purple, and magenta pile up along the horizon, noticing how the hues changed as night fell, how one color ran into and became another.

Their workshop was wonderful—writers who imagined and re-imagined with Río—but it was Pilar who'd look up from the script with her gray-blue grandmother eyes and ask gently, *But what did you feel about this?* And Río would be able to tell her because she always leaned in. *Desire Lines* wouldn't be finished until she saw it. Her witness bound all of their selves.

———————————

Pilar had just emerged from the labyrinthine halls of the Citizenship and Immigration Services building into the high noon sun when her phone rang.

"It's Julia Solis," a voice with an indeterminate accent, a mix of German and something else, said. "I'm sorry I'm just now getting back to you. I was organizing a Dark Passage event in Detroit, and then I moved there. But I'm in New York for a few days so thought I'd get in touch."

Pilar had emailed her many times. The urban exploring community remained the only one in which they'd been unable to make headway. She thanked her for calling, squinting dazedly into the sun as if Solis might walk out of it. It was no less magical that three weeks before the march, the woman who'd led her to the Freedom Tunnel wanted to meet.

As Pilar rode the subway to the Lower East Side café that Julia had chosen, her mind traveled back to those tunnels blue-lit with sadness after her father died, days when riding the subway was the only motion she could manage. Remembering Revs' underground letter, she had an idea about how to publicize the march.

Solis stood and waved at her from a corner table. She wore a black crepe dress and battered black ankle boots. Pilar imagined the hidden spaces those boots had traversed.

She told Julia how walking the Freedom Tunnel after her father's
death had reminded her of his stories. How that passage had branched to
become the march. She told her about the smoke figures she'd seen on the
tracks—something she hadn't told anyone.

Pilar was used to people pulling away from her intensity, but Solis
leaned in. She studied Pilar with her bright green eyes. "Connecting the
Beyond the Shadows movement to a march through a tunnel is a beautiful
idea," Solis said. "And I understand why you want it to happen in the
Freedom Tunnel. The resonance of that space is powerful."

They talked about safety and publicity, Solis offering advice from
events she'd organized in underground spaces. Pilar told Julia her publicity idea. She was sure she would shoot it down, but she was no longer
afraid to ask.

"Let me talk to some people," Julia said. She wasn't sure where she'd be
on May 3rd, but said she'd march if she could.

Within a week, five urban explorers had volunteered to act as safety marshals and *www.LuzOscura.net* appeared all through the subway tunnels in
purple letters shadowed black.

Río would see it. Would they try to stop the march?

Pilar remembered watching their canoe burn from the shore of the
resaca. *If it all went up in smoke, that smoke would remain.*

CHAPTER 24

At 4 a.m., Pilar holds back the fence lining the railway embankment that leads to the Freedom Tunnel. The air is cool and a crescent moon sails in and out of the clouds. The procession will exit the tunnel as dawn breaks and the march will continue down Broadway. She takes the hands of 99 marchers—Stonewall Veterans, established immigrants, queer activists, immigrant activists, street artists, urban explorers, faith leaders, drag queens (thanks to Dr. Yoon, many of the Fengs had come), drag kings, trans folx, allies, and various permutations of these identities. She helps each person up the embankment. She knows them from their town hall meetings, greets many by name. She feels the lifeline between their hands and her father's.

Flor hugs Pilar and introduces the 7 CHIRLA staff members and volunteers she brought. "I think you know these next two," she says. MJ steps forward in a white tunic, jeans, and hiking boots. "I left Mother of Sorrows." She widens her eyes as if the fact of it still surprises her. "*Love, where present, cannot possibly be content with remaining always the same.*" She laughs her deep, throaty laugh and throws her arms around Pilar. It feels like they've crossed glaciers to embrace. Padre follows in his priest's collar and rumpled lay clothes. "I'm glad to see other men of the cloth here." He puts his arm around a drag king in priest's vestments, whom he introduces as Father Cox.

Julia Solis has come. She wears a long black cloak and a bright red pageboy wig. She needs no help. Pilar takes her hand only to thank her.

Fatima and Steve, an urban planner/explorer that Julia Solis recruited, usher the last of the procession up the embankment.

Diego tries to get her attention. When Pilar turns to him, his eyes are wide, swimming behind his glasses.

"Where's Angelina?" Pilar asks, looking around.

Diego's sweet, round face collapses. "She's with her mother in the hospital."

The panic in Diego's eyes swells in Pilar's chest, but she keeps her voice calm. "Is her mother okay?"

"I think so, but Angelina needs to be with her."

Pilar looks between Diego and Fatima. "Would either of you want to speak?"

Diego shakes his head emphatically, pushes up his glasses. "I'm walking the tunnel for Angelina and her mother, but that's it."

"My place is behind a camera," Fatima says. She holds the camera around her neck up to her eye and takes Pilar's picture.

"We'll figure something out," Pilar says.

The procession walks along the raised tracks of the embankment and stops at the mouth of the Freedom Tunnel. They form a circle. The film crew turns a spotlight on Dr. Yoon, who stands under the tunnel's arch in her grandmother's stiff, white Salpuri dress, its hoop skirt rustling in the breeze. Her bald head reflects the spotlight. Musicians sit on either side of her, poised at a twelve-stringed zither and a bamboo oboe to her right, a long-bowed zither and an hourglass drum to her left. Bright graffiti bubbles around them. "Massachusetts is the only state that's legalized gay marriage, and that has to change," Dr. Yoon says. "But tonight we're after a bigger marriage. My grandmother taught me Salpuri before I could speak. It's a dance for healing divisions. That healing happens first in the body. The body brings it to the air."

The musicians begin to play, arrhythmic drumbeats and discordant bowing drifting from the tunnel's mouth. Dr. Yoon turns slowly at their center, drawing a white scarf through the air. Her silver-nailed hands dip into the tunnel, scooping shadow into light. The drumbeat accelerates and Dr. Yoon turns faster. The borders between myth and truth, male and female, east and west lift as she dances.

But not the border between Pilar and Río. Pilar thinks about Río crying the first time they saw Dr. Yoon perform. She starts when Leo puts a hand on her shoulder.

"What are you doing here?"

"I'm here to speak." He runs a hand through his pompadour and gives her a dimpled grin.

Pilar shakes her head. "It's too risky."

"Those who give up their liberty for safety deserve neither," Leo says.

"I can't let you do this," Pilar says, but Dr. Yoon steps out of the spotlight and presses a long silver nail to her lips. The doctor knows who needs to speak.

Dr. Yoon joins the circle of marchers. The spotlight illuminates the tracks and graffiti inside the tunnel—a language waiting to be spoken.

Pilar enters the cool dark of the tunnel. The speakers, and then the rest of the procession, fall into line behind her. Safety marshals walk beside the procession with flashlights, illuminating the tracks. They speak to each other and Pilar through headsets. Pilar walks until a marshal lets her know that the whole of the procession is inside the tunnel. She turns to look at the long line of shadows. One by one, starting from the back of the procession, each marcher turns their headlamp on. The lights are blue. Blue light bathes their faces. The rails shine in the blue light.

Julia Solis walks to the front of the procession. Her black cloak lights up like Yayoi Kusama's *Infinity Room* when she begins to speak. Her red pageboy wig looks purple in the blue lights.

"The Freedom Tunnel was the first forbidden space I explored when I came to the US. I grew up in Berlin and came here after the Wall fell. All these secreted lives were spilling out. The world's pores opening.

"The Freedom Tunnel was a home for the homeless then. Graffiti artists painted for hours without fear of the cops. Squatters built a tent city. The people I came to know through the Freedom Tunnel seemed connected to all of the underground communities surfacing in Berlin. I met Freedom here. I met Revs here. I huddled around fires with the people they called Mole People. Freedom's murals were most beautiful by the light of their fires. I knew then that even the lone wolves of us are not alone. Our presence in this space made us one.

"The Freedom Tunnel taught me the language of hidden spaces, which speak truths like dying people. Here we stand at the edge of certainty. Life and death run on parallel tracks. We don't have to pray. We see the other side. We walk death's border to remember life.

"I wanted to document the most marginal aspects of history. To do for history what street artists have done for art. To unearth the stories of forgotten, abandoned, decaying spaces. We not only witness history when we walk through these shadowed spaces; we write it. Revs said he wanted to tear the city to pieces and rebuild it. Here we can see the pieces. We see that we are all so much wreckage. From dust we come and to dust we return. The only meaning is what we make in the breaths in between.

"Here we reclaim the parts of ourselves the world has discarded. In this quiet, we hear ourselves breathe. In this darkness, we are the light. This is why we explore. To walk through and beyond death, to transform the decaying rooms of our pasts into a resurrection. To remake ourselves: These tracks our skeletons, this graffiti our unspoken, this tunnel our birth canal.

"They evacuated the Mole People, painted over Freedom's murals, fenced off and policed the tunnel. But we can feel the life that was white-washed—one of anger and pain, but also of resilience—life lived along the vein. What remains," she pauses in front of Freedom's Venus de Milo, "is a love letter from that past life.

"The Freedom Tunnel has waited for us. This shadow our birth light. Birth right. Tonight we reclaim it. We open our mouths and the tunnel's silenced stories tangle their tongues with ours. Its words swim through our luminous blue. We dive deep—hold in our bodies what they tried to drown. We wake the dream life of this city."

Julia's words become something else as they echo through the tunnel, absorbed by bodies of every kind, made one. The Dream reverberates off of the walls and disperses, becoming no one's, nothing, everything.

Pilar feels her father's vein opening—not blue, but silver—the procession moving inside.

Flor moves to the front of the procession. Again she and Pilar walk together through the dark. But now the shadows walk with them. Close off the space between that LA walk and this one. Memory as malleable as darkness here. Flor remembers that other tunnel. The first time she spoke these words. The words are lighter now.

The procession walks through the blackened field, inhales the ash. Together they peer in the well. Breathe in the stench of bodies. Wave away flies to look in their glazed eyes. Together they walk through the burnt church. See the splayed corpses of women, their pregnant bellies sliced open. Together they lift her nine-year-old sister Ariché's body from the pit.

Pilar listens again to Flor's story and the passage tightens, the air thins, her eyes sting.

The procession buries Ariché with Flor. Their bodies become her grave.

The Freedom Tunnel becomes the well, turned on its side, bodies spilling out. Their splayed limbs straighten to walk the tracks, roped mouths open to release the past. They walk into the desert—a plane on which to make themselves. Vultures circle their freedom. They raise their scythes. Blades swish through the air as they walk.

Leo moves to the front of the procession. "I'm a trans DREAMer from
Colombia," he says. "I migrated here with my family five years ago. I
found out I was undocumented when I started applying to colleges. For
a long time, I lived in two closets: My family told me not to tell anyone at
school about my immigration status because they could tell la migra, and
I didn't tell my family I was trans because I was afraid they'd kick me out.
I was afraid of being unhoused and undocumented. I was afraid of being
deported to Colombia, where I fear for my life as a trans man.

"When I started college, I came out as undocumented and trans. I
became an activist. I changed my name to Leo. Two weeks ago, I started
testosterone injections. I wrote this for the spoken word night I host at
Make the Road:

"I insert needles into my thighs. I stitch the self under the skin into
being. My muscles tighten. It hurts to walk the street. To be called *lady*
and *faggot*. To be frisked by cops. To be the part of them they don't want
to see."

His voice rises and cracks. "I refuse to be what they call me. I will speak
with an accent. I will speak in this cracked voice. When the mood swings
come, I will feel them. We have reason to be angry and sad. It is painful
to be the in-between, but I will not divide myself." Leo lets the echo of his
words pass backwards through the procession. His cracked anger reverberates in their lungs, so raw it is hard to move through. He waits until the
sound stills. He takes several steps in silence, then says, sotto voce: "Walk
into the in-between with me. It is beautiful here. In transition. The only
free part of you." These words break the tension like rain.

"Walk into the in-between with me. Until we come together like a scar.
Like needle and vein. Ocean and shore. Walk with me into un mundo
sin fronteras."

Pilar listens and her father's tunnel branches and expands.

She moves to the front of the procession. She looks down and sees coins,
condoms, needles, and vials bathed in the blue of veins. She looks up at

the bright scrawl of graffiti: not the words, but the crossing that matters. The way out of death is *through* it: through rat nests and cesspools, needles and debris.

"Buscamos la vena," she begins. She walks into the darkness, telling her father's story of the mines. She lets each sentence echo. The Freedom Tunnel amplifies their words. Her father's story moves into the ears of men like Leo, women like Dr. Yoon, dreamers, drowners, seekers. Ripples through the cilia of their pale pink canals like wind through the caña. Blue family stretches her father's story to hold theirs. The ricochet of words, footfall along the tracks, a prayer. The life they save—Roberto's life—their own.

Pilar's voice cracks when she comes to the place where her father stops telling the story, when she speaks about how he died. Alone. She thinks of Río flying down to the Valley to be with her.

What do you want me to call you?

You call and I'll answer.

She'd called Río before the march, but they hadn't answered. She looks back at the procession, bodies shadowed in blue light, stretching beyond her vision. She is no longer the Dreamer of this dream. It is more beautiful than she could have imagined and still not enough. *Why isn't that enough for you?* Río had demanded. The shadows wait for her to speak, but the old silence rushes in: dark hole of a mouth.

She turns back to the empty tracks stretching into the darkness. Who is she without Río? She's afraid to walk into loss.

"Who do you want to be, Pilar Salomé Reinfeld?" a voice yells from the back of the procession.

Pilar's heart leaps into her throat. *Río*: their question echoing through the tunnel. People turn to look.

"Who? Who? Who?" they hoot.

The ghostly owl of Río's voice ricocheting off of the tunnel walls is surreal. Pilar laughs in disbelief.

"I'll tell you who you are to me." Dimly, Pilar makes out their shadow, moving slowly alongside the procession. "I led you out of the library, but you convinced me to compete in the Mz. 10th Avenue Pageant, to go to prom as Carla, to go to college in New York. When I lost myself, you found me. You pushed me beyond my fear. I would never have found my way to New York, or love without you."

When Pilar accepts the reality of Río being there, elation blares in her body, drowning out their words. It takes her a moment to release her failure, take in what they are saying. And then she is a child listening to a story, the woman Río describes far off in the darkness.

"You told me I was beautiful when I first slipped on the eagle's wings dress, when I came out of 10th Avenue's bathroom all made up. You looked at me like I was a goddess. Without you as witness, those moments would have been eaten by moths in my closet."

That Río needs her is as much of a revelation as it was when they got into colleges on opposite coasts. That love rushing toward her like a train makes her want to flatten herself against the wall, turn her head, squeeze her eyes shut. But she looks out at the line of people it moves through, straightens her spine, and lets it come.

"I pulled you into a foreign world and you took it all in with wonder. You saw the beauty that most people couldn't. But when you brought me into this tunnel, I didn't even try to see it through your eyes. The truth is that I've always been afraid of the dark.

"When I was little, my mother would sit beside me singing until the night softened. This was when I was too young to know that we lived on the wrong side of the border. My mother's voice filled the room, spilled out of the windows, became the night. Became everything we couldn't see. She let me wear her dresses, called me hermosa. What was hers was mine.

"Until her boyfriend came. He left needles on the kitchen table. He tore my mother's dress off me. Tried to beat the maricón out of me. He wrapped his hands around my mother's throat, squeezed until she could not sing. She left me with my grandmother in the US when I was five so that he wouldn't kill me. Abuela tried to cast out the maricón with curandera spells. You were the first person since my mother to call me beautiful."

Río had told Pilar that their mother's boyfriend beat them, but she'd never heard the full story. She threw her body over their child body as she listened, pressed a knife to that man's throat.

"Taunting Alfonso at prom was a way of talking back to my mother's boyfriend, saying the things I was too powerless to say as a child. I knew what would happen—it had happened before—but I needed to be seen as Carla. You could have been hurt, too. You threw your body over mine. I'll never forget.

"You drove me home, protected me from Abuela. You curled up with me in the dark.

"Walking through all of this darkness, through needles and rats and god knows what, terrified me. I understand now. You were walking me through it so that we could walk out of it."

Being seen by Río—in blindness, in darkness, in blood—after she'd let go of that hope, felt like music filling her body.

"I stopped seeing you. I'm sorry. That's not who we are."

Pilar took Río's love into her veins and freedom became real.

"Everything runs back to the river, the Rio Grande, those nights of re-inventing ourselves in the resaca.

"I could not cross the Rio Grande. I could not search for my mother. I don't remember the words she sang. But I remember the feeling—I could be anything. That's why we're here tonight, right, Pilar? To witness not only our most beautiful selves, but the possibility of a world that sees that beauty.

"We parked at the border, but we never crossed. Tonight we cross into that world holding hands. Let our line of blue lights be the river and the city blinking across it. Let us be the current. Let us close off the gap between one country and another. Between masculine and feminine, wings and gutters, memory and loss.

"Do you remember singing in the resaca, rocking the canoe as we screamed? Do you remember deciding to change our lives? And we did. We made each other."

Pilar feels who they were, *are*. She believes.

"Then we searched for ourselves on opposite coasts. You told me to read Baldwin. It was years before I did. I've never forgotten that line at the end of *The Fire Next Time:* that we 'must, like lovers, insist on, or create, the consciousness of the others.' But it's only now, in this darkness, that I see what Baldwin meant.

"Patti Smith said the night—*this night*—belongs to lovers. This night belongs to us."

James Baldwin and Patti Smith—Pilar could have danced to that wild combination.

Río hums the opening chords of "Because the Night". Their Lucky Feng's Sisters harmonize, holding that dressing room space of spontaneous creation, equal parts gutters and wings. In the second stanza, Río's voice rises to a staccato call to arms, the sound bouncing off of the walls: *Take my hand as the sun descends / They can't hurt you now...* The marchers take each other's hands as they walk.

Río's voice seems to be moving toward Pilar, but it's hard to tell because everyone joins in by the second chorus, even the ones too young to know the song, the chorus' staccato syllables rounded by a beautiful jumble of accents. Without intending to, Río comes up with their protest song, its movement between ballad and chant perfect for a solidarity march that's part performance art. The brayed chorus the sort of thing that everyone can sing: *Because the night belongs to lovers / Because the night belongs to lust / Because the night belongs to lovers / Because the night belongs to us.* These words slash machete-like through the damp air. Río pulls the song back into whispered seduction. The procession pulls the song back into a rally cry. The world they shape—in which no one can hurt them—reverberates through the tunnel.

The safety marshals check their watches and shout, "*TRAIN!*" They en-sure that every marcher presses themself against the wall as they'd prac-ticed. In the seconds before a silver train shoots past, the sound of their breathing fills the tunnel. And then their breath is sucked into the wind of the passing train. They tilt their heads back to look in the windows. As if in answer, the few insomniac seekers on this night train to Niagra turn to look at them. Their mouths open. They press their hands to the glass.

As the last of the train snakes into the distance, the marchers peel their bodies from the wall and mill around, shaking out their limbs, laughing, talking. The tunnel fills with the sounds of their relief and awe. The marshals usher everyone back into line formation to get a headcount. Everyone is here, they tell Pilar. Everyone is safe.

The procession begins to chant: *Pilar! Pilar! Pilar!* The chanting grows louder, echoing through the tunnel until it's deafening. The sound wells in Pilar's chest. *PILAR.* A sturdy column of stone, wood, or metal. She knows now what her strength is for. Her heart pounds as she faces the procession. She looks at their blue-lit, waiting faces. *Shhh* moves along the length of the line until the chanting dies down and the tunnel stills.

The words form like muscled wings in her throat. "I am Pilar Salomé Reinfeld. My father came from the silver mines of Bolivia. He migrated from the graveyard of Potosi to the graveyard of San Jacinto. He learned how to breathe with lungs full of dust. He used that breath to make me a home of stories. He taught me that the stories we tell are a way out of death. He taught me to seek the vein: the silver is there.

"My mother carried me across the Rio Grande River. The dome of her pregnant belly pushed against the current, a world of its own. She left me to help others cross. They crossed at night. She wasn't afraid of remolinos, la migra, or men. She knew how to disappear into the sugarcane. She carried a switchblade. She outran fire. She was her own savior. I used to think she left me nothing, but I know now that she left me this country.

"This country is a mother of our own making, a mother we have dreamed and chased, who's evaded and abandoned us, who has always been there, buried in the light between us, a myth that might become real if we remake her in our image.

"My mother rose out of the river. Her name was Luz. She was the first light my father saw when he rose out of the mines. They conceived me in the borderlands. I was born and raised between shadow and light, river and fire, myth and truth. I grew up an old-souled ghost girl whose friends were books. Río drove me out of the library and into the world. Río taught me to laugh and dance and dive.

"My family rose out of the mines, out of the river, out of las montañas de ropa usada. We are dreamers and drowners and seekers. We are border crossers. Fronterizos.

"My mother is gone and my father is dead. I made a home of shadow and light, words and silver, and you came inside. You showed me that I am not alone. You filled the Freedom Tunnel with voices that will not be whitewashed. Our stories seeped into its walls and dirt. Now we rise into the light.

"We will write our names on the walls they built to shut us out until those walls fall. I am Pilar Salomé Reinfeld. This Country of Under is my country."

Held in the bodies of one hundred dreamers, Río, Flor, MJ, and Padre among them, echoing through the Freedom Tunnel, Pilar feels her dream become real. She lets their river of blue lights carry her the few remaining blocks to the 72nd Street exit. The procession walks in a silence that is full. They walk through and beyond death.

Dawn breaks as they walk, until light pours in shafts through the grates. At 72nd Street, Pilar finds a low gap in the fence. She crawls out, then holds back the fence to let the marchers crawl through. She helps each of them stand. She looks in their eyes.

Along with Steve, Pilar helps the last marcher in the procession through the gap in the fence. She still hasn't seen Río.

"Was there anyone else?" she asks Steve.

"That's everyone." Steve looks to Moses, the marshal who counted each marcher as they passed through the fence.

"I counted 99. Pilar makes 100," Moses says. "Leo replaced Angelina, so there were still 100, right?"

"What about Río?" Pilar asks.

"Who?" Moses asks.

"The speaker who came late." Pilar's voice is high and panicky. "The one who sang."

Steve's face clouds with worry.

Pilar walks quickly back through the tunnel, frantically searching the shadows. Her breath catches in her throat, her heart races, her palms sweat, and there is that sharp pain in her chest like she's drowning. She shakes her head to keep from crying.

She sees something in the distance and runs towards it. And then she's sure of what she sees, but unsure whether it's real: a bodily map of blue veins swims slowly toward her. She keeps running, her breath knotted. *Busca la vena.*

Río steps into a shaft of light, illuminated like an archangel, as she approaches. They wear their steel-studded *Undocuqueer and Unafraid!* T-shirt knotted over a ground-length silver tulle skirt embroidered with a glowing blue map of veins. They lift their skirt and hobble toward Pilar, blue veins swimming through the shadow.

Río and Pilar look at one another. The blue light from Pilar's headlamp plays over Río's face. Río is at a loss for words as they never are, their eyes shining. Somehow Pilar hasn't cried until this moment. She throws her arms around Río. "Are you okay?"

"I'm fine. I just wore the wrong shoes."

Río lifts their skirt and Pilar looks down at their platform Converse high-tops with four-inch rubber soles. "Why would you wear those?" she asks dotingly.

"They make me taller," Río says. "I wanted to see you. I wanted to be seen."

Pilar helps Río crawl through the gap in the fence and they walk out of the Freedom Tunnel holding hands. Javi waits at the tunnel's exit. He embraces Pilar and then Río. Pilar walks beyond them, into a roar of people strange and known, waiting in the bright morning of Riverside Park. She's never stood in a crowd like this—bodies of every kind, so dense she can hardly breathe, the air humming with their heat and electricity. Prayer is people. She closes her eyes amidst this great, shuddering love. Río lays their hand on her back and she opens her eyes. She looks out on a sea of people stretching beyond the South Lawn and to the river's edge, holding banners and screaming chants into megaphones. The light hurts her eyes, but she chooses it.

ACKNOWLEDGEMENTS

Thank you to Marcelle LaBrecque, aka Marilyn Monhoe, for being my brilliant, tireless consultant on all things NYC drag as I wrote this novel. Your radiance, work ethic, generosity, and sense of play never fail to inspire me.

Thank you to Kara Juarez, aka Kara Foxx-Paris, who, in performing drag as a teenager in the 90s in our small Texas border town, showed me what freedom felt like if you were brave enough to be it, who talked generously with me about Texas drag as she's experienced it, and whose courage is an ongoing inspiration.

Thank you to my partners in creating Our Voices: an Immigration Story: Carlos Ramos, Diana Arreaga, Dr. Shirley Leyro, Tony Alarcon, Thanu Yakupitiyage, Theo Rigby, Barbara Fischkin, and Theatre of the Oppressed, whose activism, artistry, and stories were an inspiration. Thank you to all of the inspiring youth activists with whom I connected through immigrant advocacy projects, especially Mateo Tabares, Nabila Eltantawy, Jazmin Cruz, and the students in my writing workshop at Make the Road. Marching in Make the Road's Trans Latine March and the Queer Liberation March and volunteering with the New Sanctuary Coalition were also integral to the writing of this novel.

Thank you to all of the wonderful Rio Grande Valley students with whom I've worked over the past 13 years, whose stories remind me of that incredible time of creating yourself as you leave home for college, who keep me connected to the Valley, and who give me hope for the future.

Thank you to Los Angeles Immigration Judge Rachel Ruane for the interview and for sharing research crucial to writing the novel. Thank you to immigration lawyer Stan Weber and Padre Bob Vitaglione for interviews. Thank you to Ravi Ragbir, Executive Director of the New Sanctuary

Coalition, for his interview about the New Sanctuary Movement and his experience of being held in ICE detention. Thanks to Episcopal priest and social worker Edward Sunderland for the interview on faith and activism and the Sanctuary movement. Thank you to the speakers at Greenwood Cemetery's *Living Inside Sanctuary Artist Talk*.

Thank you to Emma Taati, Katherine Mosquera, Guillermo Gomez, Justin Chan, and Felipe Alberto Herrera, who shared generously with me about their particular immigrant experiences and helped immensely with research.

Thank you to Diane Zinna and Mason Jar Press for seeing and believing in this book. I'm so grateful to everyone on the Mason Jar Press team for guiding this novel into the world with brilliance, big heart, humor, and a spirit of adventure.

Thank you to my many readers over the years, especially my Stumblers workshop and Julia Miller, my longtime writing partner, which her phone changes to "whoring partner." Thank you to my teachers, in particular my Davidson advisor Dr. Anthony Abbott; Columbia MFA professors Richard Locke, Honor Moore, and Patty O'Toole; and VCCA France workshop instructors Stephen O'Connor and Helen Benedict.

Thank you to the MacDowell Colony, the Ucross Foundation, the Saltonstall Foundation, the Edward Albee Foundation, the Jentel Foundation, the I-Park Foundation, and VCCA for writing residencies and to United States Artists, the Arts & Science Council, and the Constance Saltonstall Foundation for artist grants.

Thanks to Ryan Berg, both for reading early sections of this novel and for his book, *No House to Call My Home: Love, Family, and Other Transgressions*, which I returned to while writing this novel.

Thank you to my longtime friend Ana-Klara Anderson for her editorial eye on the Spanish passages in this novel and enthusiastic support through early drafts.

Thank you to John Drew, who made the documentary *Border Stories*, for meeting with me when I was just beginning this book and generously offering research resources.

Thank you to Dr. Francisco Guajardo, who co-founded the Llano Grande Center, for a generous early interview.

Thank you to Áine Chalmers for insights into Columbia University's First-Generation Low-Income Partnership and undergraduate student experience.

Thanks to the documentary *The Devil's Miner*, which was instrumental to researching child miners in the Cerro Rico silver mines of Bolivia.

Thanks to Julia Solis and Bob Diamond for interviews and insights into the world of subterranean exploration.

Mary Jo Weaver's *Cloister and Community: Life within a Carmelite Monastery* and Mark Salzman's novel *Lying Awake*, about a Carmelite monastery outside present-day Los Angeles, were also integral to my research.

The story of Luz Oscura was adapted from a real-life story, deftly told in Yuri Herrera's "Diana, Hunter of Bus Drivers" on *This American Life*.

Thank you to the breathtaking artist Jayoung Yoon, who in working with me on artist statements shared an artistic history, practice, and philosophy that shaped the fictional character of Dr. Yoon.

Thank you to costume designer and author Coleen Scott Trivett for the interview on drag costume and makeup.

Thank you to Ryan Boyle, for your keen insights into Patti Smith's music and for telling me about desire lines.

Thank you to Adrian Palacios, whose friendship was so important to me in those searching early years of finding ourselves as artists in New York and a touchstone for Pilar and Río's friendship. When I stare up at the Hayden Sphere, I still think of us, in our teetering 20s, claiming it as our planet.

Thank you to Katie Bond. If ever there was a friendship that deserved its own tome of a love story, it's ours, but I could never write it as beautifully as we've lived it. Here's to talking & laughing & crying & losing ourselves in time & space as long as we both shall live!

Thank you to Dr. Ben Leonel Garza (January 17, 1939 to February 5, 2021), the father who took me on as a strong-willed adolescent and brought me to the border, a man of faith—in God, medicine, music, laughter, and family. You taught me that *you can't always get what you want, but if you try sometimes, you just might find you get what you need*, and the border taught me how to see and be. When the rejections got me down, I remembered you waking up from six years of dementia to look in my eyes and say, "I'm so proud of you, baby. Your depth pleases me."

Thank you to all of my Garza family and their wonderful stories, especially my tio Dr. Marin Garza, the last living of his nine siblings; my prima Claris Garza, who shared her story of becoming a novice nun and her ultimate choice to live out her faith in the world; and my primo Dr. Jimmy Garza, who gave me the image of women crossing the Rio Grande holding hands, praying the rosary.

Thank you to my Goldfaden family, especially Josh and Brenda, who've walked with me through death, into love. Brenda, thank you for your electric empathy and the unwavering brightness of your belief in me. Thank you to my mother, who let me finish a fifth draft of the novel in her home in the Rio Grande Valley, watching snowy egrets glide over the lake that inspired Marin and Pilar's resaca. Thank you to my bighearted sister, Brennan, for her love and support and for promising to teach me how to use social media. Thank you to my father Jeff Shaffner, who shows me how to live beyond the brokenness of our bodies, and my wonderful stepmother Susan Clark, whose stories of nursing AIDS patients in the 90s also found their way into the novel. Thanks, also, for letting me write in the light in the SADdest of winters.

Thank you to my love Niteesh Elias, for believing in, loving, and creating with me. I couldn't have dreamed up a more perfect collaborator.

Thank you to all of my family—blood and chosen—whose community, love, and support carried me through the solitary work of writing this novel.

Country of Under was the PEN/Bellwether Prize for Socially Engaged Fiction runner-up and was shortlisted for Dzanc Books' Prize for Fiction and Black Lawrence Press's Big Moose Prize. An excerpt won the Asheville Writers' Workshop Fiction Contest. Brooke's work has appeared in *The Hudson Review, Marie Claire, BOMB, Litmosphere, Lost and Found: Stories from New York,* and *The Lit Pub.* She's received grants from the Arts & Science Council, United States Artists, and the Saltonstall Foundation and residencies from the MacDowell Colony, the Ucross Foundation, the Saltonstall Foundation, the Edward Albee Foundation, the Jentel Foundation, the I-Park Foundation, and VCCA. Brooke is at work on a memoir, an excerpt of which won the 2023 Lit/South Award. She grew up part Garza, part Shaffner in Texas's Rio Grande Valley. Brooke co-founded Freedom Tunnel Press with her partner Niteesh Elias to publish artivist books that straddle borders. She teaches and edits through her company Between the Lines. Find more at brookeshaffner.com.

OTHER MASON JAR PRESS TITLES

Glazed With War
poetry by Pantea Amin Tofangchi

After the Rapture
novella by Nancy Stohlman

lesser american boys
short stories by Zach VandeZande

JERKS
short stories by Sara Lippmann

The Monotonous Chaos of Existence
short stories by Hisham Bustani

Peculiar Heritage
poetry DeMisty D. Bellinger

Call a Body Home
short stories chapbook by Michael Alessi

The Horror is Us
an anthology of horror fiction edited by Justin Sanders

Learn more at masonjarpress.com

Printed in the USA
CPSIA information can be obtained
at www.ICGtesting.com
LVHW051150080324
773669LV00002B/5